Guilty
MINDS

MINDS

Little Hope Series, Book 2

ARIANA CANE

Copyright © 2022 Ariana Cane.

All rights reserved. No part of this publication may be reproduced, distributed, or transmitted in any form or by any means, including photocopying, recording, or other electronic or mechanical methods, without the prior written permission of the publisher, except in the case of brief quotations embodied in critical reviews and certain other noncommercial uses permitted by copyright law. For permission requests, write to the author at the contact form @arianacane.com

ASIN: B0B5HBGDQL

ISBN: 9798398118063

Any references to historical events, real people, or real places are used fictitiously. Names, characters, and places are products of the author's imagination.

Editor: Anna Noel.

Proofreader: Lauren Alexander.

www.arianacane.com

They say the truth will set you free. But what about the ugly truth? The one that reveals pretty as damaging and ugly as redeeming?

Dedication

To you. Yes, YOU.
The one who picked this book.
Enjoy Kayla and Justin's story.
I love those two.

Author's Note

This book touches on a few heavy subjects. If you have triggers (SA mentioning; bullying; depression), please be careful reading. Adult language and adult situations.

If you find yourself in the same situation as certain characters, please speak to someone. There's help out there. The National Sexual Assault Hotline can be reached at 1-800-656-4673.

On a personal note. This book is darker than the first one. You might have noticed Alex hinting at Justin being dark, and he is. He is a bully (to a point). He is also an asshole, has a dirty mouth and a kink, and those parts will not change. He is NOT a marshmallow, but he is with Kayla. Eventually. He grows throughout the story and learns how to be different, but it's a process. He is redeemed in my eyes, and I hope he will be in yours too. :)

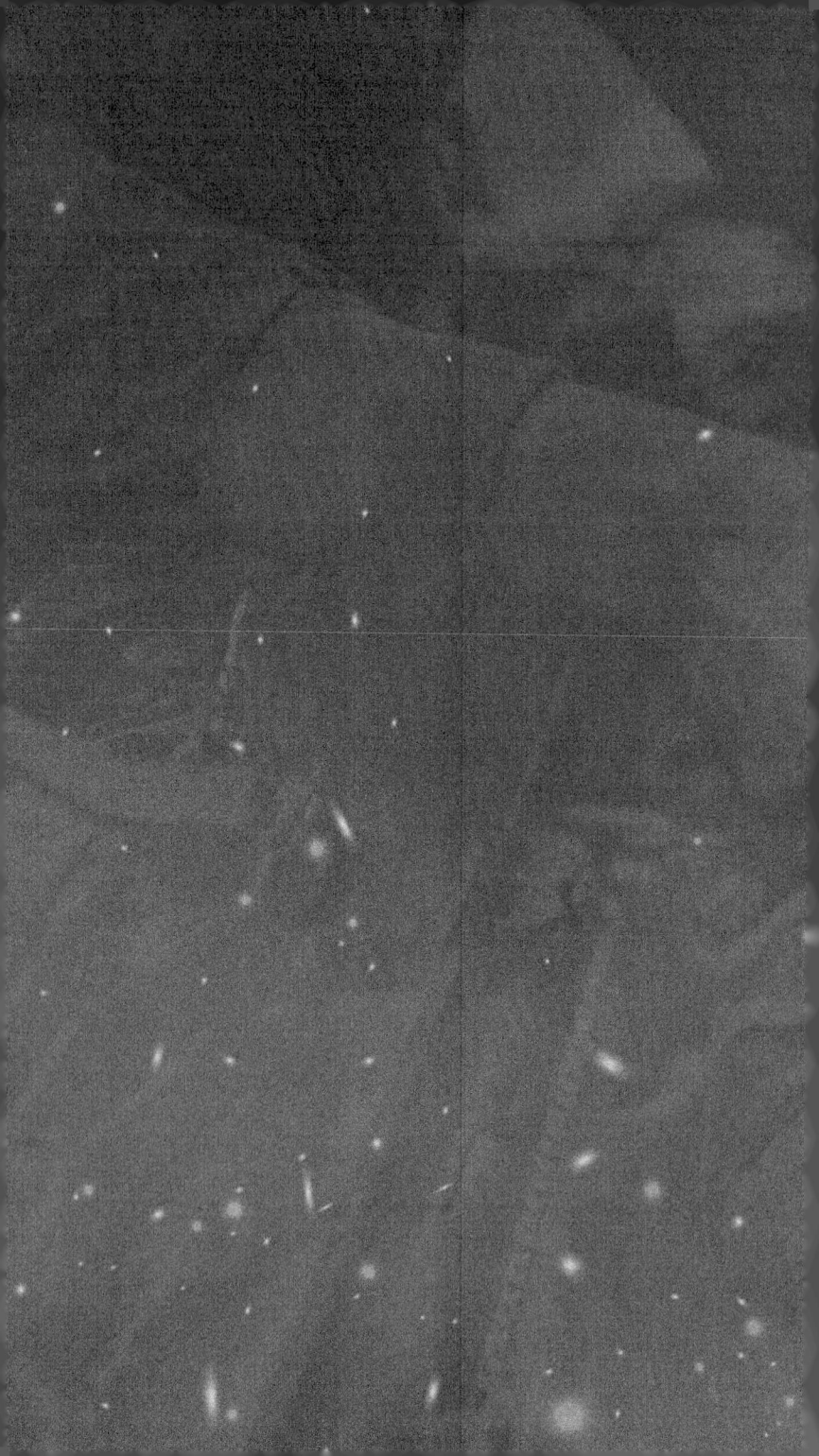

Prologue

KAYLA

The last thing I remember when I wake up is getting whacked on the back of my head after hearing an ominous male whisper from behind—*"Now she'll understand what it feels like to lose everything"*—while I was checking on the stove in the kitchen.

Marina, the owner, had texted to let me know she forgot to switch the stove off and asked me to check on it. I was surprised she did because she never forgets anything *and* lives closer to the diner than I do.

I got her text and tried calling back, but she didn't pick up. It didn't strike me as odd, though, because, well... Marina *is* odd. So, I drove to the diner, walked into the kitchen... and everything afterward is a big fat nada. I think I blacked out, considering I don't remember being put in the pantry, where I'm lying on the floor with my hands tied behind my back—the strong scent of bread and cinnamon invading my nostrils. Yeah, it had to be the pantry.

I try to pry my eyes open through the thunderous pounding in my head, but it freakin' *hurts*. I wince at another internal *boom* of pain. *Ouch*.

As I manage to finally open my eyes and look around, I start to understand the full extent of the little pickle I seem to have gotten myself into. At first, I don't see a single shred of light, but as my eyes adjust, I notice a slight flickering under the door leading to the kitchen... followed by the stench of smoke. *Oh, fuck*.

I try to yank on my restraints, but they must be formed from zip ties pulled tight, because some sort of plastic digs into my skin, worsening when I move my wrists. My attempts turn fruitless and painful mighty fast. More smoke creeps in, and my head begins pounding even more violently.

I feel like I'm on the verge of a stroke—my blood pressure must have skyrocketed after what was surely a pretty hard hit to the head, resulting in me falling into the abyss I'm slowly climbing out from, paired with the spiking anxiety from waking up in the darkness trussed up like a Thanksgiving turkey.

I've been struck in the head before—where I grew up, getting a concussion was just another Wednesday—but that was nothing remotely close to this. Smoke inhalation along with head trauma... that doesn't sound like a healthy combination.

Ceding to the ties, I peer around in hopes of finding something to cut them. Thankfully, my eyes eventually adjust to the complete darkness, so I can faintly grasp the shapes of objects around me again, but I know well enough that the only arsenal this five-by-five pantry possesses is piles of canned foods, pasta boxes, and rolls. There won't be anything sharp in here unless you consider bread a weapon—which I do, but only for my love handles.

I try to stop panicking for a second. I can still walk with my hands tied behind my back. Lightbulb moment over here.

I'm dizzy but manage to stand up and wobble to the door. With my back turned to it, I try to pull the handle down, but it's locked. Figures. If somebody went through all the trouble of shoving me in here, they'd make sure the dang door is locked. A girl can still hope the bad guy hasn't got a whole lotta brain cells floating around in his head, right?

How do I get myself out of this? I've never been abducted before, so all the knowledge I have is from movies and logic.

Well, logic is telling me that I can do much better if my hands aren't tied behind my back. Unfortunately, there are no sharp objects in close proximity. I pull the restraints again, going as far as trying to pull them through my feet from behind my back—a feat that appears much easier in movies than in reality.

There's more smoke now, and I start coughing, my vision blurring as heat rises to my face. I'm about to black out again. *Fuck.*

"Kayla!" A voice comes through the door, cutting through the haze of smoke and confusion of my fading-away consciousness. "Kayla, where are you?" The voice is louder now, and I try to peel my eyes open. I try to say something, but my tongue is swollen and refuses to cooperate, so only a pitiful moan comes out, barely audible.

"Kayla!" the voice keeps calling, and it sounds awfully like Justin Attleborough—the same Justin Attleborough who hates my guts. "Kayla!" He sounds close, and I try to say something back, but only a barking cough comes out. "She's in there!" His voice is closer now, and the door comes flying open with a loud *thud*.

Justin Attleborough's enormous frame barrels through the door, and he immediately drops to his knees in front of me.

"Fuck, what happened to you?" he says, touching my cheek with... a *shaking* hand?

What's going on? Is the end of the world upon us? I suddenly forget that I'm tied up in the pantry and the diner is ablaze because Justin fucking Attleborough, a man who only sneers and growls at me, calling me *lovely* names like 'trailer trash' and so on, is touching my cheek too gingerly for my comfort. His eyes are frantic with worry.

He draws his hand away, and a red stain is smeared on his palm. Oh crap, is that my blood? Am I bleeding? I hadn't felt it. I try to touch my head, forgetting my hands are still bound.

"My hands," I croak.

"Jus, it's getting fucking bad in here—hurry the fuck up!" A voice shouts—it sounds like Alex. Alex is here too?

"Are you hurt somewhere else?" Justin ignores the call, inspecting my head.

"I don't think so," I say with a slight headshake, causing another wave of nausea to roll through my body. *If I throw up on Justin Attleborough right now, I will voluntarily die in this fire.*

"Justin!" Alex shouts again, just as more smoke barrels inside the small space.

"We need to go," Justin says, poking his head through the pantry doorway. Whatever he sees makes him wince.

I try to move forward, but my knees meet the tiled floor with a painful thump. "Fuck," I hiss. Justin's next to me in a second. He sweeps one arm under my knees and another under my back, lifting me up as if I'm no heavier than a stuffed animal.

The restraints pull tighter, but I don't complain because smoke is everywhere, and it's getting difficult to breathe; the only thing I want right now is to get out of here and suck in a lungful of pure air.

The moment we come out of the pantry, I see the damage: flames are licking at the counters, the tables, and the walls. Alex Crawley, Justin's best friend and Freya's boyfriend, is trying to stop the spread with what appears to be wet kitchen towels.

Don't we own a fire extinguisher? I glance to where it's supposed to be, and the spot is empty. Huh. Whoever decided to make my day friggin' suck was damn thorough about it.

Outside, Justin sets me on the ground and pulls a pocketknife from his... well, pocket. He not-so-gently spins me around and cuts the ties. Blood instantly rushes to my hands, followed by a painful tingling—I must have been bound for longer than I thought. I bring my hands to my chest and begin rubbing my wrists, chafed red and raw from the tight ties.

"You okay?" Alex asks me, his words slurring a little. Is he close to a PTSD episode? Did the fire trigger something? I meet his gaze. There's no panic in his eyes. I relax a little. At least he's all right. Seeing my nod, he turns to Justin, who's sitting next to me on the asphalt and surveying the side of my head, wet with blood. "I have to go, Jus."

Justin nods. "Yeah, go. Make sure she's okay."

"Who?" Unease settles in the pit of my stomach.

"Freya got attacked by her ex."

"What?" I whip my head around, which causes another

ripple of nausea to rise up my throat—not like the previous time when it was just a slight possibility, but a real close-to-vomiting wave. I choke it down, wincing at the acidic burn.

"Is she alright?"

"She will be," he says confidently, but I know better. He cares about Freya deeply, and not in a 'want-her-between-the-sheets' way, which is new for him. He cares for her because she's his friend. The one woman who somehow managed to draw him, the resident hermit of Little Hope, out of his shell.

It can't be a coincidence, the attack on me and the one on Freya. My attack must be connected to Erik, Freya's abusive ex too.

That hissed sentence comes to mind: *"She'll know what it feels like to lose everything."* It was him for sure, thinking that I mean a lot to her. I know she means a lot to me.

"Is she hurt?" I whisper.

"No, I don't think so. Just shaken up." After a pause, he adds, "The piece of shit is dead." He squats next to me and begins timidly sifting through the hair covering the cut on my head. "Hold still, I need to check the wound."

"Oh" is all I say. I know I shouldn't feel relief hearing that somebody's dead, but I still do. For Freya. She's free now. It's the first time I truly take a deep breath since I woke up bound and alone inside the pantry.

Despite all the shock I have experienced in the past hour, I'm also going through another one: Justin's doing something with my head. Physically and mentally. *Screwing hard* (I wish), I would say. He is... *too* gentle. *Too* caring. Just this morning, he threw me the usual 'get the fuck out of the way' look when we passed each other on the sidewalk. And now he's... doing what, exactly?

The sound of sirens knocks me out of my haze. I glance

up and see Justin watching me in silence, but I can't read his face. The ever-permanent scowl he wears whenever he's around me is present, but there's no malice in his baby-blue eyes this time. Instead, they're hooded and filled with concern, a shade darker than usual.

"Justin..." I try to sound soft, not prickly as I usually do when I talk to him... which is, like, five times in the last few years. In fact, today is the most we've spoken since... yeah, since *that* night. His face changes in an instant, as if he's remembering the same.

"I didn't forget who you are and what you did," he spits and takes a step back, his demeanor turning hostile before I can even blink.

The fire truck screeches to a halt next to the diner, and firefighters pour out of it. I turn to look at Justin, but he's gone. I glance around, but he's nowhere in sight. A dang Houdini.

"Kayla? What the fuck happened to you?" Mark, one of the firefighters who used to be my neighbor and an occasional savior, drops down next to me. "Rachel, I need some help over here!" He waves to one of the paramedics that just arrived, and a tall lady in uniform rushes to me, carrying a massive canvas bag with that unmistakable medical symbol on the side.

"Kayla," Mark calls out again, "are you okay?" He touches my face and softly nudges me to turn toward him.

He's the only person from my past who is still nice to me. When you cross that invisible line from trailer park to the 'richer part,' you don't automatically become one of the 'good' ones, and the 'old' ones don't accept you anymore either. That's how you become a king without a kingdom—and being stuck in that purgatory gets lonelier every day.

So when I face him, I break down.

"Oh, shit," he mutters as he gathers me in his arms. I let out all the pent-up fear, anger, and disappointment built up over the past few hours—the past few *years*—on his shoulder.

Rachel gives me time to cry it out, but then she tepidly suggests, "Mark, I need to check her vitals. You can resume in a few once I make sure she's alright."

Mark rubs my back one more time and steps away. "I'll be back. Take care of her, Rach," he instructs, and pulls his firefighter helmet on before rushing into the diner. Now the paramedic has full access to my injuries. She checks my blood pressure and pulse before moving to address my head.

"I'm sorry this happened to you, hon." She gives my shoulder a supportive pat. "I hope whoever did it will be punished."

"I think he already was," I mutter darkly, and she hums her approval as she pulls an oxygen mask over my nose, and I begin coughing.

"Give it a moment," Rachel assures me, helping adjust the mask. As she promised, the coughing subsides in seconds, and I start to breathe easily. Swallowing substantial gulps of pure oxygen, I watch her cleaning my wrists. "I'll have to take you to the hospital for overnight observation."

"No, I'm good." I vigorously shake my head, thinking of the bills that will inevitably follow a hospital stay. I don't have health insurance. It'd be cheaper to die.

"I didn't ask for your thoughts on the matter." She throws me a stern look. "You're going to the hospital because you inhaled a lot of smoke, and the state will pay for it. Got it?"

"Yes, ma'am." She reminds me of Marina a little—scary but caring.

She helps me into the back of an ambulance and tells

the driver to go. Little Hope is not a big town, so the drive to the clinic takes less than five minutes.

I'm admitted to the trauma side. The clinic building is huge, I'd consider it a tiny hospital by local standards, but there are not enough doctors and nurses in Little Hope, so it feels eerily deserted.

I heard that a long time ago, when the clinic was built, it was famous for its family of doctors who worked there generation after generation. But at some point, one of them got bored and moved to a big city, and the clinic began dying out. A shame, really, because the place is enormous, and Little Hope could certainly use some good people.

A doctor knocks on the door to check up on me, circles under his eyes.

He listens to the paramedic repeating my vitals and the situation as his eyes scan his clipboard with furrowed brows.

"This town has changed so much," he mutters, sounding personally offended. "Assaulted. At Marina's place downtown." He shakes his head in disapproval. "Your vitals look good," he declares after a moment, glancing over me perfunctorily, "but I want to keep you overnight. The nurse will come to check on you later. Now get some rest. You look like you've been through hell."

"Thank you?" I want to laugh at his statement, but I also want to cry.

He sweeps from the room, and Rachel takes his place beside me. "I'll let Mark know the room number. He'll want to check on you." She tells me, her voice soft.

I nod with a quiet "thank you." She smiles and disappears through the door, and I'm left alone with the events of the evening. But not for long.

Mark bursts in a minute later, face smudged with ashy streaks from the fire. "Kayla, you okay? Rachel told me they're keeping you overnight." His mouth pulls down in a grimace. "Is it that bad?"

I wave his worry off. "No, they just want to make sure I didn't inhale too much smoke. I'm fine, really."

"Okay." His relieved sigh is heavy and loud. "How did you get out of the diner?"

"Justin."

"*Justin* got you out?" Disbelief is apparent in his voice.

I still can't believe it either. I loosely shrug one shoulder, shifting uncomfortably. "Yeah. He and Alex Crawley were there, and he... yeah."

"Huh." His eyes are focused on the wall, lost in his thoughts. "I guess he got one thing right."

I chew on my lip, contemplating whether I should ask Mark to do something he won't like. I decide to go through with my request. I don't have any other choice. "Can you do me a favor?"

"Sure. What's up?" He scratches his cheek, smearing the black smudges further.

"Can you find out what happened at Alex Crawley's house tonight?"

His gaze meets mine, puzzled. "But you just said—"

"Yeah, it's a long story I don't even understand myself," I explain haplessly. "That's why I need you to help me out. Can you?"

He nods, disappearing for about half an hour. When he returns, he delivers the news that Freya was admitted here, too, but is staying in another wing, and that she's got a good handful of visitors—including Justin and Jake. I ache to go and check on her, but I don't have the mental capacity to battle with either of the Attleborough's right now.

Mark's lips are firmly pressed together after he delivers

all the news about the events that he could gather. "You know what's not fair? That you're here alone—"

The door bursts open, and Marina flies in. Noticing me on the bed, she throws herself on me and envelopes me in a bear hug.

"You were saying?" I quirk a brow at Mark over her shoulder, a wry look on my face. Despite my elation at having visitors, I can't help the sting deep down when faced with the fact that I'm damn lucky even *two* people are here for me.

After hugs, a hundred questions, and apologies, Marina releases me and discreetly dabs her eyes with a tissue. She fluffs the pillow under my head, tucks the blanket around me, and takes a seat in the chair beside the bed, making sniffling sounds.

Only a moment later, Kenneth Benson, the local sheriff and Alex Crawley's half brother, bustles inside after a quick knock. "Sorry, Kayla, I was a little preoccupied with the madness happening in Little Hope today."

He takes my statement and tells me the same version of events that Mark already revealed, confirming my suspicions that I was most likely attacked by the same person who attacked Freya—her vicious ex. And that he's not a threat to any of us anymore.

I sigh in relief. Am I a bad person? And will it be too naive to hope that Justin might show up and check on me today?

Yeah, I'm too naive because he never does.

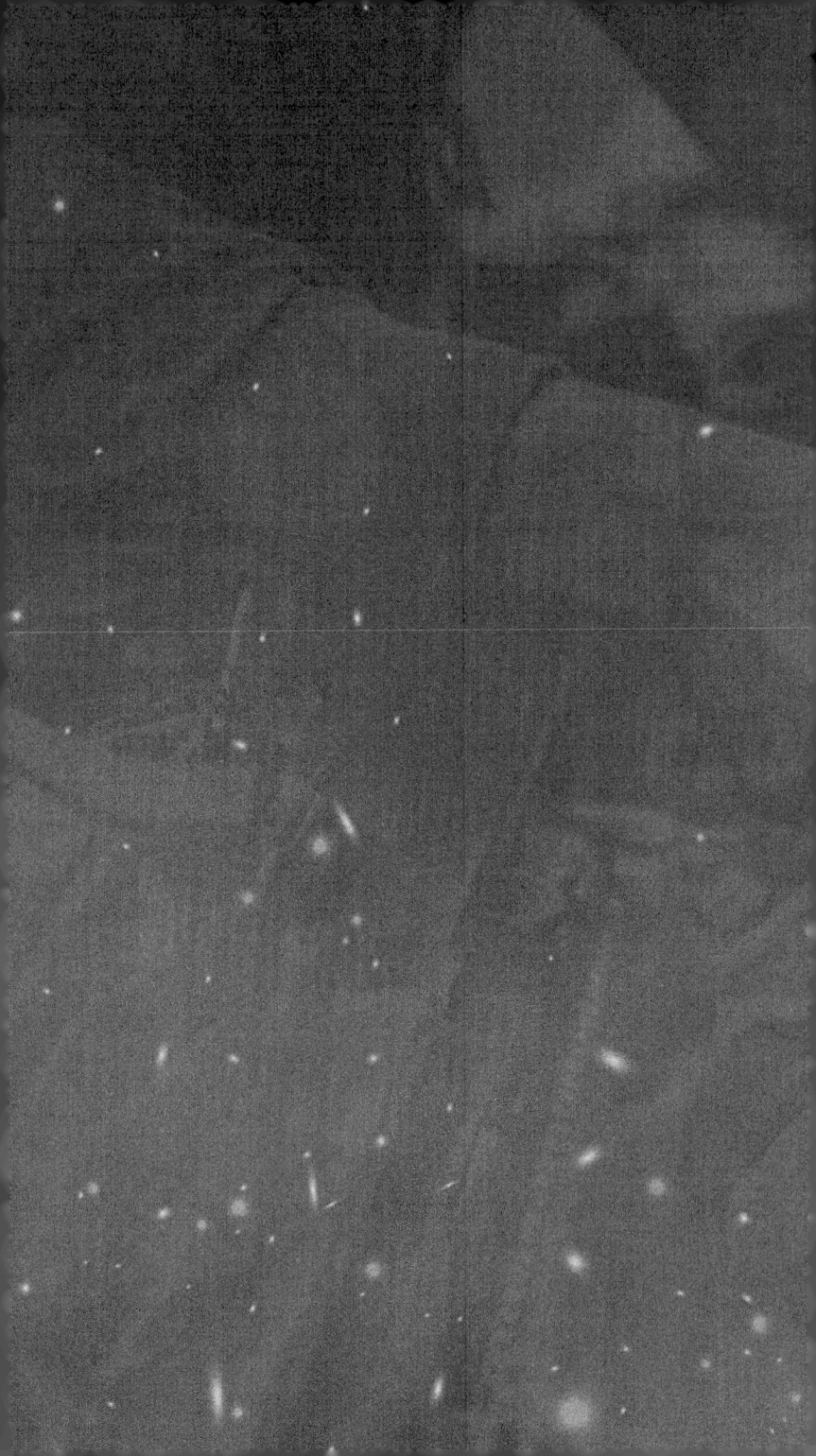

Chapter One

Two weeks later

KAYLA

A siren blares from behind me. I curse loudly, the creativity of the words shocking even me, as I pull over to the side of the road. The sirens of the cop cruiser behind me are disturbingly loud. I don't think the dude plans to turn them off despite the fact I'm already at the curb. Humiliating me is his favorite hobby. Though, for the love of everything, I don't understand the need for theatrics now: his only audience is the squirrel crouched next to a bush on the tree line.

Teeth gritted hard enough to crack the enamel, I sit and wait to see what Officer Attleborough wants with me this fine morning.

The knock on the window startles me. No matter how

many times we've done this, it always does. I should have rolled it down by now, but it's our little game we like to play—making each other as miserable as we can through even the smallest inconveniences. The rain's starting, and I want him to stand under the impending downpour. I cross my fingers, hoping fate will be on my side today.

"License and registration, please," Jake intones—how creative of him; you'd think he'd find some new words after dozens of times stopping me—fixing the bridge of his Ray-Bans I absolutely loathe with his middle finger. What a douche. I look through my window at the sky full of rain clouds.

"They're the same as they were two weeks ago, Jake. When you stopped me for driving one mile above the speed limit. Remember?" I snort, pretending to scout for dirt under my nails rather than look at him. Why would I? I've seen his face stopping my ass so many times I can recount the exact size and placement of each of the thirteen freckles on his nose. Most notably, the ones closest to his right eye. Six small freckles lined up in an almost perfect hexagram. Sometimes when I'm bored, I trace a star between them with my eyes. He's a star, all right, in his own mind. A perfect nitwit. All three of the Attleborough siblings have those tiny honey-colored dots all over their noses, and I used to think of it as cute. Now it annoys the crap out of me.

"That's Officer Attleborough to you," he says with a sneer and splays a palm toward me, waiting for my documentation. Wow, he's *extra* sassy today.

I pass him my registration and license, carefully eyeing his face and trying to assess his mood further. He's an asshole, no doubt about that, but he's also an asshole who can make my life ten times more complicated than it already is.

In doing so, I notice Officer Jake changed his hairstyle—he used to have a short military cut, and now he is growing surfer-dude blond locks. I'm not sure if I like this change or if I think it makes him look like even more of an asshole.

After taking my papers, he slowly walks, penguin-like, back to his car and gets inside. Great, now he'll take all the time in the world to check them. We both know he won't be checking crap, though, because he has to know all my info by heart by now—I bet if I woke him up in the middle of the night, he could recite my license number without hesitation. Still, he'll make sure to hold me as long as he possibly can, so I suck it up and wait. I'd love to browse Instagram to check which new tattoo designs my favorite artists have come up with lately, but my phone was destroyed in the fire, and I still haven't gotten around to buying a new one. Those things are expensive, and I don't have a spare grand just sitting around, waiting to be gloriously wasted on a shiny—though very handy—rectangle.

So, I sit and wait. And wait. And... wait. I take this ample time to muse upon why they hate me so much for the thousandth time. All I know is Jake is Justin's brother, and ever since Justin got back from jail about three years ago after the previous three he spent inside, he turned into a douche-asshole, and Jake followed his lead—though he was still a scrawny teenager at the time. Unlucky for me, about a year ago, Jake joined the Little Hope PD. And every day, there's less and less hope left for me in this wonderful place I still call home.

Around every corner, in the shadow of every building, the *brave* Officer Attleborough protects the innocent citizens of Little Hope from the devious, treacherous me. I've gotten so many tickets in the past year and a half (courtesy of him) that I eventually stopped paying them. My registration expires soon, but I'm scared to go to the DMV to see how much I'll need to pay in fines to renew it. Besides that, something tells me my driver's license is about to be suspended, and I'm so not looking forward to that either. I bet the good officer can't wait to pull me over for my expired registration or suspended license and give me the final killshot ticket that will dissolve my already empty wallet to dust.

Twenty minutes later, when I've long given up on my dentist appointment that was supposed to start ten minutes ago and accepted the possibility of having cavities in my future, he saunters back with my license, registration, and a freshly signed ticket.

"What's that for, *officer*?" I sneer.

"You're a hazard on the road," he accuses me, per usual.

"Yeah, yeah, yeah. What else is new." I snort in an unladylike fashion—there's nobody to impress here, and it's not as if he can hate me any less.

"No, your right light isn't working." He points behind me with a vindictive smile. "See? A hazard."

"Jake, Alex is out of the city, and Justin's the only mechanic in town. You know that." I remind him with a heavy frustrated sigh.

"I know that." His devious grin only grows more self-satisfied as he fixes his sunglasses higher up his nose. Then he walks back to his patrol car, its sirens having quieted about ten minutes ago. Jerk. What am I supposed to do?

The moment Jake gets inside his cruiser and closes the door behind him, the skies open and begin to pour sleet down onto the earth. What the hell is wrong with the weather lately? It's almost May already. *And couldn't you have started maybe two minutes earlier?* I ask, angrily eyeing the heavy drops of sleet bouncing off the paved road. It would've made my week to see Officer Hard-ass get drenched and know his shiny shoes would be squelching under his feet all day. Could good fortune be on my side at *least* once, please?

I tilt my head back and gently bang it against the headrest a few times. Justin owns the only auto shop in town, so I'm screwed. The closest neighboring town is thirty minutes away, which isn't bad, but the weather sucks, and I don't like driving my old boy on a slippery road. My tires are as bare as a sphynx cat—there's no tread left on them. It's a wonder I've passed inspection in the past. It pays to have connections. I drew a tattoo for a mechanic at a Springfield auto shop, so he did me a favor and signed off on my bare tires. A favor to me—yes, a favor to the society—don't think so. I might as well be skating on a mountain road without brakes. A very fun activity.

I'd love to say my Jeep Wrangler is as old as I am, but it's older. This boy has taken me through more snowstorms than I can count, but it's running on its last legs, and I'm not sure how many years—or months—it has left. If it craps out on me, I'd have to find another job. And now, I have no choice but to find a way to fix my vehicle, considering I can't afford to suddenly be without wheels.

I think about my options. I can try my luck and see if maybe somebody else is working at the garage today and pray Justin will be busy doing something else far, far away from Little Hope. Like, *Australia* far. Alex is out of town, and he's the only one who could help me besides Justin and his folks. Who am I kidding? I wouldn't go to Alex—at least, not yet. Not to him, not to Freya...

I take a deep, cleansing breath, preparing myself for the long journey to another town. Right then, my car magically stops. Just... stops.

I try to start it, frantically turning the key. It doesn't work.

And just like that, my day becomes even shittier. The battery is dead. It's been on the verge of death for a few days already, I could tell when I tried to start it on cold mornings and it resisted, but each time I just reminded myself that I can jump-start it like a pro with my generator... which is back at my trailer. Who's going to help me here, on the side of a road with no houses or cars around? I don't even have a phone on me.

The heavy, slippery slush keeps falling, and it's getting colder by the minute. Higher in the mountains, it's always colder; my trailer is parked at the bottom of one mountainside, while Little Hope is nestled in the little groove on another, and my old boy decided to check out between the two of them, right at the coldest spot. I can't even be mad. He's been giving me so many warning signs I chose to completely ignore.

I'm wearing my warmest jacket, but it's still not warm enough. My hands and nose first tingle from the cold, then begin to go numb. I pop the hood of my Jeep and get out. I can't fix it, but I know where the battery's located, and maybe I can hit it and add some kinetic energy that will allow it to miraculously start. I didn't like physics in school, but I learned enough to have a little shred of hope that this would work.

Ten minutes later, I'm back in the car. Giving the battery a smack didn't help—shocker—besides making me more aggravated with the situation. Damn it, a phone is the next purchase, even a cheap one with no internet. Anything will do as long as I can call somebody when in dire need of help. Which is now, obviously.

An hour later, I'm freezing, and not a single car has

driven by. Yes, Little Hope is a pretty secluded town, but not *that* secluded. Where is everyone? I feel like a character in a post-apocalyptic flick expecting a lone zombie to wobble out from the woods anytime now.

My fingernails are turning blue. Great. That's exactly what I need right now—to get frostbite and lose my fingers. I had big plans for these fingers of mine.

The rev of an engine startles me, and I jump in my seat. I'm so eager that I dash out of the car without hazarding a look first. Right before I start jumping and frantically waving my hands in the air in hopes the driver will stop, I recognize the truck. And the driver. Freakin' awesome. He'd rather mow me down than help me out, and there's no sense in humiliating myself even more. Deflated, I climb back inside my Jeep.

And, of course, he sails on by without even braking. Figures. I shiver yet again from the cold and blow puffs of barely warm breath onto my palms.

The car rev comes again a second later, and I get excited in hopes there's another person out there to save this damsel in distress. No such luck. The truck is coming back. Just great, he wants to rub some salt into my raw wound.

Justin Attleborough's brand-new, fancy-schmancy truck stops on my side of the road, facing me, and he slowly hauls his big body out. *I bet it has heated seats,* I gripe internally, shivering in ghostly pleasure at the thought of warming my frozen ass on one of those seats. He's not dressed for the weather, unlike I am, and I'm still an icicle. He's wearing washed-out jeans and a brown flannel with the sleeves rolled up, a dark T-shirt peeking from the collar. A black beanie is pulled over his short sandy hair. One might say it's blond, but it's not. It's the color of warm summer sand that you're just dying to feel run between your fingers to see if it's as soft as it looks.

He does a quick stretch and strides toward my driver's side in his usual overconfident manner, as if he's hung like a horse, and his balls of steel smack his knees with each powerful step. That could very well be the case, but regardless, it's just too alpha for my liking.

Ri-i-ight.

I sit and look in front of me without acknowledging him, even as he's knocking on the window.

"Open up," he orders, and as if I were an idiot, I do just as I'm told. Only halfway down, though, some brainpower might still be left in my frozen skull. "Your junker finally gave up?" he prods with a sneer.

"My car is perfectly fine," I argue, wiping at my nose self-consciously as I feel it dripping over the numbness. The tip smarts to the touch, tingling with cold.

"Sure, it is." His smirk is sardonic. "So, what are you doin' here?"

"Sightseeing," I offer, looking to the side. It *is* beautiful, that much is true: great Maine mountains after a downpour ruling over dark evergreen woods and a dirty, slippery road, with a bird chirping happily somewhere.

Idiot. It's fucking freezing out here.

"Cute," he retorts, unsmiling. "How you gonna get out of here?'

"I'll figure something out." I dare a quick glance at him and regret it instantly. His bright blue eyes are trained on my face.

"Sure, you will." He jerks his head. "Pop the hood."

"Why?"

"Just fuckin' open it." This comes out as a growl—the tone of his I'm most familiar with.

He hates me, and I sort of hate him too (*I think?*), but for the past hour, there were no vehicles driving by, and the only other living soul I saw (more like heard) was that chirping bird high as a kite, so I swallow my pride and press the button to pop the hood.

Chapter Two

JUSTIN

I'm fixing Mrs. Jenkins's steering wheel in her old CR-V when Jake shows up to my garage. Grinning like a Cheshire cat, he throws a few 'hellos' to the guys working today and proceeds toward me, leaning against the car I'm working on. *Damn it.* That smile always means trouble. Always.

"How's it going, bro?" His tone is too smug for my liking.

I keep my response clipped, seeing a carefully rehearsed follow-up in his eyes that I'd rather not hear. He begins tapping his foot on the floor like a ditz, and I just want him to spit out whatever he needs to and get the hell out of my garage. "It's going." He clearly expects me to ask about whatever shenanigans he caused this morning, but I couldn't care less.

He just smiles complacently. "Well, if you must know, I had a fine morning."

"What did you do, Jake?" Jake being in this good of a mood has only ever meant one thing.

"Well, I bumped into trailer trash on my way into town today. Where the hell does she even live?" His brows clinch, making him look older than his twenty-three years, but the crease disappears just as quickly as it surfaced. It's a reminder of how much the events of just a few weeks ago have aged him inside—when Jake took a man's life for the first—and what I hope will be the last—time. "And guess what?" He waggles his eyebrows, eager for me to join in his game, but he isn't getting anywhere with me. I hate when he messes with *her*. It was fun to watch the first few times, but now it's getting old. Only I get to do that. And for the hundredth time, I regret ever saying a word to him.

"I told you to leave her alone," I remind him through a clenched jaw, balling my hands into fists. A muscle tick starts on my right cheek, pulling at the corner of my eye. Every single conversation involving her riles me up every time.

"The fuck I will," he grits out with such hatred that my eyes dart to his, and I start to think I need to watch him a little more carefully. What happened with Freya and the shooting took a toll on him, and I've noticed he's becoming more like... *me*. And I don't wish that on my brother. "She deserves it!"

"She was just almost burned alive, for fuck's sake, Jake. Give her a break," I snap, yanking the dirty rag from my back pocket and wiping my hands on it. The thing looks in dire need of a wash, but I don't have time. Damn, I need some help around here. I'm way above my head already.

Time to hire a receptionist or something and put dry cleaning on their to-do list.

"It's what she deserves," he hisses, stepping closer to me.

I straighten to my full height, and he appears shorter by a few inches. I need to be intimidating for him to understand the gravity of my next words. "And who the fuck are you to decide who deserves to live or die, Jake?"

For a moment, I regret my words because for a second—one awful second—I see flash in his eyes the stark reaction of someone who lives with having killed another person, necessary or not. Then he looks to shake himself out of it, returning to our argument even angrier. "You know what she did, and you want me to leave her alone?" He smacks against my chest with his open palms, almost causing me to stumble back.

"What I did, Jake. *I* did!" I yell into his face and immediately feel a few curious gazes on me. My people know better than to gossip, so they quickly go about their business. "What *I* did," I repeat again, quieting my voice. "She was involved in that clusterfuck, but I'm the one to blame. You got it? *I* am."

"Jus—" he starts, but I cut him off, growling, "You got it?"

After a long hard moment, he nods and turns to leave, but I stop him with a question. It's a compulsion—I need to know. "What happened this morning, Jake?"

"She was driving with a broken taillight, and I gave her a ticket." Then he walks away.

Jake left an hour ago, and since then, I've been thinking about it. Her car's fucking dying, I've heard it around town making the telltale sounds of a rapidly approaching deathbed, and I also know she can never get it to start on the first try. I saw her hooking up jumper cables to Marina's battery a few times. After such a long harsh winter, I bet her battery is barely alive. If it's the alternator and it shits the bed while she's driving... I don't even want to think about what would happen. *What could have already happened.*

As I work on Mrs. Jenkins's car, my mind keeps drifting off to what Jake did. And that's how I find myself driving to her trailer only an hour later. Nestled into a little grove on the other side of the mountain, Kayla doesn't let anyone know where she lives, but I know. I just want to make sure there will be no more souls weighing on Jake's conscience. One is already too many. That's what I tell myself as I drive —I'm just looking out for Jake.

As I predicted, her beat-up Jeep is on the side of the road, and a quick glance confirms she's inside. I pass her and keep driving. *Fuck.* Her car is switched off, and I get the feeling she's been there for a while. It's likely Jake pulled her over there, she turned off her Jeep and couldn't get it back on. It's been raining hard this morning, so she's probably been stuck in there. *Fuck!* I make a U-turn and drive back, pulling up flush to her front bumper. She's probably going to need a jump.

I get out of my truck and instantly shiver from the cold, but I mask it with a full-body stretch. Because I'm a man like that.

Once I'm standing next to the driver's side of her car, I can evaluate the seriousness of the situation that Jake had created by making her stop nowhere near help. Her usually plump lips are completely thin and blue, the tip of her nose is red, and she's sniffling.

When she rolls the window down, I tell her to pop the

hood, but she fights me on it, of course. I win in the end, but it feels like losing when I get a look and see everything's fucking rusted and held together with duct tape. Literally. How the fuck she's managed to survive driving this old piece of junk around for so long beats me.

There's an endless list of problems that can prevent the engine from starting, but I'm guessing what's gotten her stuck on the side of the road today is her battery. I grab a cable from my truck and get her old piece of crap hooked up, then motion for her to turn the key. It rumbles to life on the first try. While I'm at it, I want to check something else quickly, so I take the positive cable off the battery, and the engine dies instantly. Fuck, it's definitely the alternator. I put the cable back and motion for her to turn the key again. Her eyes are round—she must be thinking it's dead. Which it *is*, for fuck's sake.

You need a new damn car! I gripe mentally as it sputters into another just-barely-functional purr, ignoring her gaze as I pack everything back into my truck. *I bet you can afford something better that has four wheels and can drive farther than a ditch and not be the age of a dinosaur.* The diner's been doing good since the renovation, and I know for a fact people leave her good tips. I want to tell her all of that, rant at her to take care of herself, but I don't. She'd only walk away thinking I gave a shit about her.

When I turn to her, she's sitting in her car sniffling even more; her eyes are red and puffy. *Fuck.* Just what I need. I can't stand a woman crying; I just can't—a fact that my ex knew too well and used too often.

I walk to her side while wiping my hands on the same dirty-ass rag from my back pocket and address her through her closed window. "You're good to go, but you need to fix your car if you're planning on staying alive." I pour as much hatred into my voice as I can, which honestly isn't much, considering how it feels like kicking a puppy in her miserable state. "Your alternator is dead. If it goes off while you're on the road, you're toast. Everything stops working. Power steering, brakes, everything. If it happens, you muscle the car to the side of the road." I nod at the wheel. "Carefully. No jerky movements. And pull the brake when it naturally slows down. Do you know where your emergency brake is?"

"Yeah," she mumbles while staring ahead of her. "Thanks." I look at her face once again—she looks nearly frozen to death. Besides the blotchy red rimming of her sad eyes, there are purple bags under them. Her usually *too* bright and *too* cheerful hazel gaze is dim. The corners of her lips point downward. She just looks... exhausted. Did she always? Or have the recent events at the diner made her lose sleep?

Something pinches in my chest, and it's annoying as fuck. I scratch on the place where a little ache has formed with my fist, trying to erase the unwanted feeling, but it doesn't go away.

"Are you okay?" I ask in a gruff voice after an internal battle between my brain and conscience.

She wipes her nose with the heel of her hand and answers without turning to me. "Yeah." Now that I think about it, I don't think she's looked at me even once since I first drove past her. It's unsettling. I know she had a crush on me—a lot of girls did, so I was used to it—but I always noticed her. So different from the polished type I usually went for. But now, I don't feel an ounce of interest from her. Not even a little bit. Huh. I don't know why it bothers me—probably just my ego talking.

I watch her a moment longer, then turn to walk to my truck.

The pinching sensation in my chest is still there, and I need to erase it. I need to remember why I can't stand her because I refuse to feel something other than hatred toward her. And I just happen to know one way that I can always do it.

Chapter Three

K*AYLA*

It's been three days since Justin gave me a jump, and I still remember every word he said. All few of them, because it was more than he'd said to me in the last three-odd years combined. He behaved almost humanely toward me; I actually forgot about our animosity for a single blissful moment. He gave me advice on how to stay alive. *Alive!* Before that, I'd have bet money the only advice he'd ever give me would be to go skydiving without a parachute.

I've had a crush on Justin Attleborough since I was thirteen years old, and he was eighteen. He was the boy everybody either wanted to be, be friends with, or be with. Cheerful, energetic, handsome. Dreaming of making the world a better place. Besides making him an extremely positive and likable person, the universe decided to put all eggs in one basket and make him an ultra-attractive specimen on top of it. Tall, blond, wide-shouldered, and always with that lopsided grin on his far-too-symmetrical face that I want to punch every time I see him now.

He was the boy from the right side of town. I was the girl from the wrong one. He was the guy everyone loved to see—and God, what I would've given for him to see me.

When he turned twenty, that was the beginning of the end for the female population of Little Hope and the surrounding towns. Including me. He was always attractive, but now his shoulders grew wider, his face prettier, and his abs sharper. With one physical change came another one. He stopped being that good guy who held everyone else's interest above his own.

He became a glorious man-whore, solely focused on his own pleasures and needs.

And he stayed that way ever since.

That's precisely what I'm witnessing right now in front of my face. He's standing outside the diner where I've worked since I was fifteen and flirting with a new teacher from the local school. He looks gorgeous as always, even with grease smudging his jeans and shirt, his tight, lean muscles bulked up from hard work at the mechanic shop. I imagine him carrying big heavy tires across the floor all day, every day, shirtless, and just like that, I need to fan myself.

"Wipe the drool from your chin." A rough chuckle brings me back to my sad reality.

"Wasn't even watching," I counter Marina, my boss and unofficial adoptive mother. She's watching me through her sky-high false lashes with a smirk on her perfectly contoured face. She has a pen tucked behind her ear, sticking out through her dark red bob. I'm scared for a second that she'll reprimand me, as she's tough and intimidating in her posture and Russian heritage, but I know she would never. She's loyal to a fault and equitable in every aspect of life. They say you can't choose your family. Well... sometimes you can, and we chose each other.

Marina hired me at her diner when my own family left me behind, and I had no money for food or a place to live but already had a debt to pay. She let me stay at her place rent-free for almost three years until I was standing on my own two feet and could afford a place of my own. No matter where I go next, I'll always come back to her on Mother's Day. She never had kids of her own or a husband, saying she didn't need an anchor to weigh her down. I've seen her cozying up with Paul Rogers, Justin's right hand at the mechanic shop, though. But regardless of anyone else, she'll always have me.

"He's no good for you." Marina purses her lips as if scolding an ungrateful child—me, in this case—and shakes her head. "As if you could lie to me, Kay. I knew you were ogling him way before you even thought of glancing his way." She takes a sip of coffee and throws a hand towel at me. I catch it in the air and begin wiping the new cups we just bought.

"I know." I sigh in defeat. "God, why did nature give such a hot body to an asshole like him?"

"He's okay looking, I guess," she declares with a shrug after another long assessment. "But his core is rotten. There's nothing pretty in here." She taps the left side of her chest with a French manicure, reminding me to do mine— new nail polish always makes me feel better, along with colorful streaks in my hair, which usually match. "You can't ride far on just his face." I spit out the sip of coffee I've just taken and burst into laughter. "Or maybe you actually can."

Now she is thoughtfully tapping her chin. "Yes, you most certainly can. Still not far, though."

"Do you mean he can't get far on just his looks?" I ask her, confused.

"I think you understand what I meant perfectly." She winks at me, barely containing her amusement.

"Okay, ma'am. I hear you." I finally stop laughing hysterically and wipe the tears from my eyes, trying to erase the image she put into my brain. As a matter of fact, scratch that. I should copy and paste this image into my spank bank for later use.

When I glance back at Justin, he's watching me with that hateful expression I've grown so accustomed to. It's been years since he started treating me like garbage, even though, for the love of God, I have no idea why.

It was as if he was released from prison having made the executive decision that I wasn't worth the air I breathe—and from then on, the bullying began. You would think the crush I had on him would've been shattered by that, but no-o-o—some women just love a good ol' asshole. The 'badder' the boy, the worse they treat us, the more garbage they pour over our heads, the better.

Since the fire three weeks ago and then the roadside thing a little later, he's been even worse than before. He isn't just ignoring me anymore—now he does it in style: with even more hateful glances and more malicious remarks. Why did he rescue me then? He should've left me there to die—less trouble for him. And why give me useful advice on how to stay alive driving my old boy? I shake my head, trying to clear my mind of those self-deprecating thoughts.

"I'll try to clean the wall in the kitchen; the new paint is coming tomorrow," Marina says before disappearing into the space that's left from the 'glorious' kitchen we once had.

The facility was shitty, the appliances were outdated, and with the demand we've had for the last couple of years, we were in dire need of renovation, and pronto. All the other repairs are pretty much done, and the kitchen is the last place that needs work.

"Okay, I'll come and help in a second."

After the fire, Marina pulled all her savings for the renovations we will need to re-open the diner, but it's not much. I'd put everything in, but I have nothing. Literally nothing. I don't even have the cash to get a new phone since I lost the old one in the fire, and I've recently become well acquainted with how difficult it is to live without a phone nowadays.

I sigh and look outside: he's still there. And still flirting.

Even though I grew up in Little Hope—the bad side of it, specifically—and was an obligatory participant in my messed-up family, I thought I'd developed a decently thick skin. Turns out, my thick skin becomes paper-thin where Justin is concerned. His snarky remarks and hateful stares hit the mark every time. Considering we never even dated— hell, we never even talked casually—my infuriation with him and his ability to throw me off my feet might seem a little odd. A lot odd, maybe. Marina keeps saying I need to 'get out there' and try to swim among the big fish. It's good advice, considering the tiny pool size of eligible fish in Little Hope.

Our town isn't so small, but it's not big either. All the datable guys—and I set that definition very widely and very loosely—are either taken or would never look in my direction. Or—worse—would look in my direction just to ask how much I charge per hour. Like any of them would last that long, anyway. Small-town folks don't like unorthodox, and I'm that. Unorthodox. I have colorful tattoos all over my body and piercings in 'indecent' places. My hair is ash-blonde with a few colorful streaks that tend to change color along with my mood and whatever hair dye I feel matches it. All of this paired with my family's reputation apparently lends justification to some people's perception that I'm a whore. That, and my birthplace—the trailer park where I was raised. As they see it, Little Hope is a charming little town just like any other town, and just like any other town, it has its 'bad' part.

So my dating pool is even narrower than most.

Half the people who were born in Little Hope are married to their high school sweethearts now, and I'm jealous because I never had one. Back in school, everybody knew about my mom's work in the red-light district—figuratively speaking—so nobody took me seriously as dating material, expecting me to want to hook up as if her profession translated to my preferences. But after years of being forced to watch my mother's revolving door of client-slash-friends, I kept my nose so high that they eventually just left me alone. I still do, even now.

I used to watch Justin from afar, but since Freya took over Little Hope with her energy and daytime-TV-worthy story, I was forced to spend time in the same space as him. Justin and her boyfriend, Alex, have been best friends since childhood. They went to college together and then enlisted together as well, but ended up in different branches, I believe. Had different callings, I suppose.

Three years in the Navy, then Justin came back, and Alex remained there. But nobody stays in the military forever, so a few years later, Alex got back too—scarred and nursing severe PTSD. Until Freya. She changed that hermit, making him see his worth. He deserved to invest in himself. He went to rehab because he wanted to become better for her. She's also planning to open a rehab facility for people with all sorts of PTSD. At least, that's what I've heard from the rumor mill. The town isn't accepting the change easily—small-town folks here, *hello*—but we're getting there.

Maybe the rehab will attract a few hot young doctors who like tattooed chicks and aren't scared of a few nasty rumors.

Involuntarily, I glance back outside again. The new teacher is long forgotten. In fact, she's tapping on his bicep, trying to attract his attention that is solely—and wrathfully—focused on me. I smile back at him, knowing it will drive him insane. He doesn't like me happy; he feeds off my misery and his ability to create it. So I smile wider, and his demeanor changes completely. Clouds swarm his disgustingly perfect face, and he even bares his teeth in a snarl. So different from his face when he gave my car a jump. That day, I'd felt like this monstrous thing between us, whatever it is, didn't exist.

"Oh-oh, somebody's extra constipated today." Marina nudges my shoulder, severing the weird, hate-filled connection we have going.

"Looks like it." I shrug and walk to the kitchen to help with the wall Marina has begun washing the remaining smoke damage off of, throwing one last look at the gorgeous jerk over my shoulder. Soon, I'm so exhausted that I forget all about Justin and his new conquest. Because that's all she'll be, whether she knows it or not. He could sell venom to a rattlesnake, and that lady didn't appear to need a whole lot of convincing.

When I finally look back outside, it looks like he's forgotten about me too, because I don't see him out the front window. I covertly glance at the teacher, who's still there, and notice her scowling at me. *Oops,* I think to myself with an internal snicker. Feels good to be a cockblocker. *Sorry, lady.* I go back to cleaning with a suppressed grin and begin wiping the counter. It's already sparkling since it's brand new—bought on Freya's dime.

Freya. Even thinking about her makes me cringe.

Oh man, how do I face her? And how do I even start when I finally do?

We haven't spoken since the day she was attacked and I was trapped in the pantry three weeks ago. After that chaos, which resulted in her ex being shot, I wanted to go hug the hell out of her, so grateful and happy that she was alive, but Justin or Jake was always around her. They were like big watch dogs yapping at her feet, blocking me from coming anywhere near her.

One time, when I got the courage to go and see her, Jake stopped me on the road and warned me to stay away from Freya, saying she was in bad shape mentally and I might trigger something and set her recovery back. I wanted to send him to hell—nothing new there—but something in his eyes was different. There was no glint of malice or spite, only sincere concern, which worried me more than anything he could've said aloud. I reluctantly listened, caring only about her mental health—I wanted my friend to be well again, even if that meant I didn't get to be a part of her journey and missed her something awful. So I've been waiting, hoping she'll show up when she's ready, and I'll beg for her forgiveness when she does.

But she hasn't.

If I'd doubted how much she'd come to mean to me before any of this happened, the ache in my heart that's grown more each day she's stayed away since would confirm it.

"One Lonely Kurt coming right up for our biggest sponsor!" Marina's cheerful voice pulls me out of this miserable train of thought, and I look up. Freya's standing by the door, looking ready to run for the hills.

She's here. She came.

And just like that, I start crying like a baby. She's beside me in a heartbeat, enveloping me in her friendly embrace.

"I'm so sorry!" I blubber, my throat congested. "I'm sorry I didn't come to you, but I just couldn't."

"No, *I'm* sorry for saying all that stuff to you. I'm sorry, Kayla, I don't believe that shit I said," she swears, wetting my neck with her tears and hugging me tighter.

"Screw that; I don't care about that nonsense." And I really don't. At least, not anymore. During our last conversation, she asked me what I had done to Justin's family. No, she didn't just ask—it was more of an accusation, and I got mad and hung up on her. I was tired of everybody blaming me for something I hadn't done. Something I couldn't even name. And especially Freya, who I was so happy had decided to be my friend when friends weren't so easily made or kept for someone like me in Little Hope. So yeah, I was angry.

"I—wait—I'm so confused," Freya stutters, pulling away from me.

"Why?"

"I'm confused about how you can forgive me for doubting you." She sniffs, her now-runny mascara having created a raccoon face that miraculously doesn't detract from her natural beauty.

I wave my hand. "Water under the bridge." And I mean that. In the face of recent events, the fight feels empty, and she's just said she no longer doubts me. I'd rather put it all behind us just to talk to her again. I miss my friend, and I'm just happy that she's alive and well.

She squints at me. "So why didn't you respond to my texts? Did you block me on your phone?"

"What? No! I lost my phone, man. Got no money to buy a new one yet." I tap my empty jeans pockets and add, "And before you go bananas on why I hadn't visited you at the hospital, well... I was a little *tied up* in the moment." It's a lame joke, but we both need the levity. "But honestly, I just couldn't come. Either Justin or Jake was always around you, watching you twenty-four-seven like a couple of infuriating, stupidly handsome hawks. I love you, I do, but I was waiting for you to get out of there." I decide to leave the part about Jake's warning out.

"Well, here I am." She grins.

"Here you are," I parrot, answering her grin with my own.

"I've heard you were hospitalized too." She's biting her lips nervously. "I wish I knew that while I was there so I could've visited you."

"Don't be silly." I wave her off again because after three weeks of digesting the situation, it's much easier.

"No." She vigorously shakes her head. "Someone should have been with you when you were hurt. I feel like I've taken away from you with my stupid trauma. Which wasn't even physical." She lowers her brows. "I'm sorry."

"Freya." I gently touch her shoulder. "Mental struggles can be as painful as physical ones, if not more. Don't you ever apologize for that."

"But—"

"Lonely Kurt's ready!" Marina strides in from the kitchen with a full plate, interrupting whatever Freya wanted to say. "Well, half of Kurt." She smiles sheepishly.

"We still haven't gotten everything because there's still so much to be done in the kitchen, but overall, it's usable." Then she adds with a cringe, "Somewhat."

"Marina, I told you, everything you need is on my tab," Freya promises, looking guilty. I hate that she clearly thinks she needs to pay for everything to make up for what her ex did. She's not responsible for his actions, but she insisted Marina accept her paying for the repairs. Marina's too proud for that, but she accepted it on the condition that it be a loan—though I know Freya will never take repayment. Although I'm happy Marina will save some money, I also want Freya to stop trying to buy everyone's forgiveness for things her piece of shit ex did. No one blames her. And even though everyone is grateful for her attempts to right the wrongs he did, she doesn't have to buy everyone's love. I wish she could see that she'd be loved without a cent to her name here in Little Hope.

"We can take care of this place, don't you worry," Marina insists with a broad, proud smile. "Now, you girls have fun. I'll be in the kitchen."

Freya follows Marina's retreat, sounding devastated as she tells me quietly, "God, I just feel so bad."

"Don't," I assure her. "Really. This place has needed a do-over for years. It was perfect timing. We should be thanking you." I offer her a sincere smile, hoping she believes me—it's the truth, but the guilt in her eyes kills me.

She sniffles again. "And I'm sorry for what he did to you."

"No sweat," I say with a dismissive wave, though I can't help but cringe internally. I still have nightmares of flames crawling closer to lick at my skin, but I'm not going to agonize her further by sharing that. She looks miserable, on the verge of tears yet again. "Alex isn't back?" She shakes her head with downcast eyes and wipes at her red-tipped nose. "Do you know where he is?" I ask, even though I could assume the answer—if Freya knew, she'd be there dragging his ass back here kicking and screaming.

"No." She bites her lip, her hands rubbing at her neck. "Only Justin does, but he won't tell anybody."

At the mention of his name, my jaw sets, but I refrain from sharing my opinion of him. Though it might have slightly shifted after his help—*twice*—it's still decidedly negative, and I've seen Freya and Justin around town together and know for a fact they've grown even closer. He became the friend she needed when I wasn't there. To be completely honest, I wouldn't have known what she needed from me or how I could deliver it.

I'd still been offended by Freya's accusation then—it had felt like a knife to my back. I had told her numerous times that I didn't know how I wronged Justin or Jake, and I still don't—even despite my attempts at asking either of them. They both snarl and shut me down, accusing me of being a liar. I never bothered asking Alicia, their sister, because she was never on good terms with me even before. She was always a part of the popular crowd, just as Justin was, just a bit younger. And even now, here and there, I see Alicia surrounded by the mean girls of Little Hope. Mainly Ashley, who I'd consider Justin's most consistent bedbug. Though I must admit—Alicia never looks to be participating much in their conversations.

If I hadn't undergone my own attack, I know I would've found a way to Freya sooner and ignored the Jake-shaped obstacle in my way, but I was licking my own wounds and feeling sorry for myself. While my concussed ass couldn't walk without puking for days following my heroic rescue by my disinclined rescuer, only Marina and

Mark were there for me—the latter of whom surprised the hell out of me. He's stopped by the diner twice since then to ask if I'm all right, if there was anything I needed, and if I needed to talk. He seemed a tad bit uncomfortable doing so because he's a tough guy who seems a little shy of emotional women—which I was guilty of being—but it was one of the sweetest things anybody has ever done for me.

To be completely honest, Marina's reaction surprised me too. She's been doting on me like a mother hen on her egg, which is entirely out of character for her. She didn't let me do anything more strenuous than chopping carrots till I showed her a note from my doctor saying I'm cleared to wipe my own ass and everything now. I shed a few tears upon what felt like the fiftieth time she offered me chicken broth. I think we both did. I've been shedding a lot of tears lately, really—and Marina and Mark have both seen my puffy eyes, and neither have judged me for them.

"I'm sorry, Kayla." Freya brings me back to our little diner, roused from my bittersweet thoughts.

"Stop apologizing, Freya," I soothe.

"No, I need to for all the shit you've been through because of me and my crap—"

She's going to make us both start bawling again. "Frey—"

"No," she cuts in, shaking her head. "I need to say it. Erik was an asshole, and I don't regret what happened to him. But I hate what he did to you. And I regret the things I said on that call. I was riled up—not that that's any excuse. I don't know what came over me, but I don't really believe that. I don't think you could have done anything to make anybody hate you so much. I know that." Her eyes are glassy, her lower lip quaking, and yep, we're both about to start the waterworks again. "I'll try to talk to Justin. Maybe he'll tell me. All I know is he truly believes it."

I shrug helplessly. "I hope you have better luck than me. But for God's sake, stop apologizing for your ex—he's wasted enough of your time. I hope it doesn't make me sound callous, and I don't know all the details of what happened, but I think he got what he deserved that night." Hell with details, I don't even know the major events of that night. The rumor mill has changed its mind on the facts more times than I could keep track of, so I stopped trying.

With wide eyes, Freya tells me everything that went down that night, and my eyebrows soon disappear into my hairline without any hope of reemerging. Jake shot Erik to save Freya, I find out, from long-range; that, I didn't see coming, considering the whole town knows he failed his assessment at the shooting range recently—not long before that night, actually. I wonder to myself if it was his first kill—it feels so strange and dystopian even to say that—though I'd bet with how little crime there is in Little Hope and how short a time he's been on the force, relatively, he'd never faced the need to before. In any case, I imagine it leaves an imprint on a person's mind. And is Jake really such a good shot? I can't say I'm entirely comfortable with that new piece of information.

Like Freya said before, Alex disappeared that night as well, and although Justin knows where he is, he isn't sharing it with the class. That's some strong loyalty there. I don't imagine it's easy to keep it from Freya, seeing her suffering. Alex better be suffering, wherever he is, or I'll smack him stupid with our new, cute mugs.

Then I tell Freya my side of the story, and it's *her* turn for *her* eyebrows to disappear into her hairline. When I'm done, she jumps from the stool and envelopes me in a hug once again. "I'm sorry, Kayla!"

I try to pry her off me, but she doesn't let go. "You need to chill, Freya. Really. This was a good thing, so don't worry."

"How so?" she asks, finally pulling away from me. I never was hugged much as a kid, and probably even less once I became an adult, so I'm a little uncomfortable to be on the receiving end of such strong affection.

I pointedly look around. There are new, stylish tables with matching stools, cute chairs here and there, new pictures on the walls, new curtains, and new decorations Marina and I picked out together everywhere. And everything matches. The dishes and silverware are new too, very modern and shiny. The walls are painted dark beige—the best thing we could possibly do for the diner and my poor eyes, since I always hated those weird, hospital-like green walls that Marina was so fond of. The only thing I'd add is a nice mural on the wall—that would be sick. "This place needed a makeover, and Marina would never have agreed to that unless she didn't have a choice. So, thank *you*—you saved my sanity." Her eyes are misty again by the time I finish. "Oh, for fuck's sake!"

She begins laughing, wiping away her tears. "So, we're good?"

I gently punch her shoulder. "We're good."

"Thank God. Now I'm getting you a new phone," she chirps, clapping her hands.

"No way!"

"Yes way; I have one extra already that I don't use. It's just lying in a drawer. You can have it." She shrugs.

I squint at her, fully aware that it's a ploy to give me a new phone. She knows I don't like handouts, so she lets me preserve my pride. I appreciate it. "Until I buy a new one," I reason stubbornly.

"Of course!" she agrees too soon, and I sigh as she cracks a smile.

It's good to have my friend back.

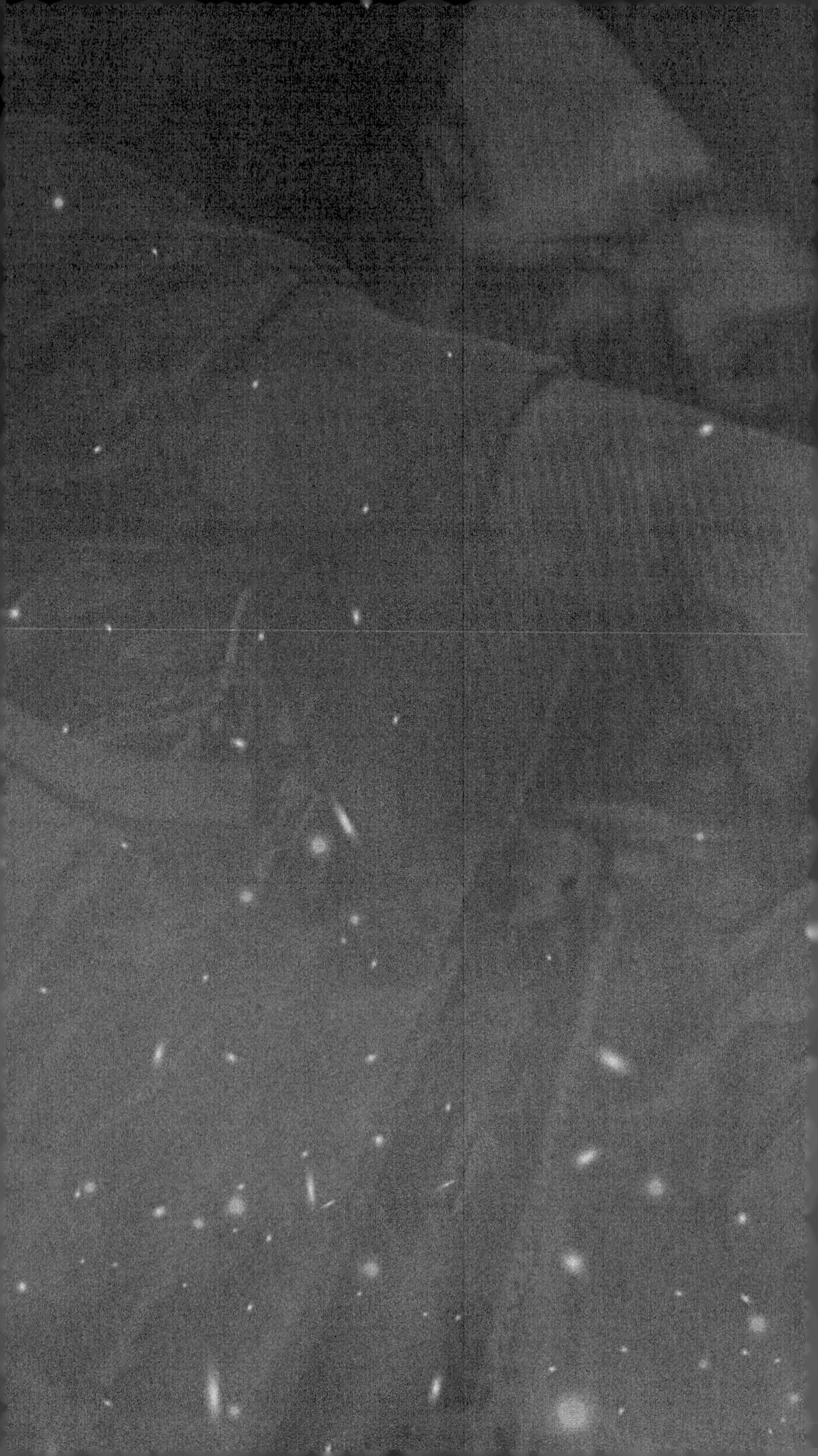

Chapter Four

JUSTIN

I've been waiting for three days till a good opportunity turned up. Now I'm hiding behind the car, trying to check the brakes while making sure nobody sees me doing it. As I thought, the brake pads are fucking worn down. Completely. I'd been hearing the loud squealing noise of dying brakes every time this rust bucket stopped at traffic lights or parked, and I could now confirm. How she hasn't been found dead in a ditch yet is beyond me. The only place she should drive this metal can ever again is to a junkyard.

I squat next to the wheel again, making sure I got the right model.

"Huh, interesting."

I jump like my ass is on fire and come face-to-face with a very smug-looking Freya.

"Lost something over there?" she asks, trying to stop her smile from spreading too wide. Her stance is that of a woman who knows a secret with which she could bury you.

"Over where?" I play dumb, even though I've been busted.

"Under Kayla's car." She nods at the old beast.

"Yeah, dropped my keys." I pat my front pockets nonchalantly.

"Did you find them?" She crosses her arms over her chest and cocks a hip, challenging me.

"Yep," I affirm and start walking toward the grocery store. Freya falls in step behind me.

"I never thanked you for saving Kayla. So thank you," she tells me.

"I didn't do anything," I grunt in the most neutral voice I can manage. "It was Alex who noticed the fire."

"Really?" She perks up at the mention of his name, even though she's heard this story a dozen times. This motherfucker better hurry the hell up because I don't know how long I can keep up with this charade he's putting me through.

"Yeah, he noticed that something was wrong and called me."

"You got her out, though." She pushes for more with a suggestive tone.

"Anyone would do the same," I cut her off too sharply.

"Yeah." Her tone dulls, indicating that she didn't like my answer. What did she expect? For me to announce my undying love for that trailer trash? I did what everybody would do in my place, and then I had to get out before the firefighters arrived. I just had to. I had my reasons.

"How is Jake? He isn't talking to me much nowadays." Great. Another sore subject.

"He's fine." He's not. He hasn't been fine since he shot that asshole. I know he and Freya made amends, but I don't think he's in the right state of mind to dive into a friendship with her. Not when he killed her ex.

"Okay, good. Do you think Alicia will want to meet for lunch or something?" Her tone is hopeful, and I don't have the heart to tell her that my sister is antisocial. And for a good reason. She hasn't really talked to anybody besides family for years now. It worries us, of course, but we don't know how to help her move on. She said she has, but we all know she's been stuck in that nightmare, that *that* moment defines who she is now, even though it shouldn't. We love her, and she's perfect just the way she is. I'd love to see her more open though, livelier, more like her old self—the social butterfly who attracted everybody to her bright light. But she refuses to change anything. Or maybe she simply can't. I wish I knew, but she doesn't share with me or anybody. Our conversations now include only safe subjects: her books, our house, the weather, and family holidays.

"Sure, I'll ask." I nod regardless of my thoughts—I don't want to be the villain and burst Freya's little bubble of temporary happiness.

"Thank you! That would be so cool!"

She then proceeds to chatter about local gossip and living with Alex's family, and I just nod and hum at the right moments. My mind's busy sorting out how to covertly fix the brakes on Kayla's car. If I didn't know about them, my hands would be clean, and I'd happily move on with my life. But now I *know*, and I can't have her getting into an accident because of worn-down brakes that I could have fixed because I fuckin' *knew*.

But then, while chatting about her recent encounters with every single person in Little Hope, Freya mentions

Jake's name again, and I get an idea. He's been giving Kayla tickets on a regular basis, and knowing her, she probably hasn't been paying them out of spite. I could remind him about all those tickets and ask why her car hasn't been towed yet. And once it's towed, I can go and replace it. Bobby, the guy who owns the towing company, owes me a favor. Yeah, sounds like a solid plan to me.

Once Freya's dutifully informed me about everything I didn't need to know, I hug her goodbye and head home to my place.

Where I get a bad fucking surprise.

Ashley's sitting on my bed, clearly naked under the comforter draped over her shoulders.

"What the hell are you doing here?" I bark, toeing my boots off.

"Waiting for you—what else?" She lifts her skinny shoulder, and the comforter falls onto her lap, baring her big tits that used to make me all hot and bothered.

"I thought we had this conversation already."

"Pf-f-f," she dismisses, waving her hand, the clicking sound of those bracelets I absolutely fucking hate grating on my ears. "It was just a joke."

"It was not," I say, clenching my jaw.

She stands up and walks toward me, trying to force her skinny hips to swing. It looks unnatural—too wide of a range. I'm surprised she hasn't dislocated her pelvis. When she comes closer, she traces her finger from my bicep to my chest and then down. Aaaaand... nothing. No movements happening *down there*. None. She used to do it for me, but not for a while now. Not at all. I'm relieved, to be completely honest.

I grip her wrist and use it to keep her at a distance. "I

said *this—*" I gesture with my free hand at the space between her and myself—"is done."

"Why?" she screeches, snatching her wrist from my grasp, and I let her. So much for staying classy—her face, growing rapidly blotchier and twisted with offended fury, doesn't predict a mature conversation to come.

"Because it was a good arrangement while it lasted." I step back and look at her with a cold stare. "And now it's passed its expiration date."

"*Arrangement?*" she parrots, her voice pitchy and loud.

"What else did you think it was?" I'm taken aback—surely, she doesn't think it was more than that. For fuck's sake, I've been sleeping with a lot of people besides her, and she knows that. So has she.

"*We were dating!*" she shrieks, turning her heel to storm back to the bed, where she picks up her watch from the nightstand.

My laugh borders on a scoff. "No, we were not. We never even went out. We fucked other people. We didn't meet each other's family—"

"I'm friends with Alicia!" she screeches again, hitting my nightstand lamp with her clenched fist, sending it flying to the floor with a loud *crash*. What in the ever-loving hell is happening with lamps recently? Alex first, and now Ashley. I'm going to have to start factoring in a monthly lamp-replacement budget if this keeps up.

"Oh, I highly doubt that." My chuckle is dark. Alicia can't stand Ashley, threatening to cut my balls off if I ever brought her to a family dinner. Not that it ever occurred to me to do so.

"Oh, you just don't know anything. Nothing, Justin." Then she begins laughing like a cartoon villain, and as melodramatic as it is, I get chills. There's something in the way she says it. As if she really knows something I don't.

"Are you done?" I level her with a stare.

"Yeah, I'm done! I'm *so* fucking done with you!" She begins collecting her clothes from the floor. She created a fuckin' mess just trying to be sexy, throwing her underwear everywhere. She was always a mess, and I absolutely hated it; there can only be one slob in this space, and that slob is me.

As she reaches the door, I stop her with a question: "How did you get in, Ashley?" I ask in my calmest voice.

"Wouldn't you like to know?" she sneers.

"How?" I repeat firmly, and she sobers up instantly. She knows better than to fuck with me when I'm in no mood for games.

"The key under the rug at the back door," she sniffs, calmer now but still thoroughly pissed.

"Forget it's there." My stare could freeze a lake to the damn bottom in a blink.

"Whatever," she says, flipping her raven hair over her shoulder.

I make a mental note to change the location of my emergency keys and tell my parents about that.

I take a shower, microwave some dinner, and go to watch some TV. Cringing at the first bite of my barely edible meatballs with pasta, I yearn for my mom's food. I need to visit them tomorrow. I haven't been for a while, plus I'm missing the home-cooked food.

My phone rings, and I pick it up without looking. "Yeah?"

"*Jus*," Alex's tired voice says.

"Hey, motherfucker. Are you back yet?" I ask through huge bites. It helps to ignore the generally disgusting taste if

I just shove it down the gullet. I probably look like a pelican eating.

"No, not ready yet. It's fucking tough, man." I hear his heavy sigh.

I stop chewing. "I know, man, I know. But you'll get better." He makes a pensive hum. "I'm really proud of you right now," I tack on. "You're doing the right thing."

"Yeah." A heavy silence follows. *"How is she?"* We both know he checked into that place because of Freya. He always needed to do this for himself, but he's doing it now for her.

"Missing you. Constantly on my ass about you." I swallow a sip of beer, washing the awful taste of the food down.

He huffs a small laugh, then pauses before adding, *"Have they been talking?"* I know who he means—he's trying to spare me because the mention of Kayla's name usually causes a burst of anger. Alex is one of very few who knows the whole story.

"Yeah, I saw them at the diner together," I answer, instinctively crinkling my nose in distaste.

"Good. That's good." He's worried about Freya and wants to be with her, but he and I both know that right now, the best thing he can do is to take care of himself and come back healthy—however he defines that. *"How's Jake?"*

"I dunno," I answer honestly. Jake seems to be separating himself from us more and more every day. I feel like I now have two siblings going through shit, and I can't help either. Some big brother I am.

"I'll talk to him when I'm back," he promises.

I roll my eyes as if he can see me. "What, you're planning on coming back now?"

"Jackass." His laughter is a hint at the old Alex.

"I appreciate it, Alex." A word from somebody who's been dealing with trauma for years might help more than me throwing in my two hugely lacking cents here and there.

I hear muffled voices on the other end of the phone. *"Okay, I gotta go. I'll call you,"* Alex tells me, sounding distracted.

"Yeah," I reply, but he's already hung up.

I try another bite of food, but it tastes like shit, so I give up on that and go grab a couple apples. At this rate, I'll turn into a rabbit soon. A visit to Mom tomorrow it is.

I open the door, and the delicious smell of freshly cooked food welcomes me to my parents' house. That's how it always smells here: mouthwatering and homey. I wonder how Alicia manages to stay skinny with all this goodness in the house.

"Mom?" I yell, taking my jacket off.

"In here, honey," my mom calls from the kitchen.

I find her beside the stove, as usual, cooking mountains of food that she'll dole out to everyone we know. That's why my father tends to eat everything he can put his hands on and fast—he knows whatever he doesn't snatch will go to friends, neighbors, and the church.

"Whatcha making?" I ask, peeking at the sizzling pan from behind her.

"Oh, just meatloaf with veggies. Nothing fancy." She's being modest as usual. I try to stick my finger into the bowl of mashed potatoes on the table, and she smacks me with a wooden spatula—the one *I* got her as part of a fancy kitchen set, by the way. Life is unfair.

"Ouch, Mom! That hurt!" I nurse my poor, offended hand.

"You'll survive," Alicia chimes in, strolling into the kitchen. As usual, she's dressed in her baggy sweatpants and a sweatshirt three sizes too big for her. My heart aches for my little sister. She used to be a girly girl, always happy and bubbly, wearing bright clothes meant to be noticed. Now, she wears clothes meant to hide. Her long blonde hair is pulled into a low, messy bun, and a few strands frame her face—which looks like a feminine version of mine. She has fewer freckles on her face—a clear indication that she hasn't seen the light of day for too long. She's turning into a vampire—like in one of her books.

"I might not. Will you miss me then?" I reply, enveloping her in a bear hug.

She mumbles something, pulling away and tapping her chin as if pondering it.

"What did you say?" I ask with a devious smile, grabbing her again and squeezing harder.

"I said 'maybe,' but I'm not so sure anymore," she jokes after she unwraps herself from my embrace. She pinches my biceps, and I pinch the tip of her nose. That's what we always do, so I feel a little better, sensing she's in a good mood today.

"Behave, children." I'm thirty-one and still live by my mom's rules when I'm in her house, and I'm not ashamed to admit that.

"Yes, mom!" we singsong, taking our usual seats at the breakfast table in the kitchen. My parents' kitchen is a work of art. I don't know how much my dad spent on it, but it must have cost a fortune. He loves my mother, though, so I'm sure it was a pleasure for him to make her happy. My parents have been married for thirty-three years and still behave like teenagers, stealing kisses in hallways, smacking each other's butts, and making all of us gag. When I look at them, I know I'll never have that, and I'll never agree to anything less, so here I am—the forever bachelor of Little Hope. I like to swim in a pool of choices, though, so I don't complain. And once our pool becomes too small or too boring, I take my truck and drive. There is always a bigger lake out there.

"I'm guessing you could eat?" Mom asks me, barely containing her smile.

"I guess I could," I reply with a grin, feigning nonchalance. I'm always hungry—always—and she knows that.

She fills my plate with steaming meatloaf, mashed potatoes, and salad before placing it in front of me. We all know it will be gone in a minute flat. What can I say? I'm a growing boy.

"So, how are you guys doing?" I ask when I'm finally full and can devote my focus to my family instead of my growling belly.

"Good," Alicia murmurs, eating her food slowly while Mom throws a worried glance at her. She's become a person of few words, and it still surprises me how she manages to write long-ass books with the number of words she says aloud in everyday life. I tried to read a book of hers once, but after seeing a few choice words—words you never want to see written by your little sister—I snapped it shut, saving myself from the trauma. Thanks, but no thanks.

"Well, your father is in Springfield, shopping for a new bed. We kind of broke the old one." She blushes and giggles like a teenager while Alicia and I gag.

"Mom!" Alicia chokes out, adding under her breath, "God, I need out of this house...."

"Alright, you boring bunch," Mom laughs, moving on to

the next topic, thank fuck. "So, how are things at the shop, Justin?"

"Good, actually. I'm thinking of hiring another mechanic and maybe even a receptionist," I reply, pouring myself another cup of tea. "The business's steady, we got a lot of customers from Springfield, and we have regulars like Mrs. Jenkins." I laugh while Alicia perks up and glances at me with interest. Weird.

"What's up with her?" she asks with apparent nonchalance, picking at her food. "Mrs. Jenkins?"

"She gives us stability by bringing her beast almost every month."

"Why? Is her car dangerous?" prods Mom worriedly.

"Her car isn't, but the way she drives is." I cringe.

"Oh, poor thing," Mom says, bringing her hands to her chest. "She's too old to drive. I expect her daughter will bring her to live in the city soon."

"I'd say she needed to do that yesterday. I love Mrs. Jenkins, I do, she's an undeniable fixture of Little Hope with her dentures always falling out while she's yelling at you, but she gets into accidents way too often." I shake my head in frustration. "I fix her car almost for free from time to time because I feel bad for the grumpy old lady; this time around, though, I'll keep her car a little longer and maybe have a chat with her daughter after all. She might not know how bad it's gotten."

"You do that." Mom nods her head. "Something might happen with her on the road, God forbid." She again presses her hands into her chest.

"When will you call her daughter?" Alicia stops chewing and asks.

"Why do you care?" I ask suspiciously.

"No reason," she shrugs her shoulders, but I know

better—my sister's plotting something and has a little spark in her eyes that I haven't seen in years. Whatever she's plotting, I'll support her. As long as I can see that sparkle again.

Guilt pierces my chest with renewed force—I'm the reason it disappeared in the first place. Me, a domino effect of actions, decisions, and their ultimate costs, and *her*.

"Hey," Alicia says quietly, gently touching my hand.

I subtly take a deep breath and plant a casual smile on my face. "Sup, sis."

"Where did you go?" she questions, holding my gaze.

"Been here the whole time." I smile forcefully, trying to master the mask I try so hard to hide behind, so no one sees what I feel.

Though from the look on my sister's face, pensive and dark, there might be one person who still can.

"Sup, y'all!" Jake bursts in, bringing a gust of cold wind along. When the fuck will this never-ending winter end? It's been lingering far too long this year. "Oh damn, meatloaf! Can I have some?"

"You sure can, baby," Mom says, causing Alicia and me to roll our eyes. Jake's the baby of the family, and our mother sure does treat him like it; he fully supports her on it too—I'd say he's a step or two away from letting her wipe his ass.

"See what I mean? I need out," Alicia complains, and I give her a commiserating smile. She's been saying the same mantra about moving out for a long time, but I don't think she can. Besides that, I want her where we can see her. Yes, I know she's a grown woman, but after everything that happened, it's hard to override the protective-brother instincts.

"What're your plans for today, Jakey?" Alicia asks with a smirk, knowing he hates the nickname.

He throws a piece of bread at her and gets a smack on the back of his head from Mom, which makes me laugh. "Ken put me on the night shift today," he tells us with his mouth full and gets smacked again, by Alicia this time—she hates open-mouth chewers. "I'll be bored to death."

Little Hope isn't super eventful—besides Freya's ex, we don't have many troubles here. Jake got suspended after something I'm still not privy to happened a few weeks ago between him and Kenneth, the sheriff and Alex's brother. He was restored to his post two weeks ago, and it's been good for him.

"So, how do you spend your shift when you're bored?" Alicia asks.

A devious smile spreads across his face. "Well, I like to torment certain citizens of our fine town."

I clench my jaw.

"I don't know why you don't just leave her alone," Alicia comments in a sour tone, leaning back on her chair. She knows who he's talking about too. "She doesn't have much good in her life. Didn't you ever learn it's shitty to kick somebody when they're down?"

That's Alicia for you. Even knowing everything, she's still trying to stick up for people. She's a mighty protector behind people's backs, despite the fact that she can be a harpy to your face when she wants to and has quite the reputation of being a bitch. Though now, she's more likely to be called aloof because she tends to avoid human interaction at all costs. I wish Ashley would get the hint and stop trying to befriend her.

Jake's face darkens. "That's exactly what I should do. Keep kicking."

"*Jacob.*" Mom's stern voice and the clang of a spoon on

the table stop him from spewing any more hate. "I did *not* raise you to treat people like that."

"Mom—" Jake starts, but I cut him off with a harsh sound from the back of my throat. He looks outraged.

"Don't 'Mom' me. You're using your position to bully this girl," she accuses. "That's an abuse of power. If that's the kind of police officer you're choosing to be, I wonder if your suspension should've stayed permanent. The sheriff gave you a second chance, but I don't know if he'll give you another one."

"Mom!" Jake yelps like a little kid, and even Alicia looks impressed with how pitiful he can make himself.

"For fuck's sake, Jake!" I bellow and smack my palm on the table, making everybody jump. "Leave it."

Jake contemplates saying something, I can tell, but he stays silent. Furious and defensive, but silent. Then he stands with a bang of his chair and leaves the room.

Mom looks between Alicia and me; she knows something's going on—she's always known—but she never asks. She always gave us the chance to share our problems on our own terms without too much meddling.

"I gotta go too. Thanks, Mom—the food was amazing, as always." I stand up and kiss her cheek. Then I position myself next to Alicia and quietly ask her, "You okay?"

"Always am," she says with a smile. It's fake.

I leave their house with a heavy heart.

I'm wondering if I should make a small stop as I drive home. Just to see her squirm. She doesn't know that I know where she lives. That more people than she realizes know that. She wants to hide in that little haven she found, but the world doesn't work like that.

When I nearly crush the wheel under my fingers, I realize that I need a breather, so I make a turn and stop by the Cat and Stallion, a local pub. It serves nearly all night long, despite the law, and I'm okay with that. Tonight, I might stay longer than I initially intended.

I walk in and take a seat at the bar. Rory, the new and very attractive bartender, comes to take my order.

"Whatcha want, Justin?"

"Some action, if you're up for it." I wiggle my brows playfully.

She rolls her eyes. "I'm not." She walks away and comes back a minute later with my usual IPA. "Open a tab for you?"

"Sure thing, hon." I smile seductively, causing her to chuckle and shake her head.

"One day, Justin, you'll find a woman you'll want to keep, but all that," she circles her finger around my face, "will fuck you over."

My smile drops for a moment before it returns in full force. "No woman like that exists."

"Sure thing, Justin. Keep believing that." She winks and walks away, and I just laugh.

Rory is new to the bar but not new in town. She's five years older than me and has a hot, lithe body and a fuck-off attitude. We had a fun couple of nights ages ago when I was barely of legal age. She knew a lot of tricks, and she was wild. Just reminiscing on all that fun, I anticipate my neighbor downstairs to stir at the thought of our old hookup and the idea of possibly rekindling things, but nothing. Fucking nada!

I look at her again and notice that her hair is too yellow,

and while she has two tattoos on her collarbone, they're the wrong sizes and placement. She's too tall for my liking.

What the fuck? *For my liking?* I used to like everything. *Love* everything. Every shape, every size, every color. What the fuck happened to me?

The memory of that vivid tattoo of a red rose with sharp green spikes creeping up a milky forearm enters my mind, and my dick roars to life. Fucking roars to full mast in seconds. Without anyone even touching it. In memory of a tattoo on a person I fucking *loathe*. In public, no less.

I chug my beer and regret… a lot.

I'm gesturing to Rory for another when I hear a familiar male voice behind me, and I still. I don't hear that voice often. I slowly turn my head, and there he is: another asshole from *that night*. Walking in like he owns the place. Like he has any fucking right to enjoy life when others can't anymore.

He looks around and tenses once he notices me. *That's right, asshole. I'm here.*

Even from my seat at the bar, I can see how tightly he clenches his jaw. I hope he fucking loses all his teeth. He rakes his hand through his hair, messing up his man-bun. A fucking *man-bun*. Who wears that?

Training his eyes on me, he walks to the other side of the bar and motions for Rory to come to him. When she hasn't even brought my drink yet. I don't think so. I stand up from my stool, about to voice my opinion, when Harry, the bar owner, comes into view in front of me, placing my drink on the bar with a loud *thud*.

"Not here, Justin. Not in my bar. Is that clear?" He looks between Mark and me (I spit his name even in my head). I feel my nostrils flaring while trying to contain my anger, but I finally nod. "Is that clear, Mark?" He raises his voice to be heard through music, and the asshole finally nods too. "Good. Enjoy your evening, boys."

Everybody knows Mark and I can't be in the same space without a fight. Often a physical one. That's why we try to avoid each other.

Mark downs his drink just as I did a moment ago and relaxes in his seat. He's alone. Probably waiting for his degenerate friends, whoever they are. Leopards don't change their spots.

I take a deep breath and try to shift my attention to my glass. I'm considering another one but decide against it. With Mark here, it's not a good idea to push any limits—Harry's warning will mean nothing to me after another drink, and I'll be banned from the only decent bar in town. Not worth it.

I drop a few bills on the counter and walk out without a glance, feeling his stare on my back the whole time. I decide to leave my truck parked at the bar and walk home; it's about ten minutes down the street anyway.

I'm leisurely strolling along the sidewalk when I notice the lights at Marina's diner are on. A brief look at my phone screen says it's past eleven—I don't know why somebody would be there so late. A weird, worrying feeling nudges at my chest—the last time something felt off was when the diner was on fire with *her* inside.

A shiver runs down my spine, and my legs pick up speed of their own accord. When I'm at the diner entrance, I push the door handle with too much force, and the door smacks on the wall, nearly making me jump. But not her, no: with headphones tucked in her ears, she can't hear a thing, not even flinching at my loud entrance. She's shaking her tight ass in those skintight black leggings that I hate with every fiber of my dark soul to some heavy beat in her ears.

That red rose with its green spikes on full display in a cropped tank top that barely covers anything. I take a deep, cleansing breath and watch her move along the wall of the diner with a paintbrush.

She has a few colorful streaks on her skin and clothes from the wet paint. Her hair's tied into a messy bun on top of her head, and from here, I don't see any color added to it. Huh—she always has some type of color in there, so that's new. If I knew her better, I'd know what color represented what, but I don't know her, nor do I want to.

I open the door again and smack it with all my might into the wall, causing the windows to shake. She finally jumps, startled by the loud noise that was able to penetrate whatever rock ballad she's been rupturing her eardrums to.

"What the hell?" she shrieks, yanking the headphones out of her ears. Then she takes me in, and her eyes go round before darting around us. "Justin? What are you doing here?"

"Why is the door open?" I ask, ignoring her question.

"What?"

"Why is the door open?" I repeat, slower this time, pointing at the entrance.

She looks between me and the door. "What's it to you?"

I take a step toward her, causing her eyes to go even rounder. "Not long ago, you were locked in that pantry," I remind her, pointing at the door where I found her, tied and nearly unconscious, "and now you're dancing around with your headphones in without a care in the world with an unlocked door where anyone can just walk in?"

"It's *Little Hope*." Like that's supposed to explain everything.

"It's not that Little Hope anymore. Times change." I clench my jaw. "You have to adapt."

Her face darkens in an instant. "That's what I've been doing all my life. Adapting."

"Have you?" I hum, my tone menacing, taking deliberately slow steps toward her, carefully watching her actions.

She looks around, but there's nobody around, and that's my point. Anybody could barge in, and she wouldn't know because she wouldn't fucking hear!

Only two feet of space separates us now, and she hasn't moved an inch, hypnotized by my slow approach. I stop in front of her and watch for her reaction—fight or flight. That's what has always been between us, and that's what will always be.

"Justin—" She wants to say something but decides against it.

"Yes?"

"I—" She clears her throat and licks her lips. My eyes instantly dip and follow the movement of her pink tongue, which makes an appearance just for a second, leaving her plump lips moist and ready... then she snaps me out of my trance. "I meant to say thank you for helping me."

"I didn't do anything." My lip curls of its own accord.

"You saved me." Her chin stubbornly sticks out.

"Not me." My chuckle is dark, and her face falls. "It was all Alex. He knew something wasn't right. Thank him."

Her face hardens. "Right. You probably wanted to leave me there. So wrong of me to assume that you genuinely wanted to save my life. Thank God Alex was there." Her voice is bitter and full of sarcasm, and I have the horrible urge to tell her the truth—that it was the second time in my life I was so scared I couldn't breathe. But no. Let her think it was Alex. He *was* the one who called me and said that something might be wrong at the diner.

She moves to leave, but I grab her elbow, stopping her in her tracks.

"I never wanted you dead." My voice is barely above a whisper as I let the words tumble out.

"Could've fooled me," she declares shakily, trying to pull her arm from me, but I grip tighter.

"Believe it."

She stops struggling against my hold and lifts her eyes. "What happened, Justin?"

I clench my jaw. "You were tied up in a burning building."

"That's not what I meant, and you know that. What happened that made you hate me so much?"

That question, passing so innocently over her lying lips, always drives me insane. I come closer to her and spit through gritted teeth, "Stop fucking with me. You know what happened. Own your shit." Her face is ashen. "Never fucking ask me that question again. I'm done playing this game with you acting so fucking innocent. *Done*," I roar as she rears back. "Do you understand? Never open your mouth again around me." I lean closer, her signature strawberry smell assaulting my nostrils, and repeat, "Never."

Her eyes fill with tears, and I hate to see them.

And I love to see them.

I'm a sick bastard.

One fat tear escapes her blurred eyes and runs down her cheek. I follow its trail and start feeling like complete shit before the recent encounter with Mark pops into my head. And just like that, I'm sober from any emotions that might make me do something stupid like rush and comfort her.

Refusing to let myself bend for her, I back away toward the door. "If you know what's good for you, stay away from me. Make sure you're not around when I'm with Freya or Alex."

Then I turn and get the hell out of that place, because I don't want to see the cascade of tears streaming down her pale cheeks.

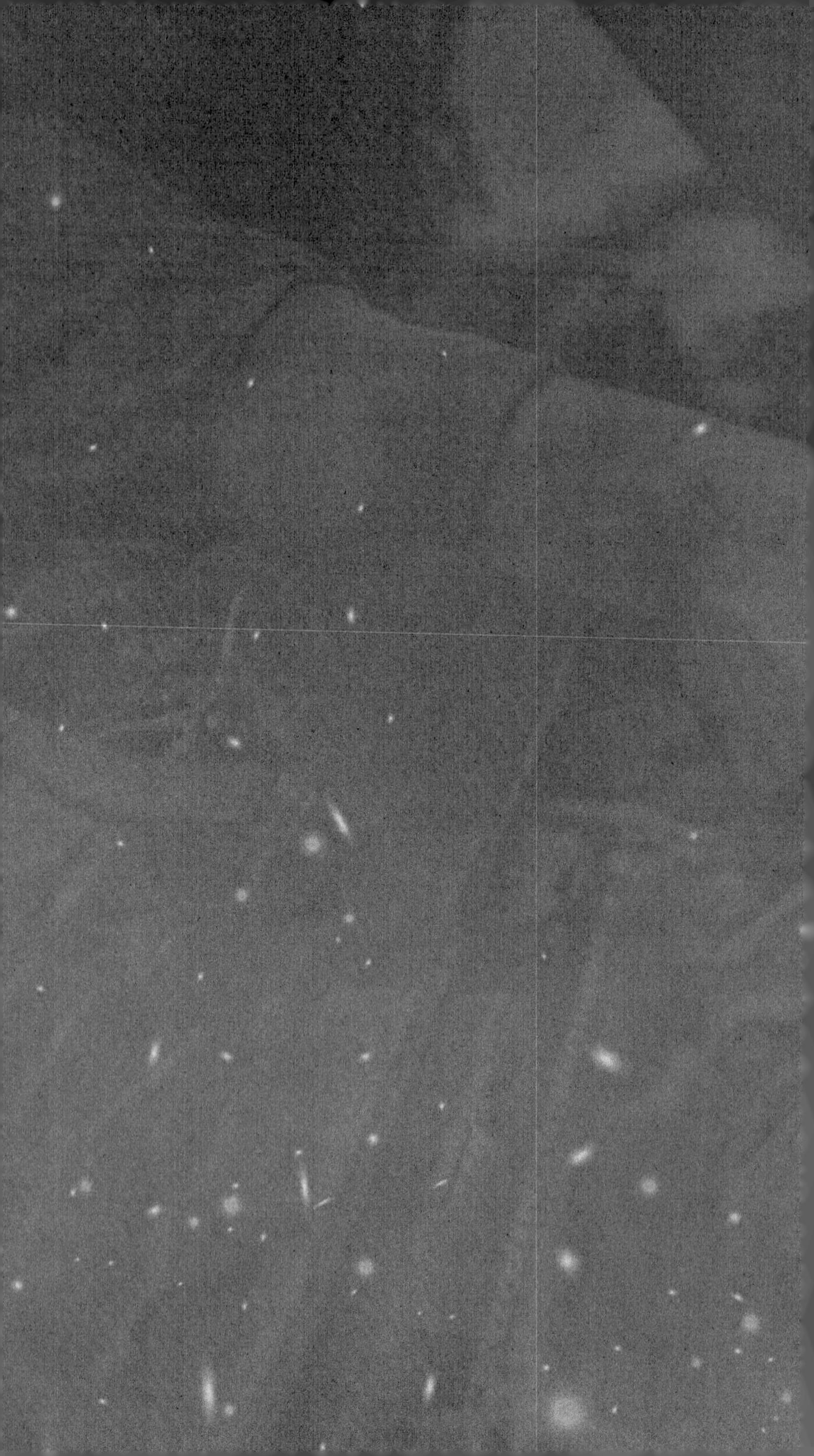

Chapter Five

K<small>AYLA</small>

Every time. Every damn time I'm close to solving that messed-up puzzle, something happens. And by 'something,' I mean Justin going off the rails. Just like right now. A weird moment of... dare I say... *care*? He stormed in demanding to know why I keep my door unlocked. I don't know why; I just always have. But he's right—given recent events, I should be more careful. You never know who might decide to visit our sleepy town in Middle of Nowhere, Maine.

I try to wipe away the tears, but they just keep burning my eyes like acid. I meant what I said: I think he wanted me dead. No matter how petty it sounds, I still do. Yes, I know I sound like a hormonal teenager, but there's no mistaking the hatred emanating from his pores when he's in proximity to me—it's palpable in the air, heavy with pent-up hatred waiting to be unleashed, and when it is, it will be hell. For the both of us, I think, because there is no way that sort of hatred would leave him unscathed.

I really have no idea why he dragged me out of the fire. He must still have some decency where I'm concerned buried deep down—way, way down.

I take a few shuddering breaths as the door once more swings open. Ready to fight, I let out a breath I didn't know I was holding when I see a familiar figure—a friendly one—standing where Justin had disappeared into the night without a second look, smacking the door on his way out.

"Hey, Mark," I croak, my voice wobbling.

"He stopped by, didn't he?" Mark's low, smoky voice washes over me like a calming pill. "I just saw him at the bar."

I try to discreetly wipe my still-streaming eyes and smile but fail miserably. "Yeah." I let out a watery laugh as I choke out my response.

"Why does he do that to you?" His face reflects the genuine puzzlement I've felt for years.

"I wish I knew." I wipe my nose, not bothering with how I must look. Not with Mark. He's known me since we were kids, living at the trailer park. He's four years older, and even as a child, he was always the protector for anyone who needed it—and always paid for it, though I've never heard him complain. You can't stick your neck out for somebody from the wrong side of town without repercussions.

"It can't be that night. You didn't do anything wrong." He clicks his tongue resolutely, like there's nothing else to it, and it sounds weirdly cute.

"Maybe he doesn't see it that way." I shrug and wipe my snotty, swollen nose again.

"He should be thanking you." He comes closer. "I do."

I shake my head. "I didn't do anything."

He gently touches my shoulder. "We both know you did, and I owe you."

I try to smile again. "Stop. You don't owe me anything."

"Do you want me to talk to him?" His voice becomes firmer, his eyes searching mine.

"No!" I exclaim too loudly, then smother a wince. "No," I add more quietly. "It's fine. Don't get involved."

"I already am," he points out.

I offer him a sad smile. "We don't know that."

"Bullshit." His voice rises slightly. "The whole town knows that's when it all started."

"Mark," I plead, waiting for him to calm down as he ignores me, pacing. "*Mark.*"

"What?" he snaps.

I walk to him, and he finally stops. I want him to *see*. "It's not your fault."

His features twist in a snarl. "Kayla, you get treated like shit by half this town for sins you didn't commit, and he just keeps adding fuel to the fire." His voice drops an octave in anger.

"Just like you were," I reason sadly. "And it's not because of that night. It's because we were born on the wrong side of Little Hope." Mark has a younger sister, who he essentially raised. Their father was—still is—an abusive son of a bitch, and Mark often drew attention to himself so his sister would be spared. Like I said—a protector. Reminds me of Alex a little, but rougher around the edges —*yes*, even rougher than Alex, if you can imagine that. Mark didn't have a supportive upbringing or caring parents, so he fended for himself. And I'm happy to see the man he's become. Doesn't hurt that he looks good too. Not that I'd ever look at Mark as more than a friend—he's practically a brother since he got his knuckles scraped for me a few times too—but objectively speaking, he's an attractive specimen. He's tall, very bulky, and very hairy. He has a man-bun, a beard, and on few occasions now, I've seen him shirtless—his chest is very yeti-like, in both size and furriness.

I poke him in the chest, testing how hard his muscles are. "Man, you got, like, super big," I tease to lighten up the mood, stepping back to look him up and down. "Are you shooting something?"

Mark was always a scrawny kid, tall with long limbs and shaggy hair, so it's a huge surprise that he filled out his long body with so much meat.

"Good diet does wonders." He pats his rock-hard belly with a laugh.

"It sure does. Speaking of which, want something to eat?"

"Nah, I'm good. I gotta go." He hikes a thumb over his shoulder. "I just got off a double shift, so I could use some sleep. I just saw *him* walking this way and wanted to make sure you were okay." He scratches his chin covered in a neat, trimmed beard.

"Everything in this town is 'this way.'" I laugh, but it's true. In small towns, there is always a Main Street, and everything usually leads there. As it happens, the diner is on Main Street, so we get more action than most.

"Yeah. Take care, Kayla. Call me if you change your mind about the talk." He waves and walks outside.

Honest to God, I considered taking him up on his offer, but Mark and Justin have a lot of bad blood between them. This is my battle with Justin, and I'll deal with it. Eventually.

I look around the diner and sigh. I've been painting the mural I've drawn for this wall for a long time, and my inspiration just got squashed by a sandy-haired asshole with a killer ass. The rest of the work will require way more time than I initially anticipated. I finish as much as I can, hoping to be done tomorrow morning, clean up, and drive home, saying a silent *thank you* to the universe when my car starts on the first try. It must have felt my distress.

The next morning, my mood is a little better. It took me a few tries and a jump start from my generator, but my Jeep was back on the road, and we were rollin', baby.

A couple hours ago, Freya dropped off her 'old' phone—in pristine condition, without a single scratch on it, and now I ditch my thousand-year-old iPod that jams every two minutes. I tried to give it back, but she refused, saying that if she ever needed me, how would she contact me? And she needs me every day, per her words. That sneaky fox.

So, I have a phone now; the only thing missing is a new SIM card I need to get from the store.

I'm finishing painting the wall in the kitchen when Marina walks in, her hands full of bags.

"What are you doing here?" She looks around and whistles. "Kayla, honey, did you spend all night painting?"

The only thing left to paint is the crown molding on one of the walls and to fix a few drops on another (I messed up a little right after Justin's visit, which I've forgiven myself for), which will take me an hour, tops. I have a ladder, brushes, and paint, so I'm good to go.

"Nah, just stayed a little longer yesterday. Almost done, though," I tell her proudly. "What do you think?"

She gazes around again, and I'm scared to hear her reaction. We've already painted it beige, but it didn't resonate with either of us, so we decided to switch it up and add my drawing. The color isn't exactly what she wanted—the brightest peach (her favorite color), but for the sake of our eyes, I bought pastel peach; it looks so gentle and easy on the eyes while still being vibrant and playful. That's why I've been here all night—I wanted her to see this color before she starts coating it in an orange monstrosity.

"This is..." She looks around again with furrowed brows.

I bite my lip, dread settling heavily in my stomach. *Oh man, I messed up.*

"This is gorgeous!" she finally bursts out at the same time I start blubbering, "I'll fix it, don't worry—wait, what?"

"The walls are gorgeous. I love them. You were right; this color's better."

I sigh, a broad smile creeping across my face. "Really?" I ask, my heart fluttering.

"Yes. I love it," she asserts with less emotion this time, back to her usual self. Oof, I began to worry there for a moment. She's never that emotional.

"Great!" I hop up from the floor where I was mixing the paint.

"Hey, hmm..." Marina begins, looking out the window.

"What?"

"I think your car is getting towed." She looks at me worriedly and then back outside.

"The hell!" I run to the window to see she's right—my loyal Jeep is getting hooked by its front bumper to a tow truck by Bobby, who owns the local towing company and is officially on my shit list. But he isn't the primary source of the problem—or the recipient of my wrath right now. A smug-looking Jake Attleborough leans on his cruiser, watching the show unfold. I can clearly tell he's eagerly awaiting me to come out screaming, thirsty for the entertainment. Like a bloodthirsty piranha. What a dick. "I'm gonna kill him," I growl.

"The shotgun is in the kitchen!" Marina calls helpfully.

I shake my head. "All I need is my bare hands."

I walk outside, noticing Jake's smile turn into a full-blown shit-eating grin as he notices me. A Valkyrie on the hunt. He doesn't know what's about to hit him. "Haven't paid your ticket yet, huh?"

My nostrils flare, and I strain to not lean over and physically bite him as I snap, "You just gave it to me. I have time."

"No, you don't." He clicks his tongue mockingly. "Your light's still not fixed, and you have a shit-ton of unpaid tickets. So yeah, your junk's getting towed."

"Jake, for fuck's sake, this isn't fair! I can't afford to pay everything at once to get my car back." His humane side clearly checked out years ago, but I make an appeal to it anyway.

"Not my problem." He shrugs, picking the dirt from underneath his fingernails. Disgusting. "And it's Officer Attleborough to you."

"It *is* your problem!" I exclaim. "The only reason I have so many is because of you constantly targeting me!"

"You're a reckless driver," he shoots back, shrugging. I see the muscles of his folded arms flex like he's imagining strangling me, but I've seen meaner and bigger than him, so his attempt to scare me is wasted effort. "And you don't follow the rules."

"Like you fuckin' do," I snap at him.

What I said must have triggered something because a dark cloud suddenly swarms his face. He pushes away from the cruiser and straightens his pose. His face grows stone-cold, no trace of his signature smirk in sight.

"Got something to say?" His voice is pure menace, and

even Bobby shoots curious looks our way while continuing to secure my baby to his truck.

I watch Jake carefully, contemplating what I'm going to say next in light of his reaction—I feel like this is some sort of critical moment that could weigh heavily on our future sparring, but I don't understand why—or why he looks almost... afraid. And then it hits me. He thinks I'm referencing what happened at Alex's cabin—what he did—and he's scared that I know the truth and could ruin him with it. I level him with a stare.

"Don't worry, *Officer*. We trailer trash do have some honor left, even if the law doesn't. Your *secret*," I inform him, curving my fingers in air quotes around the word, "is safe with me. But I'm tired of being bullied by you, Jake. Fuck, by everybody." I spread my goosebump-covered arms wide. Not only is it cold out here, but my adrenaline is spiking. "I'm done with this. Take my car. Might as well transfer the title to yourself because I don't have the money to get it back. So enjoy your win, asshole. I hope it'll make you a little less bitter."

A look of uncertainty crosses his face, but it's gone just as fast. He yanks his ever-present Ray-Bans off, sticks them in the pocket, and opens his mouth to say something, but I'm already gone. I can see Marina watching me through the window with a look of pure pride on her face. I'd be proud of myself, too, if I had any mental capacity left to feel anything.

Pride aside, I have no idea what to do. I know Marina will offer me her car and every last dollar she has—which can't be much after the renovations—but I won't take either. I can't. It's a trailer girl syndrome: scared of taking anything from anybody because we know nothing is free. It's been years, and Marina is family, but I still deal with my problems on my own.

I contemplate not sending the monthly payment for *the debt that isn't mine* but quickly disregard it—they need the money more than I do, and I know *she'll* find a way to get her green if I miss a payment, and I honestly don't want to see it happen. I get a full-body shudder as I remember the first time *she* came to demand the payment—the whole trailer park was shaken, and we're not an easily shaken bunch.

I remember Marina has an old bike—it could be good cardio, pedaling miles upon miles from my secluded location to town through the mountain. Fun times. Or I could move the trailer somewhere closer, but I quickly abandon that thought, because I don't want people to know about my problems. Or about my living situation. Which is still a trailer, just at a different location—one that's turning out to be a huge disadvantage, considering now I don't have wheels.

It's not the same trailer I used to live in with my mother and sister; this one I bought on my own. I *bought* it. It's *mine*. It was run-down and needed a lot of work, but I fixed everything on my own. *I* did it, and I'm proud of the home I've made. When Jake or Justin Attleborough calls me trailer trash, they don't know what they're talking about.

I didn't park the trailer with everybody at the park. Instead, I found the perfect spot on the other side of the mountain—so technically, I don't live in Little Hope, but I belong there. My special spot is located on the line between a field of wildflowers and a pine forest. In the morning, I sit with my beautifully mismatched dishes, have breakfast, and watch the sunrise between two twin hills across the field. And it's easy for Frank to visit me anytime he wants to.

The trailer is small but very roomy, especially for one person, and very mobile if hooked up to a car. It's more of an RV than an actual trailer, but I like to think of it as a trailer: it has all the attributes and resonates with my upbringing. I'm not sure my Jeep can handle anything heavier than a kid's stroller, but regardless, my wings aren't clipped by a house rooting me to the ground.

There is a tiny kitchen, a hybrid of a living room and a corridor, and a decent-sized bedroom. The kitchen has a loveseat and a tiny coffee table; no dining table, though. Instead, I use a two-person island connected to the kitchen structure. My bedroom fits a queen-size bed and a small nightstand. My shower is a stall with a microscopic sink and a shower. Everything is small, but it works for me. So, in my fantasy, whenever I'm ready, I'll hook this bad boy to my Wrangler (If it's still alive and still *mine* by then, which I've begun doubting), and we drive off into the night.

"You know you can always take my car," Marina offers as expected the moment I step over the threshold. "I live nearby and can walk, no biggie."

I attempt a smile. "No, it's fine, but if you could give me a ride home today, that would be amazing."

"Sure, hon." Her smile is understanding. She won't pressure me into taking her car or her money. She knows enough about pride; in the end, she refused Freya's help in restoring the diner and caved only when she didn't have any other options when the bank refused to give a loan. I feel like I might be in the same boat very soon. It's probably time to put my pride aside and look at my options.

JUSTIN

. . .

"Hey, Justin," Paul calls out from the front of the garage. "Can you come here for a sec?"

I'm buried under piles of invoices, so any distraction at this point is welcomed. I run my hand through my hair, pulling on the strands, trying to escape that haze I get into every time I see a page full of numbers. "Comin'," I holler back, then take a sip of piss-cold coffee and head to the front. Bobby is chatting with Paul. "What's up?" I ask, walking up to them.

Bobby's glancing around and nervously biting the inside of his cheek. *Huh.*

"What happened, Bobby?"

"I—" His head swivels as he shoots another look around the space. "Do you think we can talk in private?"

"Sure." I nod to Paul to give us a minute, but he's already made himself scarce. "What's up?"

He fidgets with his keys. "Not my business to say this, but—" He cuts himself off again, shaking his head.

"You can say anything. It'll stay between us."

"Alright. I just saw Jake." He swallows. For fuck's sake, he needs to hurry the fuck up with his story before I die of old age. I bite my tongue so I don't scare him off with my snippy remark. Bobby's a good guy—kind and quiet, if not a little soft—and for him to voice his opinion means a lot, so I wait. "So, I was towing this car. Kayla's car." Oh, fuck. I know where this is going. "For tickets or some shit. I don't know; Jake had a paper. But I feel like he's pushing too much. I've seen him around town hot on her heels, and I think he's using his position to harass the girl." The last sentence is so fast I barely register what he's saying. "And it's not only me who's noticed it. I've heard people talk."

I clench my jaw; Bobby thinks it's because of him and

rushes to placate me. "Sorry, man. I shouldn't have said anything."

"No, you did the right thing. I'll deal with it," I say through gritted teeth, trying hard not to punch the wall over this new information.

"Good." He nods, looking relieved. "Good."

"Do you have her car hooked up?" I glance outside but don't see his truck.

"Yeah." He points down the road. "Around the bend. Part of me thinks I should have towed it straight to the junkyard. The poor girl's going to meet her maker trying to get around in it one of these days."

I heft a sigh. "Agree with you on that one. Hey, I'm about to cash in that favor of yours." I smirk at him.

Bobby pales and swallows nervously. "Look, I can't do much—"

"Relax, Bobby, I just need to fix something in her car, but it's gotta stay between us. Feel me?" I put my hand on his shoulder, and he nods.

"Yeah, we can do that."

"I need to finish some stuff here, then I'll stop by later. Does it work for you?" The favor he owes me is big, so I know he'll agree to help me out here.

"Yeah. I'll leave you the key. We'll be good after that, though, right?" He licks his lips with agitation.

"Yeah, we'll be good."

"Okay, then. See you later." He waves and skitters back to his truck. Did I just bully him into letting me onto his lot? I did, and I have no remorse over it whatsoever.

Am I being a hypocrite, condemning Jake for pouring all his rage on *her* when I've been doing the same for years? Maybe, but I don't care. Because *only* I can do that. Only me. She is *mine*. I mean—the fun of tormenting her is mine and mine alone.

Besides that, everything is playing out perfectly: I can fix her car and be discreet about it. Nobody will ever know it was me.

We finish up at the garage early, so I say goodbye to the guys and go to load my truck with everything I need to fix her car. New brakes and a new alternator. Tools, rags, pads. Once everything's loaded up, I lock up the shop and drive to Bobby's.

He's waiting for me in his car by the gates to his lot. He hefts himself out when he sees me. "Here are the keys." He passes them to me, clearly still nervous. "Just put 'em under the can by the gates once you're done." He's about to walk back to his car when he turns to me and adds, "You're not back to the racing, are you?"

"No, Bobby, I'm here to fix Kayla's car. That's all, I promise." It sounds surreal to say her name out loud. In my mind, it's always *her* or *she*, as if she's some great and formidable god, and I dare not speak her name, so *Kayla* feels foreign on my tongue.

He nods slowly, accepting this. "Alright. I don't know why you're doing that—" I give him a look, after which he amends—"and frankly, it's none of my business, but you're doing a good thing. This girl needs a break."

I clench my jaw to barricade pure venom from spitting out. *Needs a break*, my ass. I almost change my mind about fixing her car at that. *Almost*.

While I'm contemplating whether I should follow logic or guilt, Bobby takes off, leaving me alone with the keys to his junk kingdom in my hands. Bobby has a huge lot, half of which is for towing while the other is a literal junkyard. I'm not sure which part he put her Jeep in—it sure as fuck belongs in the latter—but I get the feeling he spared it.

I get back into my truck and pull in, confirming it is waiting on the towed side, and stop there. First, I need to replace the alternator and the battery. Then I need to get the car to the rack to change the brakes. Luckily, Bobby has a car lift, so I don't have to haul her Jeep all the way back to my shop.

Once I pop the hood, I whistle. It's even worse than I remember from a few days ago. I get my tools from the truck and get to work. It takes me a good few hours to get everything fixed, and by the time I'm done, it's deep into the night. I decide to leave the broken headlight as it would be too obvious that somebody's been meddling with the car.

I lock everything up, hide the keys at the usual place by the fence, and drive home. By the time I arrive at the garage, I feel exhaustion enveloping my body and muting my feelings. I'm about to crash. I park my car and barely make it inside before collapsing on the couch.

Chapter Six

K AYLA

Yesterday evening Marina made good on her word to give me a lift home and promised to pick me up this morning. Today I need to deal with my Jeep, but I don't know how to go about fixing the problem. I don't know how much I owe, but considering there's been quite a few tickets I haven't paid over a decent chunk of time, the penalties will be embarrassingly huge, and I can't afford that. Big surprise there.

I'm just finishing my coffee when Marina's car pulls up. I shove my arms into my jacket as I head outside; it's seven in the morning, and the air is frosty. When the hell will this never-ending cold go away? I don't remember it ever lingering for so long—it's like this year, it sunk its teeth into spring and won't let go. Yes, we're higher up on the mountain than most, and the weather is unpredictable here, but still. The end of May should be much warmer.

I shiver as I run to Marina's SUV and hop inside, letting out an embarrassing moan of pleasure when I hit the seat.

"Heated seats. Oh, heated seats, how much I missed you!" I cry, patting my cold thighs.

Marina arches a perfectly manicured brow. "How can you miss something you've never had?"

"Oh, sheesh, aren't you a party pooper? Let me enjoy my fantasy." She's right, though, I've never had a fancy car with fancy features, and heated seats are very fancy in my book.

"Take my car until you know what to do with yours," she offers again.

"Nah, don't worry, I'll be fine."

"Yeah, sure you will. How are you planning on getting to work from here? I can't make it up here every morning, unfortunately. Unless you want to park your home behind mine?" She addresses a very valid point—I could have parked my trailer behind her house and been good until I knew what to do. It doesn't escape me either that she called my trailer my 'home,' warming my prickly self this cold, early morning. People who have actual houses rarely treat trailers as real homes, even though they are.

"That's an option. But let's see how much it'll cost to get my old beast back first."

Marina nods quietly; she'll support me no matter what, and I love her for that. She suddenly looks around with hawk-like attention. "I feel like someone's watching us." Her voice is suspicious.

"Oh." I look around and see the bushes move. "It's probably Frank."

She looks at me in wonder. "He's still coming here?"

"Of course. Why would he stop?" Despite us being like family, she could never understand my relationship with Frank.

"Why would he indeed." She hums and puts the car into drive.

She drops me off by the DMV. A sad building that only ever has one employee working. Today, that employee sits behind the counter reading *Fifty Shades of Grey*. She doesn't seem terribly thrilled to see me walk in. I guess I'm cockblocking Christian Grey.

"Hi, Doris!" I cheerfully greet the middle-aged lady with square black glasses matching the cover of the book she's clenching in her hands. Her forehead is sweating. She must be at the good part.

"Hi, Kayla. What can I do for you?" She sets the book on the counter face-down, like she doesn't want me to know she's been reading smut. I'm with you there, lady—the more smut, the better, but that doesn't mean I want everyone knowing what I'm into.

"My Jeep got towed yesterday," I announce, trying to keep up the contented tone, despite how inaccurate it represents my state of mind.

She puckers her painted pink lips in disappointment. "Oh, they finally got it. Sorry, honey."

"They did. Can you check how much I need to pay to get it back, please?" I force a friendly smile on my face. Even though Doris is very nice, my situation doesn't help my mood to be less sour.

"Sure, gimme a minute." She pulls on her collar, fanning herself. *Oh yeah, Doris, you do need a minute. Mr. Grey got you there.*

When she eventually gets her wits together, she takes my license and types it into the computer. I watch her face as she scans the information, trying to figure out how screwed I am. When her lips form an *o*, I start to sweat too. That can't be good. "Oh, honey, you need to pay $1,981.12 plus towing fees for Bobby when you take your car." She bites her lip like it's her fault the number is so high.

"What?" That can't be right. Did she just say that I need to pay almost two thousand dollars? "W-why so much?"

"You haven't paid quite... ahem... a few tickets in the last year and a half, honey. That comes with some hefty fees," she explains apologetically, eyeing the screen.

I'm outraged. "I paid a ton of tickets!"

"You obviously had more." She has the decency to look a little embarrassed at the system.

"Let me see!" I nearly yell.

She glances around nervously as if somebody will clock her for acting naughty—it's only myself and her, mind you, and I've already seen her fantasizing about Mr. Grey—and turns the screen toward me. *Fuck!* There are at least two dozen unpaid tickets, and I didn't even know about them. How? Some of them are for parking, while others are for weird violations that I didn't even know I made—if I even did, which I doubt, knowing Jake. Well, fuck that, and fuck Jake and his harassment. I'm so over this.

"Are you going to pay now, honey?" Doris asks quietly, already knowing the answer.

"No, I don't have the money for that. Thanks, Doris." My anger deflates—there's nothing I can do, furious or not.

"Sure thing. I hope you get it sorted, Kayla." Her smile is genuinely supportive.

"Thanks," I mumble and walk outside. Yeah, not many options left for me here. It's either take a loan from Freya or Marina (the latter has limited funds now, so she's out of the question even though she'd be my first pick) or move my trailer to Marina's property. I don't know which one would be a less catastrophic hit to my pride.

Once outside, I pick up the phone and make the dreaded call. *She* picks up on the second ring, and I mumble before I lose my nerve, "Hey, Caroline. I'm afraid I have to skip this month's payment."

"Why?" she asks in her sour, cigarette-roughened voice.

"Car troubles—I need the money to pay it off."

"Car, huh? What, not enough you can walk on two legs, now you need a car to drive you around too?"

I clench my jaw, biting back a snarky answer. "Yes, I need the car. I can't get around without it."

"Not my problem. Some people don't have the luxury of walking around at all. We need the money, so make it happen." Sudden silence tells me she hasn't bothered to wait for a response before hanging up.

Oh hell. What fantasy world was I living in when I thought she'd be understanding? She's used that line before when I've needed to skip a payment. Every single time— which isn't often because I try my best to 'make it happen,' as she put it. I long gave up on asking, but today's situation called for trying one last time, hoping she'd grow a conscience. And it's not like I can blame her, because I can't. No matter how hard I try to hate her for draining my bank account every single month, for keeping my wings clipped, I can't—because she's drowning in the circumstances of the same evil actions that I am.

I'll make it work. I always find a way to land on my feet, like a cat with nine lives... though I feel like I'm running low on those by now.

I'm slowly walking to the diner where Marina will *hopefully* make me the fattiest breakfast in the history of breakfast so I can eat away my sorrows when a car slows down to roll along beside me. I hear the sound of the window lowering and tense all over.

"When are you taking your shit back?" an annoying voice jeers. I choose to ignore it and keep on walking. "Did you hear me?" he squawks. "When are you taking your car back?"

How dare he even speak to me? I whip around to look at the asshole who's made my life miserable for *years* and snarl at him, "What the hell do you need, *Jake?*"

His megawatt smile dims a few notches. "I asked you when you plan to pick up your junker."

"I don't," I snap and keep walking.

"What do you mean, you don't?" He presses on the gas to keep up with my pace, which is close to a jog at this point. "Hey, I'm talking to you!"

"And I'm ignoring you." I keep going, looking straight ahead.

He lets out a loud huff. "You can't ignore me."

"Watch me, asshole." It didn't come out quiet, but I didn't mean for it to. Let him hear it.

"What did you just call me?" His voice drops an octave.

"You heard me," I say louder so he can hear this time, since apparently his ears are filled with wax.

"I'm the officer of the law." His voice rises to nearly a screech.

"You're a shithead."

"The fuck did you just say?" He slams on the brakes, making his shiny cop car visibly stutter.

I stop, turn toward him, and plant my hands on my hips. "You heard me: you're a shithead and an asshole, you abuse your position of power, and oh—you're a shitty fucking cop too."

"That's it," he barks, hauling himself out of the cruiser. "You're coming to the station."

I snort. "In your dreams."

"Get in the car, or I'll cuff you and put you in there by force," his voice booms over the quiet street. I notice a couple onlookers and know that in a few short minutes, the whole town will have heard that local *trailer trash* Kayla Adams was resisting arrest by the brave Officer Attleborough on the Main Street of our fine town.

"Fuck off, Jake. Last time I checked, calling someone a shithead isn't illegal," I point out, my voice pitched with shock and indignation at the realization that he's serious. "I haven't done anything to justify you arresting me."

"Alright, then." With that, he swiftly spins me around and snaps his pair of handcuffs over my wrists in one smooth movement. I didn't even know he had it in him. I'd be impressed if I didn't hate his guts.

"What the hell?" I try to yank on the cuffs, and the sickeningly familiar position of having my hands tied behind my back rings a bell of the worst kind in my head. He opens the back door of the cruiser and shoves me inside. "Ouch!" I yelp, hitting my forehead on the way in. That'll bruise. He gets in himself and peels away from the curb.

"You've gone too far this time, Jake," I hiss as I try to find a more comfortable position—not exactly an easy feat with my hands tied behind my back. It was something I learned weeks ago, a memory I try hard to shove down dragged to the surface now. "Ever heard of Miranda rights? Or, I don't know, unlawful arrest? They do teach you this shit, right?"

He doesn't utter a word, which is eerily unlike him. I lean back and try to bring my racing pulse down—I haven't been in the back seat of a cop car in years. That was back when I was a teenager, and for something I didn't do. Before Kenneth, Alex's brother, became the sheriff, we had a very old dude with very conservative views who believed that a woman's place was barefoot in the kitchen with a swollen belly. He was also a strong believer in rich white people ruling the world. He took pleasure in blaming every single mishap in town on the closest available person of color or anyone under the poverty line. So yeah, I've been in the back seat of a cop cruiser quite a few times during my teenage years simply by being born poor rather than rich.

Pulling up to the station, he gets out and opens the door for me without a word. I climb out, nearly falling on my ass in the process, but he grabs my elbow, squeezing it hard. I clench my teeth to avoid showing how much it friggin' hurts. Once steady, I yank my arms away from him and start walking to the entrance.

The station is quiet. Besides Sheriff Kenneth Benson, there is one more deputy, Jennica, easily recognized by her glowing brown skin and wavy black hair, always pulled into a low ponytail when she's on duty. I pray she's here today so she can help me, but there doesn't seem to be anyone else here. I'm on my own.

Jake grabs my cuffed wrists and walks me to the cell. Well, more like pushes me. He takes the cuffs off as he propels me inside.

"Really?" I snap at him.

"It will teach you how to talk to an officer of the law."

"You're no *officer*," I sneer, rubbing my wrists. "You're a pathetic parody of one, and I will not let this one slide, Jake. Not this one." Being tied-slash-cuffed twice in the span of only a handful of weeks is two times too many if you ask me.

The cell is standard, ten-by-ten maybe, with one cot. Look at me: placed into solitary on my first stint. I have no idea who's been here before and whether they sanitized the facility or not. I think I know the answer to that, and I cringe. Not having any choice, I plant my ass on the cot and stew in my desire to rip Jake's tiny dick into teeny-tiny pieces. I'd feed them to him with a spoon. Maybe I'd save a couple shreds for Kenneth or Jennica when they show up. They'd support me. Anyone with two brain cells can see him abusing his position, and between Kenneth trying to clean up after his predecessor's corruption and set an example, and the realities of biased police misconduct that Jennica, as a person of color and a cop, knows better than anyone else, I can't see this getting past them.

Hours pass by, and neither of them show. Why? I thought someone always must be on call at the station. What if there's a robbery? Or a murder? Who is going to respond to the call?

I hear Jake's muffled rumbling, realizing he must be talking on his phone, and I yell at him to give me some water at least. It's been *hours*, and I can see the sun setting through the window. So today's only Jake's shift. Awesome. The one day Kenneth and Jennica just decide to take the day off at the same time and leave Little Hope in the hands of the idiot. They'd better be shagging somewhere because that would be the only reason I'd forgive them for abandoning the town to Jake.

"Hey!" A male baritone thunders through the station. Jake stops rambling. "Hey, anyone here?"

"What?" Jake comes out from behind his table and walks to the receptionist's desk, currently sitting empty. It's been vacant for a few months now. I don't know if it's because there isn't enough funding for hiring another person, or they simply can't find anyone suitable. I look at Jake. The bar is pretty low, so I'd go with the funding issue.

"Hey, Officer Attleborough," the person says in a low voice accompanied by an exhale of adoration. *Uh, what?* I shift closer to the bars so I can see the person. *Well, hello, Jonah.* "I... umm... I need to get a stamp of approval for some work needing to be done on one of the properties." Jonah owns a real estate agency in Springfield and helps our locals when they need real estate help. As far as I know, he's been branching out to other cities now too. Good for him.

"Go to the mayor's office for that." Jake is being his jerky self. A little *too*... jerky? He usually reserves that particular tone for yours truly. For the rest of the human population, he's a sweet All-American boy everyone adores who can do no wrong.

"Already been there. I need police approval because we need to fix a part of the road in front of the house." He's fidgeting with the briefcase in his hands.

"Who's paying for that?" Jake sounds like an old grump.

"As a matter of fact, I am. I'm planning on moving into this house." He laughs nervously. It's adorable. We all know Jonah is gay; I remember when he came out, and everybody and their cat teased him about it. The dude held firm in his beliefs and didn't waiver, even when he got beaten up for liking somebody the local society deemed 'wrong.' I always respected him—he was a little different from the rest, just like I was. But now, his nervous chuckles and constant fidgeting of his chocolate hair tells me a very sad story: Jonah has a crush on Jake. This is so wrong. All that niceness is being wasted on this sorry excuse for a human being.

"Where's the paperwork?" Jake snaps at him.

"Here." Jonah shuffles through his black leather briefcase that looks out of place in Little Hope and pulls out a thick stack of papers.

"Leave them on the table. Sheriff Benson will look at

them," Jake says rudely without sparing him a glance. Oh yes, we all want Sheriff Benson to finally show his pretty face. The whole Benson bunch is pretty; it's annoying, really.

"Oh. Okay." Jonah sounds crestfallen, and I want to hug him to my chest and let him cry a river over this jerk.

"Hey, Jonah!" I exclaim from my cozy cell. His head whips around, looking for the source of the noise.

"Kayla?" He sounds confused when he finally notices me. "What are you doing in there?"

"Been asking myself that question since this morning." I tap a finger on my knee.

"Do you... um... need anything?" He looks between Jake and me.

"To get out of here?" I suggest helpfully.

"Is that all?" Jake interjects with his ever-present snark.

"Yeah, that's all." Jonah's helplessly looking at me, apologetically shrugging his shoulders.

"The door is that way." Jake points to the entrance. Even from here, I can see the reddening of Jonah's perfect cheekbones. He throws one last pitiful look at me and walks away.

There goes my last hope of getting out of here tonight before murdering someone in cold blood, because make no mistake—once I'm out, I'm chopping Jake's liver into tiny pieces with a rusty fork.

JUSTIN

I park my truck and walk to Donna's shop, hoping to get some coffee in me. I ended up crashing for fourteen hours;

after a long sleep, my head is always groggy. Groggy when I sleep and groggy when I don't. I just can't win with my body.

Just as I pull the door of the coffee shop open, a big body slams into me, splashing hot coffee all over my front. "Fuck!" I yell and jump like I just stubbed my toe on a table.

"Oh, I'm sorry, Justin!" Jonah apologizes, trying to wipe coffee off me. Grabbing napkins from his hands, I dab them into the mess covering my entire chest. "I'm sorry! I didn't mean to!"

"Chill, it's all good," I tell him. Fuck, this day (technically, it's the evening, but it's been a day for me) already started badly, and now this.

"Sorry again. Can I buy you a coffee?" He offers, guilt rife in his gaze.

"No, man. But you need one." I nod at what was his coffee, now splashed all over the sidewalk.

"Yeah, I need a new one," he agrees sadly, wiping his face with his hands. The gesture of a tired man.

"Got some stuff going on?"

"Yeah, been trying to get a permit for my new house and all the remodeling but looks like all the legal forces in this town are against me." He looks wiped out, and I can relate.

"Oh yeah, those people don't like to approve anything," I chuckle.

He laughs sardonically. "They sure don't. Our law enforcement seemed a little edgy today too."

"Ah, the cops. Yeah, Jake's on duty today, and he has a stick up his ass recently, so your best bet is to wait for Kenneth to be on duty," I respond while cleaning the mess. Was it a full damn gallon of coffee?

"Figured that much." He nervously laughs again. "I guess Kayla got unlucky too. Just like me." He chuckles, thoughtfully adding, "Well, not like me. At least I'm on this side of the bars."

I freeze. "What are you talking about?"

"Oh, I just saw Kayla Adams in jail," he says, wiping the rest of the coffee from his pants.

"What?" I bellow, and Jonah takes a careful step back. I try to sound calmer. "What do you mean 'in jail'?"

"I stopped by the station about an hour ago, and she was in the cell. I guess she did something wrong—I heard of her reputation. Never believed it, but it must not all be rumors if she's in there. Right? I mean, Jake," he clears his throat, "I mean Officer Attleborough wouldn't lock up an innocent person, right?" He shrugs with such certainty that I feel like I'm going insane. He doesn't know her or Jake well, and yet he's so quick to judge the situation. *Pot, meet kettle,* my subconsciousness perversely suggests.

"Was somebody else in there?" I ask through gritted teeth. Other than his incorrect assumptions, Jonah didn't do anything wrong. I try hard not to punch him in the face.

"No, just Jake—I mean, Officer Attleborough—and her." His cheeks pinken as he quickly adjusts his words.

"Okay, Jonah. Thanks," I tell him shortly and march toward my truck.

"Don't you want coffee?" he asks, but I'm already gone.

Jake is in over his head this time. Way over his head.

I'm fuming by the time I reach the station. I push the door hard and barrel inside. There's nobody there but Jake and *her*.

She sits on a cot with her legs up, leaning against the wall behind her, her palms resting on the top of her knees. Her hair is piled on top of her head in a messy bun—not the artistic kind, but the end-of-the-day, leave-me-alone kind.

"Jake!" I roar, never taking my eyes off her. She jumps at the sound of my yell, her eyes wide.

"What?' he barks, leisurely walking from the back room with a cup of steaming coffee in his hand. I can smell Donna's special roast from here, and she's very particular about who she shares it with. "What?" he repeats as he strolls to his desk and takes an easy sip.

"What is she doing here?" I jerk my head at the cell. In my peripheral vision, I see her watching us with open curiosity. She hasn't changed her pose, but her attention is definitely focused on us. I feel her eyes tracing my every move.

"Who? Ms. Adams?" He slowly takes another sip, making sure to slurp the liquid for full effect, fully knowing it will drive me nuts.

"Yes, Jake, her," I answer more patiently than he deserves.

"Well, I can't share it with you—" he starts in that annoying, overconfident manner he usually uses at work.

"Cut it out Jake." My voice resembles one of an animal rather than a human at this point.

"—but, if you must know," he continues without missing a beat, "she's here for disturbing the peace on the streets of our fine town." A loud snort comes from the cell while Jake takes another sip, and I clench my fists so I won't take his mug and throw it in his face.

"Jake." I scrub my face with my hands. "You've gone too far this time. You're clearly abusing your position."

"The fuck I am!" With that, his chill demeanor breaks, and he jumps up. "She's here because she deserves to be here, and you know it!"

I glance at her: she's set her feet down on the floor, her elbows resting on her knees. She's listening while she fidgets with something in her hand. I turn back to my brother, and I don't cushion my tone for him. "Let. Her. Go." Jake pales a little—there've only been a few times he's seen me like this to date, and none of them ended well for the parties involved. He visibly swallows, his tone changing from arrogant to pleading.

"C'mon, I'm just having a little fun, that's all."

"You are a fucking cop, Jake! How the hell do you think all this," I gesture to him and Kayla, "is okay?"

"She knows it's just for fun." His voice shrinks as he defends himself. As it fuckin' should be.

"Look at her." I wave at the cell. "Does it look like she's having fun?" He follows my hand and winces. "That's right. Let her out and pray she doesn't sue your ass."

"Don't give her ideas. Her trailer-trash brain wouldn't come up with that on her own." He smirks, throwing a patronizing look at her.

"Shut up, Jake!" I thunder. He skitters away toward the cell, the keys clinking in his hand like in an old film with a damn dungeon. Then I hear her light footsteps.

"Thank you," she says quietly to me... and just leaves. I expected thunder, yelling, and lightning, maybe a punch to Jake's face... but she just leaves without another word. And it bugs me. It bugs me more than I care to admit.

Jake returns to his desk a moment later and stands in front of me, his chest puffed like he's a little baboon. A little baboon who's about to get his ass beaten by a gorilla. I'm about one snide remark away from pounding on my chest and wiping the floor with his smug face.

"Happy now?" he asks bitterly, as if it had been my fault that he was a piece of shit abusing his position of power.

"You're gonna let Kenneth know about that." Is all I can manage at the moment without strangling him.

"Or what?" he challenges, straightening his shoulders.

"Or I will," I answer through clenched teeth.

He thinks for a second. "I'll let him know," he says dismissively, then adds with a note of disbelief, "Huh. You really put her above your own family. Above your own brother."

I take a careful step toward him, and he doesn't back down—it looks like he grew some balls after all, but he picked the wrong time for that. The worst time. "You're my brother, and that's exactly why I *will* tell him. I don't like the person you're becoming." Then I look straight into his eyes, and he flinches, unable to hold my gaze. "Hell, I don't like the person you've already become, and I don't want you to disappear farther down that road. That's why I will tell him, Jake. But I'll give you the opportunity to be a man and do it yourself first." I give him one last menacing look and stride outside, hoping to catch a glimpse of her.

She's far down the road, slowly walking toward the diner. It's a long walk from here, and it started to drizzle while I was inside the station. I jump into my truck and drive toward her. When I reach her, I stop the car and roll the window down. "Get in the truck." I sound rough after my argument with Jake. I can't help it. For the first time in forever, I think I want to sound softer with her.

She stops, startled. "No, Justin. I'm fine." She continues her walk, not paying attention to me anymore.

"Get in the truck, Kayla." I say with a sigh. Her head whips toward me, her eyes as big as saucers, big and unblinking. "What?" I ask.

"Never heard you call me by my name." And with that, somebody from above pulls the stopper on the sky, and the rain pours down, soaking her to the bone in an instant.

"In the car. Now!" I bark, and she obeys. Fucking finally.

The scent of ozone and strawberries fills the cabin of my truck, and it instantly suffocates me. I'm trying to breathe through my mouth so I don't smell it, but fucking strawberries tickle my nose. It makes my mouth water.

I quickly glance at her: she's staring ahead. She's right, though—I don't recall ever calling her by her name. Maybe, a long time ago. But not for a long while.

"Jake's an idiot, but he doesn't mean any harm," I start cautiously. But I know that isn't true. My brother goes overboard, and after recent events, he's even more edgy than usual.

She snorts and wipes her nose with her hand, staring blankly out the passenger side window. "Figures."

"What?" I ask while staring at her, waiting for her to divert her attention from the passing scenery to me.

Her laughter is abrupt. "You got me in here so you can threaten me not to report your brother. Typical." She's tapping her finger on her knee.

"No," I sigh. "That's not why I wanted you to get in here."

"Why, then?" She finally looks at me for the first time. I've never seen her this close before. Never. Her eyes are hazel, with deep chocolate streaks in them. Sparkly. Why are they sparkly? She sniffles and wipes her nose again. Oh fuck, that's why. I'm used to seeing her taking all the shit thrown her way with a raised head and a steel spine, so I didn't expect her to go all misty-eyed on me.

When I finally say, "It's raining outside, and you don't have your car," her laughter is dark, sad, and very, very tired.

"Yeah, your brother made sure of that."

I shake my head slightly. "Why don't you pick it up?"

"Really? Do you think I have two grand just lying around, waiting to be spent on a car that's older than me and probably isn't even worth that much? Newsflash—*I don't*," she spits, flustered, and turns to stare ahead of her, fidgeting with her hair.

"Two grand?" I almost whistle.

"Yep." She pops the *p*.

"How the fuck did you get two grand's worth in tickets?"

She scoffs at this. "Ask your brother how." She shrugs and pushes her hands under her thighs.

I squeeze the wheel. Yeah, he's gotta stop that. I sigh and put the truck in drive. I need to find a way to get her car back. Jake is an asshole, and I need to remedy the situation. Even just a little.

I stop in front of the diner. "Do you need a ride home tonight?"

She laughs and climbs out of the car without a word. *Okay, then.* I check the time: it's four fifty, so the DMV is closed for sure. Doris likes to slack on time, and even though her official hours are nine to five, she's nowhere to be seen by four-ish.

I'm contemplating if I should wait for Kayla or not. She looked miserable, and it's partially my fault, considering the unfortunate fact that I'm related to my idiot of a brother. I look around and don't see Marina's car. The lights switch on in the diner—okay, so she might be alone in there. How will she get to her trailer, which is on the other side of the fucking mountain?

I decide to wait for a few.

And I wait. For a whole minute. *Fuck that,* I decide, turning the truck off before dashing into the diner as I try to avoid the heavy, fat raindrops all around me.

The moment I step inside, I regret my rash decision instantly, but it's too late to run. Her back is to me as she sits on one of the high tops at the bar. She's hunched over, her face resting in her hands and her shoulders shuddering in waves of misery as she silently cries.

I want to turn around and disappear, but I can't. No matter how forcefully I will my feet to move backward, they begin moving forward. Toward *her*.

"Kayla?" I ask gently, so out of my usual range.

She jumps in her seat, startled. Vigorously wiping at her tears before turning to me, I realize that she only made an even bigger mess, reddening her face to angry blotchiness.

She takes a deep breath and asks, "What are you doing here?" Her voice trembling from recent sobs.

"I just wanted to make sure you're okay." I rock back and forth on my heels, feeling like an intruder who's become privy to an intimate act. In a way, I am.

She sniffles loudly. "I'm fine."

"You don't look fine." I take a measured step toward her.

"I said I'm fine," she snarls.

"Okay." I keep my voice neutral, like with an injured animal.

"You can go now." She dismisses me with a wave of her hand. Her sleeves are rolled up, and the colorful vine peeks out from underneath one. The dark green color on her pale skin mesmerizes me.

"Okay," I agree, but I stay rooted to the same spot, only five feet away from her. I'd move closer, but I don't want to spook her. What would I even do if I moved closer? The question of the century.

"Go, Justin. Now." The anger in her voice becomes more prominent.

So, I go. Toward her. I cross the distance in two steps

and stop in front of her. She lifts her face to mine and meets my eyes.

"Go away, Justin," she whispers.

"Okay," I whisper back. There's nothing else I can say—my brain has checked out, and what's left of my functioning mind is trying to command my eyes to move away from her pink lips she just had the audacity to lick.

"Go." Her voice is barely audible this time. The way she says it on a slow exhale, with this low tremble, unusual for her voice, causes tingles at the back of my head. I swallow a lump in my throat and lean forward. Immediately, the sweet, now-familiar strawberry smell reaches my nose.

"Okay," I exhale, and my breath fans the strands of hair around her face. She licks her goddamn lips again and opens them slightly. They're all I can think of. All I can see. I lean closer and—

A fucking car horn blasts loudly outside, and I jump back.

Fuck! I almost kissed her. What the hell was I thinking?

The sudden movement tightens my already-tight jeans further, and my poor dick weeps in pain. It got awfully hard awfully fast with just the anticipation of a kiss. Of a fucking kiss. With *her*. What the fuck is wrong with my body? It wasn't interested in anyone for a damn long time, so much so that I was about to go to the doctor to ask for a blue pill because that shit is embarrassing at my age. And here he is, ready to go in a second.

I hate her a little more for that. For how she makes me feel and for how she's broken my body without even knowing it.

I put my usual asshole mask back on and take two steps back. Her face falls, and she starts blinking. Her mouth is still slightly ajar, and I force my eyes to stay focused on the top part of her face so I don't get lured in by her pink tongue again, thinking about how it would feel against mine.

Fuck.

She's stopped crying. Mission accomplished. Time to go.

I turn around and leave without another word.

Chapter Seven

KAYLA

I sit and watch the open door where Justin just disappeared. Did I dream the whole encounter? Was he really here, and did we really have a near kiss? If not for the car horn outside, I'm pretty sure I'd know how my teenage dream tastes by now. I bet it would taste good... despite the look of pure horror on his face when he reared back. As if the idea of touching me makes him want to vomit. Such a wonderful hit to my already low self-esteem.

I take a deep breath, trying to calm my erratic heartbeat that went into overdrive the moment it sensed Justin in proximity. My situation sucks. The first couple of hours locked up, I just wanted to claw Jake's face off, to destroy his pretty-boy looks and leave my mark all over him so that every time he looks in the mirror, he'd see my face. But after hours passed, my anger dissolved into resignedness, and I just wanted *out*. I just wanted to get out of that building, curl into a ball, and forget that the day ever happened. I didn't have any energy left to fight.

When Justin appeared like my own knight in shining denim, I thought he'd come to torment me some more too. Turns out I was wrong. He was so pissed at Jake—it was glorious. For the first time in forever, I saw him angry with someone other than me. Seething. Practically foaming at the mouth. At one point, I thought he was going to punch Jake, and I wouldn't have stopped him. In fact, I'd be on the sidelines cheering him on, shaking my pom-poms.

Then in the car... I still don't know why he offered me a ride. I mean, I kind of figured he wanted to talk me out of suing Jake (a battle I'm sure I'd win if I chose to go through with it), but I just wanted it all to be over. I just want them to leave me alone.

And then he decided to follow me inside the diner. Just awesome. How did that work out for us?

So now, I'm sitting alone in the diner with no car and no means to get home. To call Marina is out of the question; she'll want to know what happened, and I can't lie to her, and if I told her the truth, I'm sure that shotgun under the table would see some action. So that leaves Freya.

"Hey." Her voice is cheerful, as usual. I don't know when this woman isn't ebullient, even though her life hasn't exactly been rainbows and butterflies lately. I admire her for that.

"Hey, Frey." I swallow down the dryness in my throat. "Can you give me a lift home from the diner?"

There is a bit of stunned silence for a moment before her voice somehow becomes even more cheerful. *"Of course! Such a good idea! I'm with Stella at their house—"* Alex's stepmom who lives nearby—*"so it's perfect timing.*

See you there!" She hangs up a moment later. I shake my head, musing that I should have probably called Marina. Freya will be grilling me the whole evening now.

She arrives fifteen minutes later with a bottle of wine and a box of pizza that she proudly shows me the moment I open the door. Her smile is wide and bright. "I got us some goodies!" she declares as I climb into the car. Thank God she traded that old Impala—I mean, it was super cool, but so impractical.

I can feel the side-eye the entire way to my place. Curiosity eating at her.

When I finally can't take it anymore, I break. "Okay, what?" I bark.

"Oh, I don't know. Is there anything you want to share with me?" She blinks her big, deceitfully innocent eyes at me.

I sigh—might as well get it over with. I tell all about The Big Tow, the tale of the DMV debacle, my little stint in jail, and Justin's visit. By the time I'm done, she's white-knuckling the steering wheel. "What a fuckin' asshole," she hisses through gritted teeth. "Both of them."

She quietly stews in her rage for a long moment before she calms down enough to form complete sentences. She promises to cut only one of his nuts off instead of both.

I keep my mouth shut, a difficult thing for me to do. While I agree with her fury wholeheartedly, I also don't want her to get into trouble with them. The three of them share their own history, especially with Jake, and my jail story shouldn't break their bond, even if I want her to beat his ass so badly. At this point, I loathe Jake, but I can't be selfish and ask Freya to share my feelings.

When we're home, she parks the car and follows me inside. "Who's picking the movie?"

"You can." I shrug. "I'm fine with whatever."

She finds *Mean Girls* on my iPad, and we spend the rest of the evening wishing we were Regina rather than Cady. Regina may be a mega bitch, but she goes after what she wants and takes no shit.

By the time the movie is over, she's ready to go. I know she alternates between staying at Alex's cabin and his parents' house. I offer her a spot to sleep here, but she makes up some excuses and goes to Alex's cabin. It's sad that she still feels embarrassed about waiting for him. I think it's sweet, and that's how it should be. He'll come home eventually, and then I can hug him, thank him for helping me that night, and then kick him in the nuts for leaving Freya for so long. In that order.

When morning comes, I'm still lacking wheels. Desperate, I call Freya again. She answers the phone on the sixth ring with a groan. *"Yeah?"* That can't be good.

"Hey, wanna play Uber again? I'll make you your favorite coffee for waking up so early." I try to bribe her. She's clearly in a foul mood at seven thirty in the morning, even with half the town buzzing around already. Small towns wake up early.

"Sure, and thanks." She yawns. *"God knows I need that. Be there in a few."*

Thirty minutes later, she beeps for me to come out. I get my purse and run outside. Once I'm in the car, I notice that her gaze is transfixed on something in the woods, and it's then that I see Frank's suspicious face locked on Freya's.

"I will never understand your weird friendship with him," she comments uncertainly, nodding at Frank.

"That's okay. The most important thing is that Frank and I do." I wink at her with a smile.

"Weird-ass town." She rolls her eyes and reverses the car, causing me to double over with laughter—seeing how Freya's adjusting to life in our small town is a whole comedy show.

"So, how is the search going?" I ask, referring to the PTSD center she's planning to open.

"Jonah promised to show me a few places today and said he has a very good feeling about one of them." Ah, Jonah. My gut feeling suggests I should thank him for sending Justin to my rescue, if that was him like I suspect. Hopefully, he'll permanently move here—we can certainly use more good people.

"That's amazing!"

"I know." She yawns. "It's exhausting. I never knew it would be like this. So many preparations."

"You're doing a good thing, Frey. I'm proud of you." And I totally mean that. Freya is one of few people who doesn't just sit on their butt complaining about the world without doing anything about it—instead, she's truly trying to change it for the better. Also, having millions helps.

Her cheeks turn a cute pink shade, and she smiles sheepishly. "Keeps me busy."

"And that too. Though you could always go back to being a nurse. I know you really loved being one," I suggest, heavily implying that she shouldn't let her creep of an ex destroy her love of helping people. She put a lot of work into her nursing career before he completely derailed it.

"Yeah, I've been thinking about that. Once we open the center, I'll see if my heart will call for it." She sounds almost shy.

"I think that's a great idea." I fully support everyone

following their dreams and their hearts. Even though I don't follow mine—I can't—I can still be happy for others pursuing their individual paths.

"What the hell?" Her eyes bulge.

"What happened?" I ask, suddenly scared—at this point, I wouldn't be surprised if the diner was flooded by a tsunami.

"Isn't that your car?" She points at something, and I follow her finger.

It is, in fact, my Jeep. My old boy is parked in front of the diner in broad daylight. I pinch my hand just to see if I'm dreaming. "That's... I mean, yeah, but... *what?*"

She looks confused. "You didn't tell me you got it back!"

"I didn't know I did."

"Huh?" Her forehead wrinkles. "I'm lost."

"Me too, man." I blink rapidly to see if the car will disappear. "Yesterday, I was told I had to pay two grand to get it back, and now it's sitting right here."

"You didn't pay it yourself?" Her voice is full of wonder.

"I don't have two grand, so no."

She turns to me with a wide smile. "I guess you got a fairy godmother."

I guess I do.

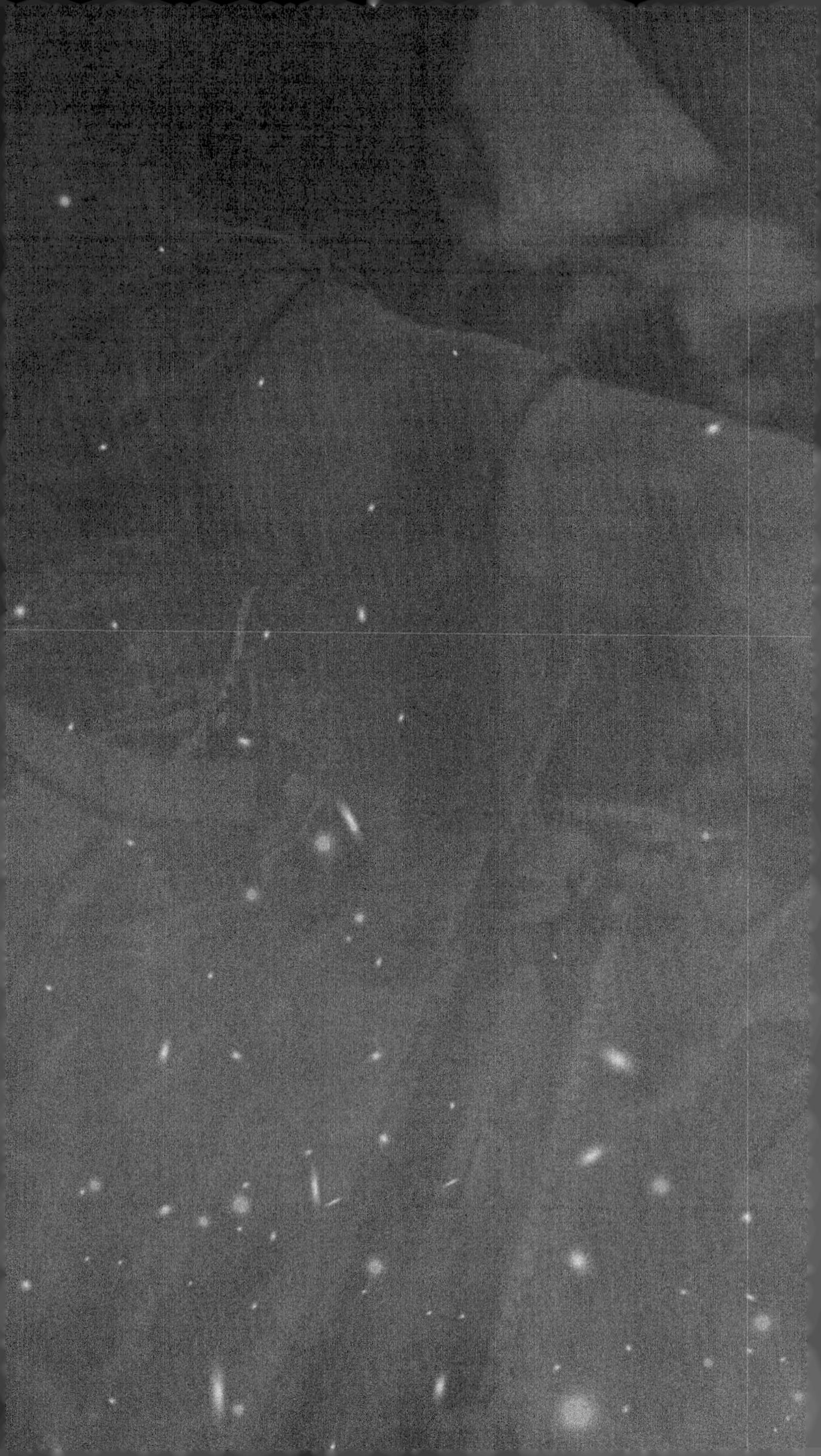

Chapter Eight

K AYLA

It's been three weeks since I got my old boy back.

Alex is back in town and has announced his undying love for Freya. Thank God he pulled his head out of his ass. I didn't want to have to kick him in the nuts. Hopefully, those nuts will be put to good use later. I must admit, the trip did him good, as he returned a seemingly brand-new person.

The diner is getting back on track after reopening a couple of weeks ago. The mornings are always busy, thanks to Marina's famous crepes laced into almost every dish we have. If it were up to me, I'd be eating them for breakfast, lunch, and dinner, but then I'd have another problem on my ass (quite literally) because they're not the healthiest meal.

Freya sits at the bar, but I don't even have time to chat with her for more than a minute while I pour her coffee. We have an extra busy day today, and since the reopening, we have so many patrons that we need to hire another waitress and a cook. Plus, Donna, the owner of the local coffee shop, has gotten sick with the flu and temporarily closed up her coffee shop, not trusting anyone with her brews. We small-town folk are no different than the big ones—we, too, need coffee to function and thrive.

Freya sees me getting overwhelmed and starts picking up her food to go. I dash around people and tables, arriving in front of her to refill her coffee at least one more time.

"Can I have a to-go cup? I think one less customer will make your life easier." She makes an apologetic face, looking around.

"Nah, stay." I wave her off, trying to wipe the sweat from my forehead with a paper towel. I've had a headache for the past two hours, and even the back of my eyeballs hurt.

"Maybe you can swing by for dinner? Alex will be happy to have you over." At the mention of his name, a rosy color spreads across her cheeks, and it's adorable. My friend is so in love, and I adore Alex a little more for making Freya so happy.

"Sure, sounds like a good idea." I force a smile through my pounding headache.

"Tonight, then? After your shift?" She looks so hopeful that I don't have the heart to refuse her.

"Of course. I'll be there." I salute her with two fingers.

She brightens up and leaves, waving her hand at me and Marina, who's absolutely overwhelmed in the kitchen.

"We need another waitress and one more cook, Marina. For real this time. You need a break from cooking," I say as I come to grab another plate from the kitchen.

"But they're my pancakes!" She makes it sound like I'm trying to take her firstborn for a debt.

"Nobody's touching your pancakes, but a new cook can help you with other dishes." Seeing the look of pure horror on her face, I add, "Following your recipes, of course."

She wipes her sweaty forehead with a paper towel, smudging her foundation, and I bite my lip to prevent a smile from spreading over my face—Marina always has a full face of makeup on. She always takes care of her skin and body. I might have to take a few tips from her. Better earlier than later. She looks gorgeous for her age. "You might be right."

"Excuse me, what did you just say?" My eyes widen in shock, and I feel a sharp pain from my headache. "Did you just agree with me? Is it doomsday?" I comically look around.

"Don't push your luck." She lovingly smacks me with a towel. "We'll talk about that after the shift." She looks outside to the floor. "Or tomorrow."

I chuckle and go back to serving the nonstop flow of customers. Good for the business and tips, but so bad for my poor back.

By the end of the day, I'm famished. I can barely stand, and my feet and butt hurt like hell. I get so excited at the prospect of going home, right up until the moment I remember that I promised Freya I'd stop by for dinner. I groan. Why did I agree to that? Why?

I'll tell you why. Because I love Freya. She became my 'bestest' friend. We clicked the very first time we met, as she isn't one to beat around the bush and is never scared to call me on my shit. I knew she was different—and now here we are.

That's why I'm driving my half-dead, enfeebled body to

Alex's cabin after a long shift, praying that Justin wasn't invited. Or was. He's like a mosquito bite: scratching it feels so good in the moment, but it's terrible for you long-term. I always make the poor choice to just keep on scratching.

I groan, grabbing the steering wheel tighter. It'll be a very difficult itch not to 'scratch' if I plan on staying friends with Freya, considering Justin's everywhere Alex is, and Freya is everywhere Alex is. You get the picture.

I'm almost at Alex's cabin, and when *it* appears in front of me, I groan loudly. Justin's truck. Luck isn't on my side today.

For the last three weeks, our interactions have been nonexistent. I still see him around town, but he avoids me just as much as I avoid him. One time though, we bumped into each other at the grocery store. He was like a brick wall, and I almost went tumbling down. While trying to prevent my body from hitting the floor, he snaked his arm around my waist and pulled me to him.

That was the first time I smelled him since the encounter at the diner. I wish I never did, though. Now, I'm dreaming of his masculine, musky smell with a note of engine oil forever engraved into his skin. Was it turning out to be my kryptonite? I'm doomed. Ever since, my usual pictures of shirtless Henry Cavill haven't done it for me anymore—now I need the real-deal sexy lifetime asshole-mechanic with an intoxicating smell. The one whose lips I can't stop thinking about being so close to me. But the moment I remember the look of horror and disgust on his face when he realized it was *me* he was holding at the store, or was close to kissing at the diner, pushing me away like I had a highly contagious disease—yeah, just like that, I'm back to Henry Cavill.

That moment of our almost-kiss... that was something I

could never dream of. He almost kissed me, and if not for the car outside, I would have let him. Why would I resist when I've been dreaming about that for so long? Is he toxic for me? Hell yes. Would this knowledge prevent me from tasting his lips only once? I don't think so, no. I'd let it happen just once, just so I know how it feels. That's it. I'm positive that the craving would be satisfied after that. Just one little taste.

I bump my forehead on the steering wheel—who am I kidding? I know Freya is trying her best to bury the hatchet between us by inviting us both to dinner in the hope we reconsider our mutual hatred, but it's just not possible. The situation between us screams not only animosity but also awkwardness, making everything more complicated.

In the last couple of weeks, I've gotten the feeling from Freya that she sees *something* that I don't, and I can tell that she's trying with all her might to prove it to the both of us. But you can't prove something that simply isn't there.

Either way, I got sucked into dinner tonight regardless, so I park my car and go to knock on the door. Right before my knuckles meet the wood (the real woody wood, not the other kind), it swings inward, and instead, my fist meets Justin's chest. Its resemblance to hardwood isn't nonexistent, actually.

He's standing there with a cup of steaming coffee in his hand, the muscles under the short sleeves of his white T-shirt bulging as he brings the cup to his lips. He takes a sip and then pointedly looks down at my hand, which is still on his chest. I quickly yank it away as if it was burned.

"Hi, Justin," I offer in a neutral voice.

Justin doesn't say anything, just looks me up and down. The corner of his lip dips as if he isn't happy with what he sees. Tough luck, buddy. I wear black leather leggings, dark olive Docs, and a baggy olive off-shoulder shirt. Last I checked myself in the mirror, I looked hot as hell *and* badass. Precisely the combination he doesn't go for. He goes for hot posh girls.

"What the fuck are you doing here?" His voice is menacing, a far cry from the gentle whisper I heard him speak before.

"You know what," I say with a defeated sigh and attempt to brush past him. His frame is solid and unmoving, so I put my hand on his bicep and try to push him out of my way. He doesn't budge—just looks down at me. I'm five-four, and he is about six-two or six-three. Normally, I'd be thrilled with that height difference because I like them tall and big (to watch them in their natural habitat, *that's it*), but not today. Today his height seems intimidating. I press harder on his arm, but again, he doesn't budge.

"Justin, for fuck's sake!" Freya yells from the kitchen, and only then does he move out of the way.

"Asshole," I not-so-quietly grumble, and his brows rise in surprise. *That's right, you're an asshole.* I've always tried to refrain from saying overtly rude things to him just so I don't aggravate the situation more, but right here and now, I decide that I am done. That masculine scent of his that's been stuck in my head enters my nostrils, telling me to climb him like a tree... and maybe even hump his leg a little. In an attempt to not embarrass myself by letting him know how much his smell impacts me, I hold my breath as I push past him, heading to the kitchen where Freya's trying to fix the food. There's a better than average chance that we'll all die, considering Freya in the kitchen is a guaranteed disaster. Her food might come out poisonous. She can cook one dish—*one*. Lasagna. And that's it. Anything else coming out of her cookbook could be used as biological warfare.

"Are you hungry?" she asks with a hopeful smile.

"Not really." My smile's forced, and my stomach clenches at the memory of what happened the last time we ate real food here.

"Oh, c'mon! It was one time!" she exclaims, seeing the look on my face. Oh yeah, that one time all three of us were puking for days following the *incident*. Right after Alex returned, Freya made dinner for us. I barely made it home before showing my car what mama had for dinner. That was the one time I wished Justin was there to suffer with us. The *one* time. But I guess he was busy fucking his longtime 'wandering vagina,' as I call Ashley, his girlfriend (or ex or fuck buddy—who knows anymore) and her friends—yes, I judge them, sue me. From then on, Alex and I decided we would avoid Freya's cooking like the plague while trying not to tell her. I don't know how he avoids it, though, living in the same house with her.

"Do you have any of that matcha tea you've been talking about?" I try to stir the conversation away from her cooking, and it works. She brightens up.

"Yes, I do! Want some?" Her wavy brown hair bounces off her back while she jumps in excitement like a little kid. It's incredible how much she's changed since she met Alex; they both had so much healing to do, and they both seem so much happier now.

"Yes, please." It's very difficult to mess up a cup of tea, but I know enough to know she can manage it. I keep my fingers crossed. She fusses over the kettle and gorgeous tea set as I look around again. I still can't believe how sophisticated Alex's house is. It's small but extremely cozy and well put together. When Freya got attacked—the first time—it was also the first time I ever stepped foot in his place. If I had to describe it, it's the love child of West Elm and

Pottery Barn. Even his dishes match. All of them. Meanwhile, I've never had two plates of the same color or style at my place. But I like it like that.

I try not to pay attention to Justin as he takes a seat on the couch, but the hatred radiating from him makes it impossible. His presence is imposing, and his scalding gaze is set on making sure I know it—he's a bigger and meaner predator, intent on making sure I remember my place. As if I could ever forget how low on the food chain I am.

"Where is Alex?" I decide to ask Freya just to take my mind off certain unsafe topics.

"He's in town. He got a new shipment for this Pontiac he's working on." Alex fixes vintage cars. Sometimes he buys, fixes, and sells them himself; sometimes, customers pay him to work on their vehicles. As far as I can tell, he makes good money. "He should be back soon." She glares in Justin's direction, and I can feel the holes he's burning into my back with his heated stare. "I have a babysitter today, as you can see. Every time Alex leaves town, he sends someone. Every damn time." She shakes her head and points at Justin. Ah, now his presence makes more sense. Alex is being an overprotective bear. Since his return, he's barely let her out of his sight. He clearly trusts Justin a lot if he asked him to look after Freya. Alex worships the ground she walks on. "Justin, do you want some tea?" Freya calls over her shoulder, making me jump.

"Not in this company," comes his rough reply.

"Justin!" Freya's voice is like that of a mother scolding a rude child. I know she tries hard, and I do miss her, but I refuse to willingly put myself through this misery, especially after the shitty day I've had.

"Sorry, Frey, I just remembered that I have an—an appointment I need to go to." I abruptly stand, grab my purse, and head to leave. My whole body feels overheated and tingly in the worst way.

"Kayla—" Freya's voice drops; she's clearly upset over my abrupt departure.

"It's fine. I really don't want to be late. Save my tea for another time, please—I like it cold too." I smile at her and run out, avoiding looking at the asshole whose ass is currently parked on the back of the couch. His face doesn't look all that happy—I guess he was eager for the long evening of torture ahead.

My mind drifts off to the first time Justin was ever mean to me—the day things changed.

He used to smile at me when passing by as he did with every other woman he saw, and those rare smiles filled my teenage years with happiness. I don't need to tell you that I tried to grab every single one of those and bottle them up so I could relive them later. Being a silly young girl, I didn't realize it wasn't real flirting—just his way of communicating with the world.

But one day, he'd changed.

One day, he was home on leave during his contract with the Navy and got sent to jail for something that could have been easily avoided. Since then, his military career was over —I had heard that his initial contract ended before the arrest, but he was planning on reenlisting. That's pretty much the moment I became public enemy number one, and the last time he looked at me like a person. That night. Mark was there, too; that was the last time I saw Justin before he went to jail. His trial was dealt with at lightspeed, and no amount of his wealthy family's money was able to save him.

On that early morning when he reappeared in Little Hope, our fates were woven together into a pattern of hate. He'd just returned from jail, and I stupidly missed his hand-

some face. He was walking down Main Street, and I saw him from the windows of the diner. When he passed by, I rushed outside to say "Hey, Justin! Welcome back home!" like the naive fool I was.

He looked at me as if I were an insect on the ground and snarled, "The fuck do you need, trailer trash? Run the fuck along."

I was crushed by the sudden hatred that poured from him. I didn't know what to think or how to respond, so I just bit back tears and retreated inside. That was the beginning of the end.

Another time, he was walking down the street with a steaming cup of liquid, returning from one of his nightly escapades, I assumed, and I was on my way to start my shift at the diner. Passing me, he bumped into me on purpose, I could tell, spilling the scorching hot coffee all over my front. He didn't even apologize, and I'd had enough. There, I decided to confront him for the first time and ask what his problem was. He gave me that look... I still remember it. Like I was... nothing and nobody, and all he wanted was to squash me under his boot. He snarled at me to get the fuck out of his way again. And I did. I got out of his way and have been ever since.

Not anymore, though. I'm Freya's friend, and he has to learn to tolerate my presence. Besides that, I might be 'trailer trash' by birth, but I'm trying to change how people see me, and I'm not planning on taking it from him any longer. He's just going to have to suck it up, because I'm not going anywhere (at least, not yet), and I'm sticking around for Freya's sake. She doesn't have many friends here, just like me. I'm tired of being an outcast. I honestly and truly am lonely. I know I'm not ugly. In fact, some have said I'm pretty. But the majority of guys around here seem to like girls who want to become a Stepford wife eventually—I could never. Of course, I get propositioned to be a hookup by the same guys. They like to get dirty like every other man—sometimes with the assumption they need to pay to play, if you get my meaning, as if I'd ever do what I watched my mother do for my entire childhood—but they don't get that from me, either.

Plus, my mind just can't seem to accept that Justin isn't interested, so I can't even consider anyone else seriously. Talk about needing a shrink. I might check myself into that rehab that Freya's opening soon.

Thank God my car starts on the first try. To think of it, for the past month since it was towed, it always starts on the first try. And it doesn't make that weird screeching noise anymore. How haven't I noticed that before? *Interesting.*

I drive to my trailer but don't get out of the car right away. I just want to be still for a moment. To get lost in the magic of the forest with unicorns and rainbows where shitty everyday problems and hate don't exist. I'm secretly hoping that Frank will show up because I certainly could use a friendly face, but even he's decided to check out tonight. Figures.

Understanding that fate isn't on my side today—just like every other day—I rest my forehead on my steering wheel and think about what I'm still doing here and why in hell I'm paying for the sins of others. A sob escapes me. Then another. Soon, the levee breaks, and I'm sobbing full force, hugging my old, worn-out wheel.

When the sobs quiet, I wipe my face and walk into my home. My safe space where I don't have to try to be liked by anyone—where I can just be me, and that's enough.

Chapter Nine

JUSTIN

"Really? Really, Justin?" Freya yells at me as soon as that little piece of trash walks out the door.

It's easier to call her that—otherwise, there's a real danger of her becoming something else in my eyes, and that's precisely why I've been avoiding her for the past couple of weeks. That moment at the diner... it knocked me off balance, planting weird thoughts in my head. Dirty thoughts. Dangerous thoughts. I have to keep my distance. I have to. For my own sake. Otherwise, I might end up doing something that would hurt a lot of people, one very dear to me in particular, all for the pursuit of following my dick. Because clearly, that's all it is: my dick talking. She is like that damn forbidden fruit that I can never have. The one I shouldn't even desire. Nothing more than the mystery of the untouchable.

Every time I close my eyes, I see her plush lips, her little tongue peeking out to wet them. A golden ring in the middle of her lower lip, and the urgency to know how it will —dammit, *would*—feel under my own lips. Every damn time since that evening at the diner.

Freya's voice thunders around the small space, almost as loud as Alex's. He must be rubbing off on her. She storms up to me, her brown hair flying behind her—that's how fast she's moving. "Justin!"

"What?" I blink innocently and take a sip of my coffee.

"You know what, you big, stupid jerk!" She jabs her little finger between my pecs, as if it can hurt me. "Why are you being like this?"

"Like what?" I raise my brows, aware I'm playing with fire.

She digs her fingernail deeper, and I can almost feel it.

"You *know* what, Justin Attleborough. Stop being an asshole to Kayla," she hisses, full mother bear mode activated.

All my humor evaporates in an instant. "She deserves it, Freya." I lean closer to her face. "She isn't as good as you think she is." And I'd be wise to remind myself of that as well.

"Really? What could she have done that would justify you treating her so badly, Justin? What?" I can tell Freya's desperate to know the whole story. Kayla probably didn't tell her everything. Of course, she wouldn't.

"Ask her." It's my turn to hiss. I know Alex won't appreciate me talking to Freya like that, but he knows my feelings on this.

"Do you think I haven't? She doesn't know the reason." Here comes the proof. Freya sounds calmer now, like she can sense my own distress and understands that only one of us can be high-strung at a time.

"And you believe her?" I almost laugh.

"I do," she claims with certainty, finding my gaze and holding it. "She doesn't know, Justin."

A moment of doubt creeps up on me. The first one I've had since that night. It's gone as quickly as it came. Of course, she wouldn't tell Freya, her only friend who doesn't know who she is—she doesn't want to lose her. Ask the whole town, and they'll tell you: she's just like her mother and sister—a whore, a liar, a life-destroyer.

"Tell me what happened."

I'm considering it for a second. Freya is Alex's girlfriend. *Live-in* girlfriend, and neither of us have had one of *those* before. It's a huge step for him; she means a lot to him. For fuck's sake, he finally checked himself into a mental health facility because he wanted to be well for her. She brought my best friend back from the dark depths of his damaged mind when we all thought he was lost forever. And yet Alex hasn't shared the secret and my shame with her. My respect for my friend grows even more. "It's not entirely my secret to tell, Freya." And then I add quietly, almost whispering, "I wish I could tell you, but I can't. I made a promise not to."

"To whom, Justin?" she murmurs like she's beginning to understand the gravity of this.

"To someone very important to me," I whisper and pull back. "Be careful with Kayla. I have no idea how Alex can stand her being around you, knowing how treacherous she really is and how she likes to run her mouth." I start walking away, but Freya grabs my hand.

"Whatever you think Kayla did, she didn't," she swears stubbornly.

"You don't know her," I snap back, my temper beginning to boil over.

"You're wrong. I *do* know her. In a short period of time, I've learned more about her than you have in the lifetime you've known her." Her face is hard with concentration, like she's desperately holding back something she wants to say.

"Why are you so set on trusting her? You've known her for what? A few months?" I'm growing angry with her blind trust in that evil little spawn, and I'm growing even angrier at myself for always noticing how good her ass looks in those black leather pants. Those fucking pants became the bane of my existence the second she started wearing them all the damn time. *All* the time. In the winter, her ass was covered by that long, ugly jacket she thinks is stylish, but now, since the weather has become nicer, she constantly has less and less clothes on. I'd prefer her in a potato sack, her body completely covered. And today, she waltzed in here wearing *that*? Does she think it's okay to walk around, tempting people left and right?

"Yes, Justin, a few short months. But I've seen a lot of shit in my life, *been through* a lot of shit in my life, and I like to think I have a pretty good radar for good people versus shitty people. And she is *good* people." Her face is flushed, her hands balled into tiny fists.

"Suit yourself," I tell her finally, giving up. "Don't tell me later I didn't warn you."

"That won't be necessary." Her eyes throw daggers at me, and I throw them right back. She should be running away from Kayla, yet she's embraced her with arms wide open. Where is Alex in this? He knows what she's done and that she can't be trusted, yet she's still allowed in this house.

Is he so pussy-whipped that he closes his eyes to everything if Freya says so? I'll never be that person. Never.

My head turns toward the door as I catch the sound of Alex's old truck. *Thank fuck, he's here*—I'm not fit to babysit his girlfriend today.

The door bursts open, and my best friend storms in. He assesses the surroundings, and I give him a few moments to adjust. His PTSD is bad, and even though it became better with Freya in his life and his new therapy, he still suffers from it. Another thing in my life I feel guilty for. If I'd just have stuck with him, maybe…

Alex takes three big strides to Freya before proceeding to eat her face.

"That's my cue to leave," I say loud enough for them to hear but not loud enough to interrupt. I'll let them have their moment.

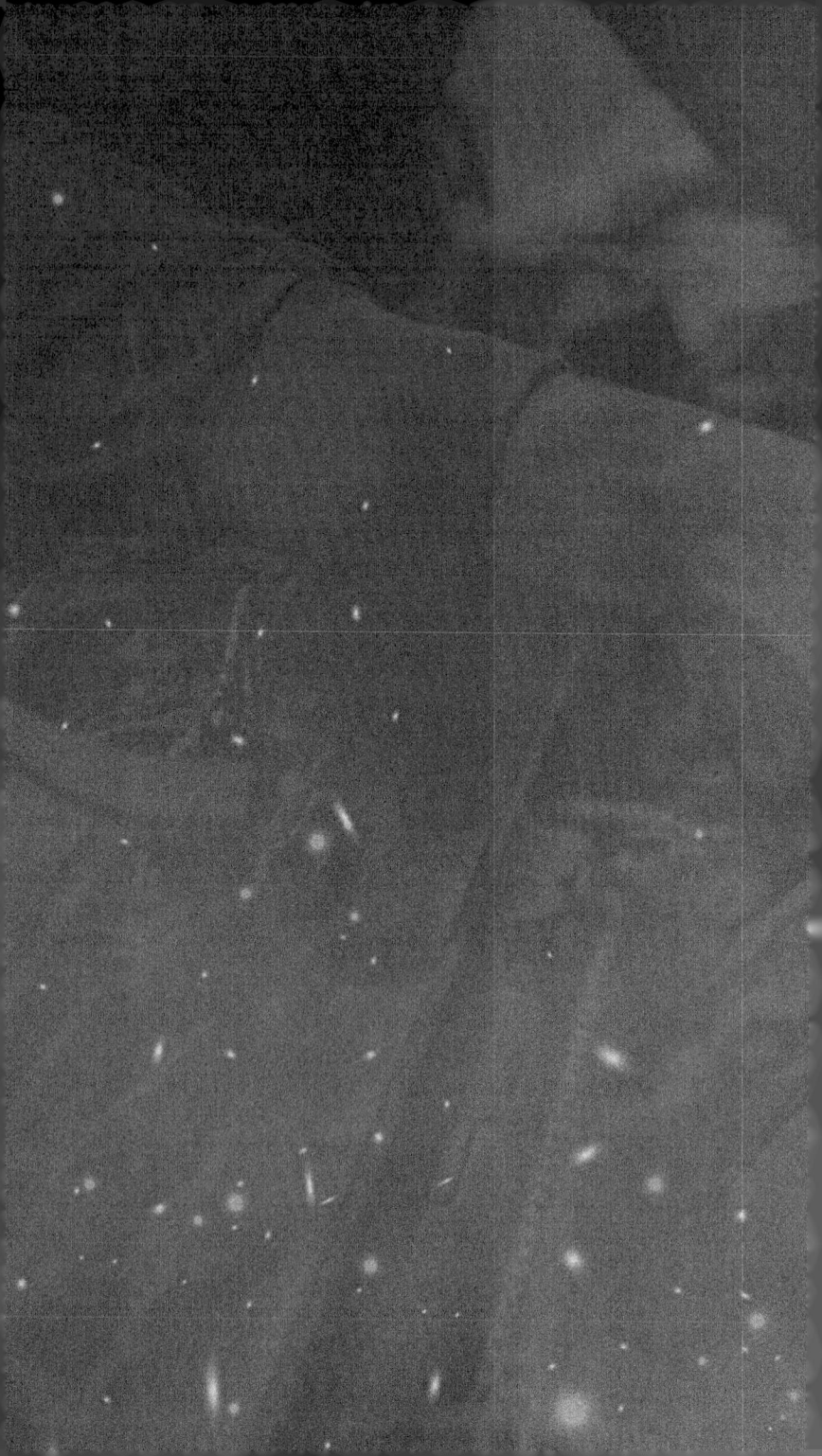

Chapter Ten

KAYLA

Today is my rare day off. I'm not working my waitressing job; I was planning to spend it with Freya and Alex for a couple of hours and then do some drawing. But considering yesterday evening, I'm in no mood for socializing, so now I have only the drawing part left.

I make myself some matcha tea—because I never got a chance to drink the delicious goodness that Freya hooked me on—swipe my pencils and a notebook off the table and head outside.

I'm sitting in my little chair, soft gusts of wind tangling strands of hair as I'm submerged in my drawing, when I hear the powerful engine of a big car roaring closer and closer to me. It's surprising because only three people know where I live, and I'm not expecting any of them.

When Justin's truck appears on the unpaved road, I

curse mentally. Who the hell told him where I live? I know Freya and Alex wouldn't do that, and the other person is Marina, who would die before she shared a breath of information about me with him. The feeling of being safe in my home, something so precious to me, slowly dissolves into thin air.

Justin parks next to my car and slowly gets out, wincing as if being here is causing him physical pain. I roll my eyes at his theatrics and keep drawing. He makes a show of taking his sunglasses off and looking around with disgust.

"Nothing seems to change for you," he announces with a scowl and strides toward me. *Asshole.* There's nothing I can tell him that's not going to end with a fight. He seems too eager for one, and that's precisely why I keep my mouth shut. He plants his annoyingly tight butt on the chair next to me that I keep for my tired feet after long shifts.

"What are you doing here, Justin?" I ask him without taking my eyes off my task: drawing horns on my anime design. How fitting.

He's quiet for a few moments, and just when I nearly lose hope of getting anything out of him, he answers. "You need to end your friendship with Freya."

"Sure," I shoot back sarcastically. I flick my eyes at him for a moment before I resume drawing, pressing the pencil harder into the paper, making the horns thicker and darker. He throws his hand out and covers the drawing, smashing the pencil across it in the process. It flies to the grass. I finally make eye contact with him. "Get. Your. Hand. Off."

"I don't know what game you're playing, but you're bad news. You need to leave them both alone." His voice is low and menacing. It's meant to hurt. And it does.

"Is it that they don't want me around, or you don't?" I lift my gaze to catch his.

He holds my eyes, and confesses after a few loud heartbeats, "I don't."

"Good thing, then. Because I don't care." I move to pick up the fallen pencil from the ground, and he follows my lead. Now we both are on our knees.

"Look, I was Alex's friend way before you were in the picture. Our friendship takes precedence over yours with Freya." He grabs one side of the pencil just as I grab the other.

"Without Freya, you wouldn't even *have* your friend, now, would you?" I pull the pencil from his hands. "And Freya is more my friend than yours."

"Freya wouldn't be your friend if she knew the truth about you," he growls, and his voice takes on a threatening tone. "Like the whole town does."

That does it.

"Get the hell out of here," I snarl. I stand, resisting making an extra hole in him with the damn pencil, and turn on my heel to walk back to my trailer.

I step inside and am about to close the door when Justin shoves his way in. Suddenly, the space feels smaller. It's enough when I'm alone, but with him in this confined space, it feels suffocating. "Get out of my house!" I point at the door.

"'House'?" He makes a show of looking around and chuckles evilly. No-no-no, no one's talking shit about my house. Especially not him, Mr. Born-with-a-Silver-Spoon-in-His-Mouth.

"Out, Attleborough! Now!" I yell. I *never* yell. Ever. Well, very rarely, let's put it that way. I'm a level-headed person because I grew up with two histrionics in the house, so I try my hardest to be the opposite of that, resolving conflict with a simple, even-toned conversation.

Well, fuck that. The time for that is way in the past.

He moves forward as I move backward. There's not much space, so in three steps, I'm cornered against the wall. His presence is looming. He puts one hand on the side of my face and leans closer. His arm is so close to my face that I can see the fine hairs on his skin and blue veins on his bulged muscles. "We both know you're no good for people. You're toxic. You need to make up an excuse and finally leave this town for good. Do us all a favor."

"Fuck you," I hiss. Did I say I had a crush on him? I hate him. That's it. That's the fine line between hate and love everybody keeps talking about. I see it clearly now, right there, that damn line blazing red, and I'm so stepping over it.

"Oh, you wish, don't you?" He smiles and inches closer, half-leaning his body on me. He trails his nose along my cheek, and I hate myself for shivering. We're in the same position we found ourselves in back at the diner weeks ago, only now I don't have an escape. He cornered me in my own home, and I'm apparently less than eager to push him away, it seems. Why aren't I pushing him away? *That'd be the right thing to do,* I tell my body. I feel weirdly too warm and too sticky. I pull my wits together and decide to follow my own advice, so I lift my hands to shove him off me, but he easily grabs them both in his large ones, folding them behind my back and using them to pin me against the wall. His fingers linger on the top of my ass, brushing along the curve ever so lightly.

"You smell good." He presses his nose into the slope of my neck and inhales deeply. "So fucking good. Like strawberries and fucking sin," he murmurs, and it feels like he's talking to himself, not me. He nuzzles his nose under my ear and nips at my skin, and I let out an embarrassing whimper.

It seems to sober him up because he releases me and rushes to take a haphazard step back. I don't know where to avert my gaze, so I look down. I mean to focus on the floor, but my gaze catches on his pants. His dick straining against them, ready to burst through the zipper at any moment. I can see the outline through the denim, and I feel my face flare.

"Don't flatter yourself." He adjusts himself, noticing where my attention is fixed. "It's a normal reaction to any pussy."

And just like that, the spell is broken. I grind my teeth, nearly breaking them down into dust. "I don't know what you're doing here, Justin, I really don't. But you need to get the hell out before I call the cops."

"Oh, you like doing that, too, don't you?" His tone becomes menacing, and he leans closer again, trying to intimidate me with his closeness. "You like calling the cops, huh?"

"What's that supposed to mean?" I ask, confused. I've never called the cops in my life; quite the opposite, actually, since I was born on the wrong side of town and therefore destined to walk a thin line with the law—and, thanks to Jake, my life has been a living hell because of police presence, so no, I don't 'like' calling the cops.

Ignoring my question, he grabs me by the hips and spins me so my cheek is plastered against the wall. I feel a pang of excitement, but I squash that little spark as if it was a bug, hoping it will freakin' die because I will not allow myself to be turned on by this.

"Justin," I ask in a calm voice despite my insides going crazy, "what are you doing?"

"Are you feeling it too?" He presses his body into my back, and I can feel every warm inch of him. His hot breath caresses my ear. "Do you want me to fuck you as much as I do?" He grinds his pelvis into the curve of my ass. He's hard. Another sparkle of excitement trickles through my traitorous body. It clearly didn't get a memo from my brain that said we should be angry and disgusted. He licks the shell of my ear, and liquid heat pools between my legs, coaxing me to give up. Just a little. *C'mon.*

I have a problem. I officially need to see a shrink.

Justin continues to grind into me and bites my earlobe again. I keep my palms plastered on the wall, scared that if I let go, they'll be wandering all over whatever body parts of his they'd be able to reach. His hands rest flat on the wall on either side of my face as he touches me with his whole body —everything but his hands, and I want them on me the most. I wiggle until I can turn in place to face him. He doesn't give me space, instead pushing me back with his frame again.

His mouth is so close to me that I can taste his warm minty breath. He's hovering over my lips, making it his purpose to torture me before the kiss. And I know it's torture; we both do. When I finally can't take it any longer, I lift my face closer to his, hoping for a kiss. Instead, he laughs abruptly and steps back, the sudden distance jolting me.

"What—you didn't think I'd kiss that lying mouth, did you? In the dark, maybe, so I don't have to see you." He laughs again, and this time, it has no humor. It's cruel. And evil. And aiming to kill.

"Seemed like you were singing a different tune just a few weeks ago." I feel a vein begin throbbing on my neck, and my face heats up, probably turning bright red.

"Yeah." He smirks. The motherfucker *smirks*! "Wanted to see your reaction."

If he slapped me, I'd feel less pain. My eyes begin to water. I step toward him and push against his chest. He stops laughing and steps back. I push harder. And harder. If he wanted, I'd never move him from the spot, but he lets me. My cheeks are getting wet—I didn't even notice when the tears began pouring down—and I push harder. He stumbles over a storage bin on the floor and looks down.

I hate him.

I hate you.

"Get the fuck out of my house!" I wail. He looks up, and his eyes don't hold even a bit of laughter anymore. They're laced with... regret? Pity? Sadness? I don't give a fuck anymore. "*Go!*"

He walks out without a word and peels off. When I'm sure he's left, I throw myself on my wonderful, cozy, worn-out loveseat I bought at a yard sale for fifty bucks and let myself drown in sorrow.

All the feelings I ever held for Justin Attleborough have died.

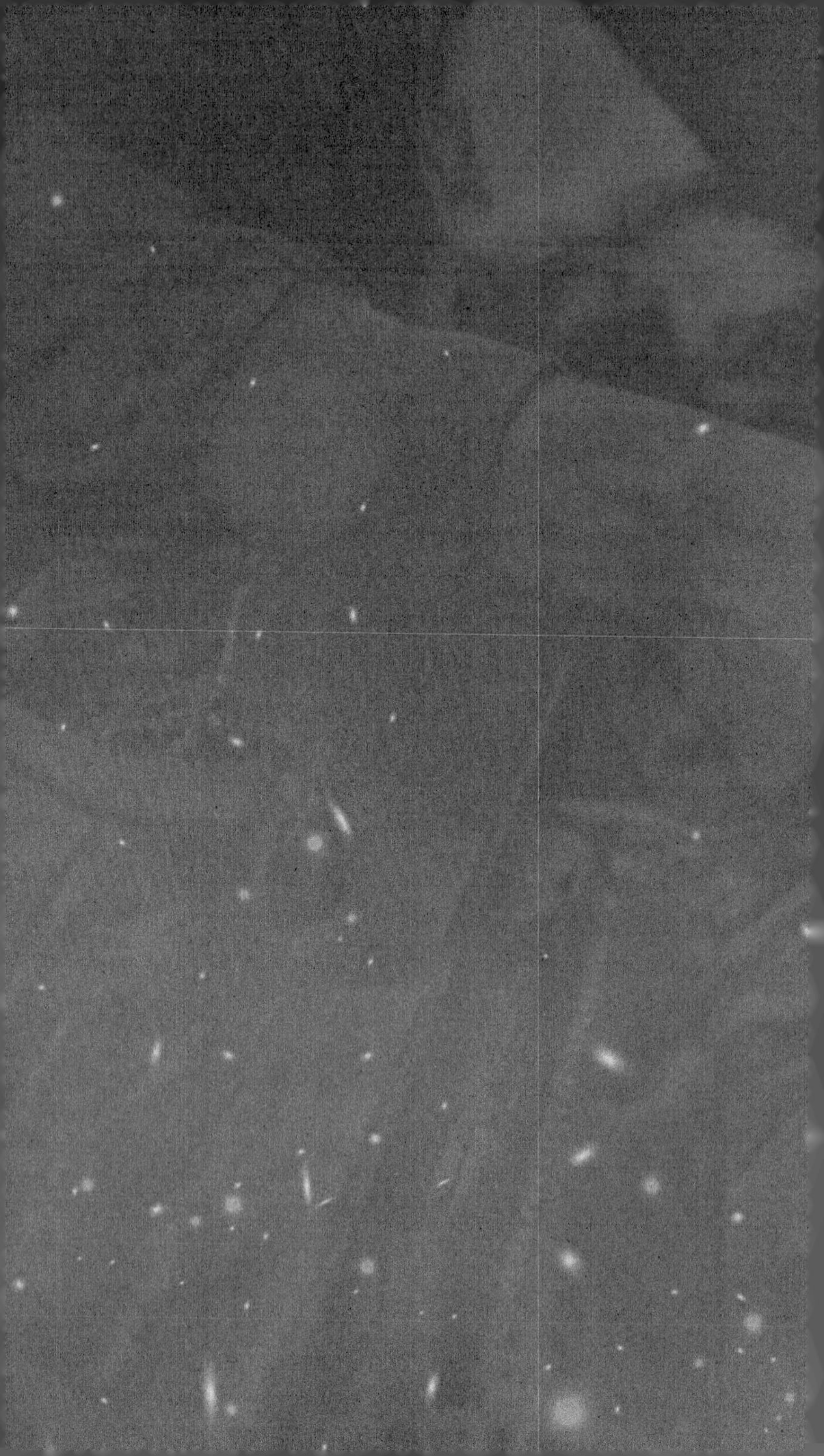

Chapter Eleven

KAYLA

The next day, I get to my morning shift at Marina's a little late. When I woke up with a puffy face after a whole night of good cleansing crying, I knew I'd have to spend a little time fixing my appearance. I couldn't show up looking like that, or I'd have to find murder-charge-grade bail money for Marina, so I called her to say that I got some food poisoning and would be late. She didn't believe me, of course, but told me to come in whenever.

I've been wiping my face with ice cubes all morning, trying to remove the redness and swelling, but as I look in the mirror, it seems like I only made it worse. So I put some concealer on, my most distractingly large glasses, and go on my not-so-merry way.

Of course, Marina knows right away that something's wrong. One look at my face, and she pours me a massive cup of coffee with cream and grabs some Baileys from her stash. She splashes some into my cup, looks at me, and pours three times more. Without a word, she pushes the cup over the counter toward me. I take it with a silent thank you and gulp down half in one go.

"Does your swollen face have anything to do with that asshole?" Her Russian accent is thicker than usual as she says this, nodding toward the door. I turn my head and freeze. Justin fucking Attleborough. I grit my teeth and groan. "Want me to get rid of him?" she asks, cracking her knuckles, and I chuckle. She *so* could—which is why I waited as long as I did to come in, because I wouldn't want her to get arrested on my behalf. I've seen this woman make grown men tremble in their boots and cry real tears. I'm glad she's on my side.

"No, I got it," I sigh.

"You sure? 'Cause I can't wait to teach this pretty boy a lesson." She finds my eyes and holds them. She usually doesn't show her emotions much, but she's loyal and fierce when protecting her family. And I got lucky that she considers me hers.

Justin walks inside and looks around. There are twenty tables in the diner, and half are already occupied despite the relatively early hour of nine in the morning. Marina makes the best breakfast on the coast, I swear, and in a few minutes, everything will be busy, and people will be calling for orders to go.

Justin's still standing by the door, looking unsure. He never comes here unless he has to, and for a very specific reason: me and his mysterious hatred for me. *Now the feeling is mutual, motherfucker.* He takes a tentative step toward us.

"The shotgun's in its usual place, should you need it,"

Marina informs me, only half-joking, before grabbing her Baileys and scurrying to the kitchen.

"I'll get the shovel," I whisper after her, nearly choking on air.

Justin stops in front of me. His hands are in his back pockets, and he rocks back and forth on his heels.

"Can I have a table?" he asks cautiously, his voice nearly pleading.

My own is curt. "No tables available."

"I can sit at the bar," he suggests with a coy smile I'd like to smack off his face.

"It's full."

He looks around at the half-empty bar. "Surely there's a spot for me somewhere...."

"We're at full capacity." I move around the counter, stashing my bag away and putting my apron on.

"Kayla," he murmurs, and I ignore him. "*Kayla*."

"I said... we're full." I start a new pot for coffee and begin washing cups.

"Can I have a cup of coffee, then?" He plants his palms on the counter, and I hate myself for noticing how huge his hands are. And how clean his nails are, despite working all day with engine oil and whatever else he uses in cars.

"We're out," I snap.

"Oh, for fuck's sake, girl. Give the man his coffee." Garry, an old Irish guy, yells from his usual table by the window. He can be a little scary in a grumpy-grandpa way. But I know his weak spot.

"Mind your business, Garry, or your next cup will be decaf," I yell back at him, and he laughs, throwing his hands up in defense.

"I tried, boy. You're on your own." He returns to his food with a broad smile on his face.

I get a travel paper cup and go to the machine. The little thing just started dripping, and it will take minutes —*minutes!*—before it's ready, and then I can be rid of Justin. Hopefully, he'll get tired and leave before that. I'm not built to listen to his insults this early in the morning. Instead, he takes a seat at the bar and watches me silently... and stays there... the whole time the coffee's dripping. I already washed all the dishes, took two new orders, and the dang thing's *still* dripping. We should have upgraded the coffeemaker like Freya suggested, but *no-o-o*, Marina's too proud.

When it's finally ready, I pour the coffee and drop the cup in front of him. He takes his wallet out and leaves a five on the counter, then he stands up. I expect him to go on with his day (preferably far away from here), but he hesitates. I can see that he has something to say, but he doesn't know how to. Usually, insults are easy for him.

"Look, Kayla. I'm—"

"Save it. I don't want to listen to any more shit from you." I throw three dollars change on the bar and turn back to the sink.

"That's not what I'm here for," he says tentatively.

"Coulda fooled me," I snort without looking at him.

"Look, I'm sorry." I hear some shuffling and turn around. He's raking his already messy hair with his hand and fidgeting with tingling keys in his pockets. Worry lines deep between his brows. If I didn't know better, I'd say he's ashamed, but I know better, and shame is an unfamiliar word to Justin. "I was way out of line yesterday."

"Okay. It's all good. Now, go." I don't mean that; it's *not* good, and it'll *never* be good. I just want him gone.

He flinches. "We're going to be in the same space

because of Alex and Freya. We should probably find some sort of truce."

There's no humor in my laughter. "Yeah, don't worry about that." Because I'm done with this town, and I'm done with Justin Attleborough. Done with letting people walk all over me.

"Why?"

"Do you need anything else?" My tone is neutral.

"Why shouldn't I worry about that?" he presses.

"A truce, as you said," I answer with a fake smile. *Just be gone already.*

"Are you planning on leaving?" The accusation in his voice audible.

"If I did, isn't it what you wanted me to do?"

He clears his throat. "Yeah—" He coughs again. "I mean, I didn't mean that. I was just mad."

"See, Justin. That's the thing." I throw a towel on the bar in front of me. "I have no idea why you were mad. Or why you took it out on me. And frankly, I don't care anymore."

"You know, Kayla." He leans closer, his voice dropping to a whisper. "Stop playing."

Our eyes meet, and his are burning with anger. Again. Almost as livid as yesterday. And mine are burning with resentment. Why did I have to poke the bear? He would have been gone by now, leaving me in blissful peace at this early hour.

"I don't, Justin. I really don't," I sigh, and there is a moment of doubt on his face. Just for a moment, before it's replaced with determination. He takes his coffee and leaves. I'm surprised he isn't scared I poisoned it—I totally should have. Or at least, I should have put some salt in it—it would serve him right.

Marina returns from the kitchen, wiping her hands on her apron, her eyes troubled. "That's new. What was he doing here?"

"He came to apologize." I cringe. Yeah, it didn't go so well.

"What for?" A wrinkle appears between her brows.

"He came to my place yesterday and was an asshole."

"I knew the tiny-whiny was the one to blame for your nonexistent eyes today." She stares after Justin, probably cursing his next ten generations. "How does he know where you live?"

"That is a very good question. I thought maybe you told him."

"What?" Now she looks offended. "You think I'd give him any information about you?" She shakes her head. "I hate that boy for how he treats you and wanna smack him stupid every time he opens his mouth." My eyes water and I squeeze her arm. She nods and goes back to the kitchen. "Maybe there's a reason why he acts the way he does." She sees my shocked expression, throwing her hands up in defense. "All I'm saying is that maybe somebody told him some shit. That's all. Good people of Little Hope are known to be nosy fuckers sometimes."

My hackles smooth out. She might be right, but it's not like I haven't tried to talk to him to figure out the problem so we could resolve it like grown people.

We're swamped for the next couple of hours, and I forget about Justin's visit. Especially after the fire, the diner's become quite famous, as drama tends to attract people more than a well-built marketing strategy. We should really thank the psycho who set the place on fire. I should probably mention all of that to Freya one more time just to be sure that it's imprinted on her brain because that woman still feels responsible for all the bad days in Little Hope.

At about eleven o'clock, Freya stops by. She floats in on the cloud of happiness of a thoroughly fucked woman, orders her usual Lonely Kurt, and sits at the bar.

"So." A small smile appears on her face as she tries to hold my gaze, widening every time I look away nervously.

"So?" I parrot, perplexed.

"I heard Justin wanted some breakfast this morning." She wiggles her eyebrows, smirking at me.

"Fucking small town," I growl, grimacing, and she laughs.

"Yeah, that's what I keep saying, but nobody's listening." She rolls her eyes, shoulders slumping. "So why did he come?" she asks, suddenly sitting tall in her seat, eyes sparkling with diabolical curiosity.

I look around to make sure nobody's listening. "He came to apologize."

She just blinks at me. "Justin? Came to apologize?"

"Yeah, color me surprised too."

"W-wow," she stutters. "I'm actually sort of proud of him for that."

"Don't get your panties in a twist until you know what he apologized for." She leans closer and motions for me to continue. "He came by my place yesterday."

"How does he know where you live?" Her eyes look worried.

I spread my arms. "The question of the century."

"You know I'd never tell him, right? After my history with men, there's no way I'd throw somebody under the bus like that. Especially not you. And especially knowing your history with Justin and his... weird obsession with you."

Freya's eyes dart around as if she let slip something she wasn't planning on.

"I know. And I wouldn't call it 'obsession.'" Her brows furrow at my words. "What about Alex?"

"He wouldn't do it for the same reason. He sees the way you interact, and he wouldn't say a word about your home where you feel safe." Her eyes cloud with concern. "You know, sometimes I'm a little scared of Justin, to be honest. He kind of gives... a *weird* vibe, maybe? You know, like he can feel... what's the right word for that? Too intense, maybe?" She bites the inside of her cheek, thinking. "And no one knows what will happen when he lets himself feel all that. Does that make sense?" She looks at me, hoping I'll understand. And I do.

"It totally does. I know what you mean. Yesterday, when he was at my place, I was a little scared of him, to be completely honest," I answer quietly, glancing around to make sure no one hears me.

"Did he do something?" Her voice rises, and she leans closer over the counter with murder in her eyes.

"Nothing to be concerned about, but it was intense. *He* was intense."

"You'll tell me if he does something you're not comfortable with. Right?" Her eyes are burying into mine, holding them hostage, waiting for my confirmation. As a woman who went through hell, she's trying to make sure no one goes through the same ever again. "I don't care if he's my friend. That shit will not be tolerated. So you'll tell me. Right?"

"I will." She clearly doesn't believe me, so I add with more conviction, "I will. I promise."

"Good." She nods. "Now, back to the mystery. How does he know?"

"Marina hasn't said anything either. Who the hell else knows?" I'm not comfortable with the idea that somebody else knows that I live remotely and there's no one around for miles. I have a shotgun, but I'm not sure I will be able to use it. I know you're supposed to point it at your target, but for heaven's sake, I assume there's a little more to it.

Freya's face creases with concern. "I'll ask Justin."

"Can you? I'd feel so much better." A mammoth-sized stone just fell off my chest at her offer.

"Sure thing. I don't like you living alone out there anyway." She waves off my concern of asking her too big of a favor.

"I'm not alone; I have Bob." I smile.

Her brows furrow in confusion. "How is your vibrator going to protect you from a big hulky man?"

"That's Charlie!" I laugh. Charlie is Bella Swan's father from Twilight. He was so incredibly hot, and I got daddy issues. "Bob is my shotgun. So, I'm not alone, see? I live with two very powerful men." I wiggle two fingers at her.

She laughs too, but her laughter is a little forced. She's still concerned about my well-being, and that right there is one of the few reasons I'd be devastated if I left. Or ran away, to be precise.

She eats her breakfast and takes one to go for Alex. For the whole time she's been in Little Hope, she's always ordered one dish. One. The Lonely Kurt. Despite all my attempts to force her to try something else, she refuses. She says Kurt will be even lonelier if she does.

The rest of the day goes by without any major events, thank God. We usually close at seven, but during the weekdays, nobody will come for dinner, so I force Marina to go. I know she has a show that's about to air. I begin getting ready to lock up when the door bursts open, and a glass of tall, dark, and handsome comes in. The very definition of those three. I usually like guys with sandy hair—*fine, one guy*—but since my last revelation, I need to switch my type. He wears a short-sleeve navy T-shirt and black jeans with rips on one knee. His arms are covered in tattoos, and I instantly sense my people.

"Hi! Sorry for bursting in, but my car just broke down, and my phone died. I forgot the charger, and everything here is fucking closed already, and—" He catches himself right before he, probably, covers our little town in shit and gives me a toothy smile. "I'll try again. I'm Archie. My car broke down on the road, and I need to use a phone." The dimple on his right cheek totally does it for me. His jaw has a five o'clock shadow, and I'm melting a little in my spot.

"You can use mine," I offer with a smile and completely forget what exactly I'm offering. At this point, I'd say everything.

"You're a godsend." He walks to the bar where I'm wiping the glasses. I drop the towel, grab my phone, and hand it to him.

"Do you know the phone number you need to call?"

He laughs. "I might be lucky because I just put my friend's new number into my phone this morning and still remember it."

"You're in luck indeed. Besides 911, I don't know any numbers anymore," I confess shamefully.

"Yeah, twenty-first century." He takes my phone, and his eyes linger on my tattoo sleeve. "Nice tats."

"Thanks." I feel my cheeks heating up.

"Never seen a similar design before."

"It's mine." I smile shyly. All my tattoos are of my own design. I have a person in Springfield, a neighboring town thirty minutes away, who inks them for me.

His brows shoot up. "Really?" He takes my hand. It's unexpected and too intimate for someone who just barged into the diner. Slowly, he moves my arm around, looking closely at my tattoo. "You ink yourself?" He gently traces the vines of the rose with the fingers of his other hand.

"No." I gently pull my arm away, and he lets me go. "I know a guy who does a good carving."

He smiles, and this time he offers me his own art. "I do mine too."

"You do designs too?"

"I own a parlor in Boston." I relax at that. So he was indeed interested in my art, not creeping on my skin. "These," he shows me his arms, "are mine."

I look closer this time and see how truly captivating and detailed his tats are. "They are amazing."

"Thanks." He smiles, and my phone rings. Archie pushes it back to me—it's an unknown number. I pick it up.

"Hello?" I say.

"Kayla?" the voice I was expecting the least asks.

"Yes. What do you need, Justin?" I sigh loudly. Now he has my phone number as well. Double torture, fantastic.

"We need to talk."

"Okay." We do need to talk, but I'm so not in the mood for him today. Hard to believe that if he said that to me yesterday, I'd drop everything and jump at the opportunity to spend some time with him, where we can talk like humans without throwing insults at each other. Or more like him throwing them at me and me deflecting them.

"I'll be there in a few minutes."

"I'm not going to talk about anything with you today. I'm tired, and I'm going home. Come tomorrow." I hang up on him. In my wildest dreams, I've never hung up on Justin.

I always thought when he'd be ready to talk, I'd be there. But he took too long, and now I have nothing to say.

"Boyfriend troubles?" Archie gives me a lopsided grin, popping that sexy dimple again.

I laugh. I've never had a boyfriend, so I wouldn't know what those specific troubles are. "No. Just fighting over turf." Assuming Freya and Alex are that turf.

He laughs. "I'm scared to ask."

"Yeah, don't." I bite my lip because it does sound weirdly funny. I give my phone to Archie. "Go ahead."

"Thanks." He punches something in, and his forehead creases. "Huh."

"What?" I ask, seeing his confused face.

"You know Alex?" His eyes are trained on my face.

"What? Did you check my phone log?" My hackles rise.

"What? No!" His voice rises an octave, defensive. "I dialed my friend's number, and his name showed up." He shows me the phone. "See?"

"So, you know Alex too?"

"Yeah. We served together. Our last two tours." His tone is light, but his eyes say there are not many light memories in there.

"Oh!" My IQ is astonishing.

"I'm actually here to see him. And I almost made it." He laughs, rubbing the back of his neck.

"Oh!" Again with that high intelligence. "I can give you a ride."

"Really?" He looks so hopeful it's almost funny.

"Yeah. I need to drop something off for Freya, so it'll be on the way." I shrug my shoulders.

"That'd be cool. I don't want to call ahead and give Alex a chance to escape somewhere." I chuckle at his statement—

that does sound like Alex. "He invited me in a moment of weakness, and I took the chance."

"I bet the moment was Freya," I suggest with a chuckle.

"She was." He smiles. Freya was what Alex needed to cure himself from that typical survivor's guilt and PTSD. He wanted to be better for her and left to get help. We never talked about that, but I'm not blind. A man can't come back whole after what he sees out there, and Alex's been hiding in his shell for far too long. Freya's got some big balls on her feminine frame, and she's not scared to show them.

"Let me lock everything up, and I'll be ready." I speed up my cleaning so we can go.

"Do you need help?" he offers, rubbing his hands together.

"That's sweet of you to offer, but I'm good. Thanks, though."

I'm about to take my apron off when the mass of Justin bursts through the door. When I say a mass, I mean it. He's rushed like somebody's chasing him. All his finesse is lost.

When he sees Archie standing next to the bar, his eyes squint. He walks to us and takes a seat at the bar, eyeballing Archie and me. I stop moving and look at him. "What are you doing here?"

"I said we need to talk," he intones through a clenched jaw, and I'm not even sure how it's possible to talk so seriously without opening one's mouth.

"And I said not today."

"Today," he parrots stubbornly.

"She said she doesn't wanna talk to you, man." Archie puffs his chest, and Justin stands up. They look like two baboons on Discovery Channel. All they're missing are red butts and tails.

"I don't remember asking your opinion," Justin tells him.

"Okay, stop." I smack the counter. "Justin, I'm not in the mood to talk today. You can call tomorrow, and we'll set up a time. Archie, thank you for standing up for me, but I deal with shit on my own. And Justin is old shit that I'm used to."

Justin looks like I just kneed him in the balls while Archie's trying to hide a smile.

"Who's that?" Justin finally stops this pissing contest—sort of—and asks me.

"That," I gesture at tall, dark, and handsome, "is Archie, Alex's friend from the Navy."

Justin's jaw clenches even more, and I fear his teeth are all but cracked. I know he's heard this name before, and he has nothing but respect for the man, but the way they met wasn't really a good start.

"And he is?" Archie asks me.

"And that," I gesture at tall, blond, and devilish, "is Justin. Alex's childhood friend."

I wait for them to shake hands, but they don't. They're still two baboons showing each other how big their teeth are. At this point, I'm half expecting them to pull out their dicks and compare sizes.

I don't understand Justin's behavior. Why he got so mad at Archie without even knowing him is beyond my comprehension. Maybe it's an alpha thing: two of those can't be in the same room.

No more cleaning can be done today, so I turn off all the machines, check the kitchen, and return to the bar to grab my bag. They haven't said a word and still are looking at each other like they're about to brawl. I roll my eyes so dramatically that I'm sure they're one step away from getting stuck at the back of my head forever.

"Alright. We need to go. We'll talk tomorrow, Justin." I grab Archie's hand and move to the door, but Justin doesn't move. I look back—he's working his jaw from side to side. His eyes are glued to my hand on Archie's. I'm about to let it go when Archie swiftly moves his, intervening our fingers, and gently squeezes my hand. I let it be. Justin notices this exchange and strides past us without a single word, smacking the door into our newly renovated wall, leaving the picture over the accent table shaking and a massive dent in its wake. He walks toward his shop without looking back and disappears into the dark.

I look over the damage again and sigh—I had a feeling we forgot a few little details. Like door stoppers, for example.

"He wants you so bad." He shakes his head.

"What?" I startle.

"That guy, Justin," he nods toward where Justin just disappeared, "he wants into your pants. Bad."

"Let me stop you right there. He wants something, but it's not to get into my pants." I start to walk around the diner to the parking spot usually taken by Marina, but today I was there first.

Archie laughs. "He *so* does. That's why I held your hand. He wanted to kill me real bad." I look at him as if he just spurted two—no, three—horns from his head. "What? You don't believe me?" He chuckles, biting his lower lip. I suppose it's meant to work to his advantage, making him look like a cute bad boy.

"You're wasting that on me." I point my finger at his face, causing him to laugh even louder. "And that guy hates my guts." I point at where Justin just disappeared.

"He may hate you, but he still wants to fuck you." His

laughter's dying. Finally. Hallelujah. "And you wanna fuck him. I say go for it. Hate-fucks are the best."

"I've known you for a whole five minutes, and you're already giving me sex advice. Moving too fast, don't you think?" I raise a brow.

"Life's short." His face sobers, and I get the feeling he knows what he's talking about.

"I'm rethinking my invitation." I tap on my chin with a finger. "You're annoying, so go find Alex yourself."

He laughs again. "You don't mean that." I scowl at him. Damn jokester. "I don't know shit about cars, and mine's fucked on the side of the road. I need to find a mechanic or something. Do you know one?"

"Yep." I say, popping the *p*. "You just met him."

"Fucking small towns." He laughs again and shakes his head. If he laughs one more time, I'll gag him with my dirty sock. That thing just went through a full waitressing shift. But I'm an evil person on Tuesdays. Archie's lucky because today's Monday, so instead, I pinch his arm a little harder than I intend to, and his eyes shift with something. And it's not a fucking annoyance. It's... *excitement*.

"Oh, for fuck's sake, dude!" I cry out, and he only laughs harder. "Keep your fetishes contained, would ya?"

"Don't start something you can't finish, honey." He winks.

We stop by Archie's car to get his overnight bag on the drive to Alex's house. He asks questions about Alex here and there, most of which I cannot answer. Well, some of them I can, but I wouldn't. So I successfully deflect them. Those things are not mine to share. By the time we reach the driveway to the cabin, I feel like Archie looks at me with much more respect. The flirting has died down considerably.

The lights are on in every single window, and I hope we're not interrupting some fun time. At least somebody's getting some.

"You're sure you're fine to drive here?" he asks again, and it makes my hackle rise.

"What? Do you think they usually throw me out, and I'm just trying to snake my way in using you?"

"No," he laughs, "I meant if it's not too much out of the way for you?"

"Ah, no, it's fine." I guess I'm used to being treated like an outsider. Any stranger who meets me for the first time automatically goes into the category of someone to beware of. My brain is so messed up. "I really needed to stop by and drop this off." I shake a package in front of me. Amazon can never find Alex's house in the woods, so Freya sends packages to the diner's address.

We walk up to the house and knock. They told me not to, but one time I walked in on Alex's naked ass plunging into my friend, and I got enough trauma for a lifetime, so I'm cautious now. It's more self-preservation than a courtesy at this point.

The door swings open. "Kay, how many times we told you not to kno—"

Alex's words cut off when he sees Archie. They both stare a moment before enveloping each other in an embrace. A brotherly hug. I can tell neither of them are the touchy-feely type, and that makes the moment even more special. My eyes swell, and I bite my lip as I try not to make a sobbing sound. Seeing Alex so accepting after years of being a repressed dude... man, that's some strong onion-cutting stuff. I look at Freya, frozen with *a spatula—dear universe, save us all tonight—*in the kitchen, and her eyes are misty as well. I guess it's even more touching for her after all the shit they went through together in such a short time.

When the guys let go of each other, they take a step back simultaneously.

"You're still one ugly son of a bitch," Alex says with a smile.

"And you're still smooth as fucking sandpaper," Archie responds with a punch to his arm. They both laugh.

Freya's light footsteps can be heard behind Alex, and she appears next to him. "Come in, guys." She smiles.

"You must be Freya," Archie says, taking her hand and kissing the back of it. Alex growls. Like legitimately growls as a beast would. I can't stop the chuckle from escaping, and he shoots me a death glare, causing me to laugh out loud.

"One smooth fucker," Freya says. Archie's brows shoot up, and he lets out a belly laugh.

"I guess I am." He lets go of her hand.

"And you're a traitor." Alex pokes my arm.

"One smooth fucker, as she said." I poke him back.

"How did you end up together here?" he asks suspiciously. His accusing gaze is fixed on Archie. *O-o-oh*. He's going all big brother on me. I'm secretly exultant.

"My car broke down in your lovely town. And my phone died," Archie says, emphasizing 'lovely.' "And everything is freaking closed at five. Kayla's a lifesaver." He gestures at me. "When it turned out that we both knew you, she offered me a ride."

Alex nods. "Where's your car now? We need to ask Justin to take a look at it."

Archie and I look at each other. "Yeah, about that. That might be a little problem." He doesn't sound happy about it. I guess it finally hit him that Justin is Alex's friend, and the situation might get messy. But then his face brightens up as if he read my mind. The guy likes messy.

"Why?" Alex looks confused.

"Because the dude was an asshole to Kayla, and I had to step in. So, we're not really on friendly terms at this very moment." He makes a sour face.

Freya and Alex groan in unison, and Archie looks from one to the other, looking confused. "Is there something I should know?"

"Too long of a story," Alex says with a shrug, and I get a suspicion that he might know why Justin behaves the way he does toward me. I notice Freya's looking at him suspiciously too, and I feel a little better. So, she doesn't know why either. I got scared for a second that she knew something and wasn't telling me. I'd feel utterly betrayed.

I squint my eyes at Alex, and for a moment, I see anger and disappointment with... *me*? It changes after a blink, but it was there. *It was there.* And now I wonder if something really happened that I don't know about. Alex has been nothing but kind to me this whole time. Usually.

Considering how my day started, how yesterday finished, and how it's going now, I should be on my not-so-merry way.

I thrust the package into Freya's hands and turn around. "Okay, guys, I gotta go."

"What?" Freya takes the box from me. "But you just came in?" Her face pinches with confusion.

"Yeah," I say, opening the door, "it's been a long day. I'm tired. See you."

"Kayla—" Alex says with a defeated exhale.

"Gotta go." I run away. That's the only way I can describe my shameful escape, but there's only so much I can take in one day. Freya and Alex are my close friends.

I know Alex has been Justin's best friend since forever, but I let myself get a little too comfortable inside with him. I'm just an occasional nuisance, something he just has to deal with a little more frequently after Freya showed up, but it hurts no less regardless. Because I thought Justin was just a jerk, and Alex was on my side, considering how he always shuts him down when he's talking crap to me. But now... now I know it's either out of pity or because of Freya. And I'm not sure which one is worse.

I feel betrayed, which is stupid. No one owes anything to anyone, and yet I thought... I'm an idiot, that's it. Now I just want to crawl into my bed with a book and a gazillion pounds of chocolate. And maybe, to cozy up with Charlie.

But I soon realize that this is not going to happen that easily. As I turn to my trailer, I see a parked truck, with Justin sitting in my favorite outdoor chair. Crap. When I thought it couldn't get any worse. I just need this day to finally end. *Please*. Is it too much to ask?

I park my Jeep in the mud (not my usual spot, obviously, because that's taken by my *unwelcomed* guest) and get out of the car. Without looking at the jerk sitting in my favorite chair, I march up to my house. I unlock the door and go inside, not bothering to lock it. He didn't come all the way here just for fresh air, might as well get it over with.

As I predicted, the door bursts open, and the fury that is Justin barrels in.

"Did you have fun?" His voice is crisp.

"Sure did." I take my cardigan and combat boots off, but stay in my long-sleeve, knee-length flowy dress, suddenly all too aware of its scoop neck. "Why are you here?"

"Why? Expecting someone else?" he snarls.

"You sound awfully close to being jealous. Be careful,

Justin; I might think you like me." I lean my backside on the counter and cross my arms over my chest.

His cruel laughter fills the small space. "As if there is a possibility of that."

"With your stalkerish tendencies, I wouldn't be so sure." I shrug. Archie's words come to mind. Maybe he does want to fuck me, and that's why he hates me so much. He hates the reaction his body has to trailer trash like yours truly. Makes sense, honestly. Considering Justin is the golden boy and all.

Well, he used to be.

"I don't take leftovers." He curls his lips in disgust.

"Really? It seems like they're the only thing you take." I refer to Ashley, of course, the current ringleader of wandering vaginas.

"Now *you* sound jealous." He smirks. I don't offer an answer. "So, when's this Archie guy coming?"

"Where?" I play dumb.

"Here." He points his nose to my floor.

"Why would he come here?" Dumb and dumber, seriously.

"Oh, so you're planning on fucking him somewhere else. A nice hotel, perhaps." He looks around. "I wouldn't bring anybody here either." He crinkles his nose. "Unless... you already fucked him in your car." His lips are thin. "You don't need much then, do you. You never did. So, the rumors *are* true." He hums the last phrase to himself more than to me.

"Why are you so concerned with whom I fuck all of a sudden?" The old tale's getting a little too old, and I'm not even offended at his words. He's trying too hard.

"Don't want to get any disease from being here." He shivers dramatically.

"I'm not holding you hostage by any means. You're free to leave." I gesture toward the door. It's not the answer he expected.

"Did you fuck him?" All emotions are gone from his voice, and the time for jokes is over. I don't want to poke the bear; I just want him to go back into hibernation inside some undiscovered cave as far from here as possible. Here, right now, I see what Freya was talking about. That *intensity*.

"I didn't." I press the heels of my palms into my eye sockets because I'm tired, and I want to sleep, and I want to cry. Again. All I want to do nowadays is cry. How pathetic.

When I drop my hands, Justin's in front of me. A foot away. His fists are by his sides like he's scared he'd use them. Well, I'm not scared of them. I sure as fuck can use mine too —I grew up in the rough part of Little Hope. You learn a lot of tricks if you want to make it there alive.

"Why?" His voice drops.

"Why what? Stop talking riddles."

"Why didn't you fuck him?" He's like a dangerous predator playing with his injured prey after it's already been defeated.

My head snaps back. "Do you think I'm a whore who sleeps with the first person she meets? Why is that? Because my mother was one? Or because I live in a trailer? That's what you think?" I poke my finger between his hard pecs.

He looks around again and shrugs. "I mean, your living situation is not perfect per se."

"My living situation is perfectly fine!" My chin lifts in defiance. "It's my home, and it's mine! It belongs to me!" I know my eyes are spitting fire right now. They may have even gotten a little red, like those crazy animals in cartoons.

"So, you bought all this shit?" He glances around with disgust.

"Yes, Justin, I bought this shit. And it's the first home I've ever had on my own. I worked hard for that, and I bought it, and nobody can come into my home and insult it *or* me. So how about you get your ass the fuck out of here and forget how to get here for good?" I push on his chest. He doesn't budge, but his eyes snap to my hands on his chest. I push harder. "Go, Justin. I'm tired of you treating me like shit. Tired of it! What's your problem? What have I done to you? Huh? That you hate me so much."

He steps forward, and I see determination written all over his face. I feel like I'm about to resolve a mystery that's been haunting me for years.

But he never delivers, this asshole. His jaw sets, his eyes become emotionless holes filled with hate once again, and he's out of here in a second. Nice. Here we go again; every time I bring this up, he looks like it pains him to talk about it, like physically pains him, so he chooses to lash out at me and storm out. Very typical Justin-around-Kayla behavior.

Once I don't hear his truck anymore, I head to the shower to wash off the disgusting feeling he left on me. A feeling of unworthiness. No matter how hard I try not to listen to him, he's the one whose words hurt the most.

I rely on the water to wash off the horrible residue he left on me. But once I lather myself, the water in the tank runs out. Great. Just what I needed to finish this already shitty day.

I wipe myself clean from soap with a few wet wipes I have left and get into the bed, writing a mental note to fill the tank tomorrow, or I'm seriously screwed. Living here for so long has taught me to preserve water and gas, but even *I*, a natural hoarder thanks to my very poor days, sometimes forget about refilling them.

In bed, I cry myself to sleep once again.

The next morning already sucks. I don't have water for a shower, to flush the toilet, or anything, really. I have a jug of water that's only enough for one cup of coffee and a quick toothbrushing. It will have to do. I pull my hair back into a low ponytail and make a mental note to buy red hair dye. The mood's calling for it. I pull on my ripped jean shorts, white off-the-shoulder shirt, and black military-style boots and am off to the diner.

My phone pings—it's a message from TJ, the guy I sometimes sell my drawings to. He works at a tattoo shop and says my drawings are in high demand. All my money from these sales goes toward my special savings account (where I can never save), from which I pay a debt that's been owed by my family. Somehow, I ended up being the only one paying it off. Somehow my ass. I dug myself into that mess on my own and have only myself to blame. Well, myself and my fucked-up family. As I said, they had left, but their mess is still here on my shoulders.

> "Need ur phoenix in large. Can u do one by this weekend?"

> "Yeah. In color?"

> "Yep. The guy's loaded, will pay a ton."

> "You're inking him?"

"Nah, he just wants the piece. Said he has somebody already."

> "Dang, sorry, man. How does he know about my stuff?"

"Said he saw the phoenix on the chick he fucked the night before, and she said where she got it from. Lol. Now he wants one 4 himself."

> "Charming. You know where the phoenix will go?"

"3/4 of the back."

> "Dang. That's a big one."

"Yeah. I got a feeling the guy is the real deal. Might be ur shot, kid."

> "Thanks, TJ. I'll make it happen by the weekend."

The first time I sold my 'special birdy,' as TJ calls my phoenix, was four years ago. I was just playing around with drawings and wasn't planning on making it a business. I took one of my pictures to a tattoo salon in Springfield to put it on my shoulder blade. TJ was inking me. He asked where I got it from, and I told him I drew it myself. Then we talked some more, and he gave me his phone number and asked me to send him my other drawings. That's how it started. He gets a special request that my art might fit and sends it to me. I'll be forever grateful to him for that.

By the time I get to the diner, I've planned the whole

piece in my mind. The head will rest on one shoulder, and the wings will go for a diagonal hug.

The morning isn't busy, which is unusual. One of the first customers is Freya. She pops her head inside the doorframe and asks. "Is it safe to come in?"

"Depends on what you're planning to do." I narrow my eyes at her suspiciously.

"Just feeding my hungry belly, that's all." She fake smiles, showing all her shark teeth. I sigh—here comes the grilling. She comes in and pops onto the bar stool, motioning for a coffee to be poured into her mouth like a cartoon character. I pour her a cup with a laugh.

"Ask what you came here to ask already."

Her face loses all humor. "What was that yesterday?"

"Just my insecurities, that's all." I plant a fake smile on my face so she won't get upset.

She's watching me carefully. "Alex was on edge the whole evening after you left."

"Because of Archie." I roll my eyes. "Your man has the social skills of a potato."

"That's true," she says with a sigh. "So true, but we're working on it."

We chat for half an hour about nothing, and I keep yesterday's encounter by my house to myself. Why? I have no idea. Freya might be able to help me answer the question. Once I can formulate it right.

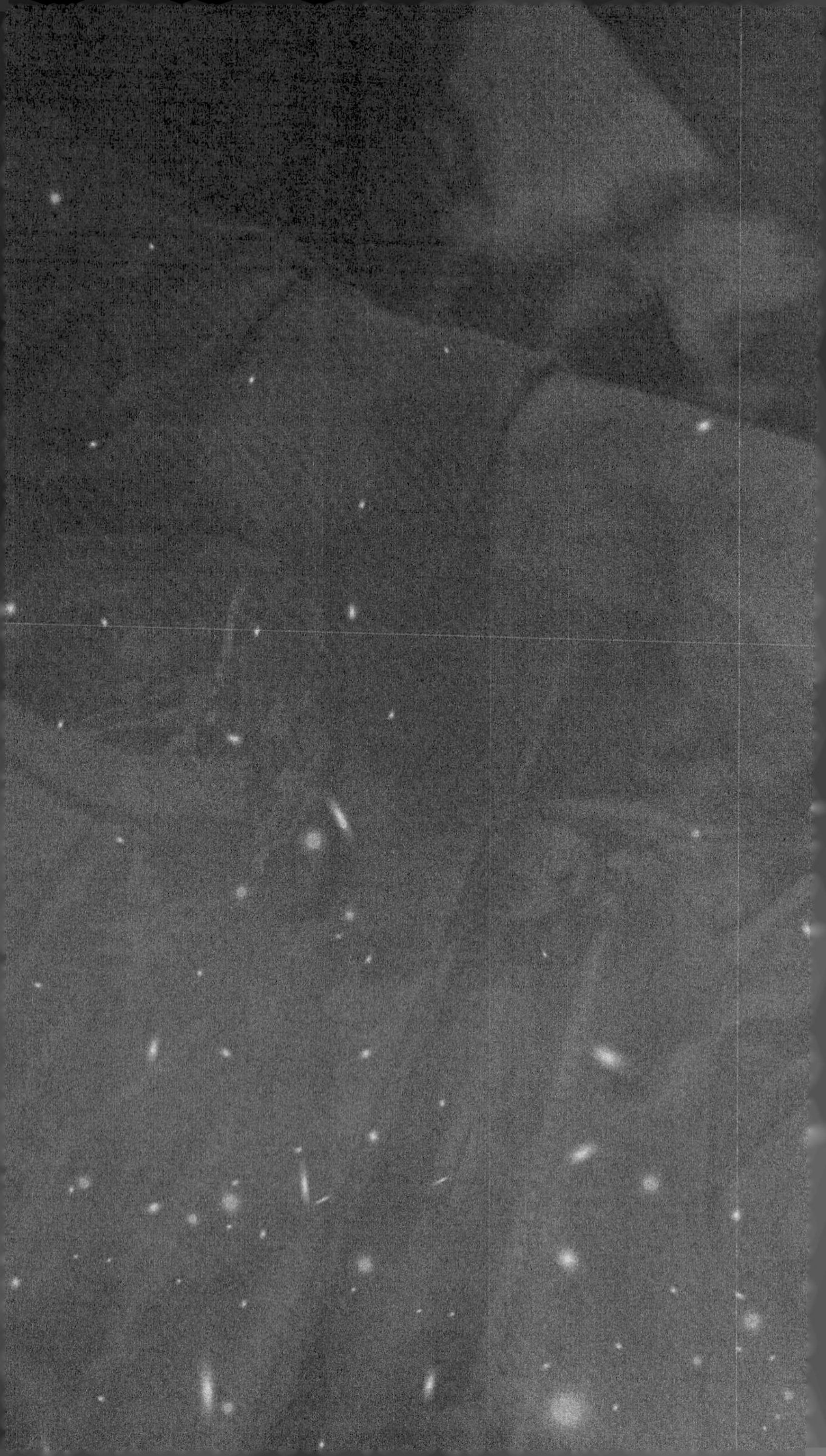

Chapter Twelve

K AYLA

A couple days pass, and I haven't seen Justin. A good thing, considering our worsening encounters and my growing murderous tendencies when I'm around him.

I sent the phoenix to TJ yesterday, and he said the client was happy. When the client's happy—I'm happy, because he pays money. The bigger and more detailed the drawing—the more money in my pocket. It's not like it's an insane amount of green, considering the person who inks gets the biggest chunk. Still, a constant stream of extra cushion into my savings account never hurts. Not that it ever gets more than a few bucks at a time, but without that, I'd quite literally go hungry. My monthly debt payments drain everything.

From a short conversation with Freya over the phone, I know Archie left two days after arriving. I secretly hoped that he would stop by for breakfast, but at the same time, I dreaded facing him. I bet he's heard a few rumors about me, and if Alex's reaction to me had anything to say... Well, it's safe to assume Archie may have changed his mind about being so friendly and flirty with me.

Thinking about it, I have no idea how they managed to fix his car. Maybe Alex did it himself, even though I know he doesn't work with modern cars. An engine is an engine if you ask me. If I wanted to know how they managed the situation, I'd have to explain how we met and what went down from my point of view. Whatever Archie told them works for me. My only shock comes from the fact that Freya hasn't grilled me about it. Yet.

Currently, I'm tired and mentally exhausted—the day has gone on for far too long, and people here at the diner are all in horrible moods, getting on me about even the most minor things—it must be a full moon. I ask Marina to let me go earlier without even getting any food for myself. I need to leave before I strangle someone. I just want out of here.

A new waitress is in today, so I get off the hook easily. She's been coming in when things are especially swamped, saving our asses. Plus, tomorrow's my day off, so I plan on starting it earlier. Marina doesn't mind; she never does. We're almost empty anyway by now, and it's closing time soon. By the time I'm out of the door, I regret not asking Marina to fix me a sandwich to take home, but it's too late to return: the diner is like a black hole, sucking you in and never letting go. So I keep on going. Remembering that my fridge at home is empty, I groan and make a note to stop by the grocery store.

As I arrive at the store, I'm not even convinced I feel hungry. Yes, my stomach is growling like a cornered animal, but my brain is too tired to get the signal from downstairs.

I'm still wearing my clothes from work that cling to me from sweat. Running nonstop around the diner and fulfilling orders of cranky customers takes *effort*. I feel filthy and very, *very* sweaty, so the idea of spending my day off tomorrow as a total stylish disaster, wearing the widest and comfiest clothes I can possibly find, sounds promising. The only people allowed to show up are Freya, Marina, or Justin if he wants to take the stick out of his ass and have an adult conversation for once. Freya or Marina won't see anything new, and Justin won't show up anytime soon since he's avoiding me like the plague. *Thank God.* And even if he does, it's not on my agenda to impress him, so it works just fine for me.

Grabbing a small bag of potatoes and a steak to make for dinner, I head down the shampoo aisle to find my usual shampoo.

My hair products are the only things I don't spare money on. Achieving the ash color I have takes a lot of work. Work that happens to decrease the health of my hair. With my constant dying, I have to keep my hair moisturized, so it doesn't break off. Good thing I have a lot of it; otherwise, I'd be left with a bald head after so much work. I might be able to pull that look off, but I'm not ready to find out just yet.

Browsing around for my favorite conditioner, I hear an all too familiar voice talking on the other side of the aisle. Glancing over to see Justin on his phone, I try to make myself scarce. Or at least try to, anyway, as I snatch up what I came for and make a b-line for the cash register. Unfortunately, I'm far too late, as I hear his stupid steps coming up behind me.

"Where are you going in such a hurry? To get to your new boyfriend on time?"

My teeth grind in response, and I suddenly feel heat

rise to my face. I cross my arms, if only so I don't punch him, and narrow my eyes in his direction. Cute. He just keeps proving what took me so many years to realize: he's a grade-A asshole. Just your typical bully. I'd never seen this tendency in him before toward anyone else, but when it comes to me, it's clear he has no boundaries.

"I smelled something foul." I look him up and down pointedly. "Plus I'm ready to go home." I keep my voice level, not wanting to get snappy with him. I don't want another argument. Yes, I decided to stick up for myself, but that doesn't mean I have to dive headfirst into a fight. Avoidance is the best tactic sometimes.

Planting the same fake smile on my face that I use at work with shitty customers, I step into the line at the cash register, expecting him to leave me alone.

"You probably got a whiff of your rotten soul." I could tell by the smug sound of his voice that his signature smirk —*meant just for me*—was plastered across his stupid face. "Maybe your new boyfriend will sense it too before it's too late." His voice, though husky and attractive despite the malice, doesn't make my heart flutter like it used to. I try to ignore him, but he acts like a child, lightly pulling on my ponytail to get my attention. I spin around and smack his hand away. "What's got you—" he starts.

"Leave me alone; I'm not in the mood for this today." I point my finger at him, trying my hardest to sound angry. Unfortunately for me, I sound more pitiful than anything. Furrowing my brows in annoyance with myself, I turn back to the line. Justin leaves me alone, thankfully.

Or so I thought. As I'm one person away from getting out of the store, his hand lands on my shoulder with a tight grip. Feeling his breath brush against my ear, I tense, sure to keep my eyes straight ahead.

"Don't expect any pity from me; you don't deserve that." Justin's tone is serious. Today isn't a day I want to talk about this mystery thing I did, so I shake off his hand, fight the urge to smack him stupid, and pay for my groceries. Somehow, I succeed without injuring him. Ten points to Gryffindor.

"I didn't do shit to deserve such a treatment." The words leave my mouth before I can stop myself, and I take all my bags and rush out the door, eager to get home. I don't care what disgusting things he had to say in response. He always seems to catch me in my weakest moments or during my rare peaceful minutes alone. I can't ever get rid of him since he's friends with Alex. Well, I'm not friends with Alex anymore, by the looks of it, so this problem is about to be resolved fast. Hopefully, I'll still have Freya because she isn't the person to sit back and do what she's told. Not anymore.

I know Freya struggles with the animosity between myself and Justin, so cutting some time spent with her might be a good idea. For her mental health. She's in the middle of a war zone without a bulletproof vest and suffers from this situation too. Just differently. I don't want to lose her by stepping out of our friendship so she can have peace. I'm a horrible, selfish person.

I settle in my seat, turning my car on. "Why the hell did I have to crush on such an asshole for half of my life! It's not fair!" I slam my hand on the car horn, scaring some birds nearby. I do it a few more times to make myself feel a little better. It works, but not by much. A lady walking by with a full cart turns her nose up in disgust. I flip her off, and her eyes turn round. Look at her, so scandalized! Her face, full of horror, makes me feel a little better. I take a breath, count to ten, and drive home.

When the sun's almost down, I sit outside in a pair of long flannel pants I've had since high school and a light, soft cardigan with no shirt or bra underneath, basking in the fresh air. A weird outfit for a not-so-hot summer evening? Sure, but oh so comfortable. My mood is better, and I slowly become calmer, surrounded by twittering birds and the fading light of a beautiful Maine sunset.

With a warm cup of tea between my hands and a small plate of food on the table I have set up, I relax and let my worries wash away as the breeze blows through my hair. This is just what I needed: a moment of peace alone with myself. I put on the perfect outfit, completed my entire skin-care routine, and made my amazing dinner. For the first time today, I can smell the scent of hope in the air.

If Freya was free, I would have asked if she wanted to join me. I have this field all to myself, and I love her company. But she mentioned something about being busy this week, so I'm alone with my tired self. Sipping from my cup and lazily chewing my dinner, I glance at my sketchbook nearby, open it, and make a quick little sketch of one of the birds perched in the tree in front of me.

And that's when I hear it.

The revving of a truck's engine and lights flashing over my eyes successfully interrupt my relaxing time. Holy hell. *Why? Why now and why today?* Zipping up my cardigan, I cover my face with my arm, pretending that if I see no evil, there is no evil. *I'm still all alone, completely al—*

"You're so fucking annoying. You're truly the most obnoxious fucking thing in this whole town. Stuck in my mind, and I can't get rid of you. Get the fuck out of my head!" Justin starts bellowing at me as soon as the truck door opens. He reminds me of a little rodent running around squeaking. I sigh, lowering my arm. I guess my plan doesn't exactly work if I can't save myself from *hearing* the evil. His steps seem to be a little wobbly. Knowing it's only been a couple hours since I last saw him, I'm guessing he had already been drinking by the time I saw him at the grocery store. If not, it's surprising that he managed to drink that much in such a short period of time to get himself absolutely drunk. Because the guy seems wasted. Just what I need today. Great.

The nonsense he's spurting is lost on me. It doesn't make any sense. If anything, he's the one who's been stuck in my head for years, so I'm in the right here, thank you very much.

He walks toward me and stumbles, barely catching himself before he falls face-first on the ground. By the time he manages to cross the path between his car and the table I'm currently sitting at, he almost falls three times.

"Justin, sit down before you fall," I sigh and push a chair closer to him. I'm a little fearful of him on a good day, and I don't know how unpredictable he can be in a drunken state. Despite everything, I'm worried about his well-being, even through his insults. He's one of my biggest weaknesses, someone I can't seem to escape. Any shrink would have a field day with me, I'm sure of it. Appearing angry, he obeys and roughly sits in the chair, making it creak a little under his massive figure. "I don't think you should drive, so when you calm down a little, I'll take you home."

I'm a bigger person. I tell myself. *I'm a bigger person, and I will absolutely not use this moment to stab this fork into his eye even if the opportunity is present.* I keep repeating the mantra, hoping I'll convince myself *eventually.*

I move back to the chair I was perched in moments ago, picking at my food until he interrupts.

"Why do you act like this? What's wrong with you?" His voice is unsteady, as are his movements. I'm surprised he managed to make it here without winding up in some ditch. "Why are you so... fucking *nice?*" He spits the word like something poisonous and foreign to him.

"Nothing's wrong with me, Justin; you've been drinking, and to deliver you home safely is the decent thing to do. You want some water?" I talk to him like I would a small child because if there's one thing I've learned, it's that you should never aggravate drunk people unless you know they're total teddy bears. Justin doesn't look or sound like one.

"No, I don't want your poisoned piss water." He snorts too loudly, making a weird noise that makes me want to chuckle.

"Tough luck, you're out of options." Rolling my eyes, I get up and give him an unopened bottle of water, watching him sniff it first. "You're such a sicko. I moved out here to get away from people. I like my privacy and peace. But here you are, interrupting my peace over and over again." My own advice not to aggravate him seems long forgotten.

Plopping back in my seat, I shovel my food in my mouth, hoping to make him want to leave sooner by being a little unmannered. Instead, I see him out of the corner of my eye, dragging his chair closer and making himself comfortable. He's watching me. Unbearably aware of his eyes glued to me, I eat in smaller bites, stopping altogether as he gets closer. The sun's light has faded by now, and my lights hanging from the camper illuminate the surrounding area in a soft glow.

"Those tattoos drive me insane. You know that, right? The needle that pierced your skin, leaving a permanent mark on it. On you. The mark that you will never be able to erase," Justin mutters and touches my arm. The sleeve of my cardigan rolls up, showing a rose with spikes. Each one represents a year of my life that I keep adding. "Like I cannot erase you from me no matter how much I try. You're tattooed on my skin." Confused, I retract my arm from his touch, frustrating him. He pulls himself closer, and his legs are touching my chair. Taking my arm in a firm but surprisingly gentle grip, he looks at the ink laid bare on my skin. "You were always around every corner I turned," he mumbles, touching a lock of my hair with his other hand. "Your hair was different back then, pink." He chuckles to himself. "I don't even know what your natural color is. I don't remember. I like it now, though; it suits you." He frowns at what he just said and drops my hair. Then it's my turn to frown as he leans down and licks the tattoo, making me reel back. "It doesn't taste weird like I thought it would."

"It isn't pen ink, you dumbass," I say and watch him sit back with a huff. "What?"

"You should wear baggy clothes." Justin's getting tired. I can tell by how pouty he's acting. Usually, he's all big-man-intimidating me and insulting my every move. Now, he almost seems like a little toddler, mumbling nonsense.

"What?" I shake my head. "Never mind. I think it's time to take you home. Get in the passenger side of my car; you can come get your truck tomorrow." *When I'm not around,* I add mentally. He tries to stand up but stumbles a little. I rush to help him, but he pushes me off and stomps toward my car, slamming the door and cursing under his breath. A little tantrum we have here. There it is, the Justin I know well these days, angry and always upset at me without telling me why. What did I do wrong now? I told him I'd drive him home, so he won't die in a car crash. I just can't win with him.

I pluck my keys from inside the house and drive him back to his, letting him mess with the radio. I don't want to argue; I just want to get back to my relaxing night and get rid of the big burly problem currently occupying my passenger seat.

Dropping him off at his garage, I speed away the second his feet hit the pavement.

Back at my trailer, it's quiet and peaceful again, but my tea has bugs in it, so I pour it out. I go to bed early, exhausted from the events of the day. I don't wake up until later to a knock on my door.

It's rather disturbing, considering I don't get visitors here. So I put on a robe, grab Bob, check if he's loaded, and check the peephole to see who's here. As it's still dark outside and about four in the morning, I groan and lean the gun on the wall.

"What?!" I ask, grumpy from getting disturbed so early in the morning. Justin stands there. Glancing down, I take a sharp breath and tie up my robe before he notices I'm wearing only a thin cami, my nipples on full display from the chilly air. By the look on his face, though, I can tell he already saw me.

"Little chilly to be wearing so little, don't you think?" Smug and standing there with his hands in his pockets, he looks as though he has sobered up. Not that he's any better than when he was drunk earlier, but a sober head is more predictable.

"Can you just get your truck and go, please?" Impatient and tired, I can see him contemplating something as he stares off to the side. "What, did you forget your keys and your dignity?"

"Would you shut up for one damn minute?" Justin snaps at me as he steps up into my trailer. The movement makes me stumble back, and I trip over my own feet. He has to move his shoulders sideways to fit through the door, and I wrap my arms around my stomach as anxiety and excitement hit me simultaneously due to his proximity to me. A sicko. "Alright, I came up here all drunk and mad before and don't remember half of it, so thanks for driving me back," he says without looking at me. Instead, his focus is solely on the wall clock above the fridge.

"Yes, I drove you back because I didn't want you to wreck. How did you get here, by the way?" I peek outside to see if anybody is waiting for him, not happy with the prospect. As I said, I like my privacy.

"Joe dropped me off at the main road."

"At four a.m.?" Whoever this Joe is, he must be an excellent friend.

"At three. I walked up here from there. Didn't think you'd appreciate any visitors." His voice is raspy. "Plus, it helped to clear my head."

So weirdly thoughtful of him, and before I melt at this one nice, tiny gesture toward me, I force my grouchy self out again. "Why couldn't this wait until morning?" My voice has a clear hint of annoyance, just as I hoped. His gaze meets mine; the hatred usually present is missing, his shoulders relaxed with both hands in his back pockets. "I've been wondering why it's so surprisingly cozy in here," he says, looking around.

"Because it's my home, and I made it cozy," I shoot back, and he sighs as if he is the one who should be annoyed. Again, with his jabs at my home. It's a touchy subject for me, so he'd better back off before I fetch Bob again.

Glancing around the dimly lit area, I turn on the lights and reach around him to shut the door so bugs don't come flying in. When I start to pull away, I can feel his arm slip around my waist, and I snap my eyes up as he leans down.

I freeze, waiting on what he'll do next. He brings his nose to my ear and sniffs at it. "Fucking strawberries." He pushes his nose into my skin, and I shiver. Then, unexpectedly, he licks the shell of my ear and blows on it. Goosebumps rush all over my body, and I shamefully whimper. *What the hell?* That's not me! I don't *make* sounds like that.

He pushes me deeper into him with his hand, and his other one goes to my chin, lifting it up as he inches away a little. Now his eyes are focused on mine.

"I've been trying to get rid of you every way I can, Kayla." His Adam's apple moves with a rough swallow. "Every fucking way. But you're always here." He taps his temple with his finger. "Always fuckin' here. I need to get rid of you the only way I know how."

"Wha—"

He doesn't let me finish before he crushes his lips on mine, far from gently. It's almost painful how he presses his mouth into mine. Almost. I like this urgency. I love it.

It's then that I feel awake and find myself kissing him back, my hand pressing against his chest, ready to push him away if he says anything to tick me off (I'm totally lying to myself here: if he opens his mouth for anything other than to devour mine, I'll just shut him up with another kiss). But instead of pushing him away, I fist his shirt and pull him toward me, biting his lip.

The taste of him... the taste I've imagined forever, is better than I ever imagined. It's the taste of overwhelming power, of a suppressed need, and my wildest dream. Of hate and desire. Of freedom and chains.

His hot tongue dances with mine, fighting for dominance that I'm all too willing to give up.

"I need this off," he whispers into my mouth as his fingers pull on the robe tie. The sound of his words fills my stomach with a kaleidoscope of butterflies; his calloused hands snake under the robe, settling against the bare skin of my back. He stops the kiss and moves his mouth to my cheek, peppering it with soft kisses. I never knew he could be so soft. Not with me.

"Justin?" Opening my eyes and trying to catch his gaze, I see the same emotions in his eyes as I feel in my chest right now. In this moment, he doesn't hate me. In this moment, he's acting on the desire he's had for me. Just like I am. In my wildest dream, I couldn't imagine Justin being my closet admirer.

Pulling him down with my arms around his shoulders, I kiss him, not caring if I should be mad, hate him back, or smack the ever-loving crap out of him for all the hurt he caused me. Not caring about anything but this one moment. We can both be embarrassed about that later.

"Step back," he commands, quickly pressing his lips against mine. Like the good girl I am (sometimes), I obey and start moving backward. Unsurprisingly, I find my legs pressed against my table on the way to the bedroom. Somewhere along the way, my robe was removed, leaving me in a thin cami that covers pretty much nothing. To even the field, I tug his shirt up, and he allows me to remove it. My eyes travel down the fit torso of a man who works with his hands and earns his muscles with hard work. His six-pack is an eight, in fact, and his pecs are so firm and smooth. I want to bite them. To leave my mark on all that perfection. My cheeks feel hot, and the smug look on his face says all I need to know.

"Like you didn't stare at me first," I huff, but my breath's taken away when he pulls me close. I can feel him. Skin to skin, his nearness causing me to swallow hard. His fingers wrap under my chin and tilt my head back, his thumb going over my lower lip, pressing it to open. "You're so hot." The words come out under my breath, but I know he heard it, the smirk on his lips growing. "I meant your body." He chuckles now. "I meant the temperature of your body. You're really hot."

His face changes into concern. "I am?"

"You are." The sexual tension begins dissolving as fast as it came. Concern rises in my chest when I see his reaction to my words.

"Oh fuck." I see a hint of... dare I say *embarrassment*?

"What?" I step back as I begin feeling uncomfortable being so exposed in front of him when the moment passed.

"I gotta get home," he slurs.

"That's what I've been saying all evening long." I grab the shirt I see on the bed and pull it over my head. The mood shifts. We missed the moment and skipped right to embarrassment.

Justin tries to walk to the entrance, but his movements have slowed. He grabs the nearest surface, a teapot on the table, and accidentally smashes it on the floor. He looks down and says, "Shit, sorry." His speech is even more troublesome, and I begin to worry for real here.

"Justin, why don't you—" Whatever I was about to say gets cut short as he crashes to the floor with a loud thud. The only thing that stopped his face from smashing is the couch that slowed his fall.

"What the hell, Justin?" I run to him and drop to my knees. I begin shaking his shoulder. "Justin, wake up! Justin!"

Yeah, he was drunk in the evening, but that wasn't a drunken stupor. He came here almost sober. Was he? *He was sober, right?* I didn't just take advantage of a drunk person. *Right?*

I shake him again. "Justin!"

Not knowing what to do, I call the only person who knows what to do in this situation. After all, she was an ER nurse in a very busy hospital. She picks up on the fifth ring. *"Kayla? What happened?"* Freya's sleepy voice drips with concern.

"Justin just crashed on my freaking floor!"

There is a moment of silence before she speaks. *"Justin is at your place?"*

"Yes! Haven't you heard the part where he crashed and is currently on the floor?" I'm nearing hysterics.

I hear Alex's voice murmuring something to Freya, and she tells him quietly, *"Justin just crashed in Kayla's home."*

"He is at her place?" There is wonder in his voice.

"Yeah. Do you know what he was going to do? He's seemed really off lately." Freya's worried, I can tell. She's worried for him, and I'm concerned for him too. I don't know Justin at all and don't know his problems. He seems like he doesn't have many unless you consider me as a problem. What if he's in trouble?

And why aren't they worried that he just collapsed? All her questions concern his general well-being, not his body splayed on my floor.

I mentally slap myself back to reality. No matter how big of a bully he is, he needs my help. Suddenly, cold fingers squeeze my chest from the inside. What if he's ill? What if he has some serious illness, and he won't be here anymore? Like forever. I feel dread settling in the pit of my stomach while Alex and Freya are still murmuring something to each other. "Freya! What do I do? Do I call 911?"

"No." She sighs. *"Let him sleep it off."*

"Sleep what off?"

"His insomnia." She yawns.

"What?"

"He's a chronic insomniac. He just crashed after probably a few days being awake," she says after another lengthy yawn.

"Justin has insomnia?" That was the last thing I expected.

"Yes. And quite severe."

I try to digest what she just said. In such a small town, it's nearly impossible to have secrets, and such a big secret like this would be difficult to hide. Yet, he managed it. Not like it's a life-changing thing that would change how people view him. "Are you sure? He acted weird. What if he just had a stroke and I don't do anything to help? Is he going to die?" My voice takes a high pitch at the end.

"He is not going to die. I've seen him crashing like that. It's normal," she explains in a calm voice.

"It's not fucking normal, Freya. He just collapsed on my floor." I wave my hand at Justin's body as if she can see me through the phone.

"I mean, it's normal for him."

I touch his forehead with my fingers. "He's cold."

"What?" Her question doesn't really hold any genuine interest.

"His skin is cold. And two minutes ago, he was burning up."

"It's a normal reaction of a body on the verge of crashing." She clears her throat. *"Well, not exactly normal, but typical for severe cases. He used up all his fuel that was left plus some more, so his body was throwing him a warning sign. I'm surprised he hadn't noticed it. What exactly was he*

doing before that?" I can almost imagine Freya narrowing her eyes with suspicion.

"Nothing." I rush my answer.

"So why do you sound guilty?" She sounds interested, if not suspicious, when she should sound concerned. Damn, what's happening with this world? And Freya, of them all.

"I'm not. What are you talking about?" My guilt is too apparent.

"R-r-r-right," she hums.

"So, what do I do?" I ask in a hurry, trying to divert her attention from the embarrassing subject.

"Check his pulse."

"Finally, some sound advice from a medical worker," I say with sarcasm, hoping she will feel a little remorse.

"Don't think I'm dropping this subject. What about his pulse?" Her tone changes to professional.

I check his neck and count the beats. "Seems steady and normal."

"Did he hit his head?"

"No, he half landed on the couch." He's lucky he did. He half sits on the floor, leaning his torso on the bottom of the couch. His head hangs on the side at an almost painful angle.

"On the couch on the way to your bedroom?" Freya asks as Alex chuckles.

"Freya!"

"Right, right. His pulse is fine; he didn't hit his head. He's fine. Just let him sleep it off." And just like that, she's lost interest again.

"Are you sure? That fall didn't look fine." I keep replaying it in my head on a constant repeat.

"He is fine, I promise. For insomniacs, it's a normal part of their lives, no matter how sad it sounds. As long as they

don't get injured during the fall, they're fine." There is zero concern in her voice, which makes me feel better.

"Okay."

"Do you want me to come over?" she offers, but I know she'd rather stay in her cozy bed with her hunky boyfriend. *"Alex can come and drag Justin's ass out if you want. He can haul him away to his place."*

I hear Alex's *"I can? Leave the fucker there."*

I chuckle; it's so Alex. "No, it's fine."

"He can be there for a while. It might take twelve hours for him to restore. Or even longer. I'm not sure how long he went without sleep this time."

"It's okay, Freya. Really. I appreciate it, but I'll be fine," I say with a sigh.

"Okay. Call me if you need us. Anytime," she tells me while unsuccessfully trying to suppress a yawn.

"Thank you, to both of you. Night!"

"Wait! Are you—"

"Night, guys!" And I hang up on her. There's no way I can survive an interrogation now, and that's undoubtedly what was about to follow; I just know it.

I look at Justin. His mouth is slightly open, his breathing is even, and his head is still at a weird angle. There's no way I could drag his muscular ass on the couch, so I grab pillows from my bed and lay them next to him on the floor. Then I carefully lower his torso on them and adjust his legs, so they don't bend unnaturally. He looks almost vulnerable like that. A little drool comes out of the corner of his mouth, and eff me, but I find it adorable. His chest rises and falls. And what a chest it is. So pronounced and so developed. Those perfect smooth globes. I saw something similar only on Alex, but Alex is a monster of a man. On Justin, it looks proportioned and well-defined. There are no hairs. None. Only a blond happy trail down his navel. It was so close to making me happy today too.

I stop my pervert-ish ogling and go to grab a comforter for him. I tuck him in, push pillows deeper under his head and shoulders, so he's comfortable, and admire my work—and his figure—for a while longer before going back to sleep.

I wake up when the sun is already high in the sky. I don't like to sleep in, but today can be excused. I dread getting out of bed to see if my night guest is still here. I try to peek at the couch from my bed; I live in a trailer, *hello*, everything's reachable from one spot.

The big body's still on the floor in the same position I left it. I stand up and go to brush my teeth as quietly as possible. I wash my hair and put some mascara on since that's what I do every day when I wake up alone, duh. A very regular thing for me on my day off when I plan on staying at the trailer in my pajamas, right.

I come out to the living room—yes, I consider it a living room, it's tiny, but it's there—and Justin's still asleep. I start a pot of coffee, drink it, and Justin's still asleep. Today is my rare day off, and I'm not planning to stay here all day. Even if the view is great.

I blow dry my hair, get dressed, and Justin's still asleep. I check his breathing and his pulse—he seems fine, so I leave him be and go outside. I don't have any particular plans, but my personal space is occupied now. I wait on people all day, all *week*, so on my day off, I want to be as far away from them as possible. The only person I might tolerate today is Freya, but she'd bombard me with questions I don't have answers to, so I'm in a bit of a jam here. Just when I'm about to go back inside, my phone rings.

"Hi, TJ."

"Sup, Kay. The guy who ordered that huge phoenix piece from you will be here in a couple of hours. He wanted to see what else you have." His smoked-up voice sounds excited.

"Oh, wow. I can send you a few pieces I have now."

"Nah, I think it's better if you come here yourself," he urges me.

"Why?" I usually don't deal with clients directly; all my designs go through TJ.

"I don't know, Kay. But I feel like you should be here. He's kind of a big deal; I looked him up. He has a few popular parlors everywhere. He might become your regular on a bigger scale than us." Wow, I'm impressed. As far as social media goes, TJ is an infant. He doesn't follow anybody and doesn't know anything.

"Wow. Okay. Wow." And I'm speechless. If TJ thinks I might have a shot, that'd be freaking awesome. It's my dream come true—to make a living out of my drawings. Wow, just wow.

"Yeah, can you take a day off and come here?" He sounds impatient.

"As a matter of fact, I'm off today. I can be there in an hour."

"Fuckin' awesome. See you, kid." And he hangs up. He never stops to listen to what else somebody has to say, but that's just how he is. So hyperactive. His mind thinks twenty steps ahead, making him always in a rush. I still have no idea how he manages to ink people being... just *him*.

Well, if it isn't a sign from above, I don't know what it is. I go back home to collect my bag and check on Justin. He's still asleep, but he's changed his position. I take it as a sign that he's about to return to the land of the living. I don't have time to wait for that—and, quite frankly, I'm not sure I want to. Considering what we were doing before he crashed and the animosity that still exists between us, I'm not sure I can face him just yet. Or myself, at this point. So I'll just run away, especially when the opportunity to do so just knocked on my door.

I stop by the diner and get a cup of coffee to go. Marina's happy for me even if she doesn't show it.

The drive to TJ's shop is uneventful, and that's how I like it. I park my car and walk to the building. A familiar masculine laugh meets me at the door. I see broad shoulders and long, lean legs covered in tight black jeans.

"Here she is!" TJ, a big burly guy with a long black beard with a few salty strikes down to his chest, exclaims like an overly excited cheerleader.

The shoulders turn, and here he is.

"Hi, Archie." I greet him with a tight-lipped smile.

"Kayla?" He looks stunned for a moment, then he recovers quickly. "You are the artist?"

"I wouldn't go that far, but if we're talking about the phoenix design, it's mine, yes." I don't play coy—I just don't consider myself an artist yet. I'd like to be one, though.

He smiles, and his face changes in an instant. What did I just say?

"About back there..." He waves his hand behind him like it should explain anything.

I narrow my eyes. "Where?"

"Back at Alex's place... That felt... *weird*. I just want you to know that whatever happened, he felt really shitty about it." He scratches the back of his head, looking extremely uncomfortable.

"Do you know what happened?" I squint at him.

"No." He looks coy. "But something was in the air?" he half says, half asks. I smile as I shake my head.

"You guys know each other?" TJ's eyes volley from Archie to me.

"We actually met a few days back," I answer, moving my attention to TJ.

"I should have known." Archie snaps his fingers. "The tats on your arms... they're the same style."

I look down automatically. "Mmm, yeah, they are kind of the same, I guess."

"Fuck." He wipes his face with the back of his hand. "Man, I'm blown away by your work. I want more. I want you to create more designs for me and my team." He shakes a phone he's holding in his hand. I guess TJ just showed him my drawings.

I blush like a schoolgirl—I don't get praised very often, especially for something I'm so passionate about.

"Why don't you ink your designs yourself?" His brows are pinched together.

"Because I can't afford school. Plus, I can't afford to be away for school. So double trouble there." I shrug. Because duh, there's no shame in being poor. There's only shame in being an asshole about it.

"I'll pay for it if you work for me," he says like it's no big deal.

"Em... no, I'm fine just drawing."

"You could be drawing for yourself and becoming a super-mega fought over artist. You're fuckin' raw talent." He's cursing a lot, something I get the feeling he doesn't often do. He sounds a little... British? How on Earth? But he's so emotional right now, so maybe his real ancestry's coming through. And besides that, *I get the cursing, Archie.* I so do. In the last few weeks, all I've wanted to do and come out to the street and yell 'fuck' so loud that they'll hear my roar on Mars.

I force a grin. "Nah, I'm good. Thanks, though."

"Are you a fucking idiot?" It's the first thing TJ says since our conversation started.

"Excuse me?" I'm half offended, but only half. Knowing him, something good is about to follow.

"She'll take it." He turns to Archie, disregarding me. "She'll go to that damn school even if I have to drag her ass to the class every single day."

I raise a brow.

"I'll help. We can switch shifts." Archie shoots me his megawatt smile, and I can't resist smiling back. For real this time.

"About damn time," TJ adds with a nod.

I raise my hands in defense. "I don't know what's happening here, but—"

"Kid," TJ interrupts me, "take this chance."

"I don't want to owe anything to anybody. I'm not some charity case." My hackles raise along with my voice.

"Nobody said you are," Archie says in a businesslike voice. "You will have to work for me. Exclusively. For five years."

"Seriously?" I narrow my eyes.

"Dead serious. Once I put your designs out there, they'll fight me to get you. That's why I need exclusivity." He firmly holds my stare.

I chew on my lips. Sounds too good to be true. Yes, to be stuck in a situation doesn't sound all that appealing, but my life isn't all rainbows and unicorns pooping lollipops. Besides that, I'm stuck here anyway, with no prospects but a life forever paying my family's debt and working at the diner. No offense to Marina, I love her, and she loves me;

that's why she always encourages me to get the hell out of Little Hope. But now I have something to lose.

I have Freya and Alex. Well, I had Alex.

And I have Justin. Well, I don't have *have* him, but after tasting those few tiny moments with him, I'm a sucker for more. I feel like we're so close to breaking the ice. There are already a few deep cracks. His words, sounding so close to a declaration of his interest in me... yeah, that one knocked me off pace.

God, if somebody ever told me they're about to throw away their dream for a man, I'd throat punch them. And yet, here I am. Considering doing the same. Thankfully I have TJ, who looks like he's about ready to beat me if I don't make the correct decision.

"I don't know, that's—"

"Sudden. I know." Archie takes a step closer and pokes my shoulder with his finger. "Take some time to think about it, but don't disregard the idea right away. Alright?"

"What's in it for you?" I squint my eyes at him.

He laughs. "So suspicious, aren't we?" My eyes narrow even more, if that's even possible. "Gathering talents is my hobby." He pokes me again. "Relax, Kayla," he says with a smile. "I wouldn't force you to do anything you don't want. But you're a big part of Alex's life, and I'm planning to be as well. We're almost family. And family helps each other. Think about it, okay?"

I scratch my nose, staring at the floor. "Okay," I tell them, feeling the weight of my decision on my shoulders.

"Good." He claps his hands once. "Alright. Now, show me some of your newest work."

I smile—that I can do. I pull over my recent work, and the men go insane over them. I don't think I've ever received this level of praise in my whole life. Archie orders pizza for the entire shop, and he, TJ, and I retreat to the back room to talk business. He shares his idea of opening a parlor in Copeland, a city thirty minutes west of Little Hope, opposite Springfield. I nervously glance at TJ—I don't know how he will take such close competition; the area doesn't have that many people after all, let alone those who get tattoos—but he looks fine to me. Excited, even. Alrighty then.

Archie says it takes a long time to become an established business, especially in small cities where people like to resist change. Oh, I can attest to *that*. And a tattoo parlor is definitely a change. Besides, it will attract more of a certain *crowd*—like me, and I'm not exactly the most well-loved person in Little Hope.

After several hours of business talk, Archie clasps his hands together, sticking them behind his head as he sits back in his seat. "Alright, pleasure doing business with you. Time to get back to work," he says with a sparkle in his eyes.

We bump fists, and he leaves. My gaze follows him all the way outside until he disappears. I feel TJ's heavy gaze on me. "What?" I ask.

"He's a lil' better than that asshole you've been pining over, but still an asshole. Plus, he got some dark shit in here." He taps his finger on his temple, his voice serious. Way too serious for him. In fact, I've never heard him speak that way before. Not with me, at least.

"What the hell, TJ?" I snap. "What are you talking about?"

"Don't mix business and pleasure. And don't piss on the golden goose." He's tapping his furry chin.

"Seriously, dude, what the hell?"

"C'mon, you know what I'm talking about." He starts shoving papers around his table; the so-called back room also works as an office. I blink a few times at him. "Oh, c'mon!" It's his time to snap. "That blond asshole you've been crushing on for years."

"How the hell do you know about that?" No matter how long I've lived in Little Hope, I always find new reasons to be genuinely astonished by the power of the rumor mill.

"A small town." He shrugs.

"You don't even live in Little Hope." My voice rises. Freaking small towns.

"I just know, kid. I just do." He says it so tiredly, so sincerely, that for the first time, I look at him from a different point of view, not just as business associates. I think he might actually care about me, and that realization makes me want to cry. A year ago, I had only Marina, and now there's a growing bubble of wonderful people around me. "He's no good for you. The dude's pining after you, but he's toxic. No good." He shakes his head while touching his long beard. He always does that when he's thinking. I watch him, speechless. I don't even think I'm blinking. How does he know that when I only found out about Justin's *thoughts* myself?

"TJ," my voice pleads, "I know, but I just can't."

"Can't what? Follow your dream?" He pulls the drawer from his table out and rummages through the contents.

"It's complicated." I let out a defeated sigh.

"I've heard about your debt." He shocks the hell out of me with this announcement and proceeds to pull a checkbook out. "I can lend you money to pay it off."

"Oh." I stand there completely dumbfounded. "How do you—"

"Don't insult me, kid." He shuts me up with a raised hand. I swallow nervously, not knowing what to say. I was hoping the sins of my family wouldn't follow me to the workplace. I've earned TJ's respect through years of hard work, and I don't want it to be ruined by the information he's unearthed.

"Yeah." My whole body loses pressure like a suddenly popped balloon, and I sag into a chair.

"How much do you need?" He's smoothing his beard again—a clear tell that he's deep in thought.

"Oh no!" I jump up from the chair. "I mean, I don't need the money; I'm just embarrassed. How long have you known?"

"Since your first day here." He taps a pen on the table. "Things like that don't happen around here unnoticed."

"True." Unfortunately.

"It doesn't change anything," he states firmly.

"But—"

"It doesn't change anything," he repeats. "You're not your mother; their sins are not yours."

"Yeah, could argue against that one." Most of the fine citizens of Little Hope would disagree with him, but my guilty mind does too.

"Let me know if you need help." He begins shuffling through the drawer again. "I'm here for you through anything." He stops moving and holds my eyes. "Anything. Got it?" He smacks the checkbook on the table.

"Got it," I answer, swallowing a huge lump.

"Good. Now get outta here; papa has some shit to ink."

I laugh and walk away, wondering what type of 'shit' he'll be inking today. For the first time in forever, I allow myself to dream that I'll be the one leaving permanent marks on people's bodies. A positive mark for a change.

Chapter Thirteen

JUSTIN

I wake to a hammer to my head. Not literally, but it feels as if someone has been knocking on my skull with one for hours. This always happens when I come back to the land of the living after a crash. My body should be rested and feeling great, but no, that would be too easy. Now I have to suffer through a killer headache and foul mood.

I sit up and get confused by my location. I look around and slowly realize I'm on the floor of Kayla's trailer, tucked in with a blanket and a few pillows. She must have left them here for me.

I lean on the couch, cover my face with my hands, and groan. *Son of a bitch.* That's embarrassing. I dropped on the floor like a sack of shit right after the kiss. *The kiss.* Fuck, that was a kiss. I'm surprised I didn't break my dick during the fall because it was hard as iron. Happens every time I'm near her, especially if I get a whiff of her smell. What happened during the kiss... I was not prepared for that. Just remembering her in my hands, feeling her skin under my fingers, her lush mouth swollen from my kiss makes my dick go full mast again. I look down. *Will ya chill already? You aren't getting shit! And we aren't buddies anymore because she's our enemy, remember? You traitorous... dick!*

I vaguely remember mentioning that she's constantly on my mind. Did I really say that out loud? Fuck. It's one thing to secretly jerk off to her ass in leather pants and another to admit it to anyone. To her, no less. I dug myself into a hole.

The first time I came to her yesterday, I was drunk and acted on something my sober brain had been itching to do for so long. I wanted to say whatever was on my mind so she'd kick me out, yelling some shit back that would make me hate her even more. But she surprised me by being a decent person and drove me back. A good thing, considering I was wasted.

The second time I came to her was of my own sober will. I was so tired of her being on my mind constantly. All the damn time. I was tired of my dick not reacting to anybody but her. Fuckin' tired of my calloused hands on it instead of a woman's body.

So, I came here for a fuck. A good hate fuck that would let me move on, and I could keep hating her afterward. But once my lips touched hers, I knew I was fooling myself. One time wouldn't be enough. I was ready to devour her, to fulfill all the fantasies I had (or at least the ones I could fit in one night), but my body once again acted against me, embarrassing the ever-loving crap out of me. She'd think of me as weak now, a freak. I can't have that.

The headache intensifies, and I get up in hopes of finding some Advil. I'm not going to snoop, but I need pills, or I'll go crazy. I go to the bathroom, almost tripping over her super fluffy, pink rug. It's so... girly. It surprises me. Kayla seems like a punk girl, but everything here is pink and fluffy. Okay, not expected. I check the mirror cabinet and find some basic medicine in there. Thank God. I pop three Advils into my mouth and go to the kitchen to wait for them to work. The coffee pot is half full and still warm, so I pour myself a cup and search for sugar. I like my coffee sweet. Once I find everything I need, I fix my cup, get a bowl of cereal, and go to the couch.

Thirty minutes later, I feel somewhat like a human again and decide to take a shower. I'm not leaving here without what I came for, so I might as well get comfortable and pleasant.

Two hours later, I'm browsing the net for some new repair tools that just hit the market when I hear a car engine nearby. A familiar one.

I drop my phone next to me and take a leisurely pose on the couch, hoping the fact that I made myself at home pisses her off. I need her aggravated so I can remember who we both are.

She walks in and groans. "You're still here?"

"Yep," I say through a mouthful of honey-crusted cereal.

"What do you need, Justin?" she asks, rolling her eyes so far into her head—I fear they might get stuck there permanently.

"We need to finish what we started." I put my feet on the coffee table, and her eyes zero in on my legs.

With a tight jaw, she says, "We finished. Now you need to go home."

"I don't think so." I cross my legs, which drives her insane. I can tell by the ticking vein on her temple.

She sucks a loud breath in and asks, "Would you be so kind as to get your feet off my table?"

"Why? It's a trashy table. I'm pretty sure my feet are cleaner than it is." I smile at her, even though I'm cringing inside. The stuff I'm spewing? I hate myself a little more for it, but if it helps keep the same vibe we usually have, then so be it.

"Get your feet off my table, Justin." When I don't move, she jumps toward me and knocks my crisscrossed feet from the table with her hands. "And get your ass out of my house!"

"I don't think so." I get up swiftly and move toward her as she takes a measured step back, but I keep going, closing in on her in this confined space. She doesn't have many choices of escape from here.

"What? Do you think that after *that*," she circles her hand over my body, "we'll just go back to where we stopped yesterday? That's what you said you're here for, right? You must be out of your mind then. Get out!"

"I think we will. You and me, we both know this," I point at the space between us, "will not go away on its own."

"What exactly?" She blinks, bemused. "You mean your hateful ass won't leave my house? Oh, I think it will." Her eyes narrow into tiny slits, her pose defensive.

"Oh no, Kayla, you owe me that much." I feel my voice drop with a malevolence that's been missing recently. "You owe me the *peace*."

"Oh, for God's sake! Stop already with this 'you owe me' crap. I don't owe you anything, and I don't know what I ever did to you. What I know is that if I ever see your face again, it will be too soon. So, get out." She points at the door, her cheeks turning pink with red splotches of that beautiful anger I crave so much. "I mean it, Justin. Get out and never come back."

Oh, here she is again with her innocent game. But I'm done playing. I will all the desire I ever had for her to dissolve into resentment.

"I will leave when I want to," I hiss just as she brings her hand up and smacks my face. I see it coming, and I let her. Now, she'll get what's coming to her. I grab both her wrists into my hand and jerk her to me.

KAYLA

I smack into his body with my hands tucked into his firm grip between us. His chest squashes mine.

"You know what, Kayla. Stop playing." His voice is furious. "You know what you did that night. People got hurt in the end." He practically spits in my face. My eyes widen. I true to God have no idea what he's talking about, but I begin to understand that Mark's assumptions might not be that far off the mark about *that* night being the catalyst to all of this. "I hope that haunts you for the rest of your life." His nose is so close to mine; his eyes are furious. His breathing comes fast and shallow. A bull before an attack.

Whatever he believes I did... he truly believes it. He looks hurt, so instead of pushing, my tone turns placid, even if I want to claw his eyes out. "I honestly don't know what you're talking about. You need to explain it to me, Justin. It's been so many years since you've started treating me like this, and I deserve to know why. I tried so many times to ask you what the hell happened, and every time you act like I'm this big fucking monster who eats children for breakfast, but you don't explain why you think so."

There, for a second, I see a tingle of doubt. For a second only. "The night I got arrested," he says slowly, carefully choosing words. His right eye is twitching.

"Yes. I remember that night. What happened?" I continue in that unfaltering, soothing voice I'm so proud of right now.

"You called the cops on me," he spats out scathingly.

"What?" I rear back. He thinks I called the cops? The thought is absurd.

His eyes contract into tiny slits. "You're the only one who saw me that night. And you called the cops on me."

"That's why you act this way? Because you think I called the cops on you?" I manage to say in dismay.

"Yes," he hisses. "Couldn't you have fucking waited one day to rat me out?"

I shove him back, but he doesn't move. "How about you not do shit to get arrested in the first place?"

"That's none of your business why I did what I did." Pure repugnance laces his voice.

I begin laughing. A good, full-belly laugh. He drops my hands and steps back. "Do you think it's fucking funny?" he yells. "My sister got raped because I couldn't get to her on time because I was pulled over by the cops! And this is funny to you?"

I immediately stop laughing. "What? Alicia's been raped?"

"Yeah, how do you feel about yourself now, huh? Knowing if you didn't call the cops on me, I could have gotten to her on time. I could have prevented what had happened to her. She called me right after I left that night. She called me and asked me to come to pick her up because she felt like she got a roofie in her drink." He grabs my shoulders and shakes me lightly. "And I was driving to her. I was driving to get my baby sister so she'd be safe. But instead, cops pulled me over and arrested me, so she got fucking raped because I couldn't get to her on time!" He's full-on yelling and raging. I hear a ringing in my ears; it's not from how loud he is but from the things he's saying. His face is red, his eyes blotchy as if he's reliving that night... or whatever followed.

I shudder violently. I can't believe it. Now it all makes sense. Why Alicia seems so sheltered, why she changed out of nowhere from this beautiful social butterfly to a hidden hermit, and why Justin and Jake act way too overprotective over her all the time. My heart's breaking for her, this poor, poor girl. Suddenly, as if he's been burned, Justin drops his hands and steps back. "I can't even look at you." He stalks toward the door. "I fuckin' hate myself for putting my lips on you. I hate myself for wanting you. I fuckin' hate you for what you've done, yet you somehow still keep making me fuckin' feel something for you!" His voice booms through the space, nearly shaking the furniture.

"Justin," I say quietly, but he isn't listening, so I gently touch his shoulder. He shrugs me off with visible disgust, so I quickly step back but keep talking. "I never called the cops on you. I've never called the cops on anybody in my life," I say before he storms out, and everything left is lost for good. I don't want him to go without hearing my truth because this hate for me and for himself is misplaced. I understand what's happening. I do.

He stops and smacks his open palm on the doorframe but doesn't turn back. "You were the only one who saw me that night."

"Was I?" I ask quietly, and he stills. Because he remembers that night too. Of course, he does. He will never be able to forget it. Neither will I. "That's right. I saw you punching the shit out of that poor guy."

"Yeah, and you were so conveniently present, rescuing your fellow trailer trash friend. He didn't deserve your or anyone's help." His lips press into a firm line, his shoulders square.

"You don't get to decide what he deserved. In fact, he deserved so much more." I shake my head. "I was there. But I wasn't the only one," I add after a pregnant pause. A heavy weight settles on his shoulders as they slump.

He finally turns to me and shakes his head. "Ashley was my girlfriend back then. She wouldn't do that, and you know it. You're just being pitiful and jealous." His voice is so gravely confident in Ashley that it makes me want to vomit. The corners of his lips turn down while he's looking me up and down as if assessing the level of disgust he feels for me.

"But I didn't do it. And he didn't do it. You know he'd be on the wrong side of the bars no matter what. Whether he was guilty or innocent, there wouldn't have been a trial. Trailer trash and all that." I shrug. "So, who does it leave?" He doesn't say anything, so I walk to him. I take his chin between my two fingers and force him to look me in the eyes. "*Who does it leave, Justin?*" I accent every word to ensure they get through to him. "Who?"

His Adam's apple bobs in a violent swallow, his mouth likely dry after such a revelation. Mine gets that way too. I drop my hand and step back, pointing at the door without a word. He walks out.

I don't hear his car start for a long time, but when it does, I breathe a sigh of relief. Part of me was hoping he would walk back in, everything forgiven so life could go on, morphing into a happily ever after. I'm clearly a glutton for punishment, clearly loving to torture myself. But part of me is relaxed. I know what happened. That I'm not at fault. I had seriously started to doubt myself. It's like gaslighting—they tell you that you've done something you never did, and eventually, you start believing it, unable to interpret true from false.

And another huge part of me just wants to weep for the poor girl whose innocent life was changed forever that night. That night changed the lives of so many others. I make a mental note that the next time I see Alicia, I'll make it up to her. Well, I can't really make up for everything she's been through—and to be honest, I can't even begin to imagine what she went through that night and the demons she's been fighting ever since—but I can help make her day a little better.

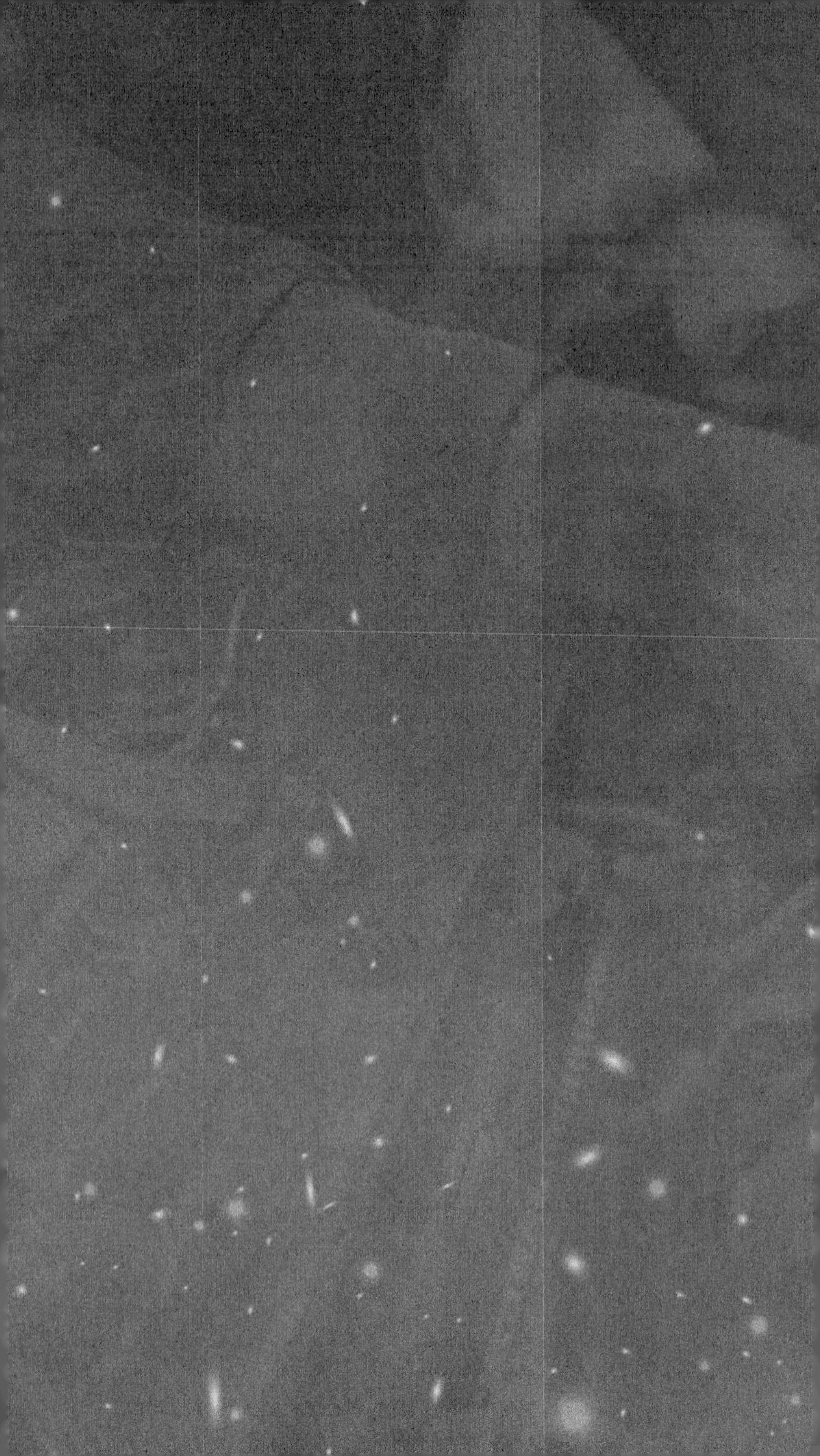

Chapter Fourteen

KAYLA

I try to recall *that* night as I lie in bed after Justin left, unable to sleep. It was almost six years ago.

I was walking down the road to my trailer. My car had just broken down again—it was a piece of junk (well, another one) that I had for one year before my loyal Jeep. It was the year I bought my RV and moved to the wilderness.

I was passing an abandoned gas station when I heard *thud-thud-thud*. I wanted to walk by as fast as possible, so I wouldn't get wrapped up in anything I'd regret. Anyone with one functioning brain cell knew not to get involved in the shit that goes down at abandoned places, and trailer park folks were especially well acquainted with this knowledge. All I needed was to keep my head down and keep on walking toward my goal: the safety of my little home cloaked between the mountains.

But then I heard a familiar voice. Justin. There were a few grunts, followed by the sound of punches being thrown. I was scared, thinking he must be getting hurt, so I ran toward the sound. What I saw was the opposite. Justin didn't need help: he was beating on a guy, barely conscious on the ground. He kept hitting him, even when the guy wasn't moving. Panic ran through me, for him and for Justin. I ran to him, tugging his arm, pleading for him to stop. I remember the mask of pure fury and a carnal thirst for blood he had on as he turned to face me. That was the very first time I feared Justin. He stopped beating the guy, stood up, and took a step back.

"He needs an ambulance," I croaked.

"No," the injured person groaned, I hadn't taken a good look at him, but I recognized Mark, a guy from my old trailer park, by his voice. His face was completely unrecognizable from the swelling and completely covered in blood. Yeah, he didn't want an ambulance, all right. At that rate, he'd need a pathologist soon. "No ambulance," he croaked again, and, no matter how much it pained me to admit, he was right: with all the illegal stuff going on, he didn't need authorities questioning him.

But I didn't need a dead body on my consciousness either. I turned to Justin. "He needs a doctor; he might have some major damage. Look at him; he's barely breathing."

"Good," Justin said, his hands pulling at his hair. His eyes were still crazed. "It'll be a great lesson on how not to try something with a woman when she doesn't want it."

"What?" I asked. I'd known Mark since we were in diapers. I knew he was doing some weed here and there, and by 'doing,' I mean 'selling,' but he'd never force himself on a woman. I'd seen this guy during the highest of highs and the lowest of lows. He's a protector to his core. I couldn't imagine *that* guy trying to force somebody.

"This piece of shit tried to rape Ashley," he spat out.

"What?" I cried out. I didn't want to come off like an asshole who blames the victim, but *c'mon*. We all knew Ashley was sleeping around while dating Justin, which only got worse when he was shipped overseas. She'd been known for telling lies of epic proportions, using her status to make other women of Little Hope look bad. And when I say epic, I mean *epic*: blaming people for stealing her stuff at the parties and getting them fired from their jobs and spreading rumors that me and my fellow trailer people were selling heavy drugs (so heavy, in fact, that we didn't even know such drugs existed), and that's just the tip of the iceberg when it came to Ashley. Everyone knew to stay away from her unless you wanted to be bullied for months. "Where is she?"

"Crying in the car," he spat out as he gestured toward his truck. I looked, and finally noticed a person in the front seat. Sure thing, Ashley was there, smeared mascara all over her face. She was smiling, a bloodthirsty look on her face, enjoying the show. I knew for sure she made the shit up. I narrowed my eyes at her as we made eye contact, and she licked her lips and winked at me. Freakin' *winked*!

"The way she's smiling doesn't make her look like a victim to me." I returned my attention back to Justin.

Justin's face changed instantly. His nostrils flared. "I wouldn't expect anything else from trailer trash. Accusing a victim instead of an actual assaulter."

"What?" A wave of nausea rose up my throat.

He turned to Mark once more. "Don't ever come near her again," he snarled before he strode out.

After five minutes of grunting and panting, I managed to drag Mark up and help him to his feet. How we were going to make a three-mile walk to the trailer park with just me basically carrying him—I had no idea. I looked over at his Challenger: he had had that car forever, so I knew it was a stick, and I couldn't drive stick. Not unless he wanted it in a ditch. So, walk it was.

"You shouldn't have gotten involved." Mark croaked while I struggled to get him standing. We kept having to stop as he was doubling over and spitting blood on the asphalt. How much did he weigh? Two hundred pounds or so versus my one thirty soaking wet? Yeah, it was a fun time for me.

"Of course, you're welcome for saving your ass, asshole!" I gripped him tighter, even though all I wanted to do was throw him to the ground and land a few punches of my own. Why was nobody just grateful nowadays? Though, to be honest, I was the one who owed Mark for all those times he protected me when I was a kid.

"Thank you, Kayla. I mean it," he said, groaning in pain. "But he's a mean son of a bitch, and it might come back to bite you."

"I didn't do anything, Mark. What would he come back at me for?" He didn't respond, and we walked slash-wobbled in silence for a few minutes. It was then I decided to ask the question that had been eating at me. Mark is a huge guy who grew up in an undeniably rough area, he could have thrown a mighty punch or two before getting smashed into the asphalt, but Justin's face was squeaky clean. "Why didn't you fight back?"

He was quiet for so long that I lost hope he'd respond, but then he said, "I deserved it."

I jumped from him, and he went down like a sack of potatoes. "What the fuck, Mark? Did you seriously rape her?"

"What? No!" He reared back, trying to pull himself back together. He looked like he was on the verge of death.

"Then what do you mean then?"

"I slept with his girlfriend while the dude was in the military, for fuck's sake. He deserved to throw a punch or two." Mark managed to pull himself up enough to sit on his butt, his hands rested on his bent knees. Did Justin seriously think he could do something that bad to a woman?

I shook my head and muttered a quiet "Idiot" before I helped him up once again.

Thankfully, luck was on our side. After thirty minutes of plodding along, struggling to keep his enormous form propped up, one of Mark's friends drove by and stopped to give us a lift. He asked what happened, but I kept my mouth shut, and Mark did too. Whatever beef they had with Justin—it was between them. From what I'd heard of Mark, he wouldn't get anyone involved. He always wanted to resolve things himself. People on the poor side of town have honor, too, you know.

As we got closer to the trailer park, Mark's friend asked if I needed a ride to my place. I declined his offer, but I could see the hesitation on his face, clearly not wanting to leave me in the middle of the road at night. Mark tried to convince me not to walk alone, telling me I should at least stay with him until the morning, but I let him know that I had my fair share of adventure for one night. After a long argument, they let me go. I appreciated how worried they were for me, I did. But I valued my seclusion, and I didn't want anyone to know where I lived. It would ruin my peace.

By the time I got to the diner the next day, everybody knew that Justin had gotten arrested that night for assault. Someone had called the police on him, and that someone wasn't me. I've been known to be on the other side of the phone call, though, as people see an out-of-place girl and think she's up to no good.

Mark didn't press charges (no surprise here), so Justin was let go. But that's when things went from bad to worse for him. Apparently, Justin got in a fight with the cop who arrested him. Considering what I know now, I feel like Justin thought all parties involved that night were to blame for his sister's assault. In his mind, Mark, me, and the cop who arrested him were the roadblocks preventing him from getting to Alicia on time and, therefore, the reason it happened.

That fight with the cop got him thrown into prison for three years. When he got out, I became enemy number one, even though I didn't have a clue why. I should have suspected something was extremely wrong when Jake started harassing me every chance he got following that night, long before he had begun working for the police. He was attending a law school in Massachusetts, and every time he was home for break, he found a way to get to me. He was so much younger, and I thought he was just fooling around. It would pass eventually, I kept telling myself. But then he became the local cop. Over time, locals started treating me like even stinkier shit than before. Jake liked to run his big mouth, which, paired with his good looks and natural charm, allowed him to easily convince everyone that I was an evil being set on destroying the good people of Little Hope. The rumors continued over time, and I still deal with them to this day. One of the *new* rumors about me being a whore started with him, I'm sure.

Guilty Minds

Only regulars at Marina's diner still saw me as a human being. They talked to me like I was a normal person with normal problems and a normal family waiting at home. I had none of that. Still don't. Even my problems suck.

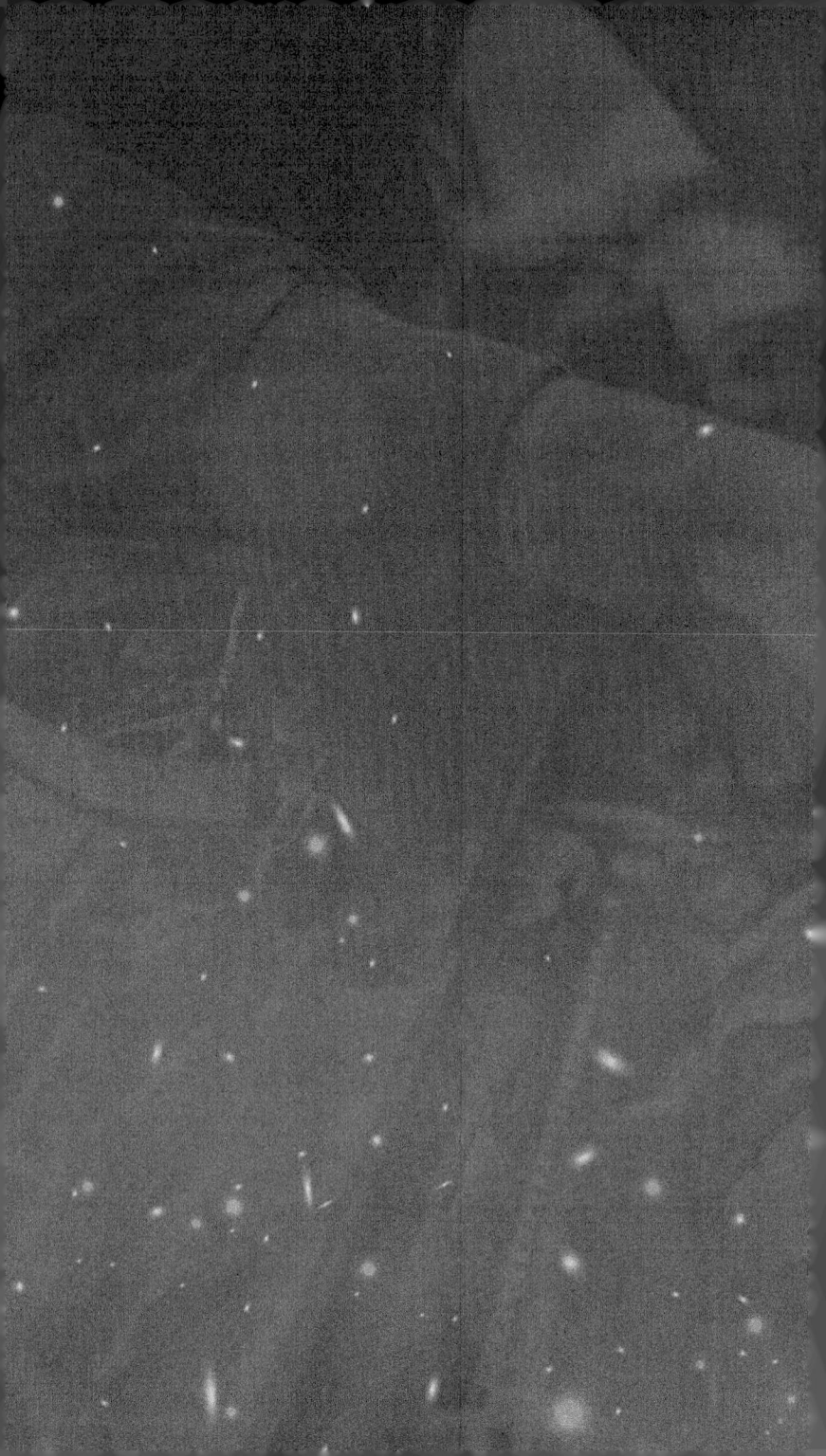

Chapter Fifteen

K AYLA

Marina's already in full cooking mode by the time I arrive the next morning. After my evening of revelations with Justin and exactly zero sleep, I feel like the walking dead. I know better than to interrupt her during her witching hour, so I go to start coffee instead. I half expect Justin to show up, but he doesn't. There's no sight of him throughout the whole day. And the day after. At the end of day two, I successfully avoid Freya's phone calls. When she texted me to ask what was wrong, I just let her know we've been swamped at the diner. It wasn't a lie. It seemed to work, and she let the subject drop. I know she was just being nice, though. She knows something is wrong.

But now Alex towers in front of me. He had finally started getting out and about around town. A stark difference from how he was only ever seen when picking up his car pieces from the delivery guy. I'm happy for him and know it's all thanks to Freya and the PTSD facility he went off to.

"Sup, Alex," I ask before fleeing to the coffee machine, attempting to avoid him like the plague. He sits at the counter. I look over at him; his ever-present baseball cap is on. Although he's made amazing progress since he went away, I can tell he still struggles with a few things. While he might be comfortable enough to be himself, scars and all, around some people, he's clearly not comfortable here, and I feel a little bad. I sigh. I think I know the reason he's here.

"Kayla—" He sighs. "I feel like an asshole."

"Why? Did you scare some children again?" I smile, trying to ease him.

"Look—" He scratches his chin. "It's not my business what you do or why you do it." I already don't like where this conversation is going. "What's done is done; it can't be changed. I shouldn't put it on you for even a second."

I place the towel I've been wiping glasses with on the table and firmly plant my hands on the bar in front of him. I adore Alex, but now that I know the truth, I'm past putting up with these lies. For God's sake, he thought I was to blame for that night? I'm sure he knows about Alicia. I dread the thought that, in his mind, I was somehow at fault for such a horrible thing. "What exactly don't you want to put on me, Alex?"

"Kayla—" His jaw ticks; it's such an Alex tell. "You know… that you ratted Justin out." Now, after all these years, he finally says it out loud. He kept quiet when I needed to know why. I was harassed and abused and kept wondering, quite loudly, mind you, why Justin hated me. But now it seems like all the stoppers have been removed from everyone's mouths. *O-okay*.

I feel my face harden and my jaw clenches. My eyes shoot ice. "I didn't rat him out." I inch closer to him over the counter. Leaning on my elbows for support, I hiss my next words, puncturing him with every one of them. "I did *not* call the cops on him. I helped Mark get to his friend's car because he was half *dead*. If I was ten minutes later, Justin would have faced *much* different charges." He tries to say something, but I silence him with a raised hand and a stern look on my face. "I'm only gonna say it once because I'm *done* being treated like an outcast for something I never did. *First*, it was with my sister and my mom. Because of them and their ways, I've been called a town whore, trailer trash, and a home-wrecker. Fuck, I *am* trailer trash. I have no formal education and no future prospects. But I've *never* been a whore." I hiss at him while his eyes bolt between mine. "I thought you were one of the few who believed I'm innocent. Of everything I've been accused of. Who actually cared about me and looked at me like a living, breathing human being who wouldn't lie about not knowing what happened. Who deserved the truth. But I was wrong, wasn't I, Alex? You saw me as a pity case. And then, after whatever you *think* happened, you were just being nice for Freya's sake." By the look on his face, I've just hit the bullseye. "So, here's a newsflash, Alex. I wasn't the one calling the cops on Justin. Instead of looking for somebody to blame, how about you look deeper and ask Justin what really happened that night, huh? I bet you don't know all the details since you weren't fuckin' there." I nearly yell the last sentence. I can feel a few curious glances on me. I bet the motherfuckers are wishing they had popcorn.

His jaw is locked, his eyes are narrowed, and he doesn't say a word. Maybe I overdid it a little bit, but I'm truly, one hundred percent done. I'll be getting my stuff in order and getting out of this town—consequences and guilt be damned.

"Kayla," his voice is quiet, "all the evidence says it was you."

"How about my word, huh?" My nostrils flare. I'm positive I look like an enraged bull three seconds short from charging at him and knocking his stubborn head into the counter. "Does it mean anything?"

"We haven't really known you that well." His voice is a little defensive.

"And you *still don't*. Talk to Justin, Alex, not me." I grab the towel from the bar like a weapon and grind my teeth, stopping myself from spitting anything else out. Maybe I should just bite into the towel, so I don't bite his neck like a rabid squirrel over a fallen nut.

Alex clearly came here to talk about that uncomfortable millisecond moment at his house. Justin hasn't spoken to him yet. For all I know, Justin still doesn't believe me. To think of it... I used to crush on that guy. Crush like crazy! He was the only man who ever awoke anything in me. I'm a mental case for accepting the treatment he was giving me for so long. Still so hopeful for a happily ever after. That he would turn out to be Snow White who wakes up from my kiss. Yep. I'm done pining for a guy who treats me like garbage. I'm going to a bar tonight and getting laid by a perfect sexy stranger. I don't care that we don't have those in Little Hope. *Strangers*, I mean. Especially perfect sexy ones. A girl can dream.

Alex stands up. A moment of hesitation lingers in the air before he strolls to the door without a second glance.

Marina comes out from the kitchen. "It's time you put everybody in their place," she says with a nod.

"And get the fuck out of this town." I nod.

"And get the fuck out of this town," she parrots with a smile. But then the smile vanishes. "What are you going to do about Maddie and Caroline?"

I sigh. "I haven't thought that far. I'll still be sending money, that's for sure. Not like I can avoid it. As for me not physically being here... It's not like I have tea parties with them. I can send money from anywhere in the world. Because that's all they need." I shrug, hopeful and sad at the same time.

"Don't let the sins of others hold you from flying, Kayla. You're destined for far better things than to be the punching bag for the whole town." I look at her wide-eyed—that's the most philosophic thing I've ever heard her say. "I still don't agree with you sending the money. What?" She notices my frown. "I don't. I have no idea why you're doing it. Well, I suppose I know *why* but I don't think you should. They use you." She shakes her head.

"I thought you loved this town." I give her a cheeky smile, letting the other part slide—we'll never agree on that one.

"I do." She nods. "But I love you more." And with that bomb, she retires back to the kitchen.

My eyes are misty. It's the first time in my entire life I've been told that somebody loves me. The first time. I furiously blink back tears. The words hold even more meaning since Marina has never said them out loud, even though I've always known she loves me.

When I'm finally composed and ready, I go to clean off the tables. The last few people have left, and we're about to close.

On the drive home, I half expect to see Justin in my chair next to my trailer. But he's not. And he's not there the next day. Or the day after.

I haven't seen or heard from him or Alex the whole week. Freya stopped by a couple times and offered to do something together, but every time I was busy (yep, so busy avoiding everybody), so she decided to give me space. I feel a little guilty for not sharing my plans with her, but honestly, she doesn't need me either. After the last encounter with Alex, I don't think I'd be very welcome in their house, and I don't want her to feel weird in the middle of this mess. She has a lot on her own plate. I know I was harsh with Alex, but it came from a place of disappointment. I had really hoped he believed in me.

Chapter Sixteen

K AYLA

A whole week has passed, and I've lost all hope of ever reconciling with Alex or fixing the situation with Justin. To be completely honest, I've been harassed by him and his brother for so long that I need some sort of closure. An apology would be nice too. One I wouldn't accept right away, demanding another one. I want groveling.

I drive up to my trailer after the Sunday shift when I notice a big familiar truck waiting for me outside my home. I can feel my heart dropping into my belly, forming a tight knot of anticipation. What will I get today: the desired groveling or another knife in the spine?

I park in my usual spot. The truck hasn't taken my designated place, like Justin let me have my spot to not upset me. Weird. Whoever comes first takes the better spot. That's the rule of the jungle.

I grab my two bags of groceries from the passenger seat and head to the door, carefully eyeing my unexpected guest getting out of his truck and following me.

"May I come in?" His voice is timid. He never asked for permission before, so I nod without a word, fearing I'll scare him off. He seems ready to run, and something tells me I want to hear what he has to say.

I put the bags on the table and begin unpacking. Justin stands by the door without moving further inside. I discreetly eyeball him: he's looking around, observing every single detail like he's never been here before, when just a few days ago, he was making fun of it. His gaze is calculating. I stay silent, curious to see how the situation will unfold.

After a few minutes of silence, he takes a deep breath. "I want you to tell me everything you know about Ashley."

I smack a can of pumpkin on the table so hard that it makes Justin flinch. "Seriously?" I growl. "You came here to ask about Ashley?"

He swallows roughly. "I need to know what you know."

"Why, Justin? Why should I waste my breath telling you something you're not going to believe?" I can practically hear my teeth grinding.

"I will believe you," he rasps.

"The whole town knows every single detail about her. Go ask them." I shove the cans into the cabinet. I'm so mad that I can't stack them properly the first time, and they all fall. Justin walks over and stands behind me, suffocating me with his delicious musk. His front is almost touching my back. He stretches his long arms around me and begins picking up the cans and stacking them neatly. I'm caged, but I don't feel trapped. My heart's beating like a hummingbird's wings. I was mad only a moment ago, and now I'm not.

"I need to ask you, Kayla," he whispers into my ear while slowly creating neat piles of everything I just dropped. It's a rare occasion, him calling me by my name. It sounds... *good* coming from his lips, in that low tremble he has going on. "What exactly happened that night? Tell me like I'm new in town and don't know anything yet." His breath tickles my ear, and I shudder.

My head drops forward in defeat. "I was walking home."

"Home where?" he interrupts.

"Here."

"You already lived here on your own. Alone," he says rather than asks.

"I've been on my own for a long time, yes." I get distracted by his heavy breathing next to my ear. His movements are deliberately slow. "So, I was walking here and heard weird noises, and then I heard you."

"Go on," he urges me.

"I saw you beating some guy on the ground." I swallow, disgusted by memories.

"Why did you stop me? Was he... close to you?" His nose touches the shell of my ear, and I know he's doing it on purpose, but my willpower is weak, so I don't stop him.

"In the moment, I didn't know who he was, but I could tell he was barely alive. You almost killed him, Justin," I whisper more to myself, reliving that horrible moment. It was the first time I saw him as a monster. "I had to stop you."

"Go on," he nudges.

"Then you said he forced himself on Ashley." I spit her name out like it's poison. Which it is, in a way. "And then I saw her in the car. She was smiling, and she winked at me. Winked! Like she was happy. What kind of person would do that?" I shake my head in disbelief.

"And?" He inhales deeply, moving the strands of hair on my neck.

"And then I put two and two together because I recognized the guy the moment I heard him speak. We grew up together at the park. I knew him well enough to know he wouldn't rape a woman. Never. I mean it." I shake my head, enforcing my statement. "Besides, I—" I stop myself on time.

"Besides what, Kayla?" He urges me to continue.

"Nothing." I bite my tongue, not knowing if I should keep going.

"Besides what, Kayla?" He presses his front into me, and I feel his hard dick along my ass. My eyes widen, and I freeze. He is a psycho too. *Hello, let's be psychos together.* "What, Kayla? What did you want to say?"

I swallow a lump in my throat. "I had seen Ashley with Mark a few times around town."

"While I was deployed?" There isn't a single note of anger in his voice for somebody who just heard that his girlfriend was cheating on him.

"Yes," I breathe out.

"What's next?" He inches his body away from mine, and I feel cold. But also free.

"Then you went off the rails and stormed away." My voice becomes small all of a sudden.

"And you?"

"I wanted to call an ambulance because he was in really bad shape. Like really bad. I was so scared he was going to die." I choke on the memory. I grew up in a bad place and saw a lot of fights, but I'd never seen that level of brutality firsthand, delivered by the man I idolized for so long.

"And what did you do?" He pushes his pelvis back into me, forcing my brain into mush.

"Mark didn't want an ambulance, so I wanted to help him to his house. So I got him up, and we started walking." I take a deep, shuddering breath, reliving the emotions of that night.

"Walking? Why the hell would you walk if his car was there?" His tone was laced with befuddlement.

"I can't drive stick. Like at all. And he could barely breathe, let alone drive." I chew on my lip, I might sound ridiculous to him, but Mark and I were far safer walking than with me driving a manual car.

"That must have been at least a three-mile walk," he says, and I'm unsure whether his tone is from surprise or suspicion.

"Mark's friend was driving by and picked him up a little after." I shrug, accidentally brushing his chest with my shoulder.

"What happened to you after?" There's a new edge in his voice.

"I went home," I answer, like what else would I do?

"Did they drive you?"

"No."

"Why?" His tone turns threatening, and I want to laugh.

"As you pointed out, I live alone. Nobody knows where I live. At the time, I had just moved, and not a single soul knew I was here. Even now, only three people know. Which brings me to the question of the century: how did you find me?"

His body goes rigid, and he takes another step back. I turn around and look at him.

"Did you call the cops, Kayla?" His face is blank, and his eyes are completely focused on mine.

"I did not," I say with an equal stare.

His next breath's shuddering and loud, like it's the last one he'll ever take. "I assume that guy didn't either." A half question, and I shake my head. He exhales loudly. "A couple hours before that, Alicia had called me and said she was at some party in Springfield. I didn't trust those fraternity boys she was with, so I just wanted to go and check on her." I'm speechless—he's sharing something with me. Scared to lose the moment, I don't move or breathe. "I was at a party myself." He rakes a hand through his hair—a tell that he's nervous. "I went to look for Ashley 'cause we came together, and I found her under that Mark guy. I didn't know his name back then but knew that he came with tr—" He cuts himself off.

"Trailer trash?" I offer helpfully, and he flinches.

"He had company there. When she saw me, she started crying and yelling, telling him to stop. I thought he was raping her, so I threw him off. I landed a few punches before his... friends," he spits out the word, "came barreling in. They threw me out of the house. Ashley left with me, of course."

"Of course." I make sure the sarcasm drips off my words, and he winces.

"Yeah, I didn't have all the details then."

"And yet, it doesn't seem to stop you from forming an opinion." I bite my tongue, preventing the remaining venom from spilling out. The first sign of regret in *forever* appears on his face.

"I was on the way to the party when I saw a car tailing us." His voice sounds dejected. "I recognized that guy."

"Mark," I offer. "You should say the name of the guy you almost killed."

"Mark. He wanted to talk. Clearly." He sighs. "There was that abandoned gas station, so I pulled in." He rakes his hand through his hair again. "You know the rest. Then, when we left…" He takes a deep breath, preparing himself. "Alicia called because she thought her drink got spiked, so I sped up. Suddenly, cop lights lit up behind me, pulling me over. I thought it was for speeding at first, but it turned out they already knew about the fight and were arresting me for assault. I begged them to let me go, or at least to let me go check on my sister, but they didn't. And the most fucked-up thing is that they weren't Little Hope cops; they were Springfield ones. They didn't listen to me." He leans on the counter, and it's the first time I notice how absurd he looks in my space. Everything here is small, cheap, and very-*very* worn out. Me included. And Justin is big, intimidating, and rich by local measurements. He doesn't fit in here. I was an idiot for even considering the possibility of something between us. First, he'd never look at somebody like me. He might like 'em all different shapes, but he definitely has a type: the definition of femininity; they are well groomed and very traditional. They'd never mark their perfect skin with ink or inappropriate piercings. They're also usually very wealthy. Well, most of them are, anyway. And I barely survive here, living from paycheck to paycheck.

And more than anything, he only *sleeps* with them. And then he goes about his business. At least, that's the rumor. He doesn't date, not since Ashley a few years ago, though I still don't know when their relationship ended. Well, according to her, they're still dating and very much in love.

And if it ever comes to *that—sleeping, that's it—*(in some alternate reality) I don't think just sleeping with this man, who's been invading my dreams for years and years, will be enough for me.

And to think, just a week ago, I decided to move on and get laid. Yep, sure. Still got cobwebs down there.

I take a deep breath and instantly regret it—his musky smell fills my lungs. The overpowering manliness in this small, confined space is lethal. I try to dodge the feelings drowning me.

"Did you figure out who called on you?" I ask while he's watching me silently. "C'mon! Do you still think it's me?" He doesn't say anything but shakes his head. A minute passes. This is getting ridiculous. What the hell am I waiting for? "You know what? It's getting late, and I have a lot to do. Is there anything else you need?" I ask. He's quiet. "Right." I pinch the bridge of my nose. "Time to go, Justin." I gesture to the door.

"If I say it out loud—" He swallows. "It means I've been fucking the person who played a huge part in what happened to my sister. For years. And I brought her around all this time...." His voice's quiet and hoarse. If I didn't know him better, I'd say he has a knot in his throat that can only be alleviated with tears. But I know better. Know *him* better.

"If you don't say it, it's still there," I tell him, pointing at his head. "It won't go away simply because you don't want to face it." I spread my arms out. "Trust the person who tries not to talk about how fucked-up her family is. Pretending the problem doesn't exist has never canceled the fact that they still are." I might try to avoid all conversations involving my sister and mother, but the facts remain. Their actions still impact my present. I pay for their mistakes.

Quite literally. "No matter where I go, it seems like I will always be trailer trash."

He winces at my words. Something flickers in his eyes, and suddenly, he's in front of me, a breath away. If I want to touch him, all I need to do is to raise my hand. "So, what do you want me to do? Shout about it from the rooftops?" His eyes are crazed.

"If it will help. You've been stuck in this limbo for how long? How long have you been dragging me into all of this?" My voice raises, and I poke his chest with my finger. "How long will it take for you to finally figure out that you're the one who fucked up?" I'm almost yelling now.

Justin's chest is heaving like a bull ready to charge. His nostrils are flared, and his breathing is loud. His eyes dart between mine and then drop down...

To my lips.

I instinctively lick them. I can't help it. I didn't mean anything by it, I honestly didn't, but he notices it. His tongue darts out to moisten his lower lip, and I'm a goner. My own breathing becomes fast and shallow. The air around us is electrified with expectations of the unavoidable, like the moment before the storm—you know it's coming. The air has changed, the silence is deafening, right before the lightning cuts the sky, followed by a punishing thunder.

And that moment of collision? It's now.

Justin snakes one arm around my lower back and the other around my neck.

He pulls me in. I don't have a chance to even take a breath before his lips are on mine. It's so unexpected that I don't know what to do.

Justin kisses me.

Justin Attleborough kisses me.

Justin Attleborough, the man I've crushed on since I was ten, is kissing me.

Justin Attleborough, the man I started to hate a few days back, is kissing me.

Justin is kissing me, and it's happening *not* in a moment of hate. It might as well be the first kiss. The previous kiss doesn't count. That one happened as a result of shedding our egos. This one is happening because he *wants* it to. I can feel it; his view of me has changed.

I don't know what to do, so I stay still. He can tell and slows down a bit. He kisses the corner of my lips, and I feel his hot tongue probing it. By now, I've collected myself from the abyss I accidentally entered, and I bring my hands to his shoulders. It's the only encouragement he needs, and he pushes his tongue between my lips. The hand around my back pulls me tighter to him, and I feel *him* against me. He's hard. And long. And pulsing. My own desperate need pools between my legs. It's warm and swirling. It's not butterflies. No, they're pterodactyls circling in my belly.

I moan into his mouth, and the hand around my neck squeezes tighter. His fingers dig in, and they're almost painful. I moan louder. His tongue dances against mine, driving me insane. I hear a groan, and I'm almost embarrassed that it's me. But it's not. It's Justin. He stops the kiss and pulls away. He rests his forehead against mine, breathing hard.

My breathing matches his, and with every inhale, I smell him. I smell his musk and the residue of aftershave on his chin.

"Why did you do that?" I whisper, trying to regain control over my own body that's currently melting—quite literally, I might add, considering the pool in my pants—into a puddle at our feet.

His chuckle's pained. "Because I finally can without hating myself." He inhales deeply. "You smell so good. What is it?"

"I don't know," I say through a haze.

"What perfume do you wear?" His voice is barely audible.

"I don't wear any," I whisper back.

He inhales again and groans, then he takes a step back. My face is flushed, and my palms are sticky. I subtly wipe them on my thighs when I notice that Justin is trying to discreetly fix the situation in his pants. My cheeks heat up even more. Oh boy, is that a situation! Now I see why *they* keep coming back for more. I avert my eyes, but not fast enough. Justin smirks at me. How arrogant of him... but there's something different about it. It's the first time he shows me the person he is with everyone else. It should make me happy, but it doesn't. I feel like everybody else.

We stare at each other, not knowing what to say. The air, full of intensity and heat just moments ago, suddenly seems one hundred degrees chillier. It's not like I can go anywhere—I'm home. And I can't ask him to leave for fear of him never coming back. Justin takes the hard decision off my shoulders and moves to the door. "Your car needs an oil change. I'll stop by tomorrow at the diner to grab it for a few hours." He steps out and leaves me with my mouth open. What the hell just happened?

Chapter Seventeen

KAYLA

The diner is unusually quiet the whole morning, and time moves at a snail's pace. I yawn half the morning because I haven't slept well. Obviously. I played fake scenarios in my head. All. Night. Long. Like, what if I said that thing differently. Or this thing with a smile. Or if I pushed my butt against him, what would have happened?

I think the last one bothers me the most. I sigh, shake my head, and go to clean up—at least I'll be busy with something. I'm mechanically wiping tables, completely checked out, when a high-pitched yell comes from outside. It sounds like a damn dying banshee, or at least that's how I would have pictured one sounding. I wipe my hand across my forehead and see Alicia sitting on the bench across the street from the diner. She holds a laptop on her knees and is typing energetically. I'd say a little too energetically. One might say *furiously*.

And then I see why. Five feet from her is the Wicked Witch of Little Hope, Ashley the Bitch herself. Even from here, I can hear what she's yelling.

"You need to tell him that you lied! You hear me? Go tell him *now!*" She stomps her foot in her high stilettos. Very well-presented lady, as I've mentioned before. Justin likes them classy. Though right now, she's a little less of a lady—or as Freya would say, she got some Dorian on her face, though I'm still not convinced I understand the meaning of that. I picture a much different thing of Dorian's that can end up on her face. "Alicia, you need to talk to him!" She keeps tapping her foot on the asphalt.

Alicia doesn't pay her any attention and just keeps on typing.

"I see it's time to put our protective amulets out." Marina walks to me, and we both watch the unraveling.

I chuckle. "Yeah, looks that way."

"Aren't they friends?" There's doubt in her voice, and I know what she means. Alicia's so different from them, but Ashley's always around her, trying to get her to join the coven. Marina and I know Ashley doesn't do friends; she does acquaintances who suit her in the moment. Our windows face Main Street, which means we see *a lot*. A good chunk of drama unfolds in front of our eyes. We should sell popcorn for the occasional shows.

I wonder what she's talking about now, though. Might have been some fallout among the wandering vaginas... or maybe Justin finally had *a talk* with her.

Please, let him believe me. For his own sake.

"I think they were," I say with a shrug, though neither of us believes it. Marina leans on the pillar and crosses her arms over her generous chest. There's never much going on in Little Hope, so any and all drama is considered entertainment. I'm just happy it's not at my expense this time. I almost turn around to keep cleaning when I hear Ashley's loud voice.

"You think you're so special? A *little damaged bird*," she mocks the last part with a pretend pout. "Everybody thinks you're so cute and innocent, huh? But we both know the truth, don't we?" She laughs. "That you spread your legs for anyone and enjoy the ride. Like you've done on a few occasions before that, huh."

Oh no, no, no. She did *not* just say that!

I look at Alicia—she smacks her laptop closed, her jaw working.

"What's she talking about?" Marina's accent is thicker, anxious after catching on to what Ashley may have meant. Nobody knew what had happened to Alicia. I only found out when Justin told me. And now everyone will be wondering what Ashley meant. It's a small town.

"I'll be right back." I drop the towel on the table and storm out. The closer I get, the more prominent Alicia's tears become. I can see them running down her beautiful, angelic face. But Ashley just can't freakin' stop. "What did you tell him, Alicia? What? Why the hell didn't you just keep your mouth shut? You don't even know what you're talking about!" she shrieks.

"Hey!" I storm up to her, positioning my body between them. "Why the hell can't *you* keep your mouth shut, huh? Didn't drink enough infant blood this morning?"

"Oh, look at that! The savior is here. The trailer trash in all her glory." She sneers and keeps tapping her foot. "Get the fuck out of here, or I'll tell everybody what you did."

"Really?" I ask, my voice flat. I quirk my brow, channeling my best Dwayne the Rock Johnson. "What is there that everyone still doesn't know?"

That shuts her up, and I can practically see the wheels turning in her head. When she finally gets her wits together, she yells in my face. "She told Justin I slept with this... this... *trailer trash!*" She spits the last word out like it's poison in her mouth.

"You mean Mark?" I ask, and she hums. "Oh, she didn't tell. I did." I cross my arms over my chest. "I'm surprised nobody else did."

"You?" she screeches again, and I wince. I swear she can bring a UFO down with that high-pitched frequency. "I *knew* you always wanted him for yourself!" She jumps closer and presses her long nail into my chest. I slowly look down and then look up.

"I strongly recommend taking your damn hand off me," I say through clenched teeth. She must see something in my eyes because she drops her hand like it's been burned. A wise choice, as I'm not known for my fancy upbringing, and living in a trailer park can teach a person a thing or two about survival.

"I always knew it," she hisses in my face. "You look at him like he's a prime rib you can never afford."

"Go away, or I'll make sure everyone knows you accused an innocent man of assault. How many more are out there? Because of people like you, real victims aren't taken seriously." I take a wide stance, showing that I'm ready to go at it if she is. She's best friends with Adison, another one of the witches of Little Hope who loves to spread lies. Maybe there's a limit to the number of bad apples the towns around us will take, so they all end up here.

"Oh, trailer trash thinks she's got some sort of power?"

"Leave, Ashley. I'm sure there are some virgins out there in need of a blood sacrifice." I try to stay unaffected, but I cringe inside that she noticed. I thought I was hiding it so well. Her nostrils flare, and she storms away. Her hair flying behind her in a perfectly silky wave.

"She's right; you're pathetic with your puppy eyes for Justin." Comes a hiss from behind me, and I turn around in surprise. "I didn't need your help." Alicia grabs her laptop and stands up. "Stay away from me and my brother. You're bad news."

I stand there dumbfounded as she almost runs to her car. When I finally pick my jaw up from the ground, I walk back to the diner.

Marina meets me with a frown. "None of the good deeds go unpunished."

"That's not the saying."

"It is mine." She shrugs and walks to the kitchen.

Indeed, she's right. The road to hell is paved with good intentions. My road was paved such a long time ago that no amount of good or bad deeds will sway the way. My dear sister made sure of it.

By the time I'm done processing what the hell happened, it's almost two o'clock, and my feet are already hurting. For such a small town, we sure have a lot of people dining in. I clean the tables and refill the waters and coffee for customers before pouring myself a cup. Just when I take my first sip, the door opens, and Justin walks in. A cloud of fury follows him, and I'm preparing for battle.

Sure, it felt like we had a breakthrough yesterday, but I don't know what to expect today.

"What did you say to her?" He grinds his teeth so hard I can almost hear it.

And we're back to square one. I sigh. "I just told her to mind her own business."

"Why would you do that? She has enough shit to deal with!" His raised voice is full of disappointment.

"What the hell, Justin? I don't give a flying crap if she has stuff on her plate. I got my own stuff too! The only thing I told her was to leave Alicia alone!" I almost yell at him. The show started, and the only thing the regulars in the diner are missing is the popcorn.

He stumbles back. "What are you talking about?"

"No, what are *you* talking about? I thought we were past this already. Stop blaming me for everything!" I smack the counter with my palm for good measure.

"I'm talking about Alicia. What did you tell her?" His voice evens a little.

"What?" Now it's my turn to be confused. "I didn't say a word to her, but she sent me on my merry way when I told Ashley to leave her alone."

Justin's shoulders sag. He wipes his face with his hand and groans. "Fuck." I wait to hear what else he has to say because I'm tired of defending myself when I'm not at fault. "Mom called me and said Alicia came home in tears and cried that you know about her secret and now, the whole town knows."

"She's right; the whole town knows because Ashley stood right there," I point to the bench where the previous event unfolded, "and yelled about it for the whole town to hear."

"Fuck. Fuck!" he says louder.

"Yeah, fuck indeed. Now, since you don't have a valid reason to rage at me anymore, can you leave? You scared all our customers." I'm hurt, and I'm tired. I'm so very-*very* tired. But our customers aren't scared; they're excited. Bloodthirsty bastards.

He presses the heels of his palms into his eye sockets. Looks painful if you ask me. *Press harder.* "Kayla," he says quietly.

I lift my hand, preventing him from saying anything that might hurt me more. "No, Justin, I'm truly, wholeheartedly done. With you and with this story. Especially with you. We talked about what happened all those years ago. I told you my side of the story. You should have known that I wouldn't say anything mean to somebody who went through what Alicia went through." I shake my head. "And yet, you're so quick to blame me. Again. And again. And again." Then I add tiredly, "Please, go." I turn around to go fetch a new pot of coffee.

For a moment there, a day ago, I thought everything was possible. Turns out, not everything.

"Kay..." he says quietly behind me. The short pet name and the tone he's using almost make me want to cave in. *Almost.* "I didn't know what to think. Alright? I didn't. My baby sister came home crying after everything she's been through, and I just..." He rakes his hand through his already messy hair. "I didn't wait for the clarification. I just want to protect my sister."

Marina comes out from the kitchen, wiping her hands on her apron. "Go home, Justin. Sort out your shit first." Her eyes are thin, angry slits.

"Kayla," he calls out, but Marina cuts him off. "Go, Justin. You've done enough." I can see his reflection in the small mirror over the bar. He hesitates for a moment, and then he walks out.

"Thank you," I say quietly to Marina. And even though I'm grateful for her mediation, I'm left wondering where the conversation would go if she hadn't said anything. I kind of understand him, I do, but I have to think of myself too.

"Don't thank me, honey. If I knew you were done with him, I'd have chopped his balls off a long time ago. He doesn't deserve you." A sad chuckle escapes me at her statement. "He doesn't." Her voice is firm. "He never did. You're so much better than him or any of his buddies. You're much better than most people in general." She walks to the kitchen. "Now, go back to work, *deton'ka*. This *durak* doesn't deserve your time."

I laugh at her calling me *a little baby* and Justin *a moron*. Phrases I became well acquainted with. She is so Marina. I don't know what I would do without her in my life.

I lock up the diner and walk to my car. A big, about six- and half-foot, surprise of a bear in human form is waiting for me, leaning on the driver's side door of my Jeep.

"What are you doing here, Alex?" I ask, stopping in front of him.

"We need to talk, Kayla." He sighs.

"We really don't." I wait for him to remove his massive body from my door so I can get in. He can be intimidating, but not to me. He never was. I've been scared of Justin at certain points in my life, but never of Alex. He just doesn't have that mean streak that Justin does. That truly evil streak.

"We do. I owe you an apology." That stops me in my tracks, and I look at him curiously. "Yeah." He sighs and wipes his face with his hand. The universal gesture of a frustrated male. "I've been thinking about it."

"About what?" I cock my head to the side.

"About *that*."

"What?" I narrow my eyes. I want him to say it.

He growls. "You know what, Kayla."

"I really don't." I'm having so much fun fucking with him at this point. Alex the Shy Grump is a better version than the old Alex. This one seems... more real.

He growls louder. "*That*." He points at the space between us. "I was quick to judge you. And I'm sorry for that."

I look at him suspiciously. "So, Justin talked to you, then."

"No." He blows out a breath. "I haven't seen him in quite some time. A few days at least." He chews on his lip. "To think of it, I haven't seen him in a week. And he stopped pestering me with this damn trip he's been asking me to go on for so long. Hmm."

That comes as a surprise to me. "So why are you here?"

"Because I've been thinking about what you said." He pushes off my car, his full height looming over me. "I know you. And whoever did that... it's just not you." He looks so sincere, and it warms my heart that he came to this conclusion on his own, without Justin's involvement or knowing the real story. He chose to *believe me*, and that right there means more than anything to me. "And besides that, I kind of owe you." At my questioning look, he explains, "You believed in me when not many people did. I should have returned the honor. Forgive me; I'm an asshole."

Poor Alex, he's referring to the situation with his ex-girlfriend Adison and her allegations against him. The whole town blamed the poor guy for something he A, didn't do, and B, didn't have control over. His situation reminds me of someone else's, hmm—mine.

I feel a burn of tears behind my eyes.

"Oh no. I'm too late, aren't I?" He wipes his hand over his face again. "I'm such an idiot, I'm sorry."

"No, no, no!" I rush to stop his self-punishing. "It's just... it means so much to me that you said that."

His sigh is heavy. "I know I shouldn't have judged you before I talked to you. It's just... not right. And also, there's something else I wanted to talk to you about." Here it goes. I knew it was too good to be true. Alex notices the change in my face and rushes to stop this train wreck in my mind. "Wait. Hold on." He lifts his hand up in a stopping gesture. "What I wanted to say is that, back at the diner, you sounded like you knew what I was talking about, and before that, you always had this look on your face."

"What look?"

"Like... you didn't know what was happening." He takes off his ever-present cap, rakes his hand through his shaggy hair, and puts the cap back on. I can't believe Freya hasn't taken scissors to it yet.

"That's because I *didn't*."

"You didn't know why Justin hated you so much?" He narrows his eyes suspiciously at me.

I grind my teeth. It was one thing to assume he hated me and another to hear it from his best friend's mouth. "Yeah, I didn't know because I didn't do anything wrong." I'm watching him carefully, trying to figure out if he sincerely believes me or is just saying as much.

"Shit." He leans on the car and pulls off his cap. "I thought you knew and played—"

"Dumb?" I suggest helpfully.

"Yeah." His shoulders sag. "That's so fucked up."

"Tell me about it." I snort loudly, sounding like an oinking pig.

"How did you find out the cause then?"

"We had... a talk." For Alex's sake, that's what I'd call my standoff with his best friend. "And Justin told me."

"What happened after *the talk*?" Yeah, I didn't fool him.

"Nothing." I shrug. "We went our separate ways."

"Is it okay if I ask you to share what happened that night?" He treads carefully.

"I have nothing to hide. You know the story about Mark and Ashley, right?"

"Which part?" His eyes dart around, avoiding my gaze.

"That they were fucking behind Justin's back."

He winces. "Yeah, I know. It's not like he was that upset, though. She wasn't exactly what you'd call 'a girlfriend.'"

"What would you call it then?" I raise a brow.

"Fuck buddies, maybe." He shrugs his enormous shoulders.

"Well, his fuck buddy, him, Mark, and I were the only ones who knew about the fight that evening. Mark didn't say anything because he was selling weed at the time—it was the most profitable job for trailer park inhabitants, and he needed the money to take care of his sister. He would have been taken in right after the phone call. He's all his sister had; he would do anything to stay with her. I've never called the cops on anybody in my life, and I'm not planning to break that record anytime soon. Who does that leave?" I look at him pointedly.

"Damn" is all he says for a while. "Why would she call the cops on her boyfriend after he tried to save her from being raped?"

"Boyfriend?" I question him with a smirk.

"Fuck buddy," he corrects himself with a sheepish smile.

"I wonder the same thing," I say, locking my eyes with his.

"Shit." He exhales.

"Shit is right." The moment he figured out what I knew for years already.

"He wasn't raping her." He lets out a short whistle.

"Nope," I say with a pop. "I saw her sitting in the car, smiling. She was enjoying the show. Mark is poor trailer trash like me—"

"Kayla—" Alex tries to interrupt me.

I stop him with a raised hand. "Don't worry, I'm used to it. Maybe Mark was better in the sack, and she didn't want to lose her new *fuck buddy*. But Mark was poor, and Justin is rich from a good family. A better choice for the long run." I shrug my shoulders. "Who really knows, that's just my theory."

"That's why he fucking disappeared. He's probably digesting this fucked-up info." He scratches his head.

"I don't know." Because I don't. I expected a bit of a different outcome after all the revelations, to be completely honest.

"I bet it stings to know you've slept with a snake for so long," he says with a sigh.

I shrug again.

"I heard he stopped by today at the diner." The tone of his voice changes, but I can't figure out what it means.

I whip my head toward him at the speed of light. "How do you know that?" He smirks. "Never mind. Small towns." I shake my head in disgust. "Sometimes, I really hate it here."

"Freya will be really upset," he says quietly.

"What are you talking about?"

"I know you're leaving. I can tell you're fed up with all

of it. And I think she knows it too. You should tell her that yourself at the very least. You owe her that much." When he puts it like that, I feel like shit.

"I know." I hang my head in shame. "I just don't know how. Did you tell her that you stopped by before?"

"Hell no, I like my balls attached to my body." He chuckles. "She'd kill me for the way I talked to you."

His words warm my heart, not the part about a possible orchiectomy, but the other part. Freya's one of those rare people who comes into your life to stay.

"How can I explain everything to her when it's not my story to tell?" I whisper, hating myself that I still think about Justin's comfort. Plus, I respect Alicia's privacy, even if she was a total bitch to me, which is why I still keep it quiet.

He touches my elbow lightly. "It is as much yours as theirs. Justin made sure of that."

I lift my eyes to him. "Thank you, Alex," I whisper. He pulls me into his broad, solid chest and wraps his tree-trunk arms around me. His presence is like a brother's hug that I've never experienced in my life. Strong and reliable. And I can't help myself. I start crying. Heavy sobs convulse through my body while he holds me tight.

When I finally calm down—one or ten minutes later—he says into my hair, "I think you should give this town one last chance."

I sniff loudly into his tear-soaked shirt. "Nmhmh."

"What was that?" He chuckles, and I finally let him go.

"I said I'm done with this town." I wipe my face with the back of my hand. "*So* done."

"You still have people here who care about you," he says earnestly, and just like that, I'm bawling like a toddler again. Heavy tears run down my face.

"C'mon," he says as he pulls me into a hug again. "Stay.

Even just to spite everybody who wants you gone. We'll back you up. You're not *them*, and you've never been." I know he's referring to my messed-up family. "I never saw you for somebody else's mistakes. And a lot of others haven't either."

"You *just* stopped thinking I'm guilty of something I didn't do," I muffle into his chest.

He gently pulls me off him by my shoulders. "Yeah, and I thought it was *your* fault. Not connected to your upbringing. Just something you chose to do, you know." He raises his brows, and I relax. He's sort of right.

"Okay, I get your point." I wipe my nose in a very unladylike manner. "I need to talk to Freya and explain to her why I'm a shitty friend." I dread this conversation. I truly am the worst friend ever.

"You know she loves you, right?" He gently squeezes my shoulder.

"She does?" I ask hopefully, feeling like an unwanted child looking for love—which I am.

"She does. I'm even a little jealous."

I playfully punch him in the chest. "You should be. I'm about to switch teams and go for her if you don't pull your head out of your ass and put a ring on that finger."

"I will. One day. We're not ready for that yet. Neither of us are." His face takes on a dreamy look. I'm just messing with him; I know they aren't ready for that yet, but I'm positive they were made for each other. When I look at them together, I believe in soulmates. They complement each other and make each other better.

"Well, isn't this cozy." A snarky, slightly growly voice inserts itself into our heartwarming, soul-mending conversation. I jump from Alex like we did something wrong.

"Justin," Alex drawls like he feels something terrible is about to come.

"Alex," Justin grits. "I need to talk to Kayla." He shoots me a pointed look. "Alone."

"I don't think that's a good idea," Alex tells him, moving in front of me protectively, hiding me from Justin. I can't figure out why he does it—it's Justin, for crying out loud, his best friend.

"I don't think I asked for your opinion," Justin growls, taking deliberately slow steps toward us.

Whoa, what? What's happening here?

I jump in front of Alex and put my hand on his chest, preventing him from boiling over. Alex has anger problems, and it's not good to poke the bear. Freya would beat us all with a pan if we let Alex go off the rails again, right in the middle of his anger management program and PTSD treatment. He's been doing so well, and I'm not about to have that thrown away over literally nothing. Nothing. Because what the ever-loving hell is happening right now?

Justin's gaze zeros on my palm on Alex's chest, and his nostrils flare.

"What's your problem, Justin?" Alex asks in an overly calm voice even though he looks as if he's about to pounce any second now.

"I need to talk to Kayla. Now." He sounds constipated, if I may say so.

"Why? What is so important that you must tell her now when we're in the middle of a conversation?" I'm about to pinch Alex for aggravating the beast when he tilts his head toward me and winks. I stop in my tracks, my jaw just about hitting the asphalt. Then he looks back at Justin. "You're just gonna regret whatever you're gonna say now."

"And you know *exactly* what she needs now *so well*, huh?" Justin cocks his head.

I'm just standing here, watching the weirdest movie of the year unfolding in front of my eyes. And I don't even say anything. I don't even *want* to say anything to Alex about speaking for me instead of... well, me. It feels nice for somebody to watch over me. God knows nobody has ever done that before.

I could ask Alex why he winked at me, but I think I know the answer: he's just trying to rile Justin up. But why does Justin follow the hook, though? It can't be jealousy.

To my utter surprise, I'm all in for a show. I step behind Alex, my eyes flickering between him and Justin.

Justin sounds... hostile? Why? I've never heard him talk that way to Alex. Even after Alex returned from the service and they were estranged. Alex was always so rude to him, and yet he still took it. Justin never gave up on Alex.

Now I see a Justin I don't recognize, and that's saying a lot considering the level of sheer undeserved hate he threw my way the last couple of years.

Alex steps forward. "I'm having a very important talk with Kayla right now. You'll have to wait. Or better yet, come back tomorrow." If I didn't know any better, I'd say he's about to chuckle.

I imperceptibly pinch Alex's side, and he lets out that chuckle he was holding in. It's gone in an instant.

Justin's nostrils flare, and something dark passes behind his eyes. Something I recognize seeing before, years ago, when he was beating Mark on that abandoned gas station pavement. *Determination.* Alex is obviously just having fun with him, but for some unexplainable reason, Justin is taking it too seriously. "I will leave when I want to," he hisses, his gaze focused on Alex. He throws me one look, just one, but in that second, I can see it in his eyes that he's wounded. Like I did something to hurt or upset him.

"Wanna go at it like old times?" Alex suggests, hope lacing his voice, and I begin to worry. Alex is bigger and more mountainous than Justin—a combination which, in my mind, means an easy win. But while I might think he's more lethal, considering his size and military background, from where I'm standing, the always cheerful and smiley Justin possesses way more danger in an unexpected kind of way. I think I see the real him now. And Alex sees it too. *He'd seen* it already, and I know he knows he's dangerous. All the masks he's been wearing around people are gone, and now, he is what he is, a wild card with a raw intensity. Who won't allow anyone to stand in his way to—

Where exactly to? To me? I'm not worth it, at least not to Justin, and everybody present knows that. Only, it looks as if Alex may have missed the memo because he snakes his hand around my wrist and tugs me deeper behind him. The man is enormous, so I'm entirely hidden behind him.

Now I see what's happening. Well, at least a little bit. Justin's been living with so much guilt on his shoulders that my big revelation probably topped it off completely, and now he doesn't know how to let his pent-up anger and resentment out. I get the feeling that Alex knows how to do it. A good ol' brawl. Of course. I'd seen Justin getting into fights with Mark around town all the time. They are balanced opponents, but I bet he hasn't completely digested the new information that Mark wasn't at fault. There's probably a piece of him in there that knows it wouldn't be right to cause a scene with him after being wrong for so long. Alex seems like an evenly matched opponent. Plus, he's probably looking to relieve some of his own anger.

Oh no, Freya will kill me.

Somebody growls. Loudly. And it's not a wild animal. Well, not a four-legged one, at least. What the hell is happening?

"Alex, get the fuck out of here." Justin's voice drips with danger.

"No." Alex shakes his head. "You wanna have a talk? Have it with me."

"I have nothing to say to you." He cuts him off.

I pop out from behind Alex's back in time to see Justin cocking his head.

"Jus, man." There's a new warmth in Alex's voice. I see Justin's shoulders relax just the tiniest bit. It must have gotten to Justin finally. "It's not gonna make you feel better. I promise. I've been there."

He looks at me, then at Alex, then back at me. "We need to talk, Kayla." Justin's voice is calmer, but there's still an edge to it.

"Okay, we will." It's getting ridiculous. Alex's game of provoking Justin might turn sideways and bite us all in the butt any second.

I move to go to Justin when Alex grabs my wrist, pulling me back once again. I look up to tell him off, but he's watching Justin like a hawk. "Alex," I whisper, trying to get his attention.

When he finally looks at me, he shakes his head lightly, his face grim. "Don't go, Kayla. Not now. That's not what he really needs." Then he adds even quieter, only for my ears. "Let him taste his own medicine."

There's something in his eyes I haven't seen before—concern—and something I've been seeing every single day—stubbornness. I suddenly look back, and there he is, the God of war, stripped of all his weapons but ready for the fight regardless. Justin's nostrils are flared, and although I expect his breathing to be fast and enraged, his chest barely moves.

I involuntarily take a small step back and bump into Alex.

Alex puts his arm around my shoulders, tugging me into him as Justin glares. "Kayla, go to the car and drive to Freya." Alex sighs.

"What? Why?"

"Just go, Kayla. I need to have a talk with Justin. Like old times." His voice is pure steel. He's never used this tone on me, so I make the right decision to make myself scarce.

I'm in my car in three big steps. It's only when I'm inside and put my key in the ignition that I dare to glance at Justin. His eyes follow my every move, and I shudder. His attention is... too *intense*. But he also looks a little crestfallen, as if he's disappointed with me. My mouth goes dry as a wave of guilt rushes over me.

I hesitate before leaving. The look on his face... it's painful. I take a deep breath and drive off, still unsure if I did the right thing.

Chapter Eighteen

JUSTIN

His hand is on her shoulders. So close to her chest. Somewhere even I haven't been. Fuck. I look at his face and imagine how I'll break his perfect nose. Just like he did mine in high school, so we can be even.

"Jus," Alex says calmly just as Kayla disappears in her junk box. "Man, you're a fucking idiot."

I let out a low growl. I need to calm the fuck down—but I'm so close to losing it. We both know what he's been doing; it works every single time. The motherfucker knows just the right buttons to push.

"Why didn't you come to me?" He wipes his face with his hand. "I could have helped you."

"And how would you do that? Erase the last six years from my memory?" I snap.

"No." He clears his throat. "But we could... you know, talk about your feelings and shit."

"About my feelings? You mean the fucking guilt that's eating me alive right now?" I hiss, smacking a fist over my chest.

"No, the guilt that's been eating at you for years." He crosses his arms.

"Yeah, and now it's ten times worse." I spread my arms as wide as I can.

"I know. I mean, wow. It's all fucked up." He whistles. He always does that when he's overwhelmed, and it's annoying as fuck.

"Tell me about that." My anger deflates. A minute ago, I wanted a fight. I was craving it. I was craving physical pain that maybe—just maybe—would replace the emotional one. A broken bone, a split lip—anything would do. And Alex knew it. The fucker wanted to rile me up. He knew what hugging Kayla would do to me. He always knew how much I hated that I had the hots for her, and now all he had to do was to touch her and my possessive side would come out to play. Fuck, why did he have to start talking about *feelings*?

Kayla's been causing a ruckus in my brain since the day I first noticed her. She was eighteen, five years younger than me but looked all twenty. I was a marine back then, in my glory years. I couldn't get involved with someone so much younger than me. Back then, five years seemed like fifteen. So I kept my distance. Even when I noticed her puppy eyes every time she looked at me. All I had to do was walk up to her and smile, and she'd be putty in my hands. But I wasn't that man.

I enjoyed watching her. I saw her change from a spirited girl to a highly opinionated woman who stood her ground. A woman who kept adding art to her body no matter what the town thought of her for doing so. And I loved what I saw. At that point, she was like a light at the end of the tunnel I was never going to reach. I never planned on acting on my obsession with her; I just enjoyed watching one woman being so different and so... *herself*. I didn't even want to get any closer. I didn't want to destroy her.

Until *that* night. That night I stopped admiring her, and the hate began.

Even through the haze of crimson in my eyes, I noticed her. Noticed that she was there. I tend to ignore my surroundings and become a one-task man. It happens with everything I do: working—that's how I got my own auto shop without the help of my dad's money, fighting—I always win, fucking—they always come back for more. But I noticed her and heard her. I still remember what she wore: black ripped jeans and a pink flowy top with open shoulders. Her hair had blue in it, and she had a few less tattoos than she has now.

I noticed her, saw her, and hated her on the spot. She was protecting the other guy. It didn't matter that I nearly beat him to death and that my girlfriend sat in the car after telling me that that asshole deserved it for forcing himself on her. No. None of that mattered. What mattered was that she protected *him*. I hated her for it.

Later that night, my sister was raped, and I hated the whole world. I thought she was the one who called the cops on me, resulting in me not getting to Alicia on time; I had a valid reason to hate her. A very valid one.

Until I didn't have it anymore.

Until I'm left to face the truth. One that I'm simply not ready to face. I can't hate her anymore, which means all that hatred gets redirected to myself. I was the only one to blame. I was. Still am. I'm not ready for that. I'm not prepared for the world as I know it to not only do a one-eighty on me but a three-sixty. All in the same week.

"So, what are you gonna do about it?" Alex rubs the nape of his neck.

"About what exactly?" I ask with a humorless laugh.

"About Kayla. Ashley. Everything, really." He whistles again. "I don't even know where you'd start with that."

"I wish I knew. I want to destroy Ashley's life. I want to so fucking bad. For Alicia and for Kayla. And for all the shit she's done over the years that I closed my eyes to. But fuck, man, someone needs to destroy me for the same thing." My eyes tingle, and I hate that my nonexistent allergies are coming back.

"Yeah, Ashley needs to get what she deserves," Alex agrees instantly.

"It's not like I can go and punch her in the face." I've thought about the many things I know and how I could use them against her, but I don't have an actual plan on how to do so. If she were a man, it would be a different story, but she's not, so the task is much more difficult than I initially thought.

"Maybe you should mention it to Freya; she'd do it in a heartbeat." Alex chuckles.

"Aren't you worried about your girlfriend?" I raise a brow.

"Please," he snorts. "You haven't seen her mad. I'd like to see the poor sucker who dares to go after someone she loves."

I chuckle, imagining Freya punching anyone. Kayla, on the other hand... A tiny Valkyrie on a war path—that I can picture vividly. Fuck, what do I do with Kayla now?

"And what about Kayla?" he asks after a pause, reading my mind.

I groan, hanging my head low. "I wish I fucking knew. I don't know what I want to do with her."

"I do," he announces with a smile.

"Please, share with the class, asshole." I wave for him to continue.

"Well," he swaggers toward me, "I'd start by explaining the maniacal intensity you had there when we were talking. How about that, huh?"

"I have no idea what you're talking about," I deadpan.

"Of course," he says with an eye roll. "You don't have a clue why you wanted to take my head off just a moment ago? Right. Everything was super cool. Super chill." His hands are on his hips, and he reminds me of a housewife chewing out her husband for coming home late. "You're gonna destroy her. You know how you are with women, and she's Freya's friend. She's my friend." He shakes his head. "You'll get her out of your system with a fuck, but where will it leave *her*?"

"I'm not planning on doing anything with her." My hackles rise. "It was a moment of weakness, that's all." I wave at him and force a smile on my face.

He slowly walks as if trying to cage a wild animal. "Dude, I always suspected that you had the hots for her, but not at that level. You were ready to kill me, and for what? For comforting her when everyone's been shitting on her?"

I feel a wave of shame shooting up my neck at his words, but I look him deep in the eyes anyway, hoping he'll understand the gravity of my words. "I won't hurt her."

"Do you want me to remind you?" He raises an eyebrow. "All you've done is hurt her."

"I haven't felt... that... yet for anybody. You know I've been a little... obsessed with her. I mean, I know it's not really healthy, but I can't change the way I feel." I lift a shoulder.

His sigh is audible and heavy. "Fuck. What are you gonna do?"

I glance in the direction Kayla disappeared. "See how I can fix this major fuck up."

"This?" He points his finger between us.

"No." It's my turn to sigh. "The years that I treated her like shit."

"Good luck with that." His chuckle is dark, and I feel like he might know more than I do. In fact, I'm sure he does. Kayla spends a lot of time with Freya. Alex must know some extra info, and he better share it with me. "But seriously though," he grabs the front of my shirt into his fist, "don't fuck it up more than you already have. You hurt her, and we repeat those bleachers. Are we clear on that?" He pulls me closer.

The bleachers. Where he punched me for talking shit to our new teacher at school. She was so young. Fresh out of college and thrown into the snake pit that was our high school. I didn't make her life easy, and at one point, Alex had had enough.

And there's nothing more I want right now than to punch him in the face, but I also respect him at the same time; he's trying to protect her because God knows, nobody else does. I sure as fuck never did; I just kept adding to her misery. She doesn't have it easy. Just look at her living condition, for fuck's sake. She lives in a trailer. One might think that when she got on her feet, she would have gotten herself a decent place. Sure, it looks super clean, and I might even say cozy, but it's still a trailer. During winter in Maine, at the bottom of the mountain where she lives alone.

Fuck, I need to check if anything needs maintaining in

there. Did her heating even work the past winter? It was cold. I had to unfreeze my car lock almost every single morning because it constantly got stuck.

Where does she get her water from? She's tiny. How does she manage to get the tank up? Does somebody come to help her? It must be somebody big to get that shit up there. Fuck! Who helps her? Is it Mark? Because that dude's been sniffing around her for a few weeks, I've noticed. And that strange feeling I had while I was there? Like someone was watching me. Was it someone who lives nearby and is *close* to her?

"Damn, man. That look." Alex begins laughing like a maniac. "You got it *bad*. I'm not even sure who I should be scared more for, Kayla or *you*." He's laughing so hard he has to bend over, resting his hands on his knees. When he's finally done, he wipes the tears from his eyes and speaks. "For real, though, don't mess it up."

"Why are you so concerned all of a sudden?" I fold my arms and narrow my eyes at him.

"I look out for you. Both of you. You did the same for me... us...." He's referring to when I warned him about messing with Freya. But I didn't do anything special, just simply told him to pull his head out of his ass when it kept getting stuck every time Freya was around. "I'm just returning the favor."

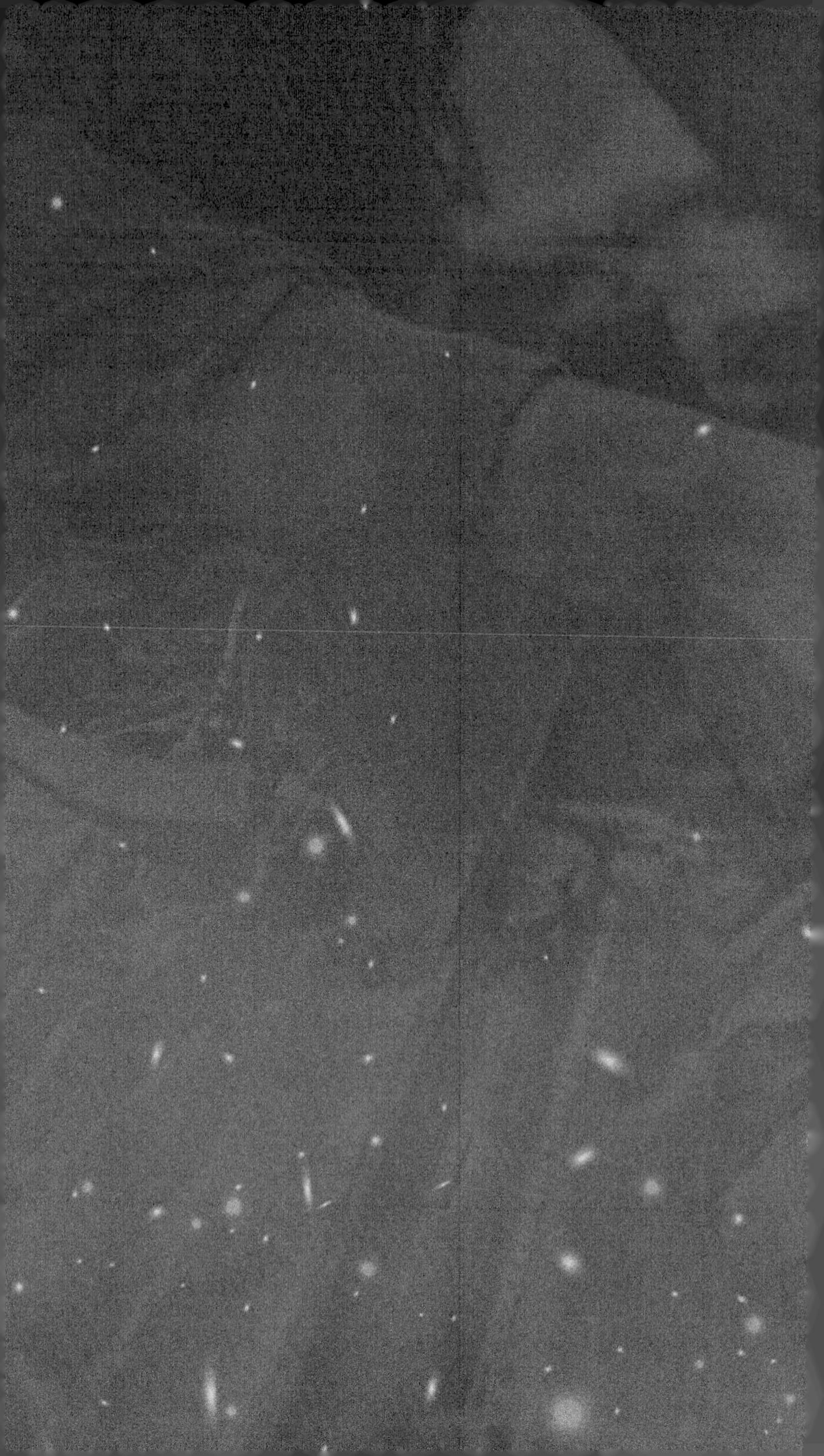

Chapter Nineteen

KAYLA

I park in front of Alex's house but don't leave my car. I don't want to. I need to figure out what happened back at the diner.

I'm mulling over every single thing I said, he said, Alex said, I did, they did, how they moved their hands, where Justin was looking when I waved my pinky on my left hand... driving myself crazy with overanalyzing every single detail.

A gentle knock on the driver's side window makes me jump, accidentally pressing down on the horn. Nice, now everyone knows I'm here, and by everyone, I mean Freya and her bears.

Freya's warm smile sets me at ease, and I roll down the window.

She shivers and pulls a fluffy throw over her shoulders.

"Wanna come in?" She nods toward the house with an understanding smile. "I made some tea."

"Yeah," I say quietly and finally exit the car. She pulls me under the throw and kisses my cheek—I must really look miserable because we don't usually partake in this girly stuff; we're tough chicks, that's it.

The couch is done up with a few extra pillows and a comforter. Freya notices my gaze and says, "Alex called and told me you might be up for a girls' night in. Or out if you prefer." She raises a brow. "He's having boys' night." My head whips toward her, and she laughs. "Don't worry, he and Justin really need some bro time; it was long overdue." She waves at the couch. "I was hoping you'd be sleeping in the bed, but just in case, I got the couch ready here."

"I'll take the couch," I say with a cringe, causing Freya to laugh. God knows what they've done on that bed. That one time I accidentally saw what they do on that counter... *shiver*... I still have nightmares. I see Alex as a brother, and that Pornhub live video traumatized the hell out of me.

"Fair enough." She keeps laughing.

I follow her to the kitchen and look around. "When are you guys going to expand? You need more space now. And I need more untouched countertops."

She prepares the tea, leaving for a moment to get cookies from the pantry. *Now, we're talking.*

"I made meatloaf. Want some?" My face must be a mask of pure horror because she throws her hands up with a loud cry. "It was one time!"

"Frey, I couldn't figure out which end needed to use the toilet for three days. Can I just have some tea?" I fake-smile with all my teeth.

"You're all sissies! Alex is still scared to eat anything but lasagna! That jerk!" she says in righteous anger. I decide to take the smart approach and wait it out, trying my hardest to hide my smile. "Yeah, go ahead, laugh at my expense." She's barely keeping herself from bursting with laughter now, but I give up first, and she follows. "Okay, that was pretty bad, I agree." She shudders, remembering. "Brr." She then returns to fixing her perfectly lined cookies on the plate. "So..."

"So?" I parrot.

"C'mon! I need details!" She throws her arms out.

"Alex didn't tell you?"

"Nope." She pops the *p*. "He said it's up to you to tell." I just love Alex some more.

"Okay, then." And I tell her everything. I mean *everything*. About that night, about all Justin's visits. About my feelings toward him and about the events of the past hour.

When I'm done, I drink the whole mug of tea in one big gulp and pour myself another. Anything to make myself busy, prolonging the silence before Freya launches into her judgment. I'm sure she will.

But she's focused on the wall behind me without blinking. I glance over my shoulder to see if there's a bear there. Why else would she be staring so hard? We all know Freya and her relationship with bears.

Finally, she speaks. "Poor, poor girl," she says as she stares behind me. The silence continues, and I begin to worry. She blinks and moves her attention to me. "It makes so much sense now."

"You need to be a little more specific than that." I'm dreading what she has to say next.

"Justin" is all she responds with.

"Again, more specific, please."

"His jokester personality," she explains, not helpfully.

I raise my brows, still not getting it.

"He adopted this carefree, funny personality and hides behind it."

"What does he hide?" I'm genuinely confused.

"Guilt, Kayla. He's hiding the fact that it's his fault." Her face is full of sadness. For Justin and for Alicia.

I jump from my stool, nearly spilling the tea from the mug. "It's not his fault, Freya. It's some monster's fault. Not his."

"Sit down, Kayla." I clench my jaw at her order. "Sit down, Kayla. Please. That's not what I meant. Trust me, I don't blame him, but I'm sure he does."

"He does." I pop back on the stool, and my shoulders sag with compassion.

"His insomnia. Man, it makes so much sense now." Freya smacks her forehead. What's up with people smacking their foreheads? It's painful.

"You think that night caused his insomnia?" I begin chewing on the inside of my cheek.

"Probably." Freya chews on her lips. "Trauma causes a lot of crap. So does guilt. I mean, look at Alex and me. One can't forget, and the other can't remember."

"Yeah, you found each other." I chuckle.

"That we did." Her eyes become dreamy every time Alex's name is mentioned. I'm so happy for them. If I hadn't met them, I'd never believe in love like that. One might say it's just passion and will fade away, but I don't think so. I never had a normal family where both parents loved each other. I never had that as a good example of how it should be, but now I see it, and I want that. Only that.

"I'm sorry you got sucked into all that. And I'm really, really sorry for Alicia. I've never even met her, you know." She lifts her shoulder. "Always wanted to, I keep inviting her over through Justin, but she's never showed up. Do you think he passed on the invitation?"

"I don't know, considering her story." I shrug. "He's probably protecting her."

"From me?" Freya looks taken aback, and I hurry to explain.

"From everything."

"Do you think she's hiding?"

"She might. I mean, she went through hell. She was always a part of a popular crowd, with beautiful hair and tight, beautiful clothes. They all wear such tight clothes! To think of it," I stop for a second, "I haven't seen her wearing any tight clothes for a long time. Or anything even a little revealing. Huh. She's always dressed in a huge sweatsuit."

"She changed her wardrobe to be invisible." Freya pours herself another cup. "That's how she's coping."

"Yeah," I murmur under my nose.

"I can't believe they tormented you for so many years for something you didn't do." She furiously shakes her head. "And every time you asked, they shut you down."

"Because they thought I knew."

"Don't defend them here. I understand where they were coming from, I do, but Jake is an asshole for using his position like that, and Justin... I don't have the words for him right now. All this could have been avoided if he just had talked to you."

"Tell me about it." I down the rest of my tea and push my cup to her for more.

"Why are you sad? I have a strong suspicion that your pumpkin is about to turn into a carriage. I'm confused why you can't sense it in the air." I don't even want to guess what she means by 'pumpkin' here, but I have a few guesses.

"Not for this Cinderella, no."

"What?" She laughs. "You've had a crush on him since forever."

"I know! But he's toxic. We are toxic. Every time we're in the same space, I want to take a shower after because that's how dirty I feel."

Her expression sobers up. "If you feel that way, then yeah, he's bad for you. I just—" She chews on the inside corner of her lips—the classic tell that she's nervous. "It's just that I picked up on a different feeling from you when you're around him."

I sigh—she has a point there. My chemistry with Justin is off the charts, but that doesn't mean we're good for each other. Toxic is what I've been running away from all my life. I don't want toxic. I don't want to be dragged into something that can make me vulnerable. I don't want to depend on or belong to anyone because nothing is forever. Eventually, Justin will want something fresh and exciting. Where will that leave me?

Nah, this new revelation won't swing my decision; I'm done with pining after Justin Attleborough. It's time to move on. Even with recent events, even with this big revelation and him telling me I'm stuck in his head. *No, move on, girl.*

"I can't just close my eyes to all the shit he's said to me. And I can't close my eyes to the fact that he's related to Jake, my biggest bully. I understand now why they thought I deserved it, I do, but that doesn't change the fact that in their eyes, I'm trailer trash from the wrong side of town. And I will always be that: trash to them. With no education or money."

"It's not like Justin finished college either. He enlisted with Alex, remember? And he never went back."

"True. But he came back and built a business from the

ground up even after spending three years in jail, and he's doing fine. Where I'm still struggling with payments for my phone plan."

"First, you're five years younger than him. Second, stop comparing yourself like that. The local hillbillies talked down to you too much; I think I need to have a conversation with a few of them." Her lips are pressed tight, closely resembling a cat's butt. I know it's a serious moment, but I'm about to laugh. "What? You disagree? So what that you were born poor. It's not a sin!"

"You know I'm called a 'whore' too?" I ask, rubbing my temples.

"Yeah, so what? Fuck them." She bumps her fist in the air. It's so cute. "Let's see what Justin thinks about you."

"That's exactly what Justin thinks about me." I raise a brow, silently reminding her about the things he'd said to me.

"No, that's what he was *saying*, but I don't think that's what he was *thinking*." Her eyes widen with meaning.

"I think you're mistaken." I try to mimic her face.

"I think I am not. How do you think your car is driving, huh?" Her lips spread into a mischievous smile.

"What?" I'm a little perplexed by her random question.

"Your car. Does it start from the first try?" She points a finger at me.

I think for a second, and her questions seem even weirder now. "Actually, yes. It starts faster."

"And what about your brakes?" Her smile spreads wider, and I'm worried her face may break in two.

"What about them?" I ask, confused.

"Do they make that god-awful sound every time you push the pedal?" She quirks a brow.

"Hmm, no. What are you trying to say, Frey?" I cross my arms over my chest.

"That one day I was at the diner, I saw Justin outside messing with your car." She's smiling like the Cheshire cat.

"Messing?"

"I think he was fixing it!" She looks like a cat who just swallowed a ton of canaries.

"What?" I exclaim as I gesticulate too widely with my hands and send a cup flying on the floor, shattering. "Oh shit."

"Yeah, that's Alex's favorite tea set." She looks at the debris on the floor.

"*Oh shit!*" I jump from the chair and begin collecting the pieces.

"Forget about that." Freya waves me off as she stands to grab a broom. "I always hated it; it looks like it belongs in a museum. I want something a little more up-to-date. Mismatched. You know?"

I know. She means 'cozy.'

While sweeping up the tiny pieces I didn't catch, she says, "Justin was checking something under your car, or behind the wheels or whatever. I'm positive he fixed your car. The whole town noticed your car stopped screeching."

"It wasn't that bad," I say in defense of my ol' boy.

"Oh, it was bad." She laughs, and I know she's right. The sound was horrible, and now it's gone. How didn't I notice that? And Justin? Fixed my car? Why would he do that?

"I think I'll be moving soon," I shoot out without any foreplay.

Her face changes in an instant, and her eyes swell with tears. She furiously tries to blink them back, but they just keep running. I move around the counter, bringing my arms around her to hug her as tight as I can.

"I need to. There is no happy life waiting for me in Little Hope." She starts crying even harder. "What? Why are you crying?"

She pulls away, wiping the tears with the back of her hand. "It's just so sad that just when I found my home here, you're losing it. And I'm losing you."

"Stop that!" I'm about to cry myself, but I refuse to. I hate crying in front of people. Even Freya. "We live in the twenty-first century, hello. Phones and FaceTime do exist, you know, grandma." I gently poke her shoulder, and she finally smiles.

"That's true. Still, it's not the same." She wipes her nose with her hand in a very unladylike fashion, and I barely keep from bursting with laughter.

"I'm not going far." And then I tell her the story about Archie and his offer. By the end of this conversation, Freya's gaping at me with wide eyes.

"What?" I ask.

"Why the hell are you still here? I'd be grabbing this opportunity with both hands! Archie's a good guy; he won't leave you high and dry if that's what you're worried about." She punches my shoulder, leaving a mild sting.

"That's not it."

"Oh ma-a-an." Disapproval is evident on her face. "You didn't want to go because of him, didn't you?" I don't answer because, clearly, it was a rhetorical question that we both know the answer to. "Don't get me wrong, I want you guys to be together, and that's where this story is clearly going, but not at the expense of your dream, Kayla. I did that already, and it was the worst thing I could have done to myself." She's referring to the time she left her nursing position at a big hospital when her ex-husband wanted her to become a Stepford wife.

"I understand... You're right—"

"But it's easier said than done." She finishes with a sad smile. "I know, Kay. Trust me, I know. And even though I'd hate for you to move from Little Hope, I think it will be good for you." She sniffles loudly and wipes her nose again, leaving it red and swollen.

"Thank you," I say quietly.

"What will you be doing about Caroline?"

Freya is one of the very few people who know about her and the money I've been sending to her.

"The same." I shrug. "Keep the paychecks steady. She can find me anywhere. Besides that, I can't take the money from Maddie."

"I still think this whole thing sounds shady." Her forehead wrinkles with concern. She's been giving me grief about sending money to them, but there isn't much I can do about it.

"You think?" My chuckle is dark.

She throws a cookie at me, and I'm surprised I catch it. "Smartass."

The topic of Caroline is always a mood downer for me, and Freya catches on quickly. We move to the living room with a large bowl of popcorn and *Magic Mike* on the big screen Alex proudly displays over the fireplace. What a man.

The rest of the evening goes just how I need it to—the healing company of a good friend.

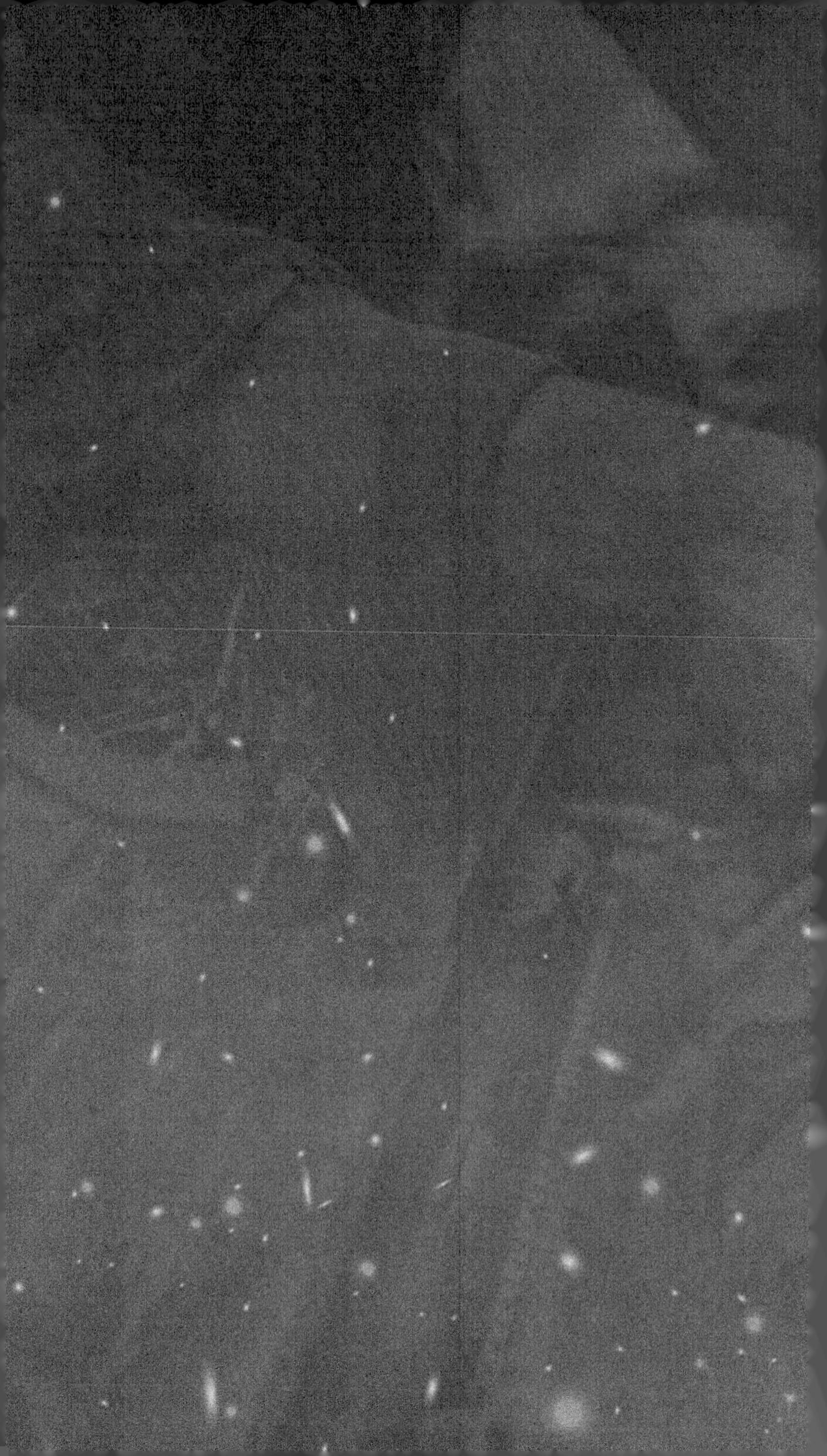

Chapter Twenty

K AYLA

The next day comes and goes way too fast. I'm currently busy cleaning this damn coffee machine. Again. It doesn't make a good espresso anymore, and I religiously descale it every week. I did everything. I YouTubed instructions on how to fix it and nothing; the machine still doesn't yield enough espresso.

I wipe the sweat from my temple.

The last video I watched recommended I open the machine's frame and clean it manually. I produce a screwdriver from the pantry (because, yes, I stocked up on more useful tools just in case—even though Freya promised that she only had *one* evil ex). I unscrew the cover from the machine that somehow stopped working after only a couple months of use and put it aside.

I sent Marina home an hour ago. She'll be here earlier than roosters wake up and will be exhausted by the time we need to close the diner. I'm alone (with a locked door, mind you, because this woman has learned her lesson), so I can blast my rock music as loud as I want. There are no residential units in this building, and all the businesses are closed at this hour.

Humming "nothing else matters" along with James Hetfield, I proceed to take apart the inside of this bougie coffee. YouTube suggested I remove the brewing system and clean it thoroughly under the water. So, I do as instructed: I remove the system and carefully move it to the sink when a knock on the door startles me, and I drop the system on the floor.

"Fuck!" I yelp. Marina will kill me! The next knock sounds louder, and I finally look up.

Justin's standing behind the door, watching me with a small smile on his face. When I see him, I expect my heart to start pounding as it usually does, but it doesn't. In fact, it's calm. I'm calm. Turns out, an evening with Freya to talk through my problems put my mind in the right place. I lift the system up and check if it's broken—it's not, thank God—and go to the door.

I open it but don't move to let him in. I wait to see what will happen.

"Need some help?" His tone is hesitant.

I look back at the sink where the system might be living its last day, which may also be my last day if it's broken, and Marina kills me. I nod and step aside. He comes in, bringing a scent of masculinity with him, and I try not to breathe so his crazy-ass pheromones won't drive me insane.

"Sorry, I didn't mean to startle you." His smile is sheepish. He is *never* sheepish with me.

I shrug, not trusting my voice. I'm not as affected by him as I was before, but I'm also not unaffected. His brows knit together but then relax just as fast. Justin walks to the sink and lifts the brewing system into his hands. "Stopped brewing enough?"

I nod. He must have expected my silent treatment because he looks at me when I respond. He takes a screwdriver from the table and unscrews the mechanism more. It's not like I know how to fix it, and he looks like somebody who knows his way around tools. I sit back and just watch his large hands move the mechanism around. A few minutes later, he puts it all together, rinses it, and installs it back into the machine. He then continues to professionally grind the beans, starting the machine. He gets the perfect amount of liquid with the most beautiful-looking crema I've ever seen. Right, I forgot that Justin's a coffee snob.

He lifts the cup to his nose and takes a deep breath before taking a sip. He licks his lips, and my eyes are glued to his throat while he takes a lazy gulp. The corner of his lip quirks up, and I know I've been caught. I look up and see a twinkle in his eyes. He stretches his arm out and offers me the rest of the coffee. The only thing I manage to do is to shake my hands and swallow the massive lump in my own throat, causing Justin to smile wider.

I cough nervously and murmur a barely audible "Thanks" before walking to the kitchen.

He follows me. "Do you need help with anything else?"

I stop suddenly and turn to him with my hands on my hips. "What are you doing here, Justin?"

"Trying to see how I can help." He looks around, but all the work is done. The diner is in perfect condition after our renovation. Besides the coffee machine, of course. But now, even that problem is fixed.

"We're good." I cross my arms over my chest. "What are you doing here, Justin? And don't bullshit me with your 'help' story."

His eyes narrow, and he takes a step toward me. There's still about six feet between us. He takes another, and I don't back down. "You looked cozy with Alex yesterday."

"Is that why you're here? To tell me to stay away from him?" My nostrils flare.

"Yes." He's curt.

"You want to take away one of my very few friends? Why? You're scared I'll do something with him? Seeing that I'm the town hoe and all that."

His nostrils flare, and he takes another small step forward. "Don't say that about yourself."

I laugh. Loudly, very loudly. "So *you* can say that about me, and I can't?" I laugh even louder. "You're delusional. Even if I was the town hoe, I'd never do anything to hurt Freya."

"Stop." His voice is louder. "I told you not to say that."

"And who are you to tell me what to do, huh? You were the one talking shit about me with your little brother all around town. What's changed?" The switch on my temper flips on.

"You know what." His voice is lower.

"I don't. Not really. I've been asking you about your hate for me for so long. And all you kept saying was 'you know, you know yourself, keep your mouth shut and blah blah blah,' like a goddamn parrot. But now, out of nowhere, you think we can do a one-eighty? Just like that?" I snap my fingers, getting more and more mad with every word. "You think now that you know the truth, everything will be normal? Newsflash: it won't be."

"Kayla," he growls.

"No. You don't get to say my name. Go back to calling me whatever else you called me, but not Kayla. No. That name is not for you. *Trailer trash* is for you. *She* is for you. *A little thing* is for you. But Kayla is not." My hands are balled into tight fists, itching to scratch them on his perfect face.

"Kayla!" His voice booms through the empty room. My eyes snap to his, and he growls. "Shut up."

"You shut up yourself. You can't tell me what to do!" I'm nearly yelling.

He moves so quickly all I see is a blur. He's in front of me, backing me up using the sheer mass of his body. I don't have a choice but to obey. Once my butt presses into the to-go order table, he stops.

"Oh, I can tell you what to do. And you will do as I say." He lowers his voice even more, making it more seductive. I'm sure it's the one he's used to using with his conquests, but as we've established, I choose a higher ground. Justin's face is right in front of me. I decide to play a little game of my own.

I move a bit so my mouth is right next to his ear and whisper, blowing air onto his earlobe, "Are you so sure about that?"

His whole massive frame shudders as he grips the edge of the table on either side of me. His body radiates heat, and I can feel it even when not an inch of his skin touches mine. It radiates off him like from a fire. "Yeah. I'm sure. And we start with," he inhales deeply, "you stop using those names for yourself."

"Why? Why should I when everyone else uses them?" I try to sound confident, but his proximity places my hormones firmly into overdrive. I can barely keep up the argument.

"Because no one ever will again." What he lacks in

decency, he makes up for in confidence. The swagger pours off him.

"You can't promise that." I laugh at his face.

"Oh, but I can. Watch me." His mouth is next to my ear, his voice barely a whisper.

I lick my suddenly dry lips and whisper back, "Why would you do that?"

He pulls back a few inches and stares into my eyes. "You know why." His voice is close to a growl. Not an angry growl, like with Alex, but a sexy growl. One that makes you shiver, goosebumps running up and down your body. The good kind of growl.

"I don't," I whisper and lick my dry lips again. He's staring at them, and I know it means he wants to kiss me. I don't want to kiss him ever again. I don't. Nope, not at all.

"You don't?" he asks. Bringing his lips to the soft place under my ear. His lips barely graze my skin, but it's enough to send my blood running south. I thought that phrase could only be used for guys, but right now, I feel that's not entirely true. All the blood has left my brain, heading downstairs to spawn a million butterflies. It makes me feel lightheaded.

"I don't. A few days ago, you hated me, and now you're all up in my space making promises you can't keep." I remind him about his recent vendetta against me that lasted for six years.

"I still do," he answers, grazing the shell of my ear with his mouth.

"What?" I think I'm mistaken through my haze of desire, but he continues.

"I still hate you," he whispers while keeping his lips strategically placed.

"What?" I rear back, staring into his eyes.

"Oh yeah, I still hate you. Because after you told me the truth, I had to come to terms with the fact that I'm the one to blame, and blaming *you* was always easier." He brings his face closer to mine and hisses, "And even when I hated you, I wanted you. And I hated you for that. And I still want you. And still hate you." He presses his front into mine, and I can feel his hardness against me. His whole body pushing into mine. All his power trying to get inside of my pores.

"Wanted me?" I parrot. It seems like all my intelligence checked out the moment Justin began spurting nonsense, and that was the only thing I caught out of all the ugly words.

He brings his index finger under my chin and gently tilts my head up. "Yeah. Wanted to fuck you till you can't walk anymore. To rip those fucking leather pants you like so much off your little round ass to see how wet you can get from just my touch. I bet you get really wet, right? You're a naughty girl, aren't you?"

My blood most definitely left my brain because I'm lightheaded and can barely think. The only thing I can do is imagine where he would touch me and where I want him to touch. Justin has very big and very capable hands. I bet his touch would feel so *good*. I squeeze my thighs together in an attempt to ease the heat between them; otherwise, I'll be begging for his help. And I won't.

"Are you wet now, Kayla?" He says my name on an exhale, and I get tingles from the tone he's using; he's switching from friendly to commanding, and I don't know why I like it so much, but I do. My breathing speeds up, and I arch my back just a little, just so my boobs can graze his chest and scratch the itch. "Oh, I bet you are. Shall we find out?"

His right hand comes behind my neck, gently massaging my sore muscles. He keeps his face a few inches away from mine, watching my face relax as his capable fingers do their magic. Once my shoulders drop, he moves his hand to my front. He follows one side of my collarbone with his index finger before turning his attention to the other. He's a large man everywhere. His palm is enormous too. It's splayed over the top of my chest, and while tracing my collarbone with his index finger, he's grazing his pinky over the top of my breast, spreading his palm wider and wider, his fingers moving lower and lower.

With a quick swipe, he grazes my nipple. They're so hard they could cut glass, I swear. And then he grazes it again. All while watching my face. My eyes are trained on his, but they're half-closed. I can barely keep them open. I'm not used to such intimacy, and every deliberate touch sends my body into overstimulated shock.

His hand comes higher, enveloping the base of my throat in his grip. He doesn't squeeze, but firmly keeps it there. His hand on my throat is enough to keep me under his total control. I never knew I liked to be dominated, but it turns out I do.

"How wet are you now, Kayla?" he asks hoarsely.

"I'm not," I croak.

"Liar." He chuckles and brings his lips closer to mine. So close, but not touching. Just hovering above. Just a hair out of reach.

He moves his hands between my breasts and trails them down to my belly, where he rests. "What will I find if I keep looking further?"

"Nothing." I'm totally lying.

He smiles wide, moving his hands lower and lifting the hem of my skirt up. His fingers hover just above the waistline of my panties. I mentally curse myself for wearing my very unsexy black boy shorts. They're my safe pick I wear in case the wind decides to blow up my ass so I don't flash my bare butt cheeks to the entire town.

His middle finger pulls on the waistband, sneaking inside, and I inhale quickly. Despite regretting my choice of underwear, I'm so happy that I randomly decided to shave this morning.

"Bare? All the way?" he asks into my lips, but again, without touching them.

I don't think he needs my answer because it's clearly a one-actor show. I let myself enjoy it and see where it goes.

His finger dips even lower, very close to its target—*my target*—but still out of reach. So close. *Just move a little lower. Please.*

And he finally does. His middle finger lands on my clit, and I shudder from the feeling of somebody else touching it besides me. His finger feels different from mine, larger and rougher, and I like it. I let out a fast exhale, and he *catches* the air with his lips. How do I know? His lips land on mine with a loud growl. His other hand comes behind my lower back and pulls me into him while his middle finger presses harder and then lets go. Harder... and lets go. It's pure torture, and I whimper. He takes it as an invitation and nudges my lips with his tongue, and I don't fight him on it.

The second the tip of his tongue gently touches mine, tasting and probing, the wetness pools between my legs, and I buck into his hand. Justin growls louder and moves his finger further. He bites my lip over my ring and pulls on it. "Bad, bad girl," he says, stopping the kiss for a moment.

He rests his forehead against mine, his finger dipping in and out. Hearing my soft moans, he adds his thumb on my clit, and I begin panting. He catches every single one of my exhales with fast kisses on my lips.

He speeds up the tempo, and I open my mouth to try to catch his lips, needing something—what he's giving isn't enough anymore. I grab his shoulders and pull him closer. His hard muscles under my grip are not enough. His enormous fingers on me are not enough. Maybe it's because he's not going deep, just here, just close to the surface, teasing. Playing. Driving me absolutely insane.

"Justin," I whimper.

"Yes, baby. What do you want?"

"Justin!" I beg.

"Yes, baby, I'll give it to you once you tell me what you want. What do you want?" His voice is collected. Too collected for such a sensual situation.

"I want to—" I'm panting.

He slows down and smiles into my lips. "Yeah? What is it, baby? What do you want?" His voice turns raspy.

"I want—" It's hard to say it out loud. I've never said it before.

"Yes?" He nudges me, nipping on my lower lip. "Tell me."

I rake my hand into his hair and pull him even closer, if that's possible, biting his lips harder than he did mine. "I want to come. I want to come, Justin." Then I lower myself to begging. "Please."

He smiles and kisses me. Slowly. Too slowly. Then, he grabs me by my waist and pulls me up on the table. My ass touches the cold metal surface and cools down my overheated flesh.

He kisses me again, deep, devouring my mouth with his, interweaving his tongue with mine. I wrap my legs around his waist. The contrast of my heated skin against the rough material of his jeans highlights every feeling I feel. I shamelessly squeeze my thighs and pull him into me with all my might, ready to hump his legs if need be—I'm close, and I'm in need; I don't care if I act like a hussy, proving the town right. I'll agree to anything as long as I can reach my high.

He must agree with me because he pushes his pelvis into mine, while at the same time pulling me into him, squeezing my ass hard. But then he suddenly pulls his warmth away, unwrapping my legs from his back. I feel like I've just been thrown under a cold shower. He notices my distress because he gives me his signature lopsided grin before he drops to his knees in front of me.

"What—"

His smile grows wider as he hooks his finger under my panties and pulls them off. "I like that your underwear makes my imagination work," he tells me. My naked pussy touches the metal surface, and I gasp at the contact. Marina is going to kill me if she ever finds out that I wiped this table with my genitalia… Even though we don't put food here, and even though it's always been a part of my fantasy, I wouldn't want Marina to do the same, because ew.

And that's the last coherent thought I have before he grabs me under my thighs and pulls me toward him. My ass is half-hanging from the table while he firmly holds me. Before I know it, his mouth is on my hot, swollen flesh, and my head rolls backward. He licks my lips down there—up and down, up and down, before he moves his mouth to my clit. It's engorged and angry. Demanding attention. The center of my ache.

His finger dips inside me and hooks to reach some magical spot I never dared to touch myself. His thrusts are shallow, but it's enough to send me into overdrive.

His tongue circles my clit and then sucks on it. Hard.

"Oh fuck," I curse loudly.

"And she speaks." I can hear the smile in his voice as he interrupts his assault for a second. I grab him by his hair and pull his head back into me.

"Shut up." It's my turn to growl.

His laughter is muted by me pressing his face into my core. He understands the assignment and goes to work, licking, sucking, and even nibbling.

"Oh fuck, Justin." My eyes roll back as the first wave of orgasm hits me. My ass rears back, and his grip on my quivering thighs becomes stronger as he pulls me back onto his mouth. My hands roam around the table, trying to find the edge so I can hold on to something while Justin's mouth assaults my pussy.

The second wave hits even harder, and I whimper. Loudly and shamelessly. Something I thought I wouldn't be able to do, but in this moment, when his mouth is doing such wonderful things to my bundle of nerves, I don't care. I don't care how I look or how I sound. Now, in this moment, I am free.

When the wave passes and I slowly descend from the high, I dare to look at Justin. His intense eyes are trained on my face as he keeps sucking, holding me in his firm grip. Once I've fully come down, I pull away. My oversensitive flesh can't take anymore. The lower part of his face is wet, his cheeks are red, and his lips are swollen.

He stands up from his kneeling position, licking the moisture off his swollen lips, and the muscles in my lower belly contract once again. His eyes are feverish. A huge bulge tents his jeans. He's trying to adjust himself but winces as if in pain. His breathing is labored.

"I... hmm... Do you need help with that?" I point at the *big* situation below his belt.

"I'd love the help, baby. But not now." He puts his hand inside his jeans and puts his dick into the right position, which is apparently straight up. I know because I'm watching like a hawk, and I swear I can almost smell his musk. Watching somebody moving their cock and catching a whiff of his scent would typically send me to the toilet to throw up. But not now, no. The opposite. My pussy clenches again, and I swallow a dry lump in my throat. A loud groan draws my attention. "Don't do that anymore, or you'll end up with your feet on my shoulders and my dick deep inside you."

My mouth hangs open; he steps closer and gives me a quick lick on my lips. My tongue darts out, tasting myself. It's not as gross as I thought. It's arousing.

I touch my lips with my fingers, still not believing what just happened. Justin Attleborough went down on me in the kitchen of the diner. While he was on his knees with his face buried between my legs. What in the ever-loving hell is happening?

While I doubt my sanity, he bends down, picks up my discarded soaked panties from the floor, and shoves them into the front pocket of his jeans.

"What are you doing?" I ask.

"Taking a souvenir," he answers with a wide smile. "For future use."

"That's gross!" I scrunch my nose.

"It's so not." He shoves his hands into his back pockets. "I meant what I said, Kayla."

"What exactly? You spurted a lot of nonsense. What exactly did you mean?" I jump down from the table and fix my skirt.

"That I still hate you, and that doesn't change anything." His words and actions are two completely different stories. This guy can write a handbook on how to be hot and cold.

My back snaps straight. "What?"

"My feelings toward you haven't changed, there's too much history with us, and there's nothing we can do about it. But we can fuck it out of our systems. We have so much fucking chemistry we can burn a building down when we are together." He adjusts his dick inside of his pants again. The little dude is clearly as confused as I am.

"What the hell?" I feel my brows furrow on their own accord.

"Yeah, a lot of chemistry." He nods like I'm an idiot.

"That's not what I meant, asshole!" I yell at him. "Do you think you're the one who's been wronged? Fuck you, Justin! You and your brother treated me like shit for years! I've been bullied by half the town for the majority of my life just because I was born poor, and here you are, coming back from jail and adding to my misery. Do you think I don't have enough to deal with already? Newsflash: I do." I walk to the sink just so I can wash my hands. They suddenly feel dirty.

"Kayla, that's... this situation between us can't be happening like that. We're going to be around Alex and Freya, and we need to keep our cool." His breathing slowly changes to normal while mine's picking up speed.

"Oh, you think?" I turn to look at him while scrubbing my hands raw.

"Yeah." He doesn't get my sarcasm, and if he does, he doesn't let on. "This tension needs to go. We just need to fuck it out."

"The only thing you will be fucking out is my foot from your ass if you don't disappear right now," I hiss, adjusting my clothes.

"Kayla, be reasonable." He tries to calm me down. The audacity!

"Reasonable? *Reasonable*!?" My voice booms through the empty space. "Do you think I price myself so low that after all these years of abuse you put me through, I'd just forget and spread my legs for you?"

"Hmm, you just did." He looks at the table.

"Fuck you!" I throw a towel at him, wishing I had wet it so the impact would be harder. "I hate you. I truly hate you, Justin. You know the truth now, and suddenly I'm not a bad guy anymore, but that doesn't mean I can just erase everything you and your brother ever did to me. Do you think so low of me? That you'd have no problem swooping in and getting me to jump your bones? That I wouldn't be able to resist you? Well, I can. Because I have some fucking dignity!" I all but screech. I can't control myself anymore. What a pathetic jerk!

"Kayla, listen—" He throws his hands in front of him in a calming manner. It does nothing but aggravate me even more.

"Nope, I'm done listening." I throw my arms out. "Get out." I point to the door.

"Kayla," he says in that voice of *reason*.

"No, Justin. Honest to God, I'm done with you. To tell you the truth, for a second there, I thought this might mean something." As soon as I say it, I regret it.

"What might mean something? Me licking you to an orgasm? *That* might mean something?" He laughs. "Yeah, it's a normal thing between two consenting adults. You don't have to be in a relationship to do it. You of all people should know that." He rolls his eyes like it's the funniest and the most obvious thing in the world.

He did not just say that. He did not...

But he did. And it hurts like hell. He, like everybody else in this town, thinks of me as a whore just because my mother was, and now I'm guilty by association. She was a shitty parent, but she did what she had to do to put food on the table for her two kids. And she wasn't a prostitute per se; she just had a few regular boyfriends (I cringe thinking about it) who helped her out with money. She had my sister when she was sixteen and me at nineteen. There wasn't much she could do for work around here, seeing that local folks don't take to the people from the trailer side kindly. As for leaving this town, well, I understand more than many how things get complicated.

I turn to face him, making sure to meet his gaze. "Get out, Justin, and never come back. The feeling is mutual—I hate you too." I feel the muscles all over my body tightening from anger pressing on my nerves.

In two long strides, he is next to me. He bends his head to my ear, his breath tickling my skin. In a whisper, he says, "You'll come to me, we both know that. I know how you've felt about me all these years." He grazes the shell of my ear with his lips. "It'll force you to come to me eventually. You just had a taste. You'll be craving it. Trying to see what we've been building up to for so long. You won't be able to get me out of your head without a good angry fuck to erase all the memories, good and bad. To wipe the slate clean. I'll wait, but not for long."

With that, he walks away, smacking the door into the wall on the way out. The wall shakes, and the huge picture of Little Hope I bought from a local artist last week falls down, clamoring onto the cute accent table Marina brought from her home, knocking the lamp onto the floor. A new, stylish rustic lamp that Freya brought for us from their house. She wanted to save it from Alex's wrath (that man has a weird relationship with lamps). I watch in slow motion as it shatters upon reaching the floor. So much for saving the beauty.

I take a deep breath and call out to the sky to give me patience.

Chapter Twenty-One

K AYLA

The following morning starts super early. I walk into the diner, greeted by Marina's loud yell.

"What the fuck happened here?"

Yeah, I didn't clean everything yesterday—besides the table with bleach, of course. I won't be able to eat there, seeing as every time I glance in that direction, I picture what happened yesterday on that exact surface. Yesterday, I ran home like a coward, hoping I could come in early enough to clean the mess from the lamp. Oops.

"Well." I pop up from under the counter where I was just fishing for the broom. "The picture fell." I smile sheepishly, and Marina narrows her eyes at me.

"Just like that? Fell on the floor?"

"Yeah, can you imagine? We must have a ghost here." My eyes widen.

"Yeah, we're about to have one when I find out who did this. That lamp was gorgeous." She looks down with tears in her eyes. I laugh—she's so dramatic today—and go to sweep up the mess on the floor. I should have just cleaned it yesterday, but I was too angry and exhausted to do anything, so here we are.

Luckily, Marina drops the subject and proceeds to the kitchen to get started for the day. Soon, people are coming in. At eight, the door chimes, and a familiar figure steps inside.

"Hey, Mark!" I wave at him. He's wearing his uniform pants with suspenders that I find super funny, but I know others find them attractive.

"Hey." He comes to the bar and leans on it, his arms straining the short sleeves of his white T-shirt.

"You're on duty today?"

"Yeah, and it's my turn to buy breakfast."

"Then you picked the right place! What can I get you?" I pull my notebook from my pocket.

"You know what, I haven't tried much here, so I'll go with your recommendations. We need to feed ten hungry men." His forehead wrinkles and he quickly corrects himself. "Well, ten men and women who have a long shift ahead of them."

"I got you." I write down the order of five of my favorite dishes in doubles and pass it to Marina in the kitchen. Returning to Mark, I pick up the coffee pot and gesture to him. "Want this too?"

"Nah, we have coffee at the station. The chief has his ways with Donna." He winks at me, and I laugh. I so do not want to know his ways, but also, I kind of do.

"Ah-huh," I hum and go to the fancy coffee maker, whipping up a latte for Mark. As far as I remember from our childhood, he likes his coffee bitter—it's not much of a preference, but a habit we grew up with; there weren't many sweets in our lives before. I sprinkle cinnamon on top of a nice pile of foam and place it in front of him. "On the house. Try it." I look at his face with anticipation.

"Looks fancy." He eyes the drink suspiciously.

"Tastes like it too. Try it."

He smiles and reluctantly brings the cup to his mouth. I'm mesmerized by his lips, and not in a sexual way; all I want is for him to love this coffee. I want to repay him in little ways for his kindness toward me. His first sip is tiny, but the second is a big gulp. The foam sticks to his lips. He licks them and takes another sip. "Alright, this is good. I think you've ruined Donna's coffee for me."

"Told ya!" My smile is wide and sincere. And that's precisely when I meet Justin's eyes through the window—with my lips stretched from ear to ear. He watches me from the outside, looking like a pissed-off God of war. The blond version of one, anyway. His nostrils are flared, his fists clenched. He slowly moves his attention to Mark, who feels his hot glare on his back. Carefully placing the mug on the table, he turns around and meets Justin's gaze. Justin's eyes turn into tiny, angry slits. He makes a move toward the door but stops in his tracks when he notices me jumping across the bar to grab Mark's hand as he stands from the chair.

"Mark, no." He tries to pull away, but my grip is firm. "Mark, chill. He's just looking for a fight."

"And I'm happy to give him one," he growls, fixating his eyes on Justin.

"Not when you're on duty, and not at the diner. We just finished renovations, for God's sake." I see Mark's body expanding with an enormous inhale as his shoulders drop.

He slowly returns to his seat, and only then do I drop his hand.

Justin watches the whole thing, his eyes glued to our hands. He clenches and unclenches his fists. Then, his eyes find mine, holding them for a never-ending minute. So much passes between us that I'm almost knocked down by the raw emotions behind his eyes. The raw feeling of betrayal prevails them all.

He glances at Mark one more time and strides away.

"What the fuck was that?" Mark returns my attention back to the present.

"What do you mean?" I swallow, trying to soothe the dryness in my throat. "That's just how he is around us, you know that."

"No, that was not it." He turns back and watches the now empty window. "That was about you."

"It's always about you or me. Today it's two of us in the same space, and he's just double mad." I shrug.

"Stop it," Mark cuts in. "You know what I'm talking about. He wanted to take my head off for being near you." He carefully watches my eyes. "Did something happen with the two of you?"

I look around, ensuring no one will hear what I'm about to say. "I found out why he hated me so much."

"Hated? As in past tense?" His eyes go round.

"Hates." I sigh. "He still hates me, but for different things now. Turns out, it's a pattern for us."

"So?" he asks curiously.

"Remember that night?"

He snorts. "As if I could forget it."

"Yeah, so that night he got stopped by the cops, and he thought I was the one who called them on him."

He looks dumbfounded for a second before letting out a

full-belly laugh. "You? Call the cops?" And he starts laughing louder.

"Imagine my surprise."

"I hate to say it, but he got himself into trouble on his own later. Nothing to do with you but with the cop he beat up." Mark's remark sounds reasonable.

"Yeah, it's not that simple." I shake my head.

"Why? He beat up that cop for no reason, and they charged him for it," he insists.

"That was the cop who stopped him, you know that, right?"

"I've heard, yeah."

"He had his reasons. It's... I can't tell why, but he had a good reason to be upset over it. Like a really good reason." All the humor evaporates from my tone, and he senses it.

"Did someone get hurt?"

"Yeah," I whisper.

He nods and takes a sip of his coffee. "I can understand that."

"Yeah."

"Wait." He puts the mug down. "Who called the cops? I sure as fuck didn't, and neither did you." I give him *the look*. "Oh fuck. Do you think she did?"

"Who else was there?" I ask, sighing.

"Holy crap." He rubs his beard. "That's so messed up."

"Tell me about it." I think for a second. "Actually, tell me one thing. What did you all find so attractive about her that you could only think with your dick the moment she appeared, huh?"

"Availability," Mark answers without a second thought.

"Huh?"

"She was always available, and she knew tricks." He shrugs.

"Ew." I scrunch my nose.

"What? You asked."

"The firehouse order is ready!" Marina's voice booms from the kitchen.

I go to fetch the food and pack everything up for Mark to go. When I return and place his order on the table, he gives me his card.

"Be careful with him, alright?" he says quietly.

"What do you mean?" I do know.

"You know what I mean. That sort of hate doesn't just disappear. He learned to live with that, and now he doesn't know how to exist without it. Just be careful, Kayla. I don't want to see you hurt." His eyes are troubled with worry for me.

"Thank you, Mark. I will." I pass his card back to him.

"See you around." He takes the food and goes to leave.

"Go save the town, hero!" I yell to him when he's next to the door. His cheeks turn pink, but I notice a slight smile on his lips before he turns back.

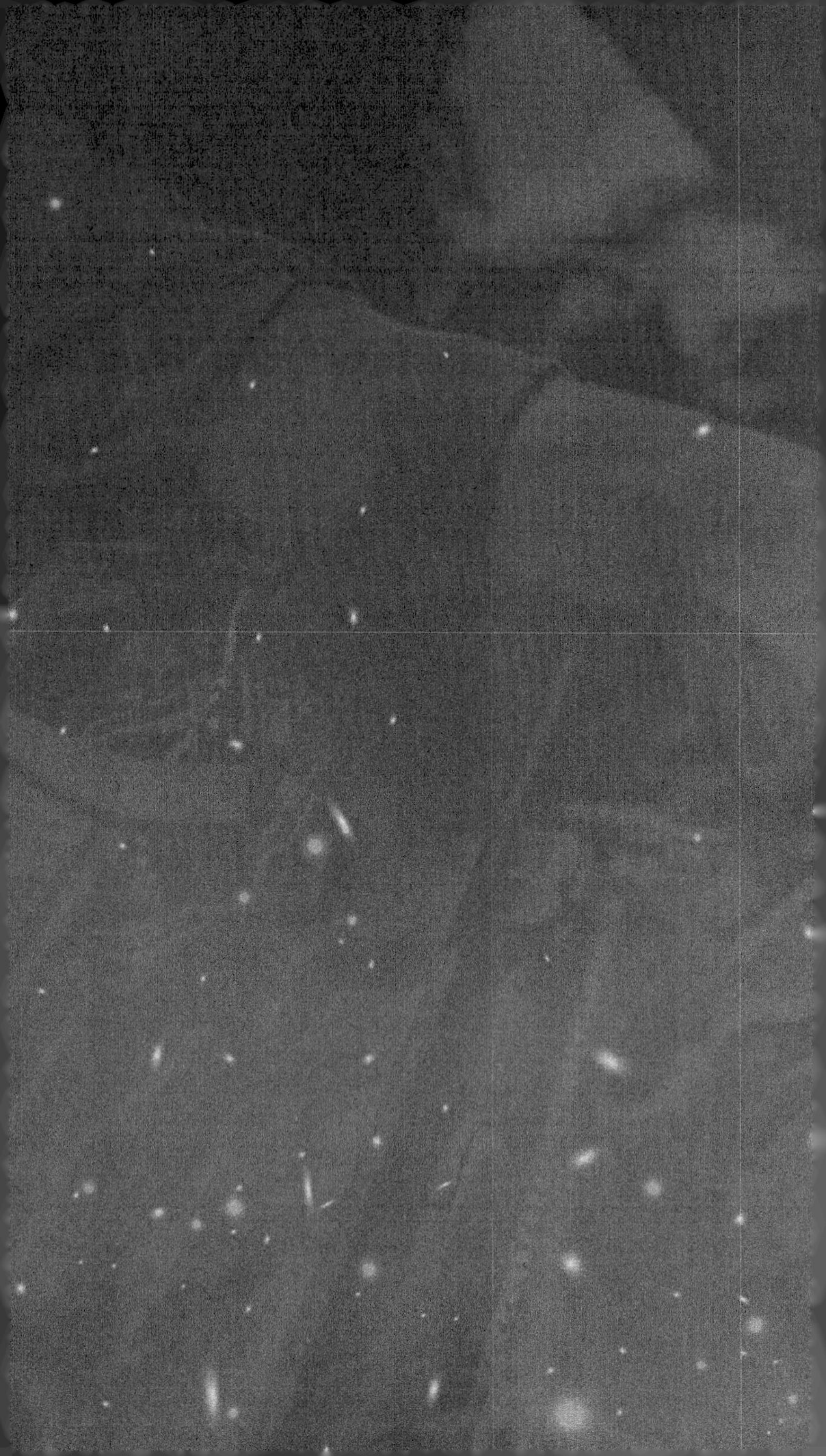

Chapter Twenty Two

J USTIN

I have to go back and smash his face into pieces. Again, I think as I march toward the garage. They looked so fucking *cozy* together. So perfect. They don't have this ugly history between them. No hurt or bullying. His family didn't poke their noses in her life and didn't try to make her miserable.

She never fuckin' smiles like that with me. Never. So carefree and happy and genuine. And so adoringly. And she's had a crush on me for ages, I know that. And yet, I've never seen her looking at *me* like that. She's always on guard around me, always alert and ready to pounce.

Do they have something going on between them? Does she want him more than me? She's mine, not his.

So why are you leaving rather than going back to demand that she be yours? My brain helpfully suggests to that burning rage in my chest. Why? Because I can't announce to the whole world that I want her for myself. Because I can't want her. I can only have her for a night, in the shadows of darkness, where no one can see us. Where I can hide from the guilt, shame, and myself. Accepting my feelings means accepting reality. She was right, and I'm not ready for that. I don't know if I'll ever be ready.

The pile of people I've been hurting just keeps growing. If I add her in there, I'm afraid I won't be able to handle it without stepping over the thin line I'm currently balancing on. I thought the only way to stay on this side of it was to fuck her and get her out of my system, but it turned out worse than I thought. Since I got a taste of her, she's been plaguing my mind with her ever-growing presence, and there is absolutely nothing I can do about it. If I ever have her, I don't think it will be enough for me, but I can't offer her anything but a shameful night full of orgasms in the darkness. Maybe it's time to try something else. Where I'm not a selfish bastard.

I can try to ignore her and pretend she never existed. That's the best-case scenario for both of us. I owe her that much.

And for the following two weeks, I do just that: I pretend she isn't walking on the other side of the road, wearing her flowy blue dress that accentuates her beautiful body. That she doesn't bend down to pat this ugly mutt the town doctor has, and that she's wearing shorts cut so low that I can see her firm ass. That she doesn't carry that heavy-ass box from her car that she almost drops, and it's not me who caves in and goes to fetch it from her hands to roughly deliver it to the diner without saying a single word. And it's definitely not me who was walking down Main Street back and forth on the night she stayed late at the diner, painting something on the wall by the door.

Nope, it didn't happen, and it was not me. I was very good at ignoring her, just as I planned.

Jake finally leaving for rehab after the shooting helped to take my mind off certain things. He became jittery and even more irritated, and our father said that he'd had enough and that it was time to fix the situation.

It's been three weeks of successful ignoring, and I'm on the verge of biting someone's head off. My guys at the shop stay away from me because of my temper. It's like I switched places with Alex and need to be put on a leash. My family stays away from me because I'm in a constant foul mood, and I stay away from them for a different reason. How can I face Alicia and Jake now? How can I tell them the truth? Especially Jake. He's going to hate himself just like I do for torturing an innocent person. And hate me for everything else.

Today will be the first time I see *her* up close. Freya's having an official opening for her PTSD facility. They just renovated the place, and she already has a full staff. Alex mentioned that she wants to introduce them to locals since some of the staff are moving from other states and could use some mingling. When Freya started this PTSD facility thing, her plans were small, a few-people-at-once kind of place. But it's turning out to be a huge place, and not only by a Little Hope scale. It took longer than we all anticipated, but, in the end, I believe it will be worth it.

I take an extra-long shower and take a shamefully long time to pick a shirt to wear to a fucking barbeque. I'll smell like a fire by the end of the day regardless of what I wear.

My phone rings right before I'm about to leave my apartment. "Yep?"

"*Jus, we need orange juice and champagne. Ladies demand mimosas.*" He says the word like it's a snake threatening to bite his ass.

"I'll get it on the way."

"*Thanks, man. Hurry up, it's a peach party here, and we need eggplants.*" He sounds like he's suffering when he's surrounded by all that beauty.

I let out a loud laugh. "Who talks like that?"

"*I don't give a fuck. All the ladies came here earlier than they needed to.*" Yeah, Alex might have worked on his PTSD, but he's still an asshole. Some things never change, and I'm grateful for that. This stability is precisely what I need after a few days of emotional turmoil.

And hormones. Fuck. I have more blisters on my hands from the past week than I've had for years working with mechanic tools. I either jack off or work at the shop, overtightening all the damn screws. Every time I turned some nice visual porn on, I couldn't do it. Got half-mast at best. I kept thinking about inviting over one of my regular fuck buddies, but every time I thought about somebody's body under mine, it gave me shivers. Bad shivers.

Fuck, I can still taste her on my lips and smell her sweet musk. Well, that does the trick, and my dick roars to life. Just great. If I had known before that tasting her would make me even more hungry, I'd never have done it. Or I would do it, but I wouldn't stop there. She was putty in my hands, and I fucking blew it by opening my big mouth. Couldn't I have fucking waited to say that I hate her for *after*? An idiot. She could be out of my mind by now if only I fucked her.

Now, more than ever, I know I have to have her. I *need*

to have her. She's the drug. The solution to my pathetic illness. One that just has a bunch of fucked-up side effects. Before, when I thought of her as guilty, I hated her with double the passion because I wanted her when I shouldn't have, and it's been going for so long that I forgot how to feel anything else toward her but hate.

Now though, I don't even know why I hate her. But I do. I hate when she smiles at everyone else but me. I hate her badass outfits. I hate her wearing those sexy short skirts that she likes so much. I hate her beautiful tattoos. I wanted tattoos, but I saw her skin covered in them, and I wanted nothing to do with them. Just to separate myself from her as far as possible. I hated her cuddled up with that asshole Mark on the curb after the fire. Oh yeah, after the fire, I stayed and watched from afar; I hated that he could comfort her without hating himself for consoling the enemy.

My feelings toward her are apparent.

Today, I'll see her up close, and nothing—I mean it, nothing—will stir. *Do you hear me, asshole? Nothing!* I glance at my lap, hoping he'll understand the gravity of the situation.

I stop by the store and grab champagne and juice. By the time I arrive at the place, the parking lot is almost full. It's an old mansion she renovated, and now she's planning to expand, considering they're already fully booked. The three-level building is about eight thousand square feet and was half destroyed by time and old owners. Now it looks unrecognizable. The first floor is fully dedicated to common areas, and I believe that's where the gathering will happen. The house itself is about fifteen minutes away from Little Hope and is surrounded by the best Maine has to offer: gorgeous pine woods, sunlit mountains in the background, and blueberry bushes.

The weather is amazing. It's warm but not suffocating because of the woods and their shadow. I'm jealous. My second-floor apartment above the garage heats up like a motherfucker. Snow is more stubborn here, though, so everything has its pros and cons.

I look around and don't see a familiar Jeep. When Alex mentioned all the chicks being here, I assumed he meant Kayla as well. She always helps Freya if needed, and I expected her to arrive earlier.

I shove a tug of disappointment down and head to the house. A lot of people are here.

"Hey, Justin!" Freya comes to hug me. "Oh, you brought goodies! Ladies," she turns to the room and yells, "Justin brought the nectar of the gods!"

"Yahoos" and "yays" boom around the living room. I quickly look around: a few girls I've seen around town are spread throughout, currently giving me bedroom eyes. I've slept with some of them. *Fuck, it's about to get complicated.* Donna's talking to Stella, Alex's stepmother, by a huge red brick fireplace; Leila, Alex's sister, is chilling on the floor-to-ceiling window with a book, her usual thing.

Alex was right—the sausages are missing. In fact. "Where is Alex?" I ask Freya as she tugs on my arm toward the kitchen with the drinks.

"He's hiding in the bathroom, I think." She laughs. "Nothing's changed there."

"He needs time," I offer gently, well aware that she knows him better than any of us do.

"That's why I don't go all storm trooper on this door and drag him out here."

I chuckle, put everything on the counter, and look around again in case I've missed her.

"She's not here," Freya says, opening a juice box.

"Who?" I've been busted.

"Kayla," she answers, passing me glasses. "Can you open the champaign, please? We have some thirsty ladies here." She gives me a pointed look and proceeds to deliver glasses to the table. Looks like a small army is about to arrive.

"Yeah." I begin unwrapping the foil from the neck of the bottle. I'm doing it slowly, very slowly, but then I give up. "Is she coming?"

"Why? So you can torment her while everybody's having a good time?"

"No," I say through gritted teeth. "Just curious why she isn't here. She's usually clingy. And always around you."

"Kayla? Clingy?" Freya lets out a loud laugh that gets us a few curious looks. "You've mistaken her for me, I'm the clingy one, and I'm the one who's always around her." She chuckles and mumbles under her breath. "Clingy, my ass."

Huh. Looks like I got the situation all wrong. Not the first time for me.

"So what about her?"

"What about her?" she parrots with the sweetest smile. My teeth begin to ache.

"Where is she?" I can't help but growl; a mischievous spark lights up her eyes.

"Archie got to Little Hope late yesterday, so she's waiting for him." Her eyes look angelic as she blinks innocently at me, but she has the smile of the devil.

I was just about to pull the cork out as she said it. Instead, I snap its neck. Champaign begins rocketing out from the bottle and onto the ceiling. A few shrieks vibrate through the space, followed by loud laughter.

Alex barrels into the kitchen with crazed eyes. "What the fuck happened?"

"Justin lost his shit." Freya keeps laughing, and I snap my mouth shut just so I don't say something I'll regret later, seeing that it's what I've been doing recently.

"About what?"

"About Kayla and Archie," she says quieter while making sure there is no one around to hear. At least, I can appreciate that. I don't need rumors flying around town that I have the hots for her.

"Oh," Alex says thoughtfully. What the fuck does he mean by that?

"I didn't lose my shit," I growl.

"You totally did!" Freya looks like a kid in a candy store.

"The bottle just got damaged."

"Yep, it got damaged, alright. When you found out they're coming together." She looks too happy with herself.

"I don't give a shit who she's coming with," I snap.

"Sure you don't." She laughs again, and Alex nudges her shoulder. "Oh, yeah, I'm gonna go and check if anyone needs anything." She rises to her tippy-toes and kisses Alex on the cheek. I feel a ping of jealousy. I haven't had those sweet kisses before. They usually lead to a fuck or end a good fuck. I don't kiss goodbyes, I don't get a supportive kiss, I don't share a kiss when I'm happy, I don't share a kiss when I'm down. I deal with my shit on my own, that's what I'm used to, and that's how I like it. So why, out of nowhere, am I jealous of what they have?

"You good?"

"Yeah," I say and go to grab towels to clean the mess I created. I wish I could clean the mess in my life like that too.

"You have something going on with Kayla?" His voice is probing.

"No," I snap at him, and I understand he doesn't like my anger, but I'm too wound up to care now.

"It's okay if you do though," he suggests calmly.

"I said I don't," I bite back. I don't need his permission.

"Okay. Make sure you keep your cool when they're here. I don't need to clean blood off the walls." The warning in Alex's voice is clear.

"Worried about your pretty boy?" I say, trying to rile him up.

"I'm not sure who I'm more worried about here, to be honest. I've seen Archie fight," Alex counters, a ghost of a smile on his face.

"You haven't seen me fight for something I want before," I say before I can think.

"So she's something you want?" He got me there.

"Fuck off." I flip him off and continue cleaning the floor while he grabs a mop, puts a cloth on it and begins wiping the ceiling. Yeah, quite a mess I've made.

By the time we're done, Freya comes back to the kitchen. She snakes her arm around Alex's torso and asks, "We're hungry. Can you start the grill, please?"

"Sure." He kisses the top of her head. Alex is a giant dude, and Freya seems so tiny compared to him. And yet, he is just a gentle giant with her. I've seen this vicious motherfucker in action, and he is so not like that. He gives her another kiss before turning to me. "You coming?"

"Yeah, let me finish, and I'll be there."

He nods, and they walk outside. Once I'm done, I go to the sink. A small hand lands on my shoulder while I'm washing my hands.

"Hey there!" a too cheerful and too... *girly* voice says from behind me. You know, one of those high-pitched ones that was surely practiced in front of the mirror for hours.

"The way you broke that bottle," she fans herself with her incredibly long well-manicured hand. Before, I would have found them attractive, "was so hot."

"Yeah?" I ask as I wipe my hands. "How is that?"

"I mean," she blinks her eyes, "you are so strong and all that." Her hand lands on my pec, and I look down. Her hand seems foreign there, like it doesn't belong. Too clean. Too boring. No tattoos.

"Yeah?" I ask again because I was done with this conversation before it even started.

She blinks and opens her mouth a few times before she says, "I'm Lou, the new designer."

"Nice." Freya probably hired her to work on something at the PTSD center before the opening.

She blinks again, clearly waiting for me to offer my name, but I'm rolling the asshole dice today. I'm giving off a strong fuck-off vibe (which is so not me when a beautiful woman is involved, and Lou *is* beautiful), but she doesn't catch it, and continues. "You must be Justin. I've heard so much about you."

"I'm sure you have. Excuse me," I say, taking her hand, still plastered on my chest, off me as I amble to the door. I need some fresh air.

There is a nice barbeque patio on the side of the building with rows upon rows of plastic tables and chairs. I'm sure the whole town could fit in here. The Dancing Pony is about to get a big competitor for theme nights.

Alex is standing by the grill alone, and I join him, looking around. Maybe I missed her arrival. But she's not here, and I feel relief and anger. What the fuck is she doing with that pretty boy? He's no good for anything.

"I see what you meant about peaches now."

"Told you." He is right, though; usually, I'd be all for

sniffing around for a new conquest. Usually. "That designer is *thirsty*, man. She's been waiting for you for two hours already."

"No shit? For two hours?" I quickly glance at her.

"Yeah, I'm telling you. Asked me all sorts of questions. I think the only thing she hasn't asked is how big your dick is, but I'm sure they already discussed it." He shivers in disgust. "And why are you here, by the way? I can't figure out why you aren't fishing over there." He points to the house with the hand he's holding his beer in. "A lot of fish in that sea."

"Not in the mood."

"Been there," he says thoughtfully and stares at the grill. Charcoal slowly smolders, creating extra heat in this hot weather. But meat grilled on charcoal is ten times better than on propane, so I'll take it.

A few cars arrive, and people come to greet us. X and Y chromosomes are somewhat balanced now. I can relax, seeing that a few needy eyes have refocused elsewhere.

I see my father's car. And Jake is in the front seat. Well, that's a surprise. Neither he nor my father told me he wanted to come to this little party. His rehab program is for eight weeks, but he's been there for only two, and a couple days ago, they let him out to visit family. A rare thing, considering rehab staff don't usually let people out until the program is done. Despite this, they signed a paper for him to be under our father's supervision.

Freya runs toward him. "Jake!" she calls. They hug, and she tugs his arm inside the house. Huh, I guess I'll say my hellos later.

Alex and I are both quiet, each in our own thoughts, when I hear a familiar engine rev. Shit, I need to change the oil in it.

The Jeep parks farther down the driveway since the front of the house is fully packed. She doesn't get out of the car for a few minutes, and I begin boiling. I can see who's sitting in the passenger seat. Fucking Archie. What sort of name is Archie, anyway?

When they're finally done whatever the fuck they were doing, they get out of the car and walk to the house. He's carrying a huge box with different veggies popping out of it. Rabbit food, my ass.

Huge smiles are plastered on both of their lips. All right, I'm about to wipe them off.

KAYLA

"Oh, it's gonna be fun!" Archie's chuckle sounds ominous. An evil bastard, he's living for the drama.

"Do I even wanna know?" I give him the stink eye.

"Your boyfriend over there," he nods toward where Justin and Alex are standing by the grill, "is two seconds away from losing his shit." I follow his eyes, and he's right. Justin looks constipated. His pose is rigid, and his fists are clenched. I don't think he ever unclenches them in my presence.

"He is not my boyfriend, and you know that," I hiss back like a rabid cat.

"Does he know that?" He sends me a curious look.

"Archie," I say to him like I would a toddler, "don't start any drama. Please."

"Okay-okay, I won't say anything until I know your positive answer to my offer." His smile is cheeky and very contagious. I find myself smiling back at him.

"My positive answer?"

"Yep. Let's go, time for fun." He moves his bags into one hand and hugs my shoulders with the other. I see what he's doing. I try to shrug him off, but he just pulls me closer and whispers, "Relax." And I do as I'm told. I relax into his embrace and let him walk me to the house.

"Alex!" Archie's voice is very staged. "We're finally here."

"That you are," Alex answers, eyeing Justin. "What took you so long?"

"Taking a shower." He winks at him, and I elbow his side just as Justin's nostrils flare and his jaw clenches.

"*Was* taking a shower. You were taking a shower. Alone." I jab him again, and he lets out an oof. I shake my head and grab both bags from him. "I'm gonna drop these off in the kitchen."

"I'll help you," Justin announces as he pulls both bags from my hands and marches toward the kitchen. Archie snickers and nudges me to follow. I threaten him with my best stink eye, but he only laughs, soon joined by Alex like they both share some super funny joke I'm not privy to.

I flip them off, causing even more laughter, and follow Justin to the kitchen. He drops the bags on the floor, about to turn back when a woman's hand lands on his forearm, squeezing it. I stop in my tracks, feeling uncomfortable. At the same time, I want to torture myself by seeing how this will unfold.

The woman is pretty. Taller than me by a few inches, the heels she's wearing definitely add to her already impressive height. Her hair is Victoria's Secret-perfect beach waves, her outfit cost more than my trailer and car combined, and her makeup is flawless. I regret not putting at least some mascara on this morning. I knew it would be a hot day and didn't want to have raccoon eyes after sweating. And now I wish I had some war paint on because clearly, it's a war zone, judging by the way she's feeling up his muscles. Like they're familiar with each other in a biblical way.

I want to turn around and run, so I don't witness the situation, knowing it will surely follow me into my nightmares, but Freya notices me and announces loud enough for all the bears around to hear, "Kayla! You're here!" She's next to me in a second and envelopes me in a hug. She became such a hugger recently—I don't even recognize her! I pull away and step back. She looks good, really, *really* good. She radiates happiness and health, and the colossal stone sitting on my chest falls off. I can breathe easily. Seeing her like that makes me happy. Makes me airy.

"Yeah, we just arrived." I can't escape now, might as well embrace the disaster.

I feel a hot glare and instinctively turn to Justin. He's watching me while the leech attaches herself to his arm permanently.

"Hi, I'm Lou." The woman waves at me with a wide smile. "And this is Justin." She pats his hand, and my eyes zero in on the movement.

"She knows," Justin says in a neutral but accusing voice.

"Oh." Lou unlatches herself from Justin's arm. "Did I step on someone's toes here?" She laughs nervously, looking a little lost. I feel a little like a dick for assuming she's just another wandering vagina.

I say "no," just as Justin says "yes."

"*O-o-oh,*" Freya singsongs.

I stare at him in bewilderment, and he holds my gaze without blinking, trying to communicate something I can't quite comprehend.

"You didn't step anywhere." I try to smile at her but miserably fail as Justin shoots me another glare and adds, "You did. I'm not available."

"Hm," she hums at him. "I see... Good luck; you'll need it," she says to me and walks away, flipping her hair over her shoulder. Freya snickers and takes the veggies out of the bags.

"Well, that was enlightening," she hums under her breath.

"Care to share with the class?" I ask her, annoyed. Did I step into a parallel universe? What the hell is happening?

"Ah, no. Oh!" She points her finger to the ceiling. "I forgot something. Be right back!" And she escapes the sinking ship.

I move my attention to Justin. This situation won't resolve on its own. "Why did you say that to her?"

"What exactly?"

"That you're unavailable."

"That's because I am." He walks to the fridge and pulls a beer out. "Want one?" he asks me, but I just shake my head.

"I didn't know you're dating somebody." I'm totally fishing here.

"I'm not." He takes a sip and leans on the counter.

"Oh."

"Why don't you ask me the question you really want to ask?" He smirks.

I fume silently as he enjoys my struggle. He got me there. He knows I want to ask what he meant, but I can't say it out loud.

"Okay, Justin. You win. *Why* did you tell her that?" I give up and ask the most important question with a new meaning.

"Because I'm interested in someone else right now."

"Oh. And who is that?"

He chuckles, finishes his beer, drops the bottle into the trash, and leaves. So much for answering the question. I'm fuming for the rest of the day. Archie left me alone with his constant attempts to rile Justin up by touching and flirting with me. Justin deflected all advances thrown his way from the ladies present and remained stoic and mysterious. I won't lie, it made me a little bit happier than I was before I arrived.

Okay, fine, a lot happier.

"Kayla!" Freya yells from outside.

"Comin'!" I call, getting up to go see what she needs. *Oh, fuck me.* She's talking to Jake. My face must have changed, becoming sour, because her eyes widen as she motions with her hand to come join them. Oh, with pleasure. After the jail incident, we haven't had many interactions. He left me alone and then went off to this rehab thing. Hopefully, they'll fix his desire to torture me along with all his other issues. Plus, now that Justin knows the truth, I suspect he told Jake as well, and maybe, just maybe, my life will be a little easier.

"I didn't think the trailer trash was invited." And... no such luck.

Freya smacks his shoulder. "Jake! Watch your mouth!"

"That's exactly what I'm doing here." He smiles like we're old friends, and from the outside, we probably look like buddies. It couldn't be further from the truth.

"I guess some things are unfixable, and asshole mode is your default." I smile sweetly back, hoping he'll get a yeast infection. "I hope they don't reinstate you. You definitely don't deserve to be a cop."

"Scared to face me again on the streets of our fine city?" His smile causes me to enter a sugar coma.

"Scared to face me in court?" I show him all my teeth in a shark smile, and his drops a notch.

"Alright, break time." Freya shakes her head, tugs on my arm, and throws at Jake, "Go get yourself a drink, Jake." And then to me, "Sorry, I don't know what I was thinking."

"I know what you were thinking because I was thinking the same thing: that Justin told him the truth. I guess he didn't." I shrug.

"I don't know why, though." She throws Jake a wondering look. "You'd think he'd crawl to you to ask for your forgiveness because his karma is so tainted. It's in desperate need of some purging. But no." Her shoulders slump. "Sorry."

"Don't be." Why didn't Justin tell Jake?

I'm deep in thought when I feel a hot glare burning my skin. My eyes dart to Justin, and I find him watching me with a drink at his lips. He's been watching me this whole evening. My every move, like a hawk preying on a little mouse on the ground before he strikes.

But Justin never does. Strike, that is. He just watches, circling around but never coming close. I don't precisely know what I've been expecting, but I leave the grand opening of a life-changing place for Little Hope feeling a little disappointed.

Archie left his car at the Dancing Pony, and because I picked him up on the way here, I feel I must drive him back. I could tell throughout the day that he had clouds hanging over his head, even with a smile plastered on his face. On the way back, I think about taking him somewhere to cheer him up.

Chapter Twenty Three

J USTIN

I always knew where she lived. Always. I found out the moment she moved her trailer here. When she asked me how I knew the other day—I completely froze. Yeah, how do you tell a woman that you followed her home when she was nineteen? Never mind that the real reason was that I needed to see where she lived so I could check on her. She was alone, and it didn't sit well with my nature. I couldn't say any of that, so I just ignored her question, hoping she would forget that she never got an answer.

And now, I'm sitting in my truck in front of her trailer, waiting for her to finally arrive home. Why is it taking so long? The drive from the Dancing Pony to here is twenty minutes; she should be fuckin' here by now unless they are doing some... *extra activities*.

At the thought of her in his hands, I squeeze the wheel

so hard it lets out a squeaking sound, and I let go. Fuck, it's been forty minutes, and she's still not here. They're fucking for sure. I'm gonna break his fucking fingers for touching her. All evening he tortured me with those little touches. Every time he touched her, he watched my reaction and just chuckled. Oh, the fuckface knew what he was doing, all right, even if she was oblivious.

I start the engine and am about to drive to the bed and breakfast where the asshole is supposedly staying when the Jeep shows up, and I kill the lights on my truck.

I left her usual parking spot empty. She slows down when she sees me, I assume, and finally parks her car. When she gets out, I get out too and walk to her.

I don't talk, I don't say anything, I just stalk her like a predator. She looks a little dazed and a lot scared and moves backward. But I don't care. Not anymore.

I grab her hand and lead her to the trailer. She doesn't resist as we reach the door, where she silently unlocks it, and we step inside. Once she closes the door, I lock it from the inside. I'm not ready for interruptions of any sort today. Not until I'm done.

She's standing with her arms crossed over her chest in the middle of her kitchen. I lean on the door and wait, making her sweat while questioning what I'm going to do.

And I'm going to do *everything*.

She's carefully watching my face, looking for clues. But you won't find any here, baby, no.

"Did you fuck him?" I growl finally.

"What?" Her eyes widen at my question.

I push away from the door and begin slowly moving toward her as she moves backward.

"Did. You. Fuck. Him," I repeat, accentuating every word. My voice descends lower.

Once her ass hits the counter, she stops moving, and I step closer to her. My feet are touching hers.

I notice her swallow nervously, the vine tattoo on her collarbone moving with the movement as if alive. I'm mesmerized by it, and for a moment, I forget what I'm doing.

"Why?" she asks as she clears her throat.

"I'm the one asking questions here. Did you fuck him," I lean in toward her lips but don't touch them, "Kayla?"

She is silent, her breathing is labored, and a drop of sweat runs down her pulsing temple.

"No," she says on an exhale.

"Good girl," I say, taking in how happy that makes me feel.

"Not today," she adds, and a wave of fury rises up my throat, threatening to suffocate me in pure rage.

"What?" My hand shoots up and grabs her by her throat on its own accord. Her eyes are trained on mine, not blinking. Challenging. "When did you fuck him, Kayla?" I hiss into her face, squeezing my hand tighter but still controlling it. Barely. She has a way of snapping my willpower. "When?" I demand, but she keeps quiet. Her nostrils flare, and both her hands snake around my wrist. I think she's scared and wants me to let go, but just as I'm about to, she plants her hands over mine and pushes harder.

A fire starts in my stomach, heaving my balls and shooting up my spine. She's kinky, just as I predicted. Hoped.

"Wouldn't you like to know?" she hisses. Her face is slightly red, and I loosen my grip on her neck. Just a little. Her normal color returns, and she takes a deep, open-mouthed breath.

"Little witch" is all I say before I slam my mouth to hers

in a punishing kiss. Her ring tingles my lips, and I get the full feel of it under my tongue. I've been wanting to play with it for a long time.

I keep my hand on her throat and snake the other behind her lower back, pulling her onto me. But she's not close enough, so I lift her up on the table and spread her legs, pushing her thighs apart. As I nestle myself between them, I return my grip to her neck and pull her into me by her ass.

Her arms come around me, digging into my back. I used to love the pang of sharp pain from long claws, but now I'm enjoying a different sort of pain as her short, blunt nails dig into my skin through my shirt. I want the barrier gone. I want her hands on me. I pull away for a second, take my shirt off, and throw it on the floor. I then grab her shirt and do the same. She's left in a sexy lace corset, like lingerie, and high-waisted tight jeans. She dressed like that for him, and I'm furious. She was planning to undress later. If I find matching panties, I'll kill him.

Suddenly, all I want to know is if she put those matching panties on, so I pull her from the counter and begin unbuttoning her pants.

I'm too focused on my task to notice her calling my name. Just as I'm about to pull her pants down, her nervous "Justin" finally gets to me.

"Justin," she calls again, and I look at her face.

"You dressed like that for him? This sexy as fuck set is for him?" I grab her by her throat and pull her to my face. She's short and has to stand on her tippy-toes. "You were planning on having fun tonight, huh."

"No, Justin, I just—"

I slam my mouth onto hers, quickly shutting her little lies down. She wraps her hands around my shoulder and tries to angle my face the way she wants. And I let her. I'll let her have this ounce of control just for a moment before I take it back.

I grab her ass with both hands and lift her up, sliding her up and down along my length through my jeans. I hear her gasp, and I press her harder into me until she begins whimpering and moving along with me.

I'm so fucking mad that I can't even talk, and I'm usually vocal in bed.

When I can feel her wetness through my jeans, I plant her back on the table and begin my assault on her neck. She is sweet. She smells like strawberries and tastes like a candy I've craved for so long but couldn't have. It was just too bad for me. But now, after I got it in my hands, I'm getting my fill.

She digs her nails into my biceps and tries to bite my neck, but she can't, because I bite her first, causing her head to fall backward, exposing her sweet little throat to me. I bite and kiss and lick until she begins shamelessly pressing her pussy onto me, trying to erase the pain. Her strong legs wrap around my back, pulling me into her. We are one at this point. We'll only be closer when I'm inside her. And I desperately need to be.

My dick is so fucking hard, I can cut diamonds with it. The wetness on my jeans is not only from her but from my precum shooting like there's no tomorrow.

I move my hand onto her corset, freeing her magnificent tits. I admire them and lick my lips. They are better than I could have imagined. Small, tight, and so fucking perky. Like they are challenging me to take them on, and I do. I lower my mouth and suck one sharp nipple in, circling it with my tongue, until she moans. And I bite. She lets out a soft cry before moaning louder as I soothe the pain with a lick. Then I move to the other. Doing the same until she wiggles in my arms.

While playing with her tits, I move my hand lower, inside the hem of her panties. Fucking matching ones. I dip my finger in and begin circling her clit, while returning my mouth to her lips.

At this point, she is a wriggling mess, and I'm so sweaty, barely able to contain myself and not spill in my jeans.

When I feel she is close, I pull my hand away, and she begins whimpering as if in pain.

"Wait, baby, you're gonna come only around my cock. Only then. Do you hear me?"

"Yes." She licks her lips. "Justin, I—"

"No." I can't hear a word she says, and I shut her with a kiss. A deep, angry, punishing kiss. She meets every stroke with increasing anger. We are a good match.

While I'm kissing her—or she's kissing me—I unbutton my jeans and free my rock-hard dick. Giving it a couple strokes, I spread the precum over its head. It feels so fucking good, but being inside her will feel even better.

Still locked in a kiss, I find her entrance and push her panties to the side. I feel her, and she's so fucking wet I almost burst on the spot. I put a finger in and then add another, giving it a few lazy, shallow pumps, stretching her entrance and preparing her for my girth. Then I grab my cock, spreading her juices over me.

I bring my dick closer to her center, and she chooses this exact moment to deepen the kiss. Little vixen. I'm out of breath and quite frankly out of willpower, so I nudge myself inside, but she is tight. Fuck. I align myself with her entrance again and push some more. The same result. My body begins to shake with anticipation, my willpower snapping. I can't take it anymore. I enter her with one rough shove.

She pulls away from the kiss and cries out as she digs her nails into my shoulders. That didn't sound like a cry of pleasure. I watch her face in horror. She is in fucking pain. Fuck!

I pull away and glance down and then back at her face.

Did I just see that?

I look down and see a few tiny smudges of blood on my cock.

Oh no. No. No. Fucking no.

"What the fuck is that?" I ask. I know I should have picked different words. "Are you a fucking virgin?" I ask in horror. Kayla is a virgin.

"Clearly. Got any problem with that?" She moves a little and winces in pain. I look down at my dick, somehow even harder now—*a sick bastard*—and it is indeed covered in blood.

"Fuck. Kayla, fuck!" That's the best I can come up with. "You let me take you like I'm a fucking animal on the counter for the first time? I almost fucking split you in two! You should have warned me."

"I tried." She's out of her sexy haze and fixes her corset, putting her gorgeous tits back inside. Such a shame.

"You should have tried fucking harder!" I yell, aggravated with her and myself.

"Well, it is what it is." She looks around for her clothes, clearly uncomfortable with the situation. And I should be too. As should my dick. But the fucker is still standing at full attention. But the way events are unfolding doesn't seem to scare him—quite the opposite. It's ready to split wood. I might join Alex's club of local lumberjacks who relieve stress by chopping wood, only I'll be using my dick instead of an axe.

I am an asshole, but even I'm not that big of an asshole to ruin her first time. *The first time.* Fuck. I've never had a virgin before. Even back in high school, it turned out all the cherries were popped before mine. I've never had the pleasure of being the bottle opener.

I probably look ridiculous: jeans down to my thighs and my nine inches standing straight up, begging for her attention. I pull my pants up and shove my dick inside. Well, I try, but it doesn't want to chill. I give up and somehow walk to Kayla, who's busy picking up her shirt from the floor.

"Come 'ere." She doesn't listen. Of course, she doesn't. I'd be disappointed if she did, so I grab her hand and pull her to me. "You should have told me so I'd be gentler. I fucking shoved inside you like you were a seasoned porn star. I'm sorry." She swallows and doesn't look at me, fidgeting with the shirt in her hands. "Does it still hurt?"

"No," she mumbles.

"Good. I'm not a small guy, Kayla. I should have never done what I did, even if you weren't a virgin. Come 'ere." I tug on her hand, and she finally looks up. "Why do you let people think you are a whore?"

"It's easier that way." She shrugs. "I've tried to prove myself to everybody, and I eventually got tired of that. Let them think what they want." She shrugs again, but not in disregard. I see hurt in the way her movement becomes jerky. She might play the part of a warrior, and she may believe herself when she says that the rumors don't bother her, but they do.

I let go of her hand, grab her by her ass and lift her up, urging her to wrap her legs around me. Her arms automatically go around my neck, and I love the feel of them there.

"What are you doing?" she whispers.

"Fixing my mistakes. I can't fix all of them, but this one, I can." I carry her into her bedroom, and it's surprisingly cozy. A queen bed with girly quilts (I didn't expect so much pink from Kayla) covered with pillows.

I carefully lay her on the bed, moving the pillows aside. She lifts her torso to lean on her elbows and watches me. I crawl on top of her and start unbuttoning her corset. Thousands of those little hooks on the front of it are about to drive me mad, and I ask. "How much do you like this one?"

"I love it," she whispers.

"I'll buy you another one." And I rip it apart, finally freeing her tits. She has a lotus sternum tattoo, in color. And it looks so fucking delicious that I lick it from top to bottom, lightly touching her breasts. Her breathing quickens as she laughs.

"It's ticklish," she says, and the happiness I hear in her voice makes me feel better. She's relaxed now, no pain. *Good.*

I move my trail of kisses up to her neck, where I suck on her skin. This vulnerable place where the neck connects with a shoulder is always sensitive. I bite it lightly, and her hips nudge forward. I smile into her skin, knowing that she just keeps proving that she will be magnificent in bed. She likes what I like, I can tell. And even if she doesn't know what she likes, I'll show her. That fuckface's never been here. Me, only me. I'll teach her everything there is to learn.

She puts her hand on my shoulders, moving them to my pecs, but I grab her wrist with one hand and bring them above her head.

"No, baby. Not now. If you touch me, the game is over, and I want it to be pleasurable for you."

"It's already pleasurable for me." She pouts, and I just

bring my mouth to hers, shutting her up. My other hand travels to her stomach, covering the lower part of her belly completely. I don't know why I do that, but I like my hand there. It feels... *right*.

Our tongues dance slowly with each other, touching ever so lightly before interweaving together like they are one. With every deep stroke of my tongue, my hips buckle forward. My dick's been hard forever, and I'm about to come in my pants.

When she wraps her legs around my torso and begins moving her hips into mine, looking for friction, I give up. I let go of her wrists and rip her panties off.

"I loved those too," she whispers through my kiss.

"I'll buy you more," I say as I grab her ass and move her pussy along my pants.

"Take them off. Now," she says in a commanding voice. I realize I like it. With a smirk, I let go of her for a second and pull my pants and boxers down as fast as humanly possible.

I look at her: she's flushed, her face and chest are pink and sweaty, and she's constantly licking her lips. She is ready. I want more.

I smile and slide down her body, reaching my target.

"Oh, hell no. Here. Now!" She grabs me by my hair and pulls me up. I start chuckling, but she silences me with a kiss. Oh, I knew she'd be wicked.

She dips her hand down and wraps her little fingers around my dick. They feel so different from mine. So gentle and soft. For the past few months, my hand was the only thing that touched him, and her hands feel like heaven. She's trying a few strokes, slower and then faster, she's trying the texture, getting the feel of it, and I let her explore.

When our kiss speeds up, her hands follow the lead, and eventually, I can't take it anymore.

"Kayla," I beg into the kiss.

She understands and aligns my cock with her pussy, but then she hesitates, so I ask, "Are you sure?"

"Yeah, I'm just..." She lets it hang in the air, and I understand.

"I got you." I give her another kiss, grab my cock and gently nudge it inside. She's so fucking tight I'm about to blow, but I slowly push forward, pulling away from the kiss and carefully watching her face for any signs of pain. But there are none. Her mouth is slightly ajar, her cheeks flushed, so I push more. And more. Then I pull back out and push more, a few times just like that, and I'm fully sheathed inside.

"Are you okay?"

"Yeah," she whispers, and I begin moving. Slow, deliberate strokes. Very slow. I watch her face with every single move. How her eyes widen with every push. How her mouth forms the cutest *o* when I hit the right spot. How her head falls backward as the feeling inside of her builds up to a breaking point.

I bring my mouth down and suck on the soft skin of her neck, causing her to inhale loudly. She loves it; I can tell because her hips are speeding up, urging me to follow. And I gladly oblige.

I move my hips faster, the strokes becoming deeper and harder. But even now, I watch her, even when I'm so deep in the passion I have to make sure she is good. It doesn't feel like my regular fucking. This feels... different.

At this point, I'm about to burst, but she's not there yet.

"Justin," she whispers. "Please."

"Yes, baby, tell me what you need," I ask through gritted teeth, sweat dripping from my temples.

"I—" She wants to say something, but she's shy. It's her first time, for fuck's sake. Even though she has that foul mouth on her, she doesn't know how to voice her desires yet. I can help her.

"My hand? You want my hand?" I say as I suck on her earlobe.

"Yes, your hand." She sighs in relief.

"Where do you want it, Kayla?"

"Everywhere," she whispers like she's letting me in on a huge secret.

I smile as I move my body a little to the side, letting the weight off her, and plant my hand on her throat, moving the other one lower. I find her clit, and I play with it, making little, fast circles. I watch her face as I do it. Her mouth is open, and she's biting on her lower lip. She is so ready. I squeeze her throat a little harder as I push into her with long, hard strokes.

And she comes undone, and I watch her ride that high.

That's the most beautiful thing I've ever seen. The most gorgeous. The most precious. Kayla Adams, during her orgasm, will be forever imprinted in my brain.

As her inner muscles begin violently squeezing my dick, I can't take it anymore and spill inside her. It's officially the longest orgasm I've ever had in my thirty-one years of life. And the most violent one. I just keep spilling and spilling and spilling inside of her until I'm fully spent.

Inside of her.

Inside of her.

Fuck!

I forgot about the most crucial part during sex.

"Kayla, I'm sorry, I'm so fucking sorry," I apologize as soon as I'm able to control my voice again.

"For what?" She looks petrified. She still has this post-orgasmic glow, but her eyes quickly sober up.

"I forgot a condom. Fuck, it's the first time I ever forgot a condom. Whatever happens, I'll help," I state and realize that I'm not scared of what might happen.

"Whatever happens?" she repeats.

"Yes, if you, you know, get pregnant or something."

Her eyes widen, and she laughs. "We're good; I'm on the pill."

"Why are you on the pill? Were you planning on doing it? With him?" A new wave of anger erases all the high I just reached.

"Oh my gosh, Justin, women can be on birth control without having a man in their lives. Shocker, I know." She grabs a comforter and pulls it over her. I stand up, so she doesn't have to move my body to get under the covers.

"So you weren't planning on having sex with him?" Whatever she said hasn't registered in my brain.

"Why are you so obsessed with him?" she throws at me accusingly.

"I'm not obsessed with him. I'm obsessed with you," I say, surprising us both.

Her eyes widen, and she blinks slowly, watching me. Once she gets her wits together (I should do that too), she says, "I'm clean, by the way. In case you were wondering. It's not like I was whoring around, as you know." She quirks her eyebrow, and I feel my cheeks pinken in shame of my assumptions.

"Me too. Never done it without a condom, and I get regular checkups anyway. Haven't been with anyone since my last one." I'm not ashamed to share it because she needs to know I'm not putting her at risk here.

"Must have been yesterday," she snorts.

"What?" I go to the bathroom for a quick cleanup, and she follows.

"Your last checkup," she clarifies.

"Actually, about eight months, I think." To think of it, maybe even nine. I clean myself with wet wipes while watching her every move. How her hand disappears between her legs, cleaning the wetness I created. How it moves across her thighs—the same ones I held onto a few moments ago. And just like that, I'm getting hard again. She doesn't notice my intense stare as she finishes cleaning up and goes to the bedroom. This time around, I'm the one following her.

"W-what?" she stutters while climbing into the bed. "You haven't been with anyone?"

"Yeah, been busy."

"For eight months?" Her face looks like she just realized Santa Clause isn't real.

"Yeah, for eight months." This conversation is making me uncomfortable. As if I should be embarrassed for not fucking the whole city. I crawl to bed and say, "Scoot over."

"What?" She looks gobsmacked.

"Scoot over so I can lay down."

She silently moves to one side, looking at me cautiously, like I can pounce on her anytime now. And I can, seeing as my dick roars to life again the second I catch a glimpse of her tits. I climb under the covers, grab her, and pull her toward me. She's surprised, as am I because I'm not a cuddler. But with her, all bets are off, or so it seems.

Her head lands in the groove of my shoulder, her tight fist on my chest. I want her to throw her leg over me and relax, but she's cautious, and I don't blame her. I wrap my arm around her and begin making small calming circles on her back. Eventually, her little fist relaxes, and her palm lands on my pec.

"You have insomnia. Why are you in bed?"

"Just to let my body relax." I sigh. I don't sleep, and it's taking a toll on me. A significant one, seeing as I've been up for less and less hours between crashing, and I'm only thirty-one. At this rate, my body would give up on me way faster than I anticipated.

"Okay," she answers quietly and yawns.

She's asleep a moment later. A soft snore tickles the skin of my chest, and I find that I like the sound. In fact, I like a lot of things that happened today.

Chapter Twenty Four

JUSTIN

I open my eyes to an empty bed and the smell of bacon and coffee.

It's bright beyond the windows, and when we went to bed, it was dark. I feel good—refreshed. A good roll in the hay can do that.

I give my body a good long stretch and look around. Yesterday, I was too preoccupied, but today, I can check everything out. The way she lives. I like it. I've been talking shit about her trailer, but it's super nice. Fifty times better than my apartment. She made it a home. Her bedroom is small, but very her. The furniture is clearly worn, and all the pieces are from different sets, but they all coordinate nicely.

My stomach growls, and I finally get out of bed, stretching one more time.

I find my pants halfway to the kitchen on the chair. Kayla's flipping pancakes at a two-burner stove. She's wearing tiny white shorts, showing off her amazing legs, and a loose black shirt with more holes than material. There's a colorful lion on her right thigh, and her hair is piled up on top of her head in a super messy bun that she didn't spend any time perfecting. She is barefoot, with one foot tapping to the song she's listening to in her headphones.

I step closer and admire the view. From here, I notice a few light bruises on her thighs, clearly from my hands. I should feel bad, but I don't. I like my mark on her.

What the fuck is wrong with me? Mark on a woman? Who am I?

She notices me and takes her headphones out. "Morning."

"Morning." My voice is raspy, as if I spent the whole night singing at a rock concert.

"Sleep well?" she asks, licking batter from her finger.

"I don't sleep," I announce stubbornly.

"Well, you did. All night." She points the spatula she's holding at the bed.

"Right." I yawn. "I just closed my eyes for a second to chill."

"Yeah, you did, and opened them many hours later." She points at the clock on the wall.

"Ten thirty?" I yelp. "How—"

She shrugs as if it's not a huge deal and keeps fixing breakfast.

Like it's not a big deal that I haven't slept like a normal human being in six and a half years. Since the night my sister was assaulted, eaten by guilt every single night. And today, I did.

Did yesterday's extracurricular activities exhaust me so

much that I just crashed? But it's not like I haven't had wild sex before, the kind that exhausts your bones and liquefies your limbs. I have, and yet I didn't sleep then. To be fair, sex yesterday wasn't just wild. It was good, and it was different. I usually end up leaving someone's place or making sure the woman leaves my place after we're done. I'm very clear about that from the beginning. I don't need people running around, talking about my problems.

"Did I really sleep?" I scratch the back of my head, looking around, lost, like a puppy. Why did such a simple thing like that throw me off balance?

"Yeah," she says, taking a sip of her coffee. "I woke up at eight, and you were still out."

"Okay." Is all I say. That's all I *can* say, so I go to her and grab the mug from her hands.

"Hey!" She wants to pull the cup back, but I take a hefty sip from it and wince.

"That shit has so much sugar in it; I think I got a cavity from just a sip."

"Good. Then you can give it back." She takes the mug back and points at the coffee maker. "Get yourself your black coffee; it'll match your soul."

"Actually, I like a vanilla latte with one spoon of brown sugar."

She chokes on her coffee and spits it out. She's trying to laugh, but the cough prevents it. I helpfully pat her on the back, and she laughs harder.

"A vanilla latte?"

"Yes," I shrug, "I'm man enough to admit it."

"Good for you." She smirks into her cup, finally done with this nonsense. "But kind of bad for you because I don't have an espresso machine. Only drip coffee."

"That's fine. Where can I get a cup?"

She points at the cabinet, and I walk to it. Inside are a few mismatched cups of different sizes, shapes, and colors. Odd, but somehow, they all... match. I take the largest mug and pour myself a coffee, filling it almost all the way to the brim.

"Got any cream?"

"In the fridge," she answers, piling the last pancakes on the plate and turning off the stove.

Her fridge is clean and almost empty. It has milk, cream, eggs, something in jars, and that's about it. I take the cream out, pour a hefty amount into the cup, and take a sip. No sugar coma for me.

She fixes two plates and sets them on the part of the counter that she uses as her table, takes her cup, and takes a seat on one side. I sit on the other.

Blueberry pancakes with chocolate chips. From scratch. No fucking way. I grab one with my hand and instantly get burned. The fucker is hot! It doesn't stop me, though, and I take a huge bite, devouring half of it in one go.

"This is so good," I say through my chewing and notice her looking at me with wide eyes. Her fork is frozen halfway to her open mouth.

"It's just pancakes."

"Do you think I get to eat homemade pancakes every day?" Her mouth is still open, I probably look like an animal, but I love food. So much. And I can't cook anything that's not microwavable. The only way I can eat good food is when I go to my parents' house, and I don't do that very often, especially in the last couple of weeks. Seeing that my mood has improved, I might visit them this week. Besides that, everyone knows the best pancakes in town are at Marina's diner, but I can't exactly go there, so right now, I'm in heaven.

"You don't?" she finally asks.

"I don't."

With that, she moves the plate of pancakes toward me, and with a sheepish smile, I pile them up on my own plate. Kayla's slowly chewing her food as she watches me devouring everything.

"Is it always like that?" she asks.

"What's like that?" I ask with a full mouth.

"One-night stands." With that, I choke on my food and begin coughing. She's waiting patiently for me to respond.

"That's what you think it was?" I put my fork down.

"What else do you think it can be?" she asks as she mindlessly plays with her food.

"I don't know. I've never had this."

"A one-night stand?" Her brows shoot up.

"No, breakfast in the morning." My eyes shamefully dart around the room.

"What?" She puts her fork down.

"I just never did." I shrug. "When I'm done, I go home."

"Why? Isn't it sad?" Her forehead wrinkles in question.

"I dunno." I shrug. "I was young, and I had this pact with Alex to not get involved in anything serious. Then I got thrown in jail, and then I just didn't want anyone to know about my sleeping problem."

"You didn't have this problem before?" She caught the main thing I didn't want her to notice.

I feel my face harden—the question bringing too many bad memories. "No," I answer, voice stern.

"I'm sorry to ask." Her face is full of regret.

I disregard her words because there is nothing I can say. Instead, I again ask the question that's been bothering me hella more than it should be. "Why would you think this is a one-nighter?"

"What else can it be?" She stares at me with wide eyes.

"I don't know. Maybe something." I honestly don't know, but to my utter surprise, I'm not opposed to the idea. I don't have a clue what's happening with me and why I'm having breakfast and a normal conversation with a woman I just slept with. Slept! Fucking slept after the most mind-blowing sex I've ever had.

"No, one-night stand. That was it," she says firmly, finishing her coffee and standing up with a half-eaten plate.

"Why?" Her words sound so final that I stop eating.

She smacks the table with her palm. "I can't believe you even need to ask. Do you really think I can just erase all those years of bullying from my memory?"

I feel a knot tightening in my stomach, a completely foreign feeling I don't like. "We are so good together. Why not?"

Apparently, it was the wrong thing to say because she turns around, fury shooting from her eyes. "Just because we fucked doesn't mean I've forgiven you. And by the way, you haven't even apologized. And a few weeks ago, you told me you still hate me. Forgot about that one? So no, Justin, forget this ever happened." She rushes to the sink and begins furiously washing dishes.

I stand up and go toward her. Plastering my front to her back, I plant my hands on either side of her, caging her in. I hear a loud intake of air and her hands hesitate before they stop moving. I bury my nose in her hair and breathe her in. The smell of strawberries, so familiar now, tickles my senses.

I press my chest into her back and feel her push back. Just a little, barely noticeable, but she did. So I take it as a yes and snake my arms around her waist, pressing my mouth to her ear. "I am sorry, Kayla," I stress, attempting to convey the full weight into my words, hoping she will understand. That she will know how incredibly sorry I am. "I'm so fucking sorry."

Her next breath shudders. "Why are you here, Justin?"

I don't give her an answer because I don't have one.

"Why were you here yesterday? Why were you waiting for me?" She sounds desperate like she needs to hear what I have to say, so I decide to go with the truth. At least for one of her questions.

"Because I didn't want you to go with him."

"Why, Justin? Is this some sort of a game where you can't let another guy have a chick you haven't fucked yet? Is that it?" she presses.

"No."

"Then what is it?" Her voice rises, and she drops the cup into the sink, shattering it. "Tell me why!" she yells, and I pull her closer to me.

"Because you are mine!" My voice matches hers. "Mine," I say quieter as I let go of her. I look for my discarded shirt on the floor, but it's neatly folded on the couch. "Do you need to go somewhere today?"

"What?" She's clearly confused by my switching subjects so fast.

"Do you need your car today or not?" I rephrase the question.

"I-I—" she stutters. "I have to run a few errands today."

"Okay. I'll pick you up later, text me the time. Where are your keys?" She silently points at the hook by the door. I grab the keychain, take off the car key, and put the rest back. All the while, she doesn't utter a word. Then I walk to her, grab her head in my hands and plant an open-mouthed kiss on her lips. She gasps, and I dive in, tasting sweet coffee, blueberries, and her. She doesn't respond, but I didn't expect her to. I think I just managed to mute Kayla Adams.

Pulling away from the kiss, I plant one last kiss on her lips before I turn on my heel and walk out the door of her inviting home.

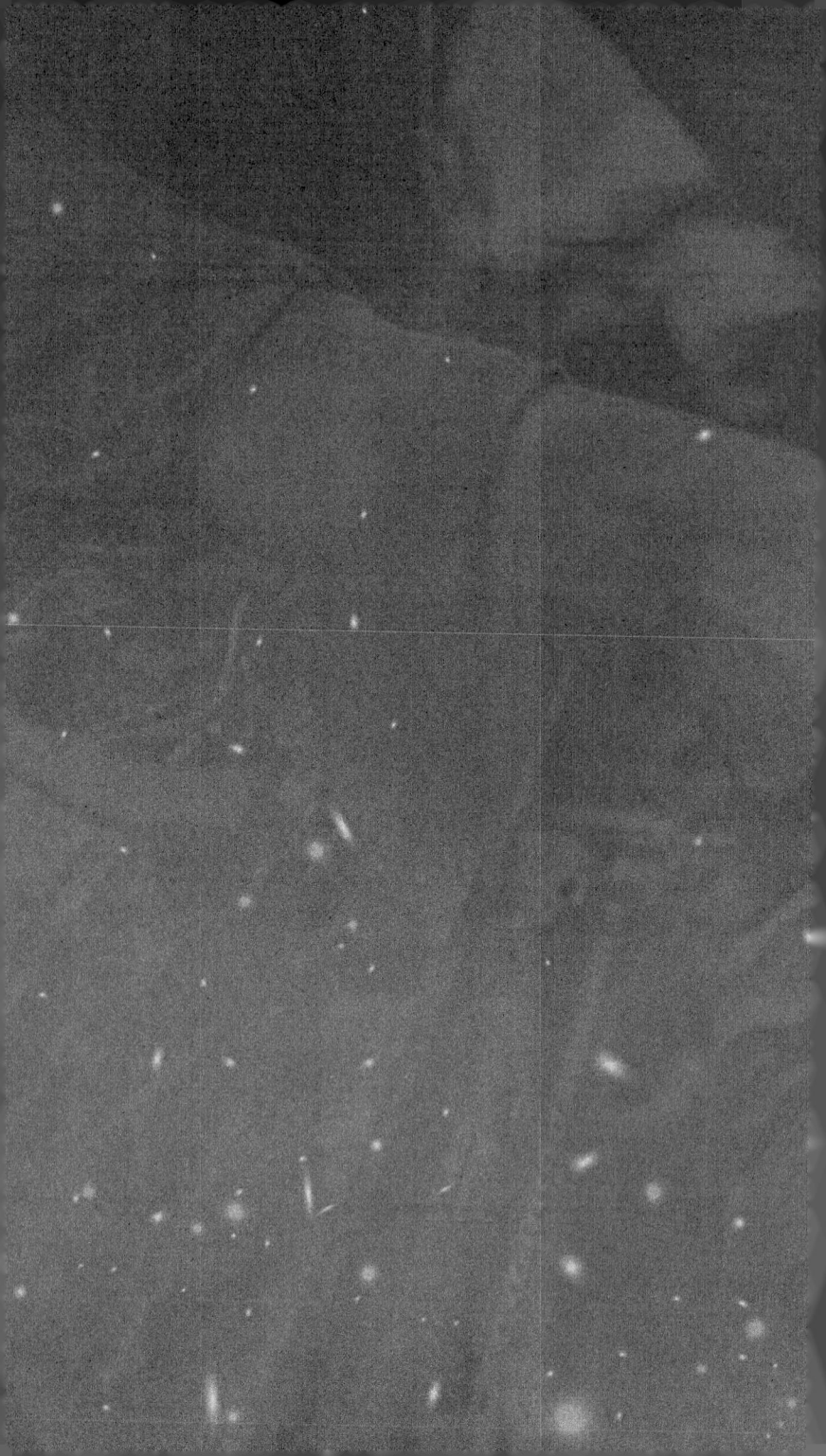

Chapter Twenty Five

K AYLA

What just happened? I'm confused. Justin Attleborough just kissed me, took my car keys, and left. Am I still alive? What's happening? I pinch my thigh and yelp. "Fuck!" That hurts. But it means I'm alive. Okay. But in what universe is Justin this sweet with me?

And let's scroll back for a second. Did he really call me 'his'? It's not like the idea of that disgusts me, not at all, in fact. It's been my dream since I was a teenager. But some dreams are just meant to be dreams: when they turn into reality, they eat you alive, devouring all senses until that dream is all you have left. I'm not ready for that. I have things to do; I'm not ready to drown in another person, even if this person is Justin. We've always been toxic as enemies. We will be toxic as lovers. Plus, I don't believe that Justin can change. He is a man-whore, and I don't want to sign up to constantly fend off his admirers. I have too many insecurities of my own to add this one to the pile.

And let's scroll back a little more. I just had sex with Justin Attleborough. How did that happen? When I saw his truck next to my trailer, I knew trouble was awaiting my arrival, but I never knew which sort.

Man, was he possessive. I couldn't even utter a word, it's like the alpha air around us ordered me to shut up, and I listened like a good girl.

I wanted to tell him about my virginal state, but every time I tried, he was there to shut me up with his mouth. Literally. He kissed me differently this time. This time, he wanted to possess, and I didn't mind one bit. Just remembering his lips on my body gives me shivers, and a silly smile spreads over my lips.

And then I expected him to leave, but he didn't. Instead, he surprised the lights out of me and climbed into the bed. More than that, he tucked me under his arm and stayed the whole night. Sleeping. I still don't know how bad his insomnia is. I mean, it must not be good from what I saw that time, but I honestly don't know his situation. From what I've googled, people can have insomnia to different degrees, and him crashing like that time in my kitchen must be pretty bad.

He didn't like the question about when his insomnia started, and I suspect that it has everything to do with what happened with his sister. Fuck, the amount of guilt he's been carrying must be exhausting. It must be even heavier than mine. How does he live with that? How does he look at himself in the mirror every day? I don't blame him, and I don't think it was his fault. The asshole who assaulted Alicia is at fault. That motherfucker needs to pay, not Justin.

And certainly not me. The ugly truth is what happened *that* night is horrible. What happened to Alicia is devastating and unfair, and I pray that one day she won't be haunted by what happened. At the same time, to my utter disgust with myself, I know I shouldn't feel guilty. The anger I feel at being made to feel guilty all these years suffocates me. I thought I did something horrible—*truly did it*—and forgot about it. I've gone all this time thinking I'm such a horrible person that I didn't even think whatever I did was important enough to remember. But it clearly left an impact on Justin's life. I'd say it's gaslighting, but I was the one feeding myself the lies.

My phone rings, and I pick it up without checking the caller ID.

"Sup, Kay." A deep voice rumbles through the speaker.

"Oh, hi, Archie." The excitement in my voice dies down...

"Don't sound so joyful." His low laughter is very sexy, but it never causes any shivers, unlike someone else's.

"I was just distracted. What's up?" It's not like I expected Justin to call so fast—if ever—but hearing another voice still deflated my bubble a little bit.

"What's up? We were supposed to meet for breakfast. Remember?"

"Oh shoot! I'm sorry, man. I forgot," I groan and smack my forehead.

"O-o-okay," he says suspiciously. *"Is something going on?"*

"No, why?" I answer too fast.

He laughs louder. *"Because I had a visit this morning from a certain blond dude whose name shall not be named. Driving your car, by the way."* Then he hums and adds, *"Or do we name him now, Kay-baby?"*

"Oh, stop it!" I say. "You're bad."

"And you probably, on the other hand, had yourself an excellent night last night. The dude has some settled look to him, like he finally got rid of his demons." He laughs. *"Happy for you. Told you, hate-fucks are the best."*

I groan at his teasing and ask, "What did Justin want?"

"So he does have a name now." He hums again. I can even imagine him smirking.

"Archie! For fuck's sake!"

"What? It was coming. Was it a good coming?" His chuckle is low and seductive but, again, does nothing for me.

"Oh, fuck you, Archie!"

"I'd love to, but no, thank you. I like my pretty face the way it is. The dude was very intense and very clear, and I'm in no mood to get my nose rearranged." I hear the shuffling of clothes.

"Pussy."

"I'm pretty." He laughs again. And he isn't wrong; Archie is very handsome, almost too handsome. He is like a dirty, sexy pirate who can sweet-talk you into doing anything. *"Do you want me to come and pick you up?"*

I like Archie, I do, but I draw the line at sharing information about my home. I'm just weird like that.

"No, I'll meet you later in town; Justin said he'll pick me up. Maybe lunch?"

"Sure. Who am I to compete with 'the one'?" he teases and hangs up. With him, it's like that: he doesn't get offended, nor does he offend. All he does is tease, even though I have a feeling he's a very deep person. And very-*very* dark. The excitement every time he feels pain, his ever-sad eyes even when he's laughing, the mastered ability to dodge every single personal question. Yeah, Archie's got

dark demons. I know he and Alex were the only ones who survived during some operation on their last tour, and neither of them came back the same. Besides that, they were both dishonorably discharged, and I can't imagine that wouldn't leave a mark on a soldier who loyally served for years. But that's pretty much it, I don't know anything else about him, but from what I see, I can tell he is good people.

Marina gave me the day off, saying I would probably be hungover after the party. If she only knew. Or maybe she did, that witch. She always knows more than anyone does. I wanted to go to town in the morning, but it's not morning anymore, and my car's taken, so I decide to clean.

The first thing I do is change the sheets because it's a laundry day, but once I step into the bedroom, I instantly change my mind—the scent of Justin and our... lovemaking? Fucking? Is still in the air. I don't know if it will ever happen again, so I quickly fix the sheets and pull the throw on top of my comforter. My little guilty pleasure, I want to bask in his smell one more night. Just one more. And screw everyone who thinks it's gross.

Then I dust, mop the floors, and collect laundry in the baskets to take to the laundromat later. We have one not far from the diner, so I can throw it in tomorrow morning and run to take it out a couple of hours later. That's why I like small towns—everything is within walking distance.

I take a shower and get ready. I blow dry my hair (blow dry my hair on my day off, mind you), put light makeup on (again, on a day off, because I do it every time, I promise), and get dressed. I don't know why I decide to dress sexy today. *Yep, I totally don't know why.* I pull on my flowy, red, sleeveless sundress that goes down to my knees and accentuates my tattoos. Others might find them weird, but Justin seems to find them intriguing, seeing as he licked almost every single one of them yesterday, so I feel encouraged to show them off and possibly even get more of them. Yeah, I'm just looking for an excuse to get a new tattoo; I still have a lot of space left.

I'm about to go change into another outfit because I feel insecure dressing for him when the sound of the engine drifts through my trailer. I peek outside—Justin's truck is already there. I grab a sweater (you never know in Maine) and run outside. I guess that's my ride to town, so I climb into the passenger side.

"Hi," I say in a neutral voice once I plant my ass on the seat—I don't know where we stand and how I should act for two reasons: one, I don't know what Justin thinks, and two, I have no idea what I think.

"Hey, baby," he says as he leans toward me and pulls me closer to him by my shoulders. My eyes widen, and my mouth opens in surprise. Justin uses this moment to slam his lips on mine. The kiss is fast, without tongue, but it's hot and wet. Then he leans back in his seat, looking no less surprised than I am, and grabs the wheel. "Where to?"

"I—" I clear my throat. "I need to go to the diner."

He throws me a confused look. "Why? I thought it was your day off."

"I need to, hmm, meet with Archie," I answer, dreading his reaction.

Justin squeezes the wheel until his knuckles turn white, and I'm sure there is not a drop of blood left in them. "The fuck do you need to meet him for?"

"Because I have things to discuss with him." I try to remain calm, but it's hard. Boy, is it hard.

"You don't have anything to discuss with him," he grunts through gritted teeth, squeezing the wheel even harder, and I fear he will break the poor thing and leave us stranded here with no means to get out. *Would that be so bad, though?*

"And who are you to tell me with who and what I can discuss?" He's quiet, so I add, "Hmm?"

"I told you, you are mine," he growls.

"Your what?" He doesn't respond. "Your what, Justin?" The only sound in the car is his clenching jaw. "That's what I thought. Can you drive me to the diner, please?"

The whole way to the diner, a thick silence looms over us. Justin's simmering, and I'm pissed. I didn't wait twenty-five years for my V card to be given away to a barbaric asshole with no boundaries. *Didn't we, though?* The submissive part of me whispers tenderly into my ear while the demoness on my shoulder sharpens a knife with an evil smirk. The latter still remembers how he handled figuring out I was a virgin, when he plunged into my fortress, and that part may or may not want to chop his balls off. But the other part is very happy with the actions that happened after. Both parts are, to be honest. And his kisses after. And all his 'babys.' But when I actually asked him the question, nothing happened, as I expected. A tiger doesn't change its stripes.

And besides that, it's not like I'd run headfirst into forgiving him for treating me like shit. I understand his motive, I do, but it doesn't change the fact that he and his brother have made my life miserable. I can't imagine forgetting him calling me 'trailer trash' every time he touches me, not remembering him looking at me like I'm the dirt under his Timberlands, or causing me pain with that fucking hot coffee on purpose.

I wonder if Alicia knows about what went down that night.

Justin parks the truck in front of the diner and gets out.

"What are you doing?" I ask.

"Getting lunch. What does it look like?"

"Justin." I walk around the car and stand in front of him. "Stop. You are being unreasonable. And quite frankly, I have no idea what you're even doing. What do you want, honestly?"

He watches my face, his jaw set. "I just want lunch. Is that something I can do in this fine establishment?"

I pinch the bridge of my nose in annoyance. "Fine. But don't come to me complaining if Marina poisons you." I turn and walk inside, where Archie is already waiting for me at the best seat in the house, the booth in the corner. And also the most private. I briefly glance back and see that Justin takes the bar seat and grabs the menu. He hasn't been here for years besides grabbing that coffee and picking Freya up once, so he doesn't know our funny menu that I put together myself.

I take a deep breath, erasing Justin from my memory just for the next few minutes, and walk to Archie, who's smiling like a cat who just ate the canary. He looks like such a bad-boy pirate with his tats, dark eyes, and tossed hair, that I can't help but smile in return.

JUSTIN

I sit at the bar and try to focus on the menu, but my eyes drift to Kayla and that sleazy fucker. I guess our morning chat didn't bring any results. No worries, I'll repeat it later. It's not like I came off like an asshole, asking him nicely not to see her again. I was very reasonable.

Is he wearing eyeliner? Yes, the fucker is wearing

eyeliner. I think? Who does that? He has a piercing in his ear, tattoos all over his body; he fuckin' matches her.

Kayla says something, leaning closer to him. He smiles and gives her a kiss on the cheek. If it had been on the lips, his hands would be broken by now.

I think I accidentally growl, because Marina, a woman I genuinely fear (she was one of the reasons I never tormented Kayla here), laughs and walks toward me. "What do you need?"

"Can I get lunch?" I try to sound timid.

"Depends." She crosses her arms over her chest, making it pop. I can see why one of my guys, Paul Rogers, has been sniffing around her.

"On what?" I squint my eyes suspiciously.

"On your answer." She quirks a brow.

"Alright." I put the menu aside and fold my arms to match her. I expected this conversation sooner or later, and I suspect the only reason Marina hasn't cut my balls off was Kayla restraining her. But now, when everything has shifted, and it can be sensed in the air, she has free rein. Knowing Kayla has no blood family here, Marina is it for her, so I'll listen to what she has to say. "Shoot."

"I just might." She glances briefly under the bar where she keeps her famous shotgun, and I shift nervously. She senses the blood like a shark and goes for the kill. "I know you two fucked." I choke on my tongue. Did Kayla say something to her already? There is no way our small town knows about that already. She sees my confusion and adds, "I've known this girl since she was a child, and I know when something has changed in her. Listen here, Justin," she leans closer, and I gulp, "I don't like you, I never liked you, and I never will. You don't deserve her, and only God knows why she gave you the time of day. But listen here, very closely, I watch a lot of true crime, boy, and I know how to use a shovel and lye. You hear me?"

"Yes, ma'am." I never let people talk to me like that, but she can. I deserve everything she's saying.

"You have no idea how many times she's cried over you and your brother. Especially you. I'll never forget it, and I doubt she will, either, so think hard about if you even want to go down that road with her. I'll get you your lunch." She walks away, and I stay silent.

I suspected she took all my jabs at her personally because that's how they were meant to be, but now, I can think of how they actually felt to her. She doesn't have a family besides Marina, and to think of it, I don't think she had friends before Freya. Jake absolutely destroyed her during those three years and made sure to make everything miserable for her. Why did she stay in Little Hope then?

I hear Kayla's loud laughter and turn to watch her. The fucker's hand is on hers, and she's laughing like he just told the funniest joke. I've *never* heard her laugh like that. Ever. It's loud, clear, and carefree. He flips her hand and moves his thumb over her wrist.

I've had enough of it. I'm about to jump from the chair, but someone grabs my hand and presses it to the table. I look up and see Marina's steady gaze.

"Drink. Your food will be ready soon." She pushes a cup of coffee toward me with her other hand. I try to pull away from her grip, but she presses harder. "Drink." Her voice is firm, but then she adds, softer, "Trust me."

I glance at Kayla again and see her big wide eyes trained on me. I look at Marina as she nods, and I try to relax. Maybe she knows something I don't.

. . .

KAYLA

Marina's talking to Justin. It can't be good.

"Relax," Archie chuckles, noticing me glancing at Justin ever since I sat at the table. "He's right where he should be."

"I don't know what you mean," I say as I begin shuffling through the menu.

"Sure you don't." I hear a smirk in his voice. "Was it good? Tell me so I can live through you. It's not like I can get some game going on here." He pouts, and it looks ridiculous with the ring in his lower lip.

"You're here for only a couple of days. You'll be fine."

"You don't know my appetite." His wink is impossible not to laugh at.

"You're really sneaky, you know that, right?"

"Oh, I do. I so do." His smile turns devious, and he grabs my hands, turning them over, and presses a thumb over my little moon tattoo. "And I'm about to be sneakier." He begins moving his thumb. "Did you know that ninety percent of people with wrist tattoos are very ticklish when you tickle them in the same spot?" He quickly switches his fingers, and he's tickling me. I begin to laugh like a maniac. My wrists are indeed sensitive, but I'm not sure it's because of the tats.

Then I feel the hot stare burning a hole in my back, and I turn to find Justin looking at our joined hands, a crazed expression on his face.

Archie tickles me one more time before pulling his hand away, and I turn to him.

"You, sneaky bastard!"

"Told ya." He leans on his chair with a self-satisfied look and says, "Let's talk business, Kay-baby."

Right, business. We wanted to discuss it yesterday, but the time got away from us. Plus, it was kind of difficult with all those death glares from half the people at the damn barbeque. We will have a chat with Freya about that.

The thing is, I decided to take Archie up on his offer. It's time for me to move on and do something with my life.

When I told TJ, I had never seen him so happy in my life; the guy usually only contacts me over texts, and rarely did we meet in person, but that day he video-called me. I almost fell from my chair.

"Are you ready to partner up?" Archie appears more excited than the butterflies of anxiety flying into the walls of my stomach.

"Yes, sir!" I answer eagerly, causing Archie to growl.

"Oh, Kay-baby, don't say stuff like that to me." He taps on his forehead with his fist.

"Shit, I forgot that you are kinky."

He shoots me a megawatt smile. I roll my eyes as I move some hair out of my face.

"You have no idea." But there, just for a moment, I can see his face darken. In the blink of an eye, he is all rainbows and sunshine again. "So, what are we doing about him?" Archie nods toward where Justin's sitting. "Do I get the story on that sometime since the tables have clearly turned?"

"Not unless you have a whole week to spare to listen to the bullshit in between." I can hear the bitterness of my tone, and I take a sip of water. "And some of it isn't even my story to tell."

"Ouch, well, you could always give me bits and pieces later. So what do you think about our partnership?" Archie sits forward.

"I'm in." The words come out, and I feel a weight being lifted from my shoulders.

"Great! I already have the onboarding papers filled out for you, so if you want, I can get you started!" Archie reaches into his pocket and grabs his phone, leaning in as if for a kiss on the cheek. "So, are you planning to leave this place?"

"You're just as bad as the locals are, nosy," I tease him and remind myself not to pinch the pervert.

"Hey, I want to know who's going to be working for me! It's not my job to do a background check, but it's definitely important to know if you're a good troublemaker or a bad one." Archie smiles at me, and I try to smile back, but something in my chest feels like it's sinking with all the emotions I've been holding back. "Oh, wait, I didn't mean anything by that."

I suppose it showed on my face, considering the immediate apologetic look he gives me. He puts his hand over mine. "No, it's fine, just that long story of bullshit I was talking about. A lot of the reason I honestly want to be done with some of the people here. Don't get me wrong, most of them are nice—"

"But not all of them."

"No."

"Got it." He moves his chair closer to me and puts his hand over mine in a reassuring gesture. "I won't pry today but expect me to be curious for a while longer." Scrolling through different classes offered and required to pass the exam, I smile at Archie being businesslike. The setting is different from the others we've been in, and I'm surprised at his flexible personality.

I glance back and see Justin staring at us without even pretending he isn't. Once he notices me watching him, his face transforms into a mask of fury, and he quickly turns around.

"Okay, we need to move somewhere private to talk," I tell him while poking his hand, still laid over mine in a comforting gesture. Unlike Alex, who despised being touched after the war, Archie seems to be a very physical person, from what I can tell. He raises his brow in question, and I use my eyes to point to Justin. Archie not too subtly stares back at him before scooting closer to me, wrapping his arm around my shoulder. "What are you—"

"It's fine; you don't have to be shy around me. Oh man, do I love to play some games." Archie winks at me, and I can feel Justin boiling like a tea kettle about to blow. "So anyway, if you want to leave this *fine* town, you can stay at my place for a while until you find something for yourself. Trust me, I have a lot of empty space." I know he's flirting to piss Justin off, but I can also see a genuine offer behind the playful look in his eye. Something tells me Archie is a reliable guy, and he understands way more than he lets on.

"I think I want to move on." With my words, I imagine an arrow sent directly at Justin's stupid face. I peek around Archie for a moment, curious to see the expression he makes. To my surprise, he looks a little regretful, *too little, too late*. His hands unclench, and he moves as if he's about to approach us when Marina smacks a plate full of food in front of him.

"I'm happy to hear that." The whispered words draw me out of my haze. Then Archie pours more oil on the fire by lightly tugging on my hair. "It's a cool idea you have—to change the color with your mood. I just tend to ink a new tattoo. Maybe I should try your method."

I'm sure from the outside, it looks intimate, and Justin has had enough. My gaze follows Justin as he stomps over.

By the big breaths he's taking, I can almost imagine he's trying to blow away a house. Shockingly enough, his tone is gentle.

"Kayla." The calmness in his voice is scarier than his wrath. He pauses for a long time, searching my eyes, and making me squirm. "I need to speak with you when you're done with your..." he glares at Archie, "meeting. Text me later." There isn't an angry bang on the table or threat to make me come see him, not even the usual huff afterward or glaring eyes. Watching him walk away, I feel Archie's arm drop down, and he puts his phone away.

"I sent you all the information, and we can go over it tomorrow if you're still walking by then. For now, go jump his bones, would you? This morning he made it very clear not to come around you, or else. Little does he know, I like pain." His eyes flash devilishly. "I kinda like the guy. Those intense people are the best ones. And besides that, I think if you don't, somebody else will." He nods outside where Ashley is approaching Justin, who's leaning on the passenger side of his truck and watching us through the window.

"Right, thanks, Archie." I wave him off as my feet begin carrying me to Justin on their own accord, just as jealousy rises up my belly.

"Take care, Kay-baby." He gives me a kiss and walks outside.

I collect our plates and carry them to the kitchen. Marina watches me with a satisfied smile on her face.

"What?" I ask.

"He finally pulled his head out of his ass, I see."

"Not by his own will." I roll my eyes.

"Who cares? It's out; live with it." She shrugs.

I face Marina with hands on my hips. "That sounds suspiciously like you're approving of him."

"Does it?" She blinks innocently and keeps churning butter in a huge mixing bowl. "And what are you even doing here? We hired a new waitress just so you can rest from time to time, you know."

"Oh, I know. How about you *resting* and finally hiring that other cook we've been talking about forever, huh?" I cross my arms over my chest, mimicking her tone.

"Busted." She smiles. "Now go, claw her eyes out." She points toward the entrance where Justin's still leaning on his truck. Ashley is saying something to him, vigorously waving her arms.

Am I jealous? Yes, I am, but I've been in this constant state for so long that it doesn't bother me all that much anymore.

I take a deep breath and go outside.

JUSTIN

I barely made it out of the diner without causing a scene. Barely. My heart is beating like I just ran here from Kayla's home, and I clench my fists to stop them from shaking.

Fuck, if I didn't know any better, I'd say I'm jealous, and the feeling fuckin' sucks. The only time I've been jealous was when I was twelve and in middle school. I had a crush on our teacher, Ms. Reacher, and on St. Valentine's Day, some dude brought her flowers during class, and that's when I learned what jealousy was. But never again. Never. Not even when I knew that half the city slept with Ashley.

Fuck, I slept with the other half. But I haven't felt a tinge of jealousy.

But seeing Kayla sitting with this fuckface and clearly flirting, letting her touch him out in public like that... I was a goner. Marina is the only reason his head is still attached to his body. Somehow, she managed to calm me.

When I saw them laughing and sitting so close together, I had to get out of there. Now, I'm waiting for her outside and see the fast-approaching trouble. Ashley. Just fucking great. How do I manage not to strangle her right here now? How do I manage to not do that in the future? I can't fucking stand her. I haven't been able to for a long time now, and after finding out the truth, the only thing I want to do is destroy her. But not like Kayla, no. Even when I thought I hated her, I don't think I ever really did. Or I did, but I also wanted her. Ashley is another story altogether. She's evil, and now I know exactly how deep her evil lies.

If Ashley were a man, I'd put her in the ground, no questions asked. Not only for calling the cops on me, but for everything she's done, and there's been a lot. Fuck, when I was younger and an asshole, I was right there with her, laughing at somebody's misery. Looking back, I'm ashamed of myself. I can never imagine Kayla doing that; she'd be the one to push me off and take a bat to the bully's head. And I fucking love that. A Valkyrie fighting for those who can't fight for themselves.

And now that guy... Mark... Fuck, where do I even start with him? I blamed the dude for raping a woman when he never did, and that's a pretty fucked-up thing to accuse anybody of. Our mutual hatred runs so deep that we'd never forgive each other. Though, at this point, I have to admit he has more forgiving to do.

I wipe my face with my hand. How did my life become *this*?

"So, are you done with your little tantrum?" Ashley asks once she stands in front of me.

"Get the fuck out of my face," I growl, not moving my eyes from Kayla. The fuckface gives her a kiss and leaves. Once outside, he winks at me and walks away down the street.

"You should be done by now, Justin. Really. It's been going on for long enough." She has the audacity to put her hand on my forearm, and I explode. I grab her wrist and tug on it. I don't know what I'm doing, and I know I'll regret it later, but she destroyed lives, and I'm done being a gentleman.

"If you touch me, talk about me *or* my family, or even show up on the same street as me, I will fucking destroy your life. And you should know I can." I lean closer and hiss into her face. "Come close to anyone in my family or Kayla, and you are done. Are we clear?"

"You don't mean that." She tries to pry my hand from hers, but I keep an iron grip.

My voice dips to a growl. "I mean every single word, Ashley. Never again."

Her face pales, and she pulls her hand harder. This time I let her go.

"Your whole family are fucking psychos—you're just too blind to admit it."

My nostrils flare at her statement as I try to control my anger. I know she's talking about Alicia. She's been hinting here and there that something is wrong with her. She knows what happened, and yet, she still runs her mouth. I can't believe I've wasted so many years on her. It's not like I was planning to marry her, God no. I'm not planning on marrying anybody. I just wanted to keep her around for just long enough, even though I knew how vile she is.

I watch her leave, and my fists clench and unclench on their own accord. I feel that I need to fight. That's how I control my anger. I fight or fuck. I used to race, too, but it got me in too much trouble when I was younger, so that option is out of the question. Fucking is not the best option either right now. I can only hope for a good brawl at the bar.

"Are you okay?" a small concerned voice asks. Kayla stands beside me, carefully watching my face.

"I'm fine," I bark. It's not how I want to sound with her, but I do at the same time. What sort of 'things' did she need to discuss with that dude, and why did they look so cozy? I begin boiling over even more and know I need to get out of here before I say or do something I regret.

"Okay," she says, deflating under my stare.

"Can you walk to the auto shop? Paul has the keys to your car." I ask like I haven't offered my help.

"Yeah. Thank you. I'll pay you for whatever repairs you did."

I shake my head silently, get inside my truck and drive off, leaving her on the sidewalk looking confused and hurt.

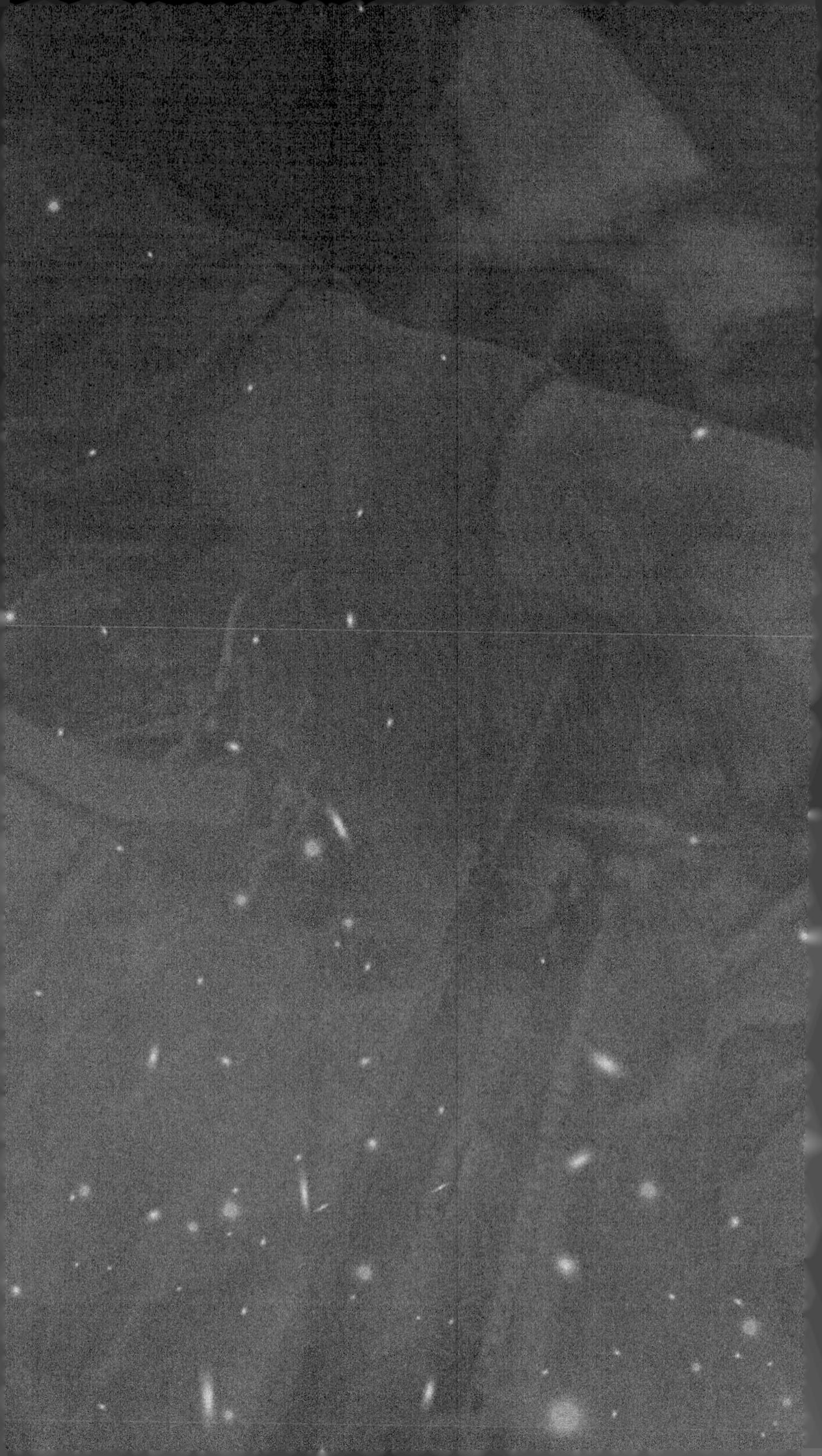

Chapter Twenty Six

KAYLA

In what universe did I think that anything would change? Nothing has. He still talks to her and still puts her first, even after everything he knows. His feelings for her must run deep for him to close his eyes to everything. I mean, they clearly had *a talk,* and yet she comes to him so casually. What did I expect after the revelation? That he'd leave her right away and come to me? *R-r-r-right.* They share years of history, whatever their relationship was, and that's hard to erase. I should know. To be honest, it hurts. Seeing them together hurts. Even if he doesn't exactly look happy right now. But I don't exactly know what they were talking about.

I sigh and walk to his auto shop. I've never really been inside, only peeked in through the open doors. There are three guys inside. I've seen two of them around town, but I don't know their names, and the third is Paul Rogers, the guy who's been crushing on Marina for years now. Even though he's a head shorter than her, he's trying. As far as I've seen, he's been successful. I shake my head, trying to forget the moment I saw him sucking her face off a few months ago.

"Hey, Kayla. I got your keys here." He digs into his seemingly bottomless breast pocket as he trots to greet me. "Here you go. Good thing you replaced that alternator. If it died while you were driving, that'd suck." He hands me my keys while I gape at him.

"I replaced what?" I almost keel over.

"The alternator," he repeats. "The new battery and the brakes are good too. Must be expensive to get the factory ones. Probably cost more than the car itself now." His chuckle makes his mustache wiggle.

I stand with my arm outstretched, my mouth still agape. "I haven't changed anything, Paul."

"Oh." His mouth forms an *o*, and his gaze darts around. "Well, someone must have done it for you." He awkwardly pats my shoulder and walks away, leaving me feeling extremely uncomfortable.

Looks like the mystery of my car's miraculous recovery just got resolved—*someone* upgraded the parts without my knowledge. And the only someone who could have done that...

I'm about to turn on my heel and leave when I decide to ask what time they close the shop. Paul says that he's about to lock up. Conflicted, I get into my Jeep and patiently wait for my brain to make a decision.

I want to thank Justin—I know it's him. But why would he do that for me when he still hated me? I don't understand. I keep bringing my thumb to the call button next to his name on my phone screen but decide against it every time. He clearly didn't want to see me a few moments ago.

Soon, the guys leave the garage. Justin still isn't here. I start my car, reluctantly about to drive off, when there's a loud knock on my window. I jump in my seat with a yelp.

"It's just me." Justin's standing there with his hands raised in a gesture of surrender. "Don't freak out."

"Oh." I let out a relieved breath and roll the window down.

"What are you doing here?" He lost a little of that anger, but it's still there. His not-exactly-friendly question indicates that I'm not really welcomed here.

"I'm—" I clear my throat. "Actually, I was waiting for you."

"Why?" He narrows his eyes.

"I wanted to thank you."

"For what?" He leans his hands on the hood.

"For my car."

He sighs. "Let's go talk inside. I'm starving."

I know it's not a very good idea, and I can thank him right here and right now—it would take literally thirty seconds. But I like some emotional pain, apparently, so I roll the window shut, get out of the car, and follow him inside. To be honest, I'm curious to see how Justin lives. He saw my home; it's only fair I see his.

We go to the back of the building; there are stairs to the second level. We go up, and he unlocks the door, heading inside. I follow him.

Looking around, I see that my old crush is a slob. Different pieces of clothing are splayed everywhere, pizza boxes and soda cans are chilling on the table, and in the living room, dishes are piled up in the sink. Nice.

He walks to the fridge, pulls a beer out, and offers it to me. "Want one?"

"No, thank you."

He opens a can for himself and asks, "What did you want to talk about?"

"I wanted to thank you for fixing my car."

"No problem. It's just an oil change." He shrugs.

"Yes, but also the other things you fixed." I look at him impactfully.

His cheeks turn a soft shade of pink. I think I've seen luxury brands sell that same shade under the name 'screaming orgasm.' "I don't know what you're talking about."

"Really?" I quirk a brow.

"Really." He looks everywhere but at me, and it's adorable.

"Justin. We both know you fixed my car, and I thank you for that. You're probably the only reason I haven't slid off the road somewhere." And then I go off on a limb here and touch his shoulder. It freezes and instantly bunches under my palm.

"Don't touch me," he growls, and my hand drops just as bile rises up my esophagus. I'm nauseous all of a sudden. Well, that was a clear message.

"Ah, okay. Sorry." I all but run to the door, begging the universe to swallow me whole as soon as possible.

"Shit," he says, but I'm out of the door and already running down the stairs, nearly breaking my ankle when I miss a step. "Kayla," he calls out.

But I'm not listening. This is so incredibly embarrassing. Like, oh-my-gosh-I'm-leaving-this-planet-right-now embarrassing. Blood roars in my ears from how fast I run, and I can't hear a thing. I feel a strong arm wrap around my waist, and I scream bloody murder. It pulls me into a hard chest.

"Stop yelling," Justin hisses into my ear, and I calm down a notch. "For fuck's sake, stop flailing, Kayla."

But I don't stop, and I keep trying to kick him, so he lets me go. When my foot finally lands on his shin, he growls, throws me over his shoulder, and heads back to the apartment. When we're upstairs, he walks to the couch and drops me on it. I land with a loud thump, my hair falling over my eyes, and I can't see anything.

While I'm trying to clear my view, Justin growls like a wild beast. "The fuck did you run for?"

"Seriously?" I hiss, trying to pull myself up, but he leans over and pushes me back, and I land on the couch once again. "Seriously, Justin? You just hissed at me and told me not to touch you. I only offered a friendly gesture. I don't think you're capable of changing, no matter how much I wish you would. You're still an asshole! Every time I start to think you're not, you prove you are!" I try to stand up again, but he pushes me back.

Standing in all his six-foot-two glory, he clenches and unclenches his fists. His nostrils flared. His eyes wild.

"Do you think I can tolerate your touch when I'm like that?" He gestures at himself.

"You tolerated my touch just fine yesterday." I look at him from my low position.

"Oh, no. I wasn't mad like that. No." He shakes his head and takes a deep breath. "Now I'm mad."

"For touching you? Seriously? You got so mad over me touching you? What the hell, man? Really." I can't say I'm not offended because I am.

"Oh no." He puts one knee on one side of me. "That's not why I'm mad." He then puts his hands on the back of the couch, framing my head, and leans closer. "I'm mad at you for doing something I told you not to do." Then he brings his face closer and whispers, "Kayla."

"What?" I croak.

"Oh yeah." He licks his lips, and my eyes dip to watch his tongue. "I told you not to talk to him. Not to spend time with him. And here you are, flirting," he inhales deeply, "mingling your scent with his, rubbing on him like you're some cat in heat. You're fucking lucky you still smell like you and not him." My heart stops beating. I've never seen Justin so possessive, but now, he is an alpha pissing on his territory.

And I fucking love it.

"What are you doing, Justin?" I whisper after I lick my own lips, unconsciously wetting them.

"I'm thinking the same thing, Kayla." He dips his head and quickly presses his lips to mine in a butterfly-like kiss. "What am I doing? I'm still fucking mad at you. At him. At fucking Ashley."

"Oh, *Ashley*." Horny clouds over my head dissolve in a second at the mention of her name, evaporating completely into oblivion. *Way to go, Justin.*

"Yeah, I hate her."

"Just like you hated me, but still wanted to fuck?"

His chuckle is dark. "I never hated anyone as much as I hated you." He plants his other knee on the couch, and now he's straddling me, but holding his weight off. "Just like I never wanted to fuck anyone as much as I wanted to fuck you."

My breathing quickens. He admitted he hated me the most, but I didn't hear that part. No, all I heard was that he wanted to *fuck* me the most.

"And I'm still so fucking mad at you for letting the fuckface near you. So mad." He strokes my cheek with the back of his fingers. "Should I punish you for that?"

He straightens, and his huge dick is straining his jeans right in front of my face. I swallow nervously and look up. When I meet his eyes, he smiles. "That's what I like to see." He brings his finger under my chin and lifts it up. "You, right where you're supposed to be, with your mouth open, looking so innocent and scared."

I think my panties just evaporated. I knew Justin was a very experienced man, but I never expected him to be so dirty.

And I never expected myself to be the one to like it.

"Should I punish you for that?" he says as he plants his hand on his cock and strokes it a few times over the jean material.

"I think you should." I surprise us both with my answer, and his hand stills, his mouth dropping open. I surprise us both some more when I bring my hands to his front and pull the zipper down. He takes a shuddering breath.

Once the zipper is down, I pull his fully hard cock free. I lick my lips and glance at him. His nostrils are flared, his mouth ajar, his eyes trained on my mouth.

"Have you done this before?" he croaks, his voice low and strained.

"No," I answer honestly.

"Fuck. Me." He growls as he looks up at the ceiling. Then he wipes his face with his hand and shifts his attention back to me. "I'm kind of big; you don't have to—"

I don't let him finish. I grab the base of his cock and lick the tip. I've watched enough porn to know the basics; I can figure out the rest as I go. It's not rocket science.

"Oh, fuck, Kayla. Your mouth is so hot." He clasps his hands behind his back, clearly restraining himself, his muscles all over his body strained. But he's still in control, and once in a blue moon, I want to be the one. So I grip his cock tighter and guide him on. His breath hitches and I suck him deeper, hollowing my cheeks. Once he hits the back of my throat, my throat constricts at the intrusion, and I gag. He immediately pulls back, but I grip him by the ass and push him back to me, taking him as deep as I can.

"Baby, you don't have to—" I suck him harder, and he inhales loudly. "Kayla, you don't need to—"

But I don't let him finish because I take him as deep as I can, overcoming my gag reflex. And it's deep. Man, is it deep. Justin growls something incoherent and leans forward, resting his hands on the back of the couch, accidentally inserting himself even deeper inside my throat with the movement. I gag again, but this time he doesn't pull back. He keeps thrusting, meeting my mouth halfway. At this point, I don't even bobble my head anymore; he's just making use of my mouth. And he's right, he is fucking big, so I work the rest of his length that doesn't fit with my hands. Eventually, I drop them. Justin's too far gone, and I'm enjoying it.

He keeps thrusting and growling while I dig my fingers into his ass.

"Oh fuck," he says as he pulls out with a loud pop. Saliva is dripping from my mouth, but he drops to his knees on the floor and pulls me to him. Covering my mouth with his, he suffocates me with the kiss. I barely had any oxygen while his dick occupied my mouth, which is only replaced by his tongue. But I don't complain.

Suddenly, he breaks our kiss, grabs me by the back of my thighs, and pulls me closer to him. I'm half-lying on the couch while he rips my underwear off.

"I'll buy you another one."

"So I've heard." I should keep a count of all the underwear he keeps destroying.

His voice takes a dangerous tone. "Did you wear this dress for him?"

"What if I did?" Seems like I can't help but challenge him today.

"Then I'd have to punish you again."

At this idea, sparkles ignite inside my belly, and I laugh. It's low and sensual, and very, very unlike me. "Maybe you should."

"Yeah, I definitely should," he says as he brings his mouth to my completely soaked pussy. I relax into the cushions, knowing I'm up for a very good time. "Fuck, Kayla, you are so wet just from sucking me off." I can feel him breathing the words on my heated core. I'm aching and sore, and I just need release.

"Shut up, Justin," I say as I grab him by the hair and pull him into me. His low chuckle is the last comprehensible sound he makes before my moaning fills the room.

When I'm close, so deliciously close, he pulls away with an evil smile.

"Justin!" I yelp.

"Punishment, baby. Don't forget." He stands up, pulls his pants off, and grabs me by my ass, twisting us in the air as he lands on the couch, and I'm the one straddling him. "You're on the pill, right?" I nod. "Is this okay...?" He let the thought trail off as he helps to lift me up on my knees with one hand and grabs his dick in his other, moving its head under my core.

"Yeah." I swallow a huge lump in my throat. After feeling his raw skin inside me, I don't think I'll ever be able to settle for any barrier between us.

He guides himself in, and I get ready for pain. It doesn't

come. I'm so wet and ready that he can slide halfway inside in just one go.

"Ah," I breathe out.

"Is it painful?" His neck is straining, and his breathing is hard.

"No." I sigh. "It's good."

"Thank fuck." And he drops me all the way in. I let out a yelp. "Kayla?"

"I'm good, I'm good," I answer as I begin moving. I don't think Justin understands how big his dick is. For him, it's something to brag about; for me, it's something I have to accommodate for.

His hands come under my thighs as he helps my movement and I feel my own muscles begin to shake. I'm so out of shape; who knew that riding a dick could be so physically taxing.

Justin quickens the pace when I lean to kiss him. He tastes like sin... and me. I dive deeper into the kiss, and he speeds up even more. I grab his face with my hands, angling for a kiss, when he growls, lifts me up, and throws my back on the couch. Switching positions, he plunges into me with a force that knocks the breath out of me.

"Fuck, I can't control it anymore. I'm sorry, Kay," he says as he delivers punishing thrust after punishing thrust. He grabs my ankles and puts them on his shoulders, causing his heavy balls to begin slapping my ass.

In this position, he hits just the right spot. It's close. It's there. But not quite yet.

His movements are deliberate and hard. He grabs my waist as he slams himself into me with every thrust. He's imprinting me with the hate we shared for so long, his newfound jealousy, and this overwhelming need with every thrust. Someone moans, and I think it's me.

"You need to come, baby. Now." Sweat is dripping from his body onto me.

"I can't," I whisper in shame.

"Oh, baby. I'll help you." He tilts his head to the side, licking my ankle while still plunging in. "Do you need me to do that for you?"

"Yes," I whisper. How broken am I if I'm just beginning my sexual journey but can only come from certain things?

"I love how naughty you are." He bites the exposed skin on my ankle, leans forward, and plants his hand on my throat, squeezing it just a bit. He then presses his finger on my clit, rubbing it in circles, all the while thrusting in.

And I feel the wave coming. I open my mouth for a breath, but I can't take one. Justin squeezes my throat tighter, not stopping the airflow, but just enough to make me a little lightheaded, and I explode.

I don't feel anything but waves of pleasure wash over me again and again and again. The feeling of being powerful, boneless, and soulless is wonderful, and I don't want it to end.

A loud growl shatters my haze just as Justin grabs my thighs and pulls me onto him. He does a few powerful, jerky thrusts before spilling inside. His head falls back, and he growls. That's easily the hottest and the most gorgeous thing I've ever seen.

Once he comes down, he falls on top of me and buries his face in the crook of my neck.

We are silent for the next few minutes, trying to return from the fog our brains are in now.

Everything around us is wet. He is sweaty, I'm sweaty, and the couch is wet from our liquids. There is a sea of us combined between my legs, and it's pouring out.

"Justin, I need to use the bathroom."

"Yeah." He lifts himself up and looks like he's struggling to do so. "There." He points to the door. I stand up and scuttle to the bathroom. As expected, it's a mess. I dig under the sink and find a few packs of wet wipes. I clean myself as best as I can, fix my dress, and walk out.

He's standing by the fridge, drinking water from a bottle and looking like he just got thoroughly fucked. By me. A feeling of pride spreads in my chest. When he notices me, he walks over and hands me the bottle. "I'll be back. Don't go anywhere."

"Okay," I whisper as I take a huge greedy sip.

He's back a moment later, finding me in the same place. "Let's go." He grabs my hand and tows me to the bedroom. He lets go of me, walks to the dresser, and digs inside. "This should fit," he says as he passes me a gray T-shirt.

I look at it as if it's a spider. "Why?"

"Why what?" He sounds genuinely confused.

"Why do I need a shirt?"

"To sleep in. Unless you want to sleep naked. I don't mind." He shrugs.

"Am I sleeping here?" I look around.

"Of course, you are." He walks to the bed, falls onto it, and pats the space beside him. "C'mon."

I shrug off my dress, put his shirt on, and crawl into bed with him, keeping my distance. He grabs my waist and pulls me to him. I end up in the same position as back at home—with me half sprawled on top of him.

"I'm sorry, Kay." His sigh is full of remorse.

"For what?" He has so much apologizing to do, so he'd better clarify every time, so it counts.

"For what happened." He closes his eyes in shame.

"What are you talking about?" I perch on my elbow.

"I was fucking rough." He wipes his face with his hand.

"I don't know what came over me; I swear, I've never been like that."

"I liked it," I say quietly.

"You did?" His eyes widen.

"I think it was hot."

"Of fuck." I feel his cock hardening against my knee.

"I like you all... beastly and growly." I put my finger on his bicep.

His dick twitches. "Fuck."

"I'm sorry. I wish I could come easier, though, so you don't have to work so hard or do kinky shit," I say with a shrug, voicing my own shame.

His eyes grow even wider, and he flips me on my back in one swift movement.

"Never ever apologize for that." His eyes are serious.

"Never?"

"Never ever. It's my job to make sure you come. And if you don't, I fail, not you. You got it?" His eyes dart between mine. "Got it?"

"Yes," I say in a small voice.

"And asphyxiation is a very popular erotic play, and there is nothing to be ashamed of. You have no idea how happy I was when I figured out you liked it." A dimple appears on his cheek.

I stop drawing circles on his bicep. "Why?"

"Because I like to be in control."

"Oh."

"Like you haven't noticed that." His grin is wide. "Now, you woke the beast; what can we do about that?"

The rest of the night is an orgasmic haze as we try to tame the beast. By the time we're done, I'm deliciously sore and in absolutely no condition to move anywhere.

Chapter Twenty Seven

JUSTIN

The second morning in a row, I wake up to the smell of food. I don't remember my place smelling so good before. Ever. I look around—Kayla isn't in bed, of course, though it would be nice to wake up to her warm body snuggled up to mine.

To wake up. To fucking *wake up*? Did I sleep again? I listen to my body, and yes. I slept again. Two nights in a row. Like a normal human. Those orgasms must be pretty magical if they knock me down that fast.

I pull sweats on and walk toward the smell.

And stand shocked. My apartment is clean, like spotless clean. I look around and don't recognize my place; there are no more food boxes or cans lying on every surface, no more trash, cushions are neatly placed on the couch, dishes are done, and the counter is sparkly.

"Hey." My voice is rough.

She jumps, startled, and turns around. "Oh, hey."

"Expected someone else?" I smirk.

"No." She laughs nervously. "Just didn't expect you to wake up so early."

"It's eleven," I deadpan.

"I've seen you around town looking for coffee at ungodly hours before." She rolls her eyes with a hidden smile.

"Yeah, with insomnia, you never know when it hits and when you will wake up." I scratch the scruff on my chin. I probably need to shave. "Why are you up so early?"

"I'm used to waking up early. The diner opens up at six-thirty." That's right. Normal people have normal patterns.

"You cleaned." Somehow, it sounds like I'm accusing her, and her cheeks turn pink.

"I didn't mean anything by that. I mean, your place is nice."

"My place is a shithole that needed a good cleaning. Thanks for the help here." I go and kiss her cheek. Her lips form a cute *o*.

"Welcome," she squeaks.

"You didn't have to do that, though."

"Who would do that, though?"

"Touché." I laugh and go to the coffee machine, where a full pot of fresh brew is waiting for me. Did I wake up in heaven?

"Want some breakfast?" she offers, pointing at the stove.

"That would be amazing." I take a seat at the table with my coffee and relax. "You look good this morning. Though limping a little. Why is that?" I don't want to sound smug, but I can't help myself. Last night was off the charts, and Kayla woke something I never thought I had in me.

"Awfully full of yourself, I see." She narrows her eyes at me, but there is no anger in them, only a twinkle of good humor.

I lean back in the chair. "Well, I'm kind of responsible for that, I guess." But there is no remorse in my voice, only the pleasure of knowing she'll be walking around the whole day, remembering me with every step she takes. Then I stop smiling, reminding myself that Kayla doesn't have much experience, even if she could have fooled me. "Are you really that sore?"

"Yeah."

I wince. "Fuck, I'm sorry. I didn't mean that."

"You did." She laughs. So carefree and loud. Just like she did with the fuckface. Like she had never done with me before. Like I'm *her* people. Her face changes; it looks brighter, her eyes sparkle like diamonds in the sun, I swear, and I'm about to spontaneously produce some poetry. "You totally did, especially because of that last time when I was trying to crawl away, but you pulled me back into that never-ending marathon." Fuck, how do I explain to her that my dick has been on hiatus for months, and now it's regaining its appetite for only her, and she's the only one who can feed the fucker.

"Alright, I did mean it, but I didn't want you to be sore today." I totally did. She needs to know who was between her legs all night. Me. Only me. But I also hate to see her wincing in pain every time she walks.

"It's a good kind of sore." Her cheeks pinken, her lips turn into a cute bow, and I find myself smiling like a fool.

"Oh, yeah?" I lean my elbow on the table. "How good?"

"Very good." Her cheeks turn bright red. "Now shut up and eat." She places one plate in front of me and the other in front of the chair across from me. I grab it and move it next to mine. She watches and carefully sits at the newly assigned place. I casually put my hand on her thigh like it's the most natural thing in the world and grab my fork with the other.

She stills for a moment, then grabs her own utensils and digs into her food. My plate is overflowing with home fries, bacon, and eggs. I didn't even know I had anything even remotely potato-looking.

"You have a weird obsession with apples. You have all sorts of them, and they take up half of the fridge."

I chuckle at that. Alex was always busting on me ever since we were kids, telling me that I would turn into a rabbit with my next apple. "I love them; what can I say," I say with a full mouth of food. "What are you doing today?"

"Well, hopefully, not getting fired, for a start."

I choke on my food. "What? Why?"

"I overslept, and when I woke up, it was eight-thirty. The diner has long been open by now."

"Ouch. I'd be scared to call Marina." I wince as if in pain, imagining the wrath of that woman.

Her laughter is light. "Trust me, I was. Turns out, she called the new girl in this morning, so everything worked out."

"You know she would never fire you, right?" I ask between bites.

"I know." She sighs. "It's just that I hate to let her down. It's hard work to cook for so many people, especially in the morning, and if you also have to wait on them, you're toast by nine."

"Yeah, she has a lot of customers." To think of it, the diner always has people in it, unlike any other place here.

"That's because her food is good." She looks at me pointedly, daring me to contradict her.

"I had the pleasure of trying it myself yesterday." I pat my belly.

"Speaking of yesterday..." She drinks her coffee and swats my hand away from her thigh where it took a permanent residency. "What was that?"

"What?" I blink at her, hoping like hell she doesn't mean the *feelings* part.

"You were clearly jealous of Archie. Why?" She crosses her hands over her chest.

"Because I don't like the fuckface."

"What did he ever do to you for you to hate him so much?" Then she laughs. "Wait, nothing, right? That's the pattern with you."

"Kayla," I growl as I put the fork down.

"What? You were acting like a possessive gorilla the whole time. And then when I asked you why, you didn't have an answer. Then, mind you, you proceeded to chat with your girlfriend, who you're clearly still hung up on, and then you had the audacity to blame me for spending time with Archie." There is a bitter note in her voice that I don't like.

"She is not my girlfriend," I say through clenched teeth. "And I'm not hung up on her."

"Could have fooled me," she snorts.

"What did you expect me to do? To rip her hands off for touching me?"

"Sounds like a good idea to me." She shrugs.

"What did you do when the fuckface was all over you?" I counter her.

Her spine straightens. "If you must know, we were talking about business."

I snort. "What sort of business can you have with him?"

"He wants to hire me to work for him, you asswipe! Do

you think I'm too stupid to do any sort of business with anyone?" She jumps from the chair and goes to the bedroom.

I follow her. "Kayla, wait. That's not what I meant."

"Yep, sure." She takes my T-shirt off but stays in her bra and panties, and my dick takes notice. *Not now, fucker. Down, boy.* She then proceeds to pull her dress over her head, and I have to take action before this amazing morning is completely destroyed.

"Kayla." I try to sound gentle and not needy, but she keeps going without acknowledging me, so I bark an order. "Kayla, stop." It seems to work because she stops and focuses her attention on me. A win. I slowly move toward her, careful not to scare her away. "I didn't mean it like that. I meant that he's too dangerous to do any business with. Especially for you."

"Why is it especially for me?"

I swallow the dryness in my throat, contemplating if, for once, I should just go with the truth. "Because of how fucking beautiful and sexy you are."

"Oh." It's all she says, her mouth ajar. Her cute little tongue peeks out and licks her lips, and I'm a goner.

I groan and close the last little bit of distance separating us and pull her into me. She doesn't fight me, and plants her hands on my chest. It's a glorious feeling, her in my arms. The right one.

I take my time with her this time, exploring every single detail of every single tattoo that I neglected yesterday with my tongue.

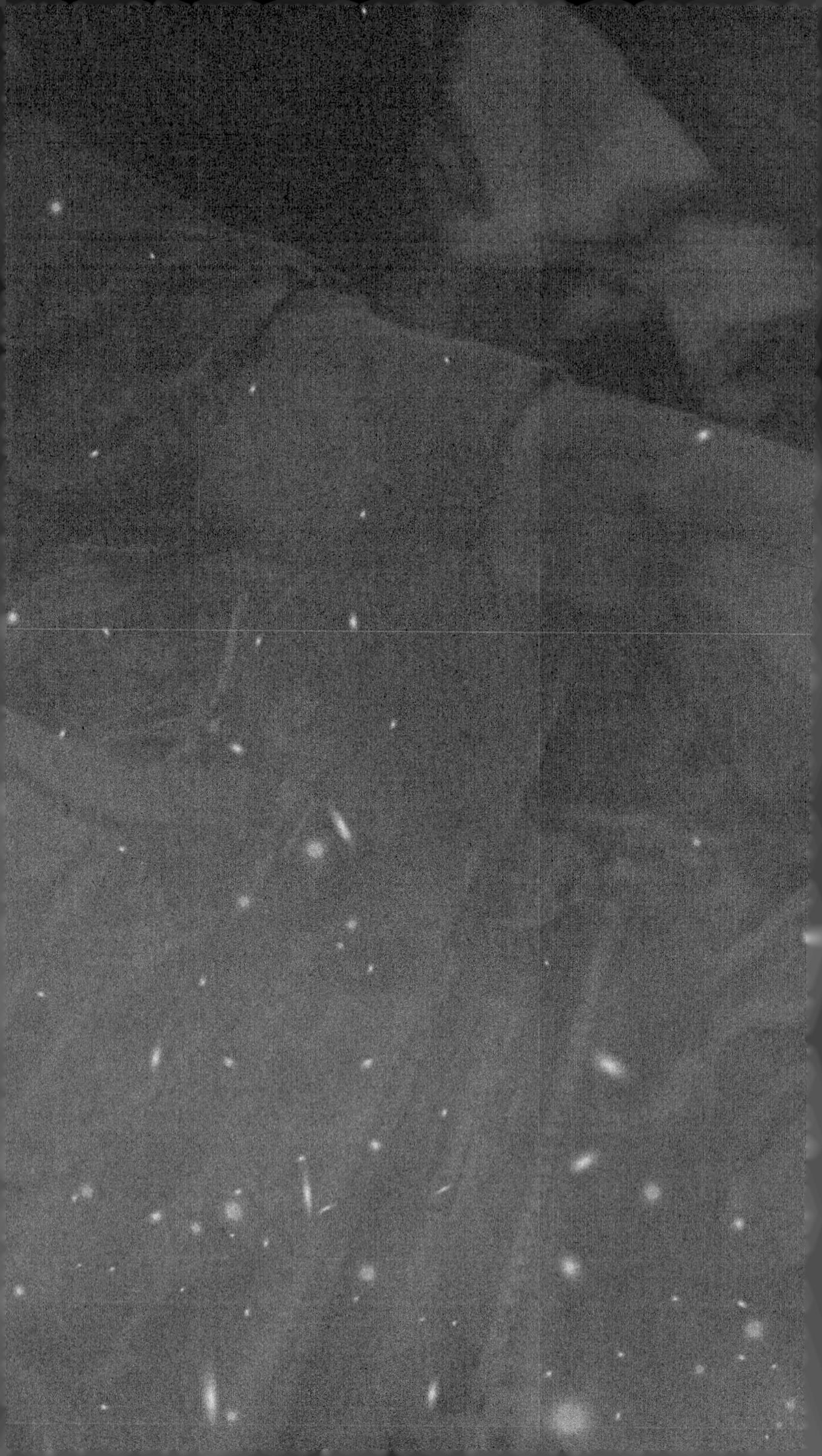

Chapter Twenty Eight

JUSTIN

I sit in my truck, still parked by my house, thinking. It's two in the morning, and I'm back to my usual self, meaning no sleep whatsoever. It's been two days since our night together at my place, and I haven't slept since then. My body is aching, and my mind is foggy, but I still can't shut down.

After we had slow, lazy morning sex, I drove her to the diner and left her car parked beside it. I wanted to ask again what sort of business she was discussing with that fuckface, but every time his name is brought up, we fight, and I didn't want to ruin those rare moments of real conversations we had.

Because of her, I had to jerk off these last two days. A lot. Thinking that was the cause of my two good nights of sleep before—empty balls. Turned out it was not. I look at my palms—they're worse for wear from the past two days, more so than if I were to use my bare fingers to screw the bolts at the shop. My hand is tired, my dick is tired, my body is tired, but I still can't fuckin' sleep.

I dig the heels of my palms into my eyes. Even they ache and feel like they're seconds away from falling out of my eye sockets.

Fuck it. I start my engine and drive through the mountain to the place I felt at peace for the first time in forever. She's probably sleeping, and I'm about to scare her shitless, knocking on her door at night. But I don't have a choice; I need to test my theory.

And I hope I'm fucking wrong.

I park my truck behind her Jeep and slowly walk to the door, giving myself time to escape, if needed. There are no lights on in the windows, obviously. Before I knock, I contemplate if I should turn back and go home before I make things even more complicated than they already are, but before I can decide, the door swings open, scaring me shitless.

Kayla greets me at her threshold, wearing a white worn-out off-the-shoulder shirt, nearly see-through, and black panties, looking sleepy and cozy. A weird, tingling feeling spreads in my chest and dips into my belly, without reaching my dick. Even though she is sexy as fuck, especially right now, the fuzzies stay in my chest, and it scares the living crap out of me. I can deal with the horny but don't know how to deal with anything that runs deeper.

I try to say something—*anything*—but my throat is dry, so I cough to clear it. "Why are you not sleeping?" I croak.

"I was." Her voice is a mess, in a feminine way, with sleep. "But had to pee and saw lights through the window."

"Sorry." I truly am—she looks tired.

"It's okay. What happened?" She shivers from the cold air seeping through the open door.

I swallow a lump in my throat and look around.

"Justin, are you okay?"

"Yeah." I hide my hands inside my pockets.

She looks me over and steps aside, leaving the doorway open. "C'mon in."

I silently accept the invitation and follow her inside, locking the door behind me. She walks to the bedroom and crawls under the covers, scooting over to one side of the bed. Silently too.

I take my pants and shirt off and follow her. It's warm in here and smells like her. I wrap an arm around her middle and pull her back toward me, enveloping her in a hug. She nestles her head on my bicep and sighs. I pull her closer and bury my nose in her hair. The strawberry scent now represents calm and quiet, like a chill pill for me.

I'm asleep within minutes.

A few days pass in a blur. I stay at Kayla's, or she stays at my place. I mostly prefer to have her stay at my place with me, only because there is some weird Frank dude living in the woods next to her, and I'm totally not comfortable with it. Every time I bring the subject of him up, she laughs it off and keeps quiet. This Frank is the bane of my existence. I'm thinking of just hiding somewhere around the trailer one day to see what this fucker does when he shows because he sure as hell doesn't show up when I'm around. All I see is the rustling of bushes—this Frank is a fuckin' ghost for all I know.

Every time we are together, I sleep. After mind-blowing sex, of course. A few rounds of that. My appetite was always over the top (well, before my dick refused to work for anyone but her), and she's insatiable. She's made for me, a perfect version of sinful paradise.

In the mornings, I drive her to work, where Marina has a breakfast already ready for me that she passes with a stink eye. Yet, she still gives it to me. It's adorable, really. I think I'm growing on her.

Freya and Alex invited us over for a few dinners, and we went as a... *couple*, I guess? We never really put a label on it, but we've spent every free moment we both have together. Throughout the whole meal, Alex watched me like a hawk, conscious of my every move and every word, but I didn't restrain myself. I can't restrain myself when Kayla's near. So I kept touching her every moment I could, brushing her hair behind her ears, feeling her skin under my fingers, pressing my palm onto her thigh, making her giggle like a schoolgirl. God, I love that sound. So carefree and happy.

Jake came back from rehab and claims to be a changed man. I have yet to see that. We talked where he announced how unhappy he is with my relationship with Kayla, but I quickly shut him up, saying that it's none of his business. Since then, he's been staying away from me. I still haven't told him the truth. I just don't want to ruin this little bubble of happiness I happen to have here. And I know—I just know—that the moment the truth is out, our lives will be forever changed, and I'm not sure I'm ready to see just how changed they will be.

For the first time in my life, I feel like I might be ready to settle. To stay with one woman because I don't *want* anyone else. I just need to test one theory before making such a big decision. Before discussing putting a label on us, because for the first time in life, I want one.

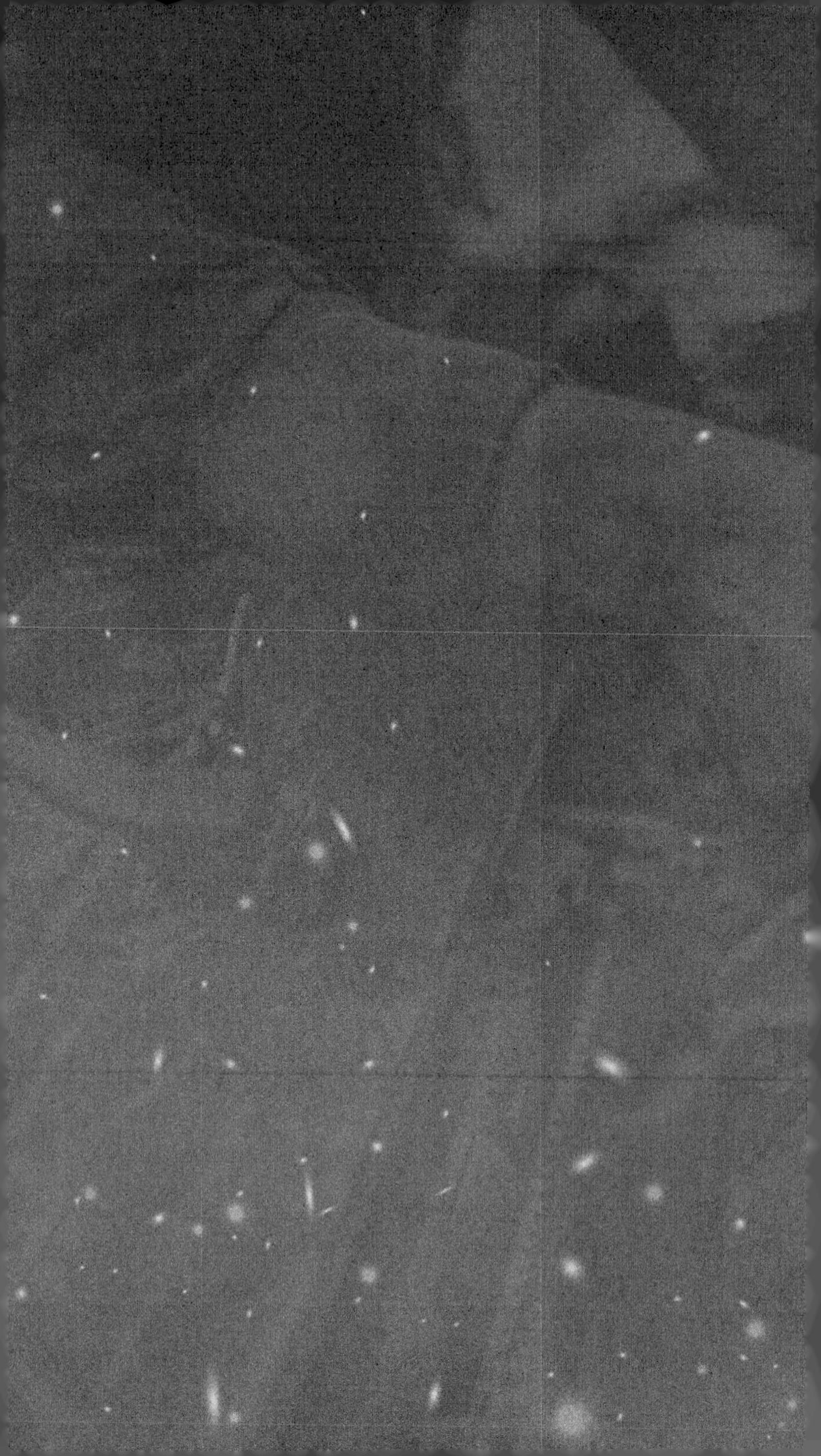

Chapter Twenty-Nine

K AYLA

I try to call Justin all day long, but he doesn't pick up the phone. Then I text him, and all of the messages stay 'unread.' It's not like him. We haven't seen each other in a couple days, and the last time we spoke was yesterday. He seemed a little off, saying he had some things to take care of. I let it go because if he wanted to, he'd tell me. Plus, I'm not in a position where I can demand answers—our relationship is very new and not even official.

By four in the afternoon, I begin to worry.

"Hey, Marina."

"What's up?" she asks from the coffee machine, chugging her fifth cup of coffee today. Well, someone must have been busy last night. Any other time I'd ask, but today my mind is ten thousand miles away.

"I feel like something might be wrong with Justin." Her

face changes from relaxed to concerned—it looks like somebody's grown to like the rough guy. "Do you think you'll be okay if I take a break now?"

"Sure, go ahead." She waves me off. "Call if you need me."

"Alright." I take my apron off, grab my purse and hurry to Justin's place. I don't bother taking the car because it's only a ten-minute walk, but I make it in six.

The garage is open, and the guys are working. I spot Paul and walk to him. "Hey, Paul. Have you seen Justin today?"

"Nah," he says. "He's probably sleeping." He points to the stairs at the back.

"Okay. I'll check on him."

"Sure." He shrugs and goes back under the hood of the car he's working on. "Holler if you need my help."

"Will do." I will not. I don't know the extent of their relationship, so I'll keep whatever I find to myself.

I run up the stairs and go inside the apartment.

"Justin?" I call. "Hey, Jus, are you here?"

He doesn't respond, so I walk around to check on things.

When I push the bedroom door open, I see a person on the bed.

On top of Justin.

He's sleeping on his stomach, and a woman's body is wrapped around him like a snake around a tree. When I see them, I let out a cry of pain. An arrow shoots through my chest, leaving a hole. All my happiness evaporates in an instant. It's slowly dissolving into nothingness. I can't breathe, and I can't move.

He doesn't wake up from my cry because he doesn't hear me. I, out of anyone, should know that he sleeps like the dead after a good fucking. Every time we do it, his lights are out for hours. I can blast music in the morning and start vacuuming at the same time, and he would still sleep through it.

The woman stirs and looks up. I don't know her name, but I've seen her with Adison, one of Ashley's friends, around town. I think she is from Springfield. She looks thoroughly fucked: her eyelids are heavy, her hair is a mess, and she has burns on her face and neck from his stubble. I know what they look like because I see them every morning in the mirror… Used to see.

Disheveled pieces of clothing are scattered everywhere around the room.

I swallow a huge lump in my throat, not bothering to wipe the tears that begin streaming down my cheeks. The woman smiles as she places a hand on Justin's back and starts massaging it while he's out cold. I don't want to face him when he wakes up, so I don't plan on waiting, and besides that, I don't think he'd want me here. He made that pretty clear.

I turn around and walk outside through the back door.

When I'm on the ground, I find Jake leaning on his cruiser, looking happy and smug.

"What happened, trailer trash? You look like somebody's kicked your puppy." He chuckles at his own unfunny joke. I ignore him. "Oh, let me see. You probably just met Claudia, Jus's friend. Yeah, they've been hooking up for a few weeks now." His face changes to thoughtful. "Oh, wait. You didn't really think that he was into you, did you? It's clear as day for everyone that he was fucking his anger out on you." He smirks, delivering the last blow.

I don't respond, but I wipe my tears away and go to my car. And he follows.

"What? You don't have anything to say?" He falls in step behind me. He keeps chatting as I wipe the wetness from my face away. "C'mon, what did you expect?" He laughs, and I try not to listen. When we are at the front of the building, he is still there, still following, delivering death blow after death blow, and each one lands in just the right place. I don't know what he wants. I'm already on the ground, so he can stop any minute now.

A huge truck slows down and then completely stops. The door opens up, and a big body steps outside. I don't look at his face because my eyes are trained on the asphalt in front of me. I think if I look up, I'll lose it.

"Kayla, are you okay?" Mark's low voice sounds concerned.

"Go mind your own business," Jake hisses.

Mark ignores him and asks again, "Kayla?"

I sniffle and wipe my eyes with my sleeve. "Yeah."

"Get out. It's like all the trailer trash got together in one place. Fuck."

"Shut your mouth," Mark growls, and I know he doesn't care about being called names, but he doesn't want Jake saying it about me. "Kayla." He steps in front of me, grabs my chin, and lifts it up. "What happened?" His eyes dart between mine.

My lower lip trembles and more tears pour out of my already swollen eyes.

"Get out of here. It's none of your business." Jake just doesn't know when to stop.

Mark drops my chin, steps around me, and hisses at Jake. "Right now. One warning. Go. Now."

"Or what?"

I turn around just in time to see Mark grabbing the front of Jake's uniform. Oh fuck, this can't be good. I don't want him to get in trouble, so I jump on Mark, tugging him by his hand, the one holding Jake, and say, "Can you drive me home?" He slowly moves his attention to me. "Now, please." I tug on his arm, and he lets go.

Wrapping his enormous hand around my shoulders, he pulls me into his massive body and walks me to his truck, where he opens the passenger door and practically shoves me in.

"You won't get away with it," Jake says.

"Can't wait to see what you got." Mark throws back and climbs into the driver's seat.

"You shouldn't have done that. He'll be an asshole to you now," I murmur, staring at the steaming Jake.

"He always has been. Nothing new. Don't worry." He pats my knee. "Wanna tell me what happened?"

I violently shake my head, fighting a wave of tears.

"Okay." He takes a deep breath. "But are you *okay*? I mean physically. Did something... that you didn't want to..." He inhales soundly. "happen?" It pains him to ask, his jaw is clenched, and his words are just a note above a real growl.

"No. Nothing like that." I shake my head again.

"Okay. But you would tell me if it had. Right?" He sounds like a person talking to a child.

"Yeah." I sniffle.

"Kayla." His voice is stern.

"Oh, for fuck's sake, nothing happened with me. He didn't force himself on me or something, if that's what you're assuming. I just walked in on Justin sleeping with another woman. Happy now?" I yell.

"That stupid fuck." He grips the wheel. "Fuck him, Kayla. You're better than him anyway. Never thought he deserved you."

"Yeah."

"I'm serious." He glances at me while keeping his attention on the road. "He doesn't. Though I'm confused, I've seen you with him around town and... never mind."

"What?" I ask, but he keeps his mouth shut. "What, Mark?"

"I mean, I thought he was into you. Like *really* into you. At least, it looked like that to me. Are you sure, though, about him cheating?"

"I just saw a naked chick on top of him. Both soundly sleeping. So yeah, I'd say I'm pretty sure." My voice is drowned in sarcasm.

"Fuck. I'm sorry." He pats my knee again. He reminds me of Alex a little, gruff and rough around the edges, but Mark has one of the biggest hearts I know, and his awkward attempt to comfort me makes my chest ache with a new force.

"Me too." I sniffle.

"Where do you want me to take you?" he offers with a sigh.

"Can you take me to my car?"

"Sure." Hesitating, he adds, "Can I follow you home just to make sure you're okay?"

I sniffle and nod.

He looks surprised. "Are you really gonna tell me where you live?" He lifts a brow, and I feel a tug of a smile on my lips.

"Ready to feel special?"

He chuckles and drives me to my car and from there follows me to my home.

When he comes out of his truck and sees my trailer, he whistles. "Wow, you got a fancy one."

"Yep," I say proudly. "Wanna see?"

"Sure." He follows me inside. I'm not scared of him in

my space because it was never like that between us. He always protected everybody, me included. That's it. I feel safe with him. Like with a big brother. It's not only that I trust him but also that he never, even once, has made me doubt my trust. "Nice place. I'm proud of you, Kayla," he says after he looks around. His tone isn't mocking; it's genuine. I feel my cheeks heat up, and the ache inside my chest subsides a notch.

"Where do you live now?" I ask him, realizing I never have before. He just always showed up at the right time in the right place, but I don't know his story.

"I bought a house three years ago." Then he adds with a cheeky smile. "On the good side of town."

"Oh, I bet 'the good side' loved it!" I laugh, imagining those uptight people being neighbors with trailer trash. We are allowed to call ourselves that because we don't mean it.

"Didn't they?" He joins in, laughing. "My new neighbor, Mrs. Jenkins, we literally share a driveway. She used to call the cops on me every day. But once I started cutting her grass when I was doing mine, she turned into a fairy godmother and started bringing me cold lemonade, batting her lashes." He shudders.

"Don't tell me the lemonade was so bad," I say as I open the fridge, and he laughs. "Want something?"

"No, I'm good. Just wanted to make sure you are okay. Give me your phone." He stretches his arm with an open palm, and I pass him my phone. He punches digits in and returns the phone. "Here, call me anytime." I nod. "Anytime. Got it?"

"Yes," I whisper, feeling a new wave of pain descending upon me.

"Oh, Kayla." Mark grabs my hand and pulls me into his

embrace, where I shed all the liquids I have left in my eyes to the point of hiccuping. "This will pass."

"I know," I muffle into his shirt. "But it hurts."

He doesn't say anything but just keeps me tight to his body. When I'm finally done, he makes sure I'm okay and leaves me to my business, forcing me once again to promise to call him if I need anything. I promise him with a sincere smile. Mark was always there, even though we were never considered actual friends. But when anyone needed protection, Mark was there, like a solid wall you can lean on or hide behind.

When he's gone, I call Archie.

"Hey, Kay-baby." He's ever flirtatious.

"Hi, Archie." My voice cracks a little, and he senses it immediately.

"Are you okay?"

"I'm ready to start that thing we were discussing anytime now." I sniffle into the phone.

"Did something happen?" His voice borders the edge of dangerous.

"Sort of. I just need to get out of town." I'm vague, but I'm not about to go into details. At least, not yet.

"Okay. I'm gonna send you my address; come here anytime."

"Alright. I just need to get my trailer ready."

"What for?" Genuine confusion laces his voice.

"To hook it up to my Jeep." Duh.

"Oh no, don't do that. Just pack your bags and come here, you'll be staying with me. I have five extra bedrooms I'm not using, so you can bring half of Little Hope with you."

"Okay." I don't fight him. I got no energy left for that.

I get my bags ready. A suitcase would be nice right

about now, but I've never traveled and never needed one, so I get three small bags packed with my clothes, toiletries, and art supplies. I load everything into my Jeep, then I gather all the stuff I have outside and bring it inside the trailer.

When I lock everything up and go to the car, I see a movement in the bushes. A familiar, sad face greets me.

"Hey, Frank. I'm not leaving forever; I'll be back, I promise."

He only looks at me with big brown eyes in response. I wave at him and climb into the car.

I have two stops to make on the way. First is Freya.

She opens the door, and her face falls at the sight of me. "You're leaving, aren't you?"

"Yeah, I'm taking Archie up on his offer." I force a smile on my face.

"What about Justin?" she asks, looking behind me as if he's there.

"What about him?"

"I thought you two were together." She sounds crestfallen. Just how I feel.

"I thought so too." My face hardens as the memory I'm trying to suppress with all my might returns to the surface.

"I see." She's chewing on her lip. "Asshole," she mutters under her breath. "What did he do?"

"Nothing. It's all good. It's just time for us to go our separate ways." I don't want to say too much because Justin is a big part of Alex's life, and Alex is Freya's life, and me mentioning what I saw will not go well.

She's carefully watching my face. "Okay. But you will tell me when you're ready, right?"

"Yeah, I will." I smile sadly.

"Okay." I see a battle of emotions on her face. One side of her wants to grill me for information. Another wants to comfort me. And one more wants to rip Justin's balls off; I can tell because she still blames him for whatever happened. Mission failed.

"Kayla?" A low growl, Alex's regular voice, comes from inside the house. "You're leaving?"

"Yep. Going to school. Yay!" I try to sound enthusiastic, but by the look on his face, I fail.

"Good for you." He comes out and gives me a bear hug. Then Freya nudges him to the side and throws her arms around me, and I bury my face in her neck because I'm shorter, and she smells good.

"Call me when you get there, okay?"

"Of course," I assure her because she looks so worried, and I don't want to dump my problems on her.

We say our goodbyes, and I go to my next stop—Marina. Her face is full of the bad kind of surprise when I tell her I'm leaving.

"What? Now?" she exclaims.

"Yeah."

"Why? What about Justin?" she asks, way too upset. Would you look at that? Someone's becoming Justin's advocate.

"Justin's done."

"Why? What happened?" Marina brings her hand to her mouth.

"I wasn't planning on telling anyone, but I know you can keep it a secret." I take a deep breath. "I just found a naked woman on top of him."

Her hand goes to her braless chest. "No way? Can't be true!"

"Marina! I thought you were on my side!"

"I am. That's why I can't believe it. That boy is in love.

Why would he sleep with anyone else?" She's tapping her chin with her finger, lost in her thoughts.

I begin laughing. "Justin? In love with me? I don't think so." I shake my head.

She finally focuses on me with the words "Foolish kids."

We hug and kiss goodbye, and I give her the address I'll be staying at.

The drive to Boston is uneventful. I don't cry a single tear after the waterfall with Mark. All I want now is to fall flat on a bed—any bed—and get lost in sleep.

When I stop at Archie's driveway, I need to make sure if I'm at the right place because *ma-a-an*, that house is enormous. It's made of red brick, the entrance has four white columns, and the door is a double with painted glass on either side. The landscaping is marvelous. All types of plants from different climate zones perfectly match each other. I'm not sure how he keeps all of them alive, but he probably pays a fortune to his landscaping company.

I check again—yep, the address is correct. I get out of the car and walk to the door. Right when I'm about to ring the bell, it opens, and Archie steps out with a broad smile across his face.

"Welcome home!" He spreads his arms. And I begin bawling. Again. "Oh shit," he says, pulling me inside and giving me a hug. "Do you want me to go and break his nose?"

A muffled laugh escapes me. "How do you know that it was him?"

He makes a *tsk*ing noise. "Please. Why else would you be here at night? The idiot messed up. My gain. I just got myself a future star. C'mon in." He gently leads me inside the house.

And with that, a new chapter of my life starts. I get into

the school and work at Archie's parlor in my free time. It's not so much a job but also experience I put toward hours at school. A win-win.

That first night I cry. A lot. I thought we shared something. There was something special—it turns out I was wrong. The second night I cry too. Same with the third and the fourth. And many nights after. During the day, I put a brave face on, but at night I take the happy mask off and let my real feelings pour out of me. Quite literally—waterfall nights follow every single day.

I talk with Freya daily on the phone, and she asks me if I'm ready to share every time. At this point, I don't even want to remember. I don't want to relive that horrible moment when I understood that my feelings were shit on by the one person I let myself be vulnerable with.

After four weeks, I stopped crying at night, but the ever-present ache in my chest remained there forever.

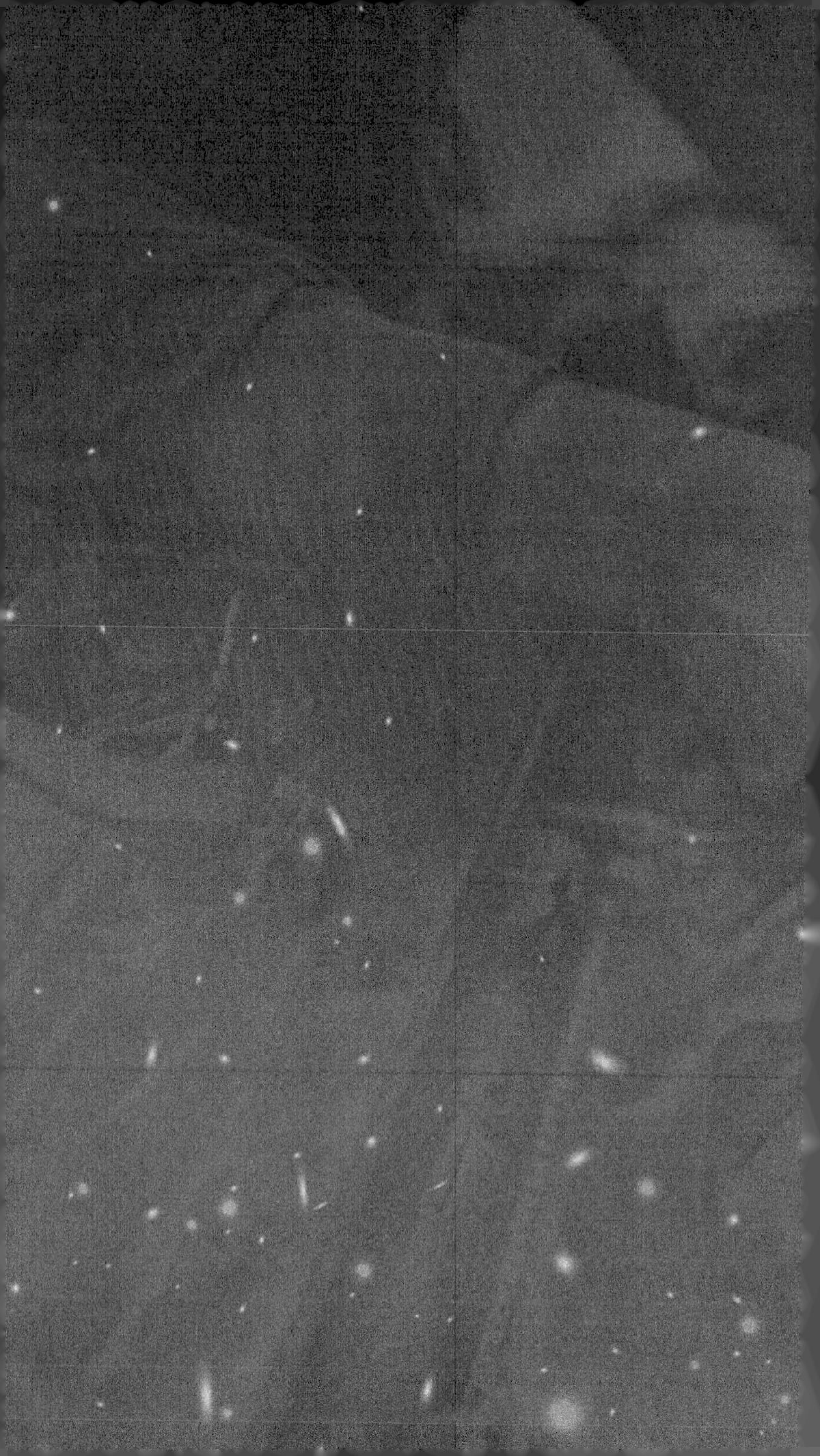

Chapter Thirty

JUSTIN

I wake up to a weird smell surrounding me. It's too sweet and suffocating. I scratch my throat because it's literally hurting me.

After a quick look around, I note that everything is the same, but I'm undressed. Weird. When I crash, I usually don't have time to get prepared.

I try to find the source of the weird smell, but I can't, so I decide to just strip the sheets. But first, I check my phone. *Damn*, it's dead. No wonder, I was probably out for hours. Plugging it in, I head to the shower.

Good thing I fucking made it home before crashing. Otherwise, it'd be embarrassing. Yesterday—or was it the day before yesterday? I'm lost with this time shit after so many hours of being out—I wanted to go to the trailer park she used to live at and talk to Mark. Since I've decided to find peace for myself, I need to make amends, and fuck do I need to apologize to that guy. And also, I wanted to test the waters and see what sort of relationship they have. I'd be a fool not to admit that he's been around a lot, and they grew up together. So I hoped to find him there. Color me surprised when it turned out he doesn't live there anymore. Instead, his old trailer is still occupied by some drunk who sort of reminds me of Mark. Can it be his dad? I don't blame the dude for leaving then.

I stuck around the trailer park longer than planned, but I got some valuable information from the neighbors. Some folks who saw Kayla growing up still remembered her mother, and they told me a few horror stories that will keep me up at night for many years to come. Stories about Kayla running away from home whenever her mom brought her new boyfriends home, and how she would always hide at Mark's place, waiting for the men to leave, and how she was left alone when her mother and sister checked out of town after hitting a woman and her child with their car, leaving Kayla with the shame and unrequited guilt. That's where the story got interesting. They told me that said woman visited her a few times before she'd moved in with Marina, right after the accident, and she brought 'friends' with her. And that word 'friends' bugged the hell out of me. I couldn't pinpoint why exactly. Kayla was fifteen when her mother checked out of town so that 'friendship' seems even weirder.

So, I drove to Springfield to ask if anyone knew any information. My search turned out fruitless, but I had spent far too many hours awake by then, and my body was crashing. I barely made it home before my lights were out. That's how my last two days went.

I miss Kayla, and all I want right now is to hold her in my arms, preferably not telling her where I was these last couple of days. I can't wait any longer, so I speed up my shower.

Twenty minutes later, I make myself a coffee and pick up my phone. It's nine-thirty at night. Fuck, just awesome. Now the next few days will be thoroughly fucked. I have a bunch of phone calls and messages from Kayla, a few from my parents, and a couple from Freya and Alex. All right. I've been out for maybe fourteen hours, but judging by the number of missed calls, it might as well have been a week.

I dial Kayla's number, and it goes straight to voicemail. Okay, odd. I try again with the same success. I shoot a quick text asking her to call me back, but it's undeliverable. *O-o-okay*, now I begin to worry a little. I finish my coffee in one big gulp and run downstairs. The garage is locked up, and everything is neat and in its place. I can always rely on Paul. He's a loyal guy and a good worker. I pay him handsomely for that.

The whole drive to her place, I'm nervous; my knee can't stop jumping.

And for a good reason.

There are no lights on in the trailer and no Jeep parked next to it. No folding chairs out front that she likes to sit in and draw. None of her stuff around.

I swallow the bile rising up my throat.

Pulling the door handle, I already know that it will be locked. I knock, but I already know that no one will respond. I feel dread settling in my stomach.

Where is she? And why is all her stuff gone?

I dial Alex.

"Yeah." His gruff voice isn't exactly welcoming on a good day, but now it's even more menacing.

"Hey. Do you know where Kayla is?"

He's quiet.

"Alex?"

"Not in Little Hope," he says shortly.

A stone, the size of Mars, drops into my stomach. "What do you mean 'not in Little Hope'? Where is she then?"

"She left." He's curt. Way too curt for somebody who rooted for us to get together.

"Where?" He's quiet. "Fuck, Alex, where did she go?"

"I have no idea, you fucker. You messed this one up, just how I told you you would." And he hangs up.

What the fuck? I look at the phone. Where did Kayla go? And why didn't she tell me anything? I try to redial her with no success. Fuck. Fuck! I don't know what's happening, but my gut tells me it's bad.

So I shoot her another message with the same results.

Then I call Freya.

"Yes?" Her voice is tepid, but I feel I might have some luck here—at least she isn't pissed at me.

"Hey, Frey. Do you know where Kayla is?"

"I do," she says, her tone suddenly terse. Never mind, she's definitely mad at me for something.

"And where is she?"

"She specifically instructed me not to tell you that."

"Why the fuck not?" I'm getting pissed at this charade.

"Calm your voice." She's enraged now. *"You're getting what you deserve."*

"What do I deserve? I don't even know what happened. And if she's okay. Is she okay?" Freya's quiet. "Is she okay, Frey?"

"She will be," she says after a pause. Well, that sounded ominous as fuck.

"Is it something I did?" I rack my brain, trying to figure out if anything even remotely bad had happened that would send her out of town without saying a word, but I can't come up with anything. The last time we talked, we had a sweet, quick chat. She had to run somewhere in Springfield, where she's been a few times in the past week to talk with her tattoo guy, TJ, who buys her incredible art. That's it. What could have happened between our last conversation and me waking up from my crash?

"She didn't tell me."

"Freya." My tone turns to a growl. I know she knows more than she says.

"I don't know, alright? I tried to torture the answers out of her, but she never said anything."

"Why? You are her friend. Why wouldn't she share it with you?" I pull on my hair.

"My guess is because I'm your friend too, and she didn't want to put a strain on our relationship. Even though I'm on her side, no matter what you did," she says harshly.

"I don't know what I did!" I shout into the phone.

"Oh, how does it feel to get a taste of your own medicine, huh?" Freya isn't a mean person per se, but at this moment, she sounds evil as fuck.

I still. "Is that what this is about? To punish me?" It can't be true; that's just not Kayla. But on the other hand, I don't know jack shit about what's happening.

I hear a loud sigh on the other side of the line. *"No, Justin. I don't think it is, but you clearly did something big enough to finally send her out of town, and she didn't tell me what."*

I, indeed, taste my own medicine. She asked me what she had done so many times over the last six years, and every time I snapped at her, demanding she leave me alone without giving any explanation when she really wasn't even the one to blame. Yeah, that shit tastes terrible.

I stoop to begging. "Can you at least tell me if she's okay?"

"*She is.*" She's quiet, and I can almost hear her thinking. "*She took Archie's offer,*" she mumbles.

I feel the world around me crumbling down, like a house of cards when someone pulls a card from the bottom. The one card that was holding the whole thing together. "What?" I ask.

"*It's good for her. She needs to move on; she can't do that by being stuck here. She's an artistic person; she has a talent, and she's wasting it here.*"

"I know," I growl. God, do I know. Every time she touches paper, a work of art appears. I wanted to ask her to make a tattoo design for me because I'm finally ready, and I know I'll be more attractive to her. She loves tattoos so much, and she likes me, so I figured she'd like me even more if I had one or two. Or liked. So I thought.

Then Freya asks the question of the year. "*What did you do, Justin?*"

"I don't know, Freya. I really don't." I hang up and climb back into the car.

What do I do next? What are my options?

Marina! She'll either shoot me, or she'll talk to me. Worth trying.

I drive to her house and knock on the door. She doesn't answer, so I keep knocking until Marina appears in the doorway a minute later.

"Oh, you got some nerve showing up here." She takes a defensive pose, her hands on her hips.

I ignore her battle stance. "Do you know where she is?"

She snorts at my obviously stupid question. "Of course, I do."

"Where?"

"Seriously?" She quirks a brow, her eyes narrowing into slits.

"Can you at least tell me why she left?" I plant a hand on the doorway.

She laughs and closes the door in my face, barely missing my fingers. At least she didn't shoot me.

Back in my truck, I sit and think about where it all went wrong. Why am I hurting so much, and why does this heavy weight stay on my chest? And why can't I breathe? And why do my eyes sting?

By the time I'm back home, the suffocating smell is gone, but it doesn't make me feel any better. Not in the slightest. I want Kayla's strawberry smell back.

My apartment is clean—of course, not my doing. But it's missing the most vital piece that made it home for me: *her*. It's missing Kayla. *I'm* missing Kayla. And I'm so fucking mad at her for leaving like that. Did our relationship mean so little to her that she could just up and go? Did *I* mean so little?

The days blur into one. I ask everyone the same questions over and over again, and I drink, and I crash. I pick a fight or two with people, but it doesn't make me feel any better. My parents tried to talk to me to figure out what's happening, but I shut them down. Alicia doesn't try, but she calls. Every single day. She's never called so many times in her entire life, but now she suddenly wants to know how my day is going. Only Jake avoids me. Weirdly, he hasn't called even once, and it's been weeks since I've entered this constant alcoholic rage.

Today, Alex barrels into my place as I'm slumped on the

couch, nursing a bottle of my friend Jack in my hands. He stops in the middle of the room and looks around in disgust. I blink at him, my head cocking to the side in question.

"Look at you, man. What the fuck happened to you?" he asks me reproachfully. I wish I could care, but I don't.

I spread my arms, accidentally splashing some Jack on the couch where we spent so many hot nights—and days—both of us learning so many new things. Turns out, Kayla is adventurous; the second I found out, I knew I had hit the jackpot. Now I'm just sad that those days are gone. "Kayla happened. That witch."

"You leave women left and right, and they don't mope like this." He rolls his eyes. "Did you lose your dick somewhere along the way?"

I point an accusing finger at him. "None of them were Kayla," I say her name with care, even when I'm pissed at her. "And might as well have." I shrug at the second part. Even porn doesn't do it for me these days. How pathetic I've become.

"Are you gonna wallow in your sorrows for the rest of your life?" He stands in front of me, arms crossed over his chest.

"Are you gonna tell me where she is?" I counter.

He sighs and sits next to me. "I know she's in Boston, and she's doing good. That's all I know."

A sliver of hope sparks in my chest. "Do you know why she left?"

"Nah." He shakes his head, and I stare at him, trying to figure out if he's lying. "I swear I don't know. I don't think Freya knows either, or she'd cave the second she saw you like this, looking like a miserable piece of year-old shit. My guess is Kayla doesn't want us to beat the shit out of you, so she's not telling us."

My hope dies in an instant. Marina would never tell me how I can find her, and no one else knows.

Suddenly, Alex smacks me hard on the back and says, "Take this one last day to lick your wounds, and tomorrow be a better man for when she returns."

"Will she?"

"I'm sure she will." He smacks me again, gets up, and leaves.

Do I want her to return? Fuck, I do. I'm still pissed at her. Fuckin' furious, but I've missed her. And I want her to tell me why she left. What the fuck could I have done so wrong for her to just disappear one day without even a simple goodbye?

I decide to follow Alex's advice and get my shit together. But today... today I'm getting piss drunk.

Chapter Thirty One

M ARK, the guy who happens to be at the right place this time around

I walk into the Cat and Stallion, hoping to get a drink and get lost in the sounds of the crowd after a difficult shift. We couldn't save someone. Those calls always take a toll on me. I relive those moments many times over, thinking about what we could have done differently, hoping the outcome could be changed. But I'll meet with those thoughts later, at my house, when I'm alone with no barrier between us.

Rory, a pretty bartender, shoots me a flirty smile that I don't have the mental capacity to return. She reads my mood and brings me my usual drink without a word.

"I made you a double. It's on the house." She pats my hand, plastered on the counter, and walks away. Bartenders. They're a special breed. Better help than a therapist and better at reading people than damn tarot cards.

I nod gratefully and chug half of it. Just as I'm about to

feel that warm fuzzy feeling in my stomach, a loud laugh comes through the door. A very fake and a very familiar laugh.

Justin fucking Attleborough. God, I hate this guy. And after Kayla, that pure soul... I squeeze my glass, nearly breaking it.

"Oh, look who's here." He walks over to me. Of course. Today of all days, he wants to fight. I chug the rest of my drink and smack the glass on the table. On the other hand, a fight is just what I might need right now.

"Got a problem, golden boy?" I ask. I know he hates that.

His eyes turn violent.

"Possibly." He leans his elbow on the counter next to mine. He smells like a rotten vineyard, and my desire to fight evaporates. I don't pick fights with drunk people. I don't want to end up in jail for accidentally killing someone. A good, nice brawl with a decent opponent, on the other hand —sign me up. We've had quite a few of those throughout our lifetime. I always felt better after each one, if I'm completely honest. All the anger and hurt leaves your body after you get that first punch in. It doesn't matter whether you're the one to deliver it or receive it—it's just a different sort of pleasure.

"Go home, Justin. Sleep it off."

"Can't do." He spreads his arms wide. "Haven't done that in a while."

"What? Gone home?" My chuckle is sarcastic. The dude is in desperate need of a shower.

"Slept." Then he looks around, looking almost uncomfortable. Like he overshared. I take pity on him, even if he doesn't deserve it.

"Yeah, I bet you haven't. With all those women who

occupy your bed. I bet they keep you busy." My jab is deliberate, but it doesn't hit the mark. Instead of rattled, Justin just looks confused.

His forehead wrinkles. "What are you talking about? I've been a fucking monk for months."

"Yeah. Did you tell that to Kayla when she found you in bed with a piece of ass?" I motion to Rory to get me another drink.

I expect him to spit something dirty and sarcastic at me, but he's quiet. I glance at him. His eyes are trained on me, and I can tell he's quickly sobering up.

"What do you mean found me in bed with a piece of ass?"

Oh shit. Did I say something I wasn't supposed to? Fuckity fuck. Rory brings me my drink, and I'm saved by the glass. I bring it to my lips to keep myself busy. Fuck, did I betray Kayla's trust by saying something I wasn't supposed to? He was the one in bed with another woman, so he should know what I'm talking about.

But he doesn't. It's clear as day that he has no idea what I'm talking about at all.

"No fights, boys," Rory reminds us before leaving us to our business.

I gulp down my drink, wave for Rory to put it on my tab, and quickly walk toward the exit.

I shouldn't be driving with two drinks in my system, especially after a full sleepless shift. I gotta get home somehow, so I decide to walk and pick up my truck tomorrow morning. I don't have a shift, and I don't need to be anywhere early anyway.

Heavy footsteps soon follow me, and the situation feels all too familiar.

"Wait," Justin calls, but there is no malice in his voice, only urgency, so I cave and turn around.

"What?"

"What did you mean back there?" He points to the bar. I look between him and the bar as if I'll find answers between them. "Look. I'm lost here. She left without a word, and I have no idea what happened. The whole town rioted against me, and no one will say a word. Just tell me what you know. Please." His 'please' does it. He wipes his face with his hands, looking miserable. I don't give a shit about him being a miserable fuck—he deserves that and so much more. But I care about Kayla, and if my senses are right, there may have been a colossal misunderstanding, resulting in poor Kayla suffering for nothing.

I sigh. "I drove her to her place the day she left." His jaw clenches tight, and I chuckle. One possessive fucker. I'll never be like that if I ever find the right woman to settle with. Never. I'll always be the rational one. "Chill. I drove by your garage and saw her being harassed by Jake, so I had to stop." His nostrils flare, and his eyes suddenly turn a dangerous shade. The one from that night. "Did you talk to Jake?"

He shakes his head. "I didn't think he knew anything."

"Oh, that little fucker knows." I hear my teeth grind with irritation. "He was following her from your house and talking shit. I had to step in because he was being a total asshole to her while she was crying her eyes out."

His face twists in pain, and I'm one hundred percent sure a big revelation is imminent. He swallows and asks, "Do you know why she was crying?"

I level him with a stare, taking a deep breath. "Because she saw another woman sleeping with you. Naked."

"Fuck!" he yells, pulling on his hair. "Now that fucking smell makes sense."

I'm glad it makes sense to him because it doesn't make any sense to me.

"Of fuck. Thanks, man." He begins pacing and suddenly stops, looking at me with crazed eyes. "Wait. You said you saw Jake there. Are you sure?"

"Pretty damn sure. He was following her from the back of your building and threatened me with the law like he always does."

His fists clench, his jaw sets, and for a moment there, I'm a little scared for that poor fucker. He nods and walks down the road toward his house.

Did I do a good deed or a bad one?

Chapter Thirty-Two

JUSTIN

Driving to my parents' house, I know this isn't how I wanted this evening to go, namely murdering my little brother. I believe Mark (not in a million years did I think I'd say that). Jake's hands are dirty in this situation; I feel it in my gut. He's been so intent on hating Kayla for so long that he doesn't know how to stop. Plus, it's not like I shared the news of her being innocent with him. Why did I keep it to myself? What is wrong with me?

Fuck, how did I mess up so badly? I wasted years bullying an innocent woman—one I realized seems to have been created specifically for me—for something she never did. All of it could have been avoided with just one conversation. Just one. And like when I couldn't find her, I just needed one conversation to see what I had done wrong. Just one.

My grip on the wheel is too strong, and I force my fingers to flex so I don't accidentally pull it off and die before I get to kill this little bastard.

A complicated puzzle slowly comes together in my head. The only thing that doesn't make sense is the naked woman in my bed. With me in it. I sure as fuck didn't invite her in there. I haven't been with anyone besides Kayla in a really fucking long time. The last time I had sex with someone else was even before Freya showed up, or around the same time. How on earth did a naked chick get in my bed?

I stop the truck in the driveway and run toward the house. Jake's car is here. Good.

I rush in and find my father sitting in his favorite chair, concentrating on something on his iPad. Mom is chatting on the phone, but once she sees me, she says her goodbyes and comes to give me a hug.

"I didn't know you were coming, honey. You hungry?"

"No, I'm good." Her forehead wrinkles in concern—I never turn down food. Never. "Where is Jake?"

"He was doing something for Alicia in her room. I think he was fixing the shelf or something."

I'm running upstairs before she even finishes. The door to Alicia's room is open, so I walk right in. Jake's attempting to hang a floating shelf on the wall while she's curled up with her laptop on the bed. As I barrel in, they both look at me with wide eyes.

"Sup, bro," Jake chirps cheerfully. "What are you doing here?"

"Do you know why Kayla left?" I demand.

His eyes widen even more, and he begins looking around as if searching for an escape route, but the only one is behind me. He's not going anywhere.

"Do you?" I bark, drawing his attention back to myself. He runs his hand through his hair and scratches his chin.

"I mean, I may have seen her around your place." He tries to smile.

"Around your place?" Alicia turns to look at me, unanswered questions clear in her eyes.

"Yeah." He turns to her with a sneer. "Our brother here," he points a finger at me, one I'm very much willing to break, "has been sleeping with that trailer trash for a while. Isn't that right, Justin?" He finally turns to me, a self-satisfied smile on his lips.

"Really?" Alicia's voice is small, and I look at her. I take a deep breath, preparing to say something I'll never live down.

"Yes," I say firmly because I'm finally done hiding. I finally know what I want. I just picked shitty timing for it.

"How could you?" she asks, her eyes brimming with tears.

"Yeah, after what she did... I don't know what kind of brother you are. She's fucking trailer trash and will always be."

"Shut up!" I yell, grabbing him by the front of his shirt. "I warned you to never call her that again. Didn't you get it?"

"No!" he spits in my face. "Who are you to dictate what I can say and where? Huh? She destroyed our lives!"

"She didn't! She didn't, Jake. I did!" I yell back. I take a second to calm down before adding, "I am the one to blame here." He looks crestfallen, and Alicia's face is covered in tears. I regret hurting her all over again the most, but I have to tell them. "I made the wrong decision that night. I did. I stopped to fight instead of driving to Springfield and trusting my gut, and I trusted Ashley."

"Ashley was almost raped. Don't blame her." Alicia's whisper is barely audible. She can't stand Ashley, but as someone who went through that horrible experience, she feels terrible for her. It's the only reason she tolerated Ashley hanging around. The keyword is 'tolerated.' Nothing more.

A lump settles in my throat. "She wasn't," I choke out. "She was sleeping with that guy for a long time, and that night was no different. I read the situation wrong, believed her, and picked a fight that could have been avoided." I take a deep breath, preparing for the rest of the story. "Kayla stopped me from killing him at that gas station. She helped when I could have gone off the rails and did something irrevocable." Jake opens his mouth to say something, but I silence him with a raised hand. "Kayla didn't call the cops that night. She didn't."

"Fuck." Is all Jake says. "Fuck!" he adds, louder. "Who did then?"

"Ashley did," Alicia whispers.

"Yeah, she did," I confirm. It hurts to admit. "While she was waiting for me in the car."

"While you were beating the dude?" Jake's brows are raised.

"Seems so, because she didn't touch her phone after I got in the truck."

"Fuck." He puts his hands behind his back. "So..." But he doesn't finish and shakes his head. "All this time..."

"Yeah." I close my eyes, wallowing in the guilt threatening to suffocate me.

"How long have you known?" Jake asks, his voice rising an octave.

"A few weeks. Didn't know how to tell you."

"Why the hell didn't you?" he shouts.

"How about because I had been sleeping with the person responsible for our sister's pain?" I yell back. "For years, Jake. For years. I couldn't fuckin' look in the mirror."

"No one is responsible for my hurt but the assholes who did that to me," she says, her voice calm. Way calmer than I've heard her for the past couple of years.

A pained cry comes from the doorway. I turn. Mom stands there, her hands raised to her mouth. "*Assholes?* There were more than one?"

A horrible feeling of an approaching disaster sets in my stomach, and I feel my blood begin boiling. I slowly turn to Alicia and notice Jake doing the same. Alicia pales once the weight of what she let slip settles.

"Alicia?" I try to sound calm, but I'm mad as hell.

"No. It's just a figure of speech." She raises her hand, attempting to calm me down.

"Alicia!" My voice booms through the small space of the bedroom. For the past couple of years, she never mentioned who it was, despite all our attempts to find out. No one was brought to justice. No one. I spent years trying to find the asshole. Now it turns out he wasn't the only one.

"I promise it's just a figure of speech." Her eyes dart between all of us. I glance at Mom, making sure she's okay. My dad is hugging her shoulders, and she's leaning on him for support. "What happened with Kayla?" she asks nervously, switching her attention. I'll take it for now, but we're revisiting the matter later.

"Yeah, Jake, what happened with Kayla?" My eyes meet his, and his cheeks pinken. Good. Probably the first time he's genuinely felt embarrassed in his life. He swallows roughly and glances around the room, looking for a friendly face. But he finds none. Mom and Dad never knew the whole story and never understood why Jake was harassing

Kayla. Alicia has always been forgiving and has tried to move on. She really did. She took what had happened to her as fact and didn't look for the guilty ones. I just didn't tell her about Kayla and me because I didn't want to trigger any memories from that night, and for so long, we thought that Kayla was involved. I thought it would be hard on her, even if she'd forgiven her. I was the only one who found Kayla guilty without a trial. I am an idiot.

Jake takes a deep breath. "Do you remember Claudia? You hooked up a few times last year," he says, scratching his two-day scruff.

"Language!" Mom reprimands from behind me.

"You *went on a date* with her a few times," Jake corrects, scowling at Mom.

"And?" I urge him.

"Well, she was in town."

"And?" My blood's boiling by now. I'm sure as fuck he is not about to say what I think he's going to say.

"And I was there to borrow your PS5, and she was there too, knocking on your door." He swallows loudly and continues, "Well, I let her in because she was there, and I was there; I didn't see any harm in it. I didn't know you crashed, man. Besides that, I knew where the key was; it's not like I've never been to your place without you." He shrugs. "Then she asked for a drink, and you didn't have anything, so I ran to the store to get something."

"Why the fuck would you do that?" I growl.

"Justin!" Mom shouts in horror, but I ignore it.

"Because you were shagging the enemy, man, and it wasn't funny anymore. I thought if Claudia stayed at your place, you would wake up and just carry on your previous relationship; you would all but forget about the trailer trash." He snaps his fingers.

"Jake." My growl is his last warning.

"Sorry, I mean, Kayla. When I came back from the store, I saw Kayla going up the stairs to your place and thought that everything turned out even better than I hoped, because she saw Claudia getting comfy with you firsthand." He winces.

"What?" My voice booms through the room, deafening everyone.

"Yeah, not my proudest moment, but in my defense, I thought she was to blame, you know. If you only told me earlier, it could have been avoided." He dares to look sheepish.

"Avoided what?" I yell. "Sending the only woman I ever loved away so I would never stand a fucking chance with her?" It's the first time I say it out loud. My real feelings for her. I just wish she'd heard it first.

Jake's face twists with dread, while my mom lets out an excited cry, followed by Alicia's whistle.

"I don't know where she is. I don't know how she's doing. She left the only town she ever lived in because she thinks I cheated on her. Because you fucking let a naked chick into my house! Are you out of your fucking mind, Jake?" A curtain of red clouds my mind.

"You love Kayla?" my mom coos from the door.

I pause, pinching the bridge of my nose between my fingers. "I do, Mom. I do. But I don't think I stand a chance now. She moved to Boston, and she's gorgeous and smart. There is no way that some stupid red socker hasn't snatched her up."

"But if she loves you too, she'd wait." She's clutching her hands to her chest, eyes full of hope.

"That's the thing, Mom. I don't know if she ever did. I never told her how I feel. I was too much of a coward to let her know anything about me. I lost the only one who's ever made me feel like I could have what you guys have." I motion between her and Dad, who's still hugging her while making little, calming circles on her shoulder with his finger. It makes the hole in my chest grow even larger. I'll never experience that because the only person I want that with, doesn't want anything to do with me. And for a good reason. I'm the one who started this snowball of problems.

"That's messed up, Jake. Really horrible. Letting another girl into Justin's house with a spare key just to drive Kayla off... You're a sicko," Alicia voices from the bed. Closing the laptop and putting it aside, she gets up and walks toward me. "I think Kayla loves you, and if I'm right, it wouldn't be that easy for her to move on. Look at yourself; you're a man-whore, yet you never did."

"Alicia!" Mom exclaims. "Who did I raise?" she mutters, throwing her hands up.

"What if you're wrong?" My voice sounds unsure, even to my own ears.

"I write love stories for a living. Trust my gut." She shrugs.

"Do you know where she is?" I ask, but I already know the answer.

"No." Her enthusiasm deflates.

"I do," Mom says quietly from the door.

"What?" Our heads snap to her in unison.

"What *what*? I'm friends with Marina." I feel my mouth drop open at her words.

"Since when?" I ask, stunned.

"Since always. And close your mouth. You'll catch a fly." She walks toward me and puts her hand on my chest. "We always knew you two were meant for each other but were too stupid to see it."

I blink in astonishment. "We were?"

"Yeah, you were. Marina bet it would happen earlier, though." She pouts. "You made me lose a hundred bucks."

"Mom!" I exclaim as Alicia snickers. "You bet on us?"

"It's a small town, and we were bored." She shoots me a sheepish smile and shrugs.

"So, where is she?" I can feel my heart pump in my chest with anticipation.

"She's in Boston. She goes to school and works at this guy's place. What was his name?" She taps her chin with her finger.

"Archie?" I spit.

"Yes!" She points her finger up. "Archie! I thought it was a weird name."

"Do you know how I can find this place?"

"No, honey." She looks crestfallen. After a second, her face brightens, "But I know where she lives!"

"Where?" This charade is getting on my nerves, but this is my mom, so I keep my trap shut.

"With Archie!" She smiles brightly while I explode with rage.

"What?" I roar.

"Chill out, Justin, or you'll get your nose broken. Again," my dad mutters. It's the first time he's spoken throughout the argument. He never lets us talk back or raise our voices to our mom.

"Yes, sir. Sorry, Mom." I take a deep, shaky breath. "Are you sure that's where she lives?"

"Marina mentioned it. She said apartments in Boston are very expensive, and he has a lot of space," Mom suggests helpfully with a sweet, all-knowing smile.

My blood is boiling, and along with my sadness and misery, a new feeling emerges. Jealousy. Raging jealousy.

There is no fucking way she is just staying there; that fuck-face was onto her for a long time. I have to go. I gotta get to her before it's too late. What if it's too late? What will I do?

"Whoa, bro. Relax," Jake tells me, his hand outstretched.

"Don't talk to me, Jake. I don't want to hear a word from your mouth."

"He is your brother, honey. He tried to help you." Mom tries to mitigate again to break up the fight.

"Mom... Just don't." I raise a hand to stop her, silently begging her not to mediate. At least not now.

"I think you should talk to Marina. She'd know where Kayla is." She gently pats my cheek, and I feel a lump in my throat. Why does it feel like I've already lost her?

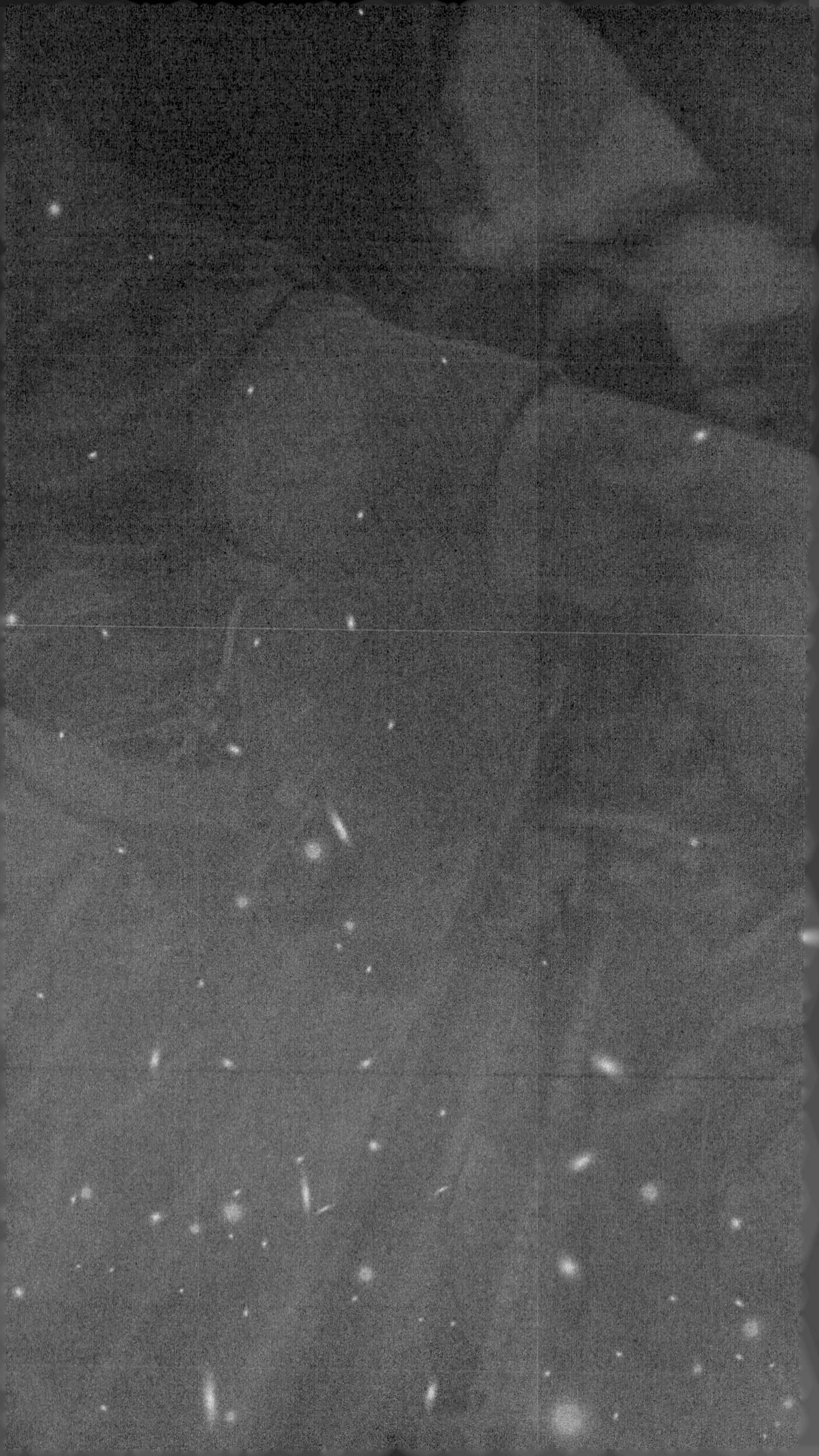

Chapter Thirty Three

J USTIN

When I leave my parents' house, I call Freya right away. After yelling at me for bothering her with the same question (even though I remind her of the similar questions she asked me when Alex was gone) before listening to my story about Jake and his stupidity, she says, *"I'm sorry, Justin. That's awful. I don't know why Jake would do something like that."*

"Yeah, that makes two of us. Can you give me her address?" I don't need anyone's apologies now; I need information.

"I don't have it." She sounds defeated.

I bite back the harsh remark I really want to yell and calmly say instead, "Freya, I thought you were my friend."

"Justin, I don't have it. I swear. And I don't think Alex does. Hold on." She yells so loudly I almost lose hearing,

"Alex, do you have Archie's address?" I hear a grunting noise, and his *'no'* comes through.

"How the fuck doesn't he have his address?" I growl at Freya. But I feel bad. I know she doesn't deserve my anger.

"They just reconnected, so chill." Freya's voice takes a defensive tone, just like every time someone talks ill of Alex. "Alex is saying he can ask for his address."

"Please," I beg.

There's silence on the other end.

"Freya?" *Please, don't tell me it got disconnected.*

There's a gasp. *"D-did you just say please?"* she stutters slightly.

"Have Alex text it to me when he knows it." And I hang up.

The next stop is Marina.

By the time I pull into her driveway, I'm a sweaty mess. I thought she didn't like me, and I'm still convinced she doesn't, but her unexpected friendship with my mom gives me hope.

I take a deep breath before raising my fist to knock on her door. I have to admit, I'm scared of Marina. Like, really scared. I never know what's going on in that woman's head.

The door swings open, and Marina appears, a smug smile plastered on her face. She's cutting an apple with a small sharp-looking knife. I swallow—it's better than a shotgun, at least. "Your mother called and said you might be coming by."

"Yeah." I meet her eyes and hold them. "Did she tell you why?"

"She might have mentioned, yes." She smirks, chewing her apple.

"Will you help me?" I ask hopefully.

"Why would I do that?" she asks, eating another slice of the apple.

I stare into her eyes, praying she'll believe my words. "Because you love Kayla, and I love Kayla, and we both want what's good for her."

She stares back at me. "And you think you're good for her?" She quirks her brow.

I answer with a nod. "I'll do my best to be good for her."

She shakes her head. "Trying your best is not enough. You've been making her miserable for a really long time."

"I can promise it'll never happen again." I place a hand on my heart, meaning every single word.

"Can you?" She pops her hip, eyebrow quirked.

"Yes, ma'am." I nod firmly. I genuinely believe it.

"Alright." She turns around and walks back to the living room, leaving the door open. *What am I supposed to do? Follow her? Wait for her here?* I decide on the latter.

She returns with a piece of paper, an address scribbled across it.

"She hasn't changed her phone number, just blocked you everywhere, so I don't really have good news for you there," she says with an apologetic shrug. "You can try texting her from a different phone number, maybe. This is Archie's address and the place she works at."

"She's already working?" I thought she was only studying there.

"Archie's teaching her. She's very talented. She needs five times less practice than her peers do." Genuine pride shines in her eyes, and I understand how lucky Kayla got when she met Marina. She's more of a mother to her than I ever thought, and their connection runs deep.

"Thank you, Marina," I say with as much sincerity as I can muster.

"I'm not whooping Jake's ass only out of respect for your mother." She levels me with a stare.

"I'll do it for you."

"I expect nothing less. I got money to bail you out of jail." And then she closes the door in my face, leaving me to wonder if she was joking.

Now that I have the address, I decide to get my shit together and figure out what I want to say to her. I want nothing more than to go to her right this second, but I can't show up looking like this. That's if I even make it to Boston. So I go home and drink all the alcohol I have left in an attempt to knock myself out. By the time I'm out, I'm pretty positive my liver is about to say bye-bye.

In the morning, I feel like shit, but I force myself to get it together. I take a very long shower, shave off the lumberjack beard I have going on, and go to Marina's diner to get a ton of coffee for the road. I can go to Donna's, of course, and get the good stuff from her, but I feel like I need to see Marina to connect to Kayla through her. Like, Marina's known Kayla forever, and if I'm close with Marina, I can be close with Kayla too. Stupid, I know, but I'm desperate.

By the time I park my ass at her diner, she leaves me speechless by passing me a huge thermos already filled with coffee and a humongous sandwich.

"Drive safe" is all she says before walking away. I leave a fifty on the bar and go to my truck, ready for the long trip. Kayla's waiting for me at Point B, which makes it feel even longer.

And I'm right—the drive feels never-ending.

I park and look at the building in front of me. Am I sure it's the correct address? I take a look at my GPS again, and yes, I'm in the right place. The red brick house in front of me is enormous. The columns, those colorful mosaic windows, and the landscaping make it a true work of art, I must admit.

Fuck, if Kayla's been living here all this time, I better up my game. My dusty bachelor pad seems miserable compared to this.

I get out, walk to the door, and ring the bell, half expecting a butler to show up. But instead, I come face-to-face with the fuckface. Wearing only jeans. Is that how he walks around the house when Kayla is here?

"Took you long enough." He smirks and opens the door wider, silently inviting me in. "Want a drink?"

"Where is she?" I walk past him, knocking into his shoulder. He lets out a chuckle.

"She's at school. C'mon." He gestures for me to follow him. His house is the size of the whole PTSD center in Little Hope, the downstairs just as spacious.

When we get to the fancy kitchen with new appliances and pristine white cabinets, he puts a pod in his fancy coffee machine and places a mug under. I make a mental note to buy the same one for Kayla for my place, just so she has it there if she ever visits. He repeats the same with another and takes a bottle of whiskey from the cabinet. Pouring himself a hefty dose, he offers to do the same for me.

"It's eleven in the morning, for fuck's sake." I'm a hypocrite, considering I've been drinking even earlier for the past couple of weeks.

"Yeah, I started late today," he says with a sigh and takes a sip. "Heaven." He takes a seat at the island bar and gestures for me to join him. Just to spite him, I stay standing. "So why are you here, Justin?"

"I'm here to take Kayla back."

"To do what exactly? To be a waitress for the rest of her life? To bury her talent?"

I swallow roughly and grab the mug. I just need my voice to return. *Fuck*. He hit a sore spot. What will happen when I try to convince Kayla to go back with me? Of course, she'd have to believe me. Because fuck, that story would be far too ridiculous to make up. But what if she has feelings for this fuckface?

"I see your wheels are turning." He leans back in his chair and places his mug on the table. "She's in a good place now, Justin. She really is."

I must be a selfish prick because it pains me to hear that. Here I thought she's been suffering from the abrupt ending to whatever we had like I was, but she's really doing great. I'm ecstatic for her success—I am. She has a rare raw talent that must be seen, but I was selfishly hoping I'd be by her side for it.

"Are you two...?" I let the question trail off, hating myself for asking him.

"God, no." He pushes away from the chair. "She's gorgeous, don't get me wrong. But she's not my type." He notices my scowl. "The unavailable type. She's already taken, and I don't mess with that."

My nostrils flare, and I let out a loud exhale. "She's dating someone?"

"Gosh, you are dense." He rakes his hair with his hand. "She's still hung up on you. Plus, Alex would rip my balls off if I ever went near her. I'm surprised you still have yours attached."

My ass hits the chair on its own accord, and I grab my head with my hands, defeated. "Is she really doing well?"

"Very well. She's going to school and passing her classes with flying colors. Fuck knows how, but she is. In the evenings and on the weekends, she works at my shop." He nods. "She clearly misses you, but if you show up right now with whatever story you have, whatever it is, she'll drop her schooling in a heartbeat and move back. The decision is yours."

Yeah, that's a tough one. Coming here, I thought I'd be going back with her. Even if she was dating him, I'd still be going back with her. I'd kiss her senseless so she could see that I'm the only one for her. Of course, after I knock the shit out of that guy. But not when she's happy, no. Not when she's following her dreams and doing something with her life. Something that she always wanted.

Is he right? Would she really go back with me if I asked? It's so tempting to find out. So tempting. But what if she does? What's next for her?

"How is she doing with money?"

"Tough, man. But she doesn't accept any help. She's even paying me rent, believe it or not." I pointedly look around as he speaks. "Yeah, I don't need money, as you can imagine. I just want her to finish school so she can be my number one artist."

"Can I somehow... I don't know, help financially?" I'm lost here. I feel useless, a feeling I've never enjoyed.

"I don't think it will go well. And I repeat, I don't need the money, but the stubborn mule refuses to accept it. I feel bad; these monthly payments she's sending somewhere are draining her dry." He waves his hand at something in the air, clearly annoyed with Kayla.

"What monthly payments?" My ears perk up.

"You don't know?" He hesitates.

"No." I shake my head, hoping he'll keep going. "I know

she's been having money trouble for a long time but could never figure out why."

"Oh fuck." It's his turn to grab his head in his hands. "Alright, you didn't hear it from me. She hasn't said anything *directly* to me, but I've heard her talking to someone named Caroline about sending money to her late this month because she was short on cash or something. I offered to help, but you can guess how that went."

"Caroline?" What the fuck?

He perks up. "You know who it is?"

"God, I hope I'm wrong." But I don't think I am; little pieces of Kayla's puzzle are slowly coming together.

"What do you mean?" His brows furrow with concern. Can I trust him? I can't stand the dude, but he's helping Kayla and doesn't seem to be eager to creep under her skirt.

"Oh fuck." I take a deep breath. "Years ago, I don't even remember when exactly, Kayla's mother and sister hit somebody on the road and left town right after. Nobody has heard from them since."

"And Kayla?"

"She stayed in Little Hope. I don't remember much about it, but I do remember she wasn't in the car when it happened. She was a kid herself." The thought of her own family leaving her must have hit hard. She was just a kid.

"And her mother and sister just left?" His jaw sets in anger for Kayla, and maybe—just maybe—I can tolerate him a little more.

"Yeah, and I don't think anyone knows where they are, including Kayla. As far as I know, she detests them."

"How does Caroline fit in the picture?" he asks.

"Caroline is the mom of the girl they left paralyzed." The unfairness of the situation eats me. For all parties involved.

"Shit." He rubs the back of his neck. "That's where she sends money every month?"

"Looks like it. For many, many years, I assume, since no matter how much she works, she can't even buy new tires for her Jeep. And they're meant to keep her alive in snow, for fuck's sake. She was maybe fifteen when it happened? That's how she ended up with Marina. I don't remember all that much from then because she was way younger, but the rumors circulated around town." I sigh. "I'll take that drink now." I point to the bottle.

He stands up, grabs the bottle, and pours me a generous amount. "Wanna see her?"

"Yeah," I croak.

"Let's go."

He walks off, coming back fully dressed only a couple minutes later. We walk to his car. The drive to wherever we are going is silent. My stomach is tight with knots of anticipation. I'll finally be seeing the woman I love. The only one I ever loved, and I'm sure the only one I ever will.

We stop at a multistory building with a full wall of windows.

"There." He points at one of the windows, and I see it.

I see her. She's leaning on the counter and talking with a dark-haired chick covered in so many piercings I can barely see her skin. Kayla's hair is gathered on top of her head in that signature messy bun I know she wastes no time making. She's wearing an oversized white shirt, those black leather pants that I love to hate, and her favorite Dr. Martens. She's laughing at something the woman said, and her whole face brightens. She looks happy and carefree. Someone walks in and calls to her. She turns around, and her face shines. She hurries to give them a hug, and they walk together into the back.

"That's Cherry." Archie's voice fetches me from dreamland. "Kayla's supposed to help her ink her regular today, but I bet she'll be the one doing the inking. Cherry lets her get away with a lot."

"She's so talented."

"That." He laughs. "And Cherry has a crush on her."

I don't blame her; anyone would.

"Now, do you see?" I feel his eyes on me.

"I see."

The drive home is miserable. I make the decision for the both of us: I decide to keep the truth to myself so she can have her dream. If she wants to stay in Boston by the time she's done with school, I'll move there too. I'll find mechanic work and do what I do best—fix cars and give her orgasms.

Yeah, my heart whines. *Then what? How long will it take? A year? Two? What if she finds someone else?*

I seriously contemplate returning just so I can explain to her what went wrong. Just so I can tell her that I love her. Hoping she'll give me a chance when she knows the truth. If I were her and found out what my brother had done, I wouldn't want to be anywhere near me or my family. We've been messing with her for so long. I can do that. Return to her... but then it will be about me again, about us, and not about *her*.

I groan and grip the wheel tighter. I can't do that to her. I can wait. In the meantime, I'll deal with her problems any way I can.

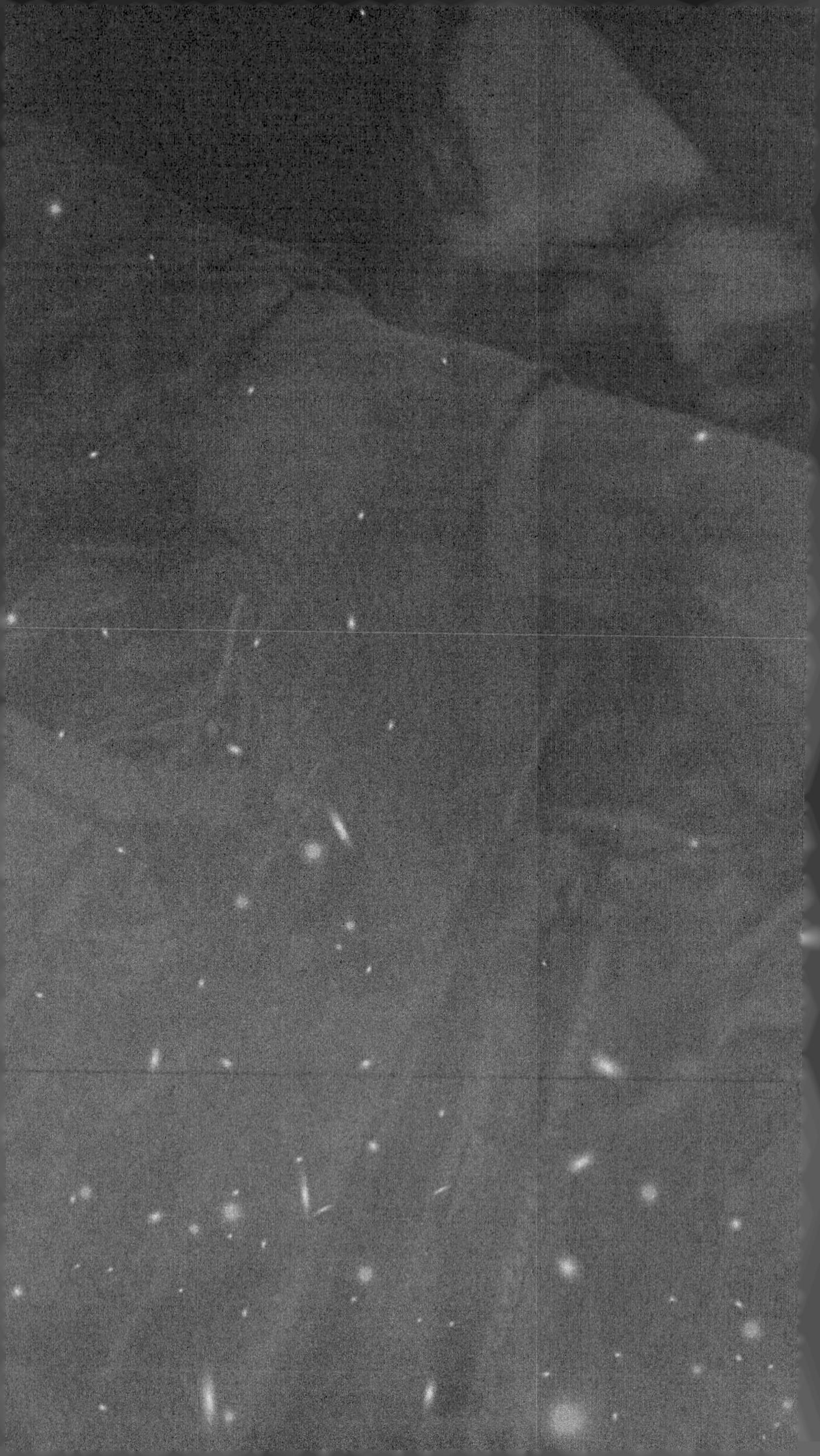

Chapter Thirty Four

K AYLA

Caroline keeps calling me, and I keep not picking up. I already sent her money this month, but two days after the payment, she called again and asked for more, claiming that Maddie needs more medicine this month, but I don't have anything to send her. Nothing. I feel awful because a child needs medicine, but there is nothing I can do right now.

I woke up this morning with a homesickness that only Marina, Freya, Alex, and the diner could fix. And... maybe just a glimpse of Justin.

Freya tried talking to me about him a few weeks ago, but I cut her off right after she mentioned his name. I was in too good a place to destroy it with the bitter memories of the last time I saw him. But now I have to admit, I miss him like crazy. Working at one of the most popular parlors in New England (even as a newbie) comes with a lot of good perks, and one of them is meeting so many interesting and super-hot people. Some of them—okay, most of them—hit on me, but I just laugh it off. They don't make it weird—it feels more like extra attention rather than creeping, considering the atmosphere in the parlor is so light and friendly and flirty. But never in all those months I've been in Boston have I responded to any of the flirting. Never. Both my mind and my heart were still dead set on missing Justin and weren't interested in anyone else.

The drive back to Little Hope was uneventful, but I couldn't help but rack my brain for other ways I could obtain extra cash to pay Caroline. I'm so lost in thought that I don't notice the car parked next to my trailer until it's too late.

There's three people in the car, but I only recognize one: Caroline in the passenger seat. The other two are a bald man who looks to be in his early thirties in the driver's seat and a guy in the back seat sporting tribal tattoos on his neck and arms. Come to think of it, I think I've seen the bald guy before—when I was fifteen, he and Caroline had come to have a 'chat' for the first time.

How Caroline found out where I live, I have no idea. But the fact that she brought a party along with her only meant one thing for me: bad news.

I climb out of my Jeep and walk to the trailer just as they do the same.

"I called you," Caroline snips as she approaches me. I haven't seen her in two years. We only ever talk on the phone, and she's never allowed me to visit Maddie. To think of it, the last time I saw Maddie was a long time ago, right after they were released from the hospital. Caroline only sends me occasional photos of her face, but that's about it.

"I know. I was busy." I hesitate to unlock the door, even though I don't have anything valuable in there.

"I don't care if you're busy," she says, her voice terse. "You haven't replied to me in days."

I turn to her. "And why do I have to be available to you at all times?"

"Because you owe it to us." She bares her teeth like a feral coyote.

"I've been paying you every single month for nearly eight years. I think I'm entitled to a little break from double payments."

"When your family caused the kind of suffering they did, you don't get breaks. Mario?" she yells toward the car. "We have a problem here." At her voice, the familiar dude with big biceps and no neck gets out of the driver's side and calls to the other one. The guy nods and gets out too—holding a huge freakin' bat—and they both slowly walk toward us.

I lick my lips, suddenly feeling the thrum of my pulse. My gaze locks on Caroline's, and I squint at her. "So, what exactly is your plan here?"

Her face turns evil. "To teach you a lesson." And at that moment, I see through all the bullshit. For once, I see her for who she really is to her core. How did I never see that before? Have I felt so guilty for what my family did that I completely ignored it?

"About what, exactly?" I try to keep a brave face, but the situation's quickly heading downhill for me. No one knows I'm here—no one. I didn't tell anybody that I decided to come home today. Not even Archie, because he wasn't home—probably exploring more kinks at some private party. Why did he have to pick this day of all days not to be around? I usually yell to him that I'm off here or there, so he knows which river to look in for my body in case I don't come home again.

Is she really going to beat me up? Why else would she bring two dudes with a clear lack of working brain cells, compensated by their sheer muscle mass? It feels like a scene from some Mafia movie, only in reality, it feels terrifying.

I make a move toward the door to unlock it—maybe I could sneak inside and slam the door, buying time to call somebody—but Caroline quickly steps in front of me. "You're not getting out of this."

Now I really begin to worry. What are my options here? And more importantly, what are their intentions? I swallow a lump of fear and look around. The bushes are moving, but there's no wind. To hope for a random bear to show up right about now sounds too good to be true.

"What are you gonna do? Break my kneecaps?" I ask as my eyes dart around.

She clicks her tongue. "Hmm, that sounds like a good idea. Don't you think?" she asks the man with no neck. He looks at me with his beady eyes, nodding.

"Not really. Who's going to pay you then?" I counter, appealing to her logical side—there must be one somewhere, hidden deep down.

Her chuckle is dark. "You'll be paying me my money no matter what."

"How would I make money with broken legs?" I ask her, rolling my eyes.

"You think that's my problem?" She shrugs her leather-clad shoulders, and at that moment, I think I lose my love for leather jackets forever. "Sometimes lessons need to be taught. This is one of those times. I promise you'll never skip a payment ever again after this."

"I didn't skip it! I just didn't have the means to pay you twice this time."

She looks me up and down, the disgusted frown on her face deepening. "What about that fancy house in Boston you're living in with your fancy boyfriend? He looks like he has a lot of money." She pats the front pocket of her jeans with a sleazy smile.

Now it makes more sense. Somehow she found out where I've been living and thinks Archie and I are dating. She wants more money because she thinks I have more money.

"He's not my boyfriend."

"Sure, he isn't," she drawls. "He just lets random people live at his place. Right, boys?" A disgusting cackling comes from the doofus duo.

Another movement comes from the bushes, and they all turn toward the sound. Using the distraction to my advantage, I fidget with the keys, but Caroline grabs my braid—*why did I decide today of all days to be fancy?*—and pulls it with all her might, dropping me to the ground on my back. The bald dude is on top of me in a second, kicking me in the ribs, and I let out a yell. "Asshole! Get your dirty feet off me!" I attempt to scramble back, but another kick comes from the other side.

"Teach her a lesson, boys. She should know never to fuck with me again." Caroline leans on my trailer door as if it's her property. Unfortunately for her, we—trailer park kin —never go down without a fight, so I crawl backward from the feet of the two gorillas.

"You've sure changed a lot. You used to be so nice. Suffering, but nice," I taunt, trying to anticipate their movements. So far, they have managed to kick me twice on each side. Pff—just a Monday-morning warm-up for trailer folks. "Just trying to take care of your daughter."

"That's why I'm here, you bitch. I'm still taking care of my daughter. She'll never walk because of you! Do you know how much work goes into helping her? How much time and money?"

I sigh, telling myself not to fall for it. Not this time. "Caroline, I'm so sorry about what happened to her; I really am. But I wasn't there, and you know that."

"Your *family* left a child paralyzed." She picks at her fingernails. "I can't work. Someone has to foot the bill."

"Yeah? And who's paying for the goons?" I eye the jerks.

"They're family." There is so much love in her voice that I want to puke. Goon number one, the one with the bald head, tries to kick me again, but I kick him back right in the groin and scramble back at his bellow of pain. "Get her!" he calls to goon number two through gritted teeth.

Goon number two swings his bat and charges at me. *Now* it's getting hot in here. How will I avoid a bat in the hands of a giant psychopath—I have no idea. I try to stand up, assessing the likelihood of having time to run away, considering that's the only way I can think to keep all my limbs attached, when he jumps forward and swings his bat at my head. I close my eyes and throw my hands out, trying to protect myself. The blow never comes.

Time seems to slow down, and the silence is followed by the sound of a huge body slamming into the goon, knocking him down before the bat reaches me. I keep my eyes shut, scared of what's to come. It's only when I hear grunting, followed by a pained cry, that I open my eyes.

Frank, my Frank, has bitten into the goon's shoulder and is currently dragging him around, stomping on his limbs in the process. The goon is screaming and trying to punch

Frank, but Frank is a big motherfucking moose; it's not that easy to catch him, especially if you're hanging from his mouth in the air, bloody and broken.

"Get the bitch!" Caroline yells to Baldy, who has finally gotten his wits together. I turn just in time to see him charge at me. I can take one down. I think. Right? I can?

I'm trying to stand up, but the kicks they did manage to deliver landed at the 'right' places, and it's hard even to move.

"You're done, bitch!" he says as I almost manage to pull myself up.

I almost give up hope when I hear it.

The rev of a powerful engine cuts through the crying of goon number one, who's still getting dragged around like a broken toy by a toddler. The vehicle is speeding up—the ground vibrates beneath me as it gets closer.

"Who's that?" Baldy's attention focuses on the truck as it whips into view.

Justin jumps out of the car before it even comes to a complete stop. He reaches Baldy with an almost super-human speed, punching him in the face and sending him to the ground like a sack of potatoes, but he quickly recovers. He charges Justin, but unfortunately for him, Justin's already too far gone. His face is a stoic, emotionless mask, the one people should fear the most. That's the face of a person who's removed all feeling from his being and has nothing to lose. He's ready and enraged.

Why is Justin even here? How did he know?

Baldy jumps forward, attempting to punch him in the face, but Justin easily deflects his advance, punching him in the stomach, sending the bat flying to the ground before delivering another jab to the side of his head. Baldy is shaky—very shaky.

From the corner of my eye, I see Caroline lunging for the bat. *Oh no, you don't.* I use all my strength to jump toward it, knocking it farther into the bushes with my foot. She lets out an annoyed yell and runs after it. I jump on her back, knocking her onto the ground.

It's then that her tune seems to change. "Don't hurt me!" she pleads. "Who's going to watch after Maddie? She can't walk!" her words come out in a screech as she covers her head. I keep her pinned to the ground.

"Oh yeah?" Justin shouts just as he punches Baldy one more time, sending him to the ground, unconscious. Justin takes one more look at him, kicks him once for good measure, and walks toward me. "I've heard a different story, Caroline. A very different one. It's interesting, really." He draws closer to me, and it's the first time our eyes meet after months of being apart.

I swallow the lump in my throat and slowly drag my eyes over his frame, returning to his face. His eyes are trained on mine, the moment intense. It's our reunion, but Caroline ruins it. "Get off me! I'm calling the cops!"

"Please do," I shoot at her and crawl away. Justin's watching my every move, and I'm drinking in the intensity that only he can generate. Only his presence. Only his eyes. His nostrils flare, and he opens his mouth to say something when goon number two bursts out from the bushes and runs toward us. Frank's following him like a silent predator, his big brown eyes focused solely on him, steam practically pouring from his flared, velvety nostrils. It's hilarious, really. Frank is a teddy bear—well, a teddy moose—yet I've never seen him so focused on a human being with such a bloodthirsty look on his cute furry face. I thought he only ate twigs and leaves. Turns out, my Frank is full of surprises. He looks like he's about to turn into Hannibal Lecter.

"Call him off!" the goon yells when he passes us in his attempt to flee Frank.

"I can't. Frank is a free spirit—he does what he wants." I shrug. I'm so proud of my moose right now and so grateful that I momentarily forget the situation in front of me, thinking about what nice bush I can plant for him in return for his services.

A low, choking chuckle comes from my left. "So *that's* Frank?"

I missed his voice. Missed it so much.

"Yeah. We've been neighbors for so long, we're practically family." I quickly glance at Justin, who's fascinated by Frank. Not a big surprise there; he's a magnificent animal. While Justin's busy watching the unfolding events, I watch him.

He's lost weight. A lot. His cheeks are hollow, and there are dark circles under his eyes. He's probably had periods of insomnia again and again and again. My heart aches for him, even as I remember the heartache I felt when I saw another woman in his bed.

"Call him off, Kayla," Caroline pleads from the ground. I lift a brow, and she adds, "Please."

"Why would I do that? You came to my home, angry that I didn't pay you money I don't owe you, threatening to break my bones with a damn bat, and now you want me to help the man who was just kicking me on the ground only a couple moments ago?" I glance at Frank, enjoying my lap-moose playing Doberman. Looks like Frank's enjoying it too.

Her voice turns beseeching. "He's helping take care of Maddie."

Fuck, even when I tell myself not to let that get to me, it always does. A pang of guilt hits me like a lightning bolt.

I'm about to call out to Frank when Justin interjects. "What exactly is he helping with?" I eye his posture. His arms are folded over his chest, his stance wide.

"To take care of the child who was injured by *her*—" Caroline points at me—"family."

"Really?" Justin's voice is suspicious. "How bad were the injuries?"

"Justin," I go to stop him, but he lifts his hand up, silencing me.

"You know how bad they were. Everyone in Little Hope knows." Her voice raises an octave.

"How about Springfield? Do they know there?" He narrows his eyes at her, but she's looking everywhere but him.

I look between them. "What? What are you talking about?"

"You gonna tell her, or should I?" he asks, but she doesn't respond. "Alrighty then." He turns to me and explains, "I did some digging, and it turns out Maddie was never paralyzed."

I feel ice down my back. "What?" I gasp.

"Yep. She had a broken leg and a concussion. A horrible thing to happen to a child, but she recovered quickly and is currently on the school soccer team. She's a pretty great scorer, isn't she, Caroline?"

I look between them. "That's not true, right? Tell me it's not true! I've been struggling for eight whole years for nothing? You played on my guilt for nothing?" I watch Caroline squirm, and the dreadful feeling of unfairness settles in. I'm so relieved and happy to hear that Maddie is living a full and happy life, but what about me? What about the guilt I felt every single month when it was time to send money— money I didn't have to spare? I thought my family was responsible for destroying her life, and I was ready to help her as much as I could for the rest of my own, but it was all a lie. It was all a fucking *lie*!

"Eight years, Caroline!" My voice cracks. "I was a child when you asked for money the first time. You told me to go and do what my Momma taught me and get some extra cash. How could you?" For a split second, all I feel is a sense of mourning wash over me for all the things I lost out on—over a lie. I don't let it linger for too long. Not right now.

I hear a loud intake of air from beside me, followed by a growled, "What the fuck?"

Justin slowly moves closer to me and tries to touch my hand, but I swat it away. Not now. I don't want to be touched by anyone right now. That feeling of heavy, back-breaking guilt I carried for so many years slowly melts into another emotion—stupidity. I should have sensed something wasn't right sooner, but I was too busy digging a hole for myself inside my own head. Too busy trying to coexist with this guilt for something that wasn't even my fault but became my responsibility. And it was all for nothing.

"I'm sorry, Kay. I'm really sorry," Justin murmurs. He doesn't try to touch me this time.

"How did you find out?" I whisper, glancing at him.

He looks down and away, and only then does he answer. "I needed to know how I could help and where you send money every month."

"How did you know about the money?" I ask, shocked. I thought I was hiding it well.

"The fuckface told me." Justin's smile is a little embarrassed, and the tips of his ears turn pink.

"Archie?" My head jerks back. "When did you talk to him?"

He finally looks up. "When I came to see you in

Boston."

"You came to see me?" I'm having a hard time keeping up right now.

"Yeah."

Another pained cry comes from the woods, and Caroline looks around, worried. *Good.* "Please," she starts again. "I really need you to call off your beast."

"Fuck off," Justin and I say in unison.

"We'll leave," Caroline promises. "Just call him off."

I sigh. "Frankie boy! Let the bad guy go." There is a commotion in the bushes, a struggling sound, and a smug-looking Frank gallops out from the woods. He stops next to me and nudges my shoulder. "Good boy. Momma is proud of you. A very good boy." I pat on the top of his nose, where he likes affection the most, before moving behind his ears, just like with a dog. "You saved Momma, but I can't kiss you because you have blood all over you. You need to wash up in the lake, okay?" Frank nods.

"Did he just fuckin' nod?" Justin sounds surprised. Why, though?

"Yes, he's a very smart boy. Right? Go wash yourself, and then we can cuddle." Frank nudges my shoulder one more time and trots away.

"Is he really going to take a *bath*?" Justin watches Frank leave with round eyes and an open mouth.

"He's a free spirit." I shrug. "We'll see."

Baldy groans and writhes to life on the ground. Caroline rushes toward him. "Alfonso, what did they do to you?"

I raise a brow—the asshole was about to take a bat to my face, and now she makes it sound like we're the bad guys here. The second goon limps from the bushes. "Let's get the fuck out of here." Caroline helps Baldy stand up, and he limps to the car.

"Good choice. And never come back," Justin growls, grabbing Caroline's elbow as they pass by. "*Never* come back. You got it?" Identifying the true ringleader, he addresses Caroline with the same emotionless expression that I still fear sometimes. Caroline nods, and they all climb into their car.

Soon, it's only the two of us left.

The air is starting to feel weird. The memory of the last time I saw him washes over me, and I feel a ping in my chest that wasn't there for a long time.

"Kayla." He exhales my name as if a prayer, and it reaches that damn ache in my chest, soothing it. "I didn't do that." I shoot him an accusatory glare, but he continues. "I didn't do that. When you left... fuck." He wipes his face with his hands. "When you left, I couldn't figure out what happened. No one told me. No one."

"Sounds familiar," I whisper, though with no malice.

"Yeah, it does." He smiles sadly. "That night, what you saw... that wasn't what happened."

"It's pretty difficult to interpret any differently, Justin. There was a naked woman in your bed with you." Against my will, I recall the picture I've been trying so hard to forget.

He sighs. "That's partially my fault."

"Partially?" My voice rises.

His gaze grows agitated. "Yeah, I know what you think."

"Stop telling me what I think!" I snap at him.

"Let me finish then!" His voice grows louder too.

"Stop playing around and just spit it out already!"

He groans and turns on his heel. "Fuck, I forgot how infuriating you can be." He turns back and explains, "It's my fault because I should have explained how bad my insomnia is to you."

"What does that have to do with this?"

"Everything. When Alicia—" He cuts himself off. "When *that night* happened, I had so much fucking guilt in my head that I couldn't sleep even for a minute. And that continued happening for days. Then months. Then years. I'd go days without sleep and then crash for hours, even days, completely dead to the world."

"Like you did after our first kiss?" I half-ask, half-confirm what I've already heard from Freya.

"Yes, like after our first kiss."

"Why did you never say anything?" My anger has simmered down a little—I'm well acquainted with guilt. We're old pals.

His cheeks pinken. "Because it's embarrassing."

"What is? That you have insomnia?"

"That such a small thing can knock me down dead. That's what. I'm not used to being weak. I hate that." His voice turns raspy, like he's truly embarrassed by his condition—something he can't control. "Those knocked-out hours were a fuckin' nightmare in jail. No one gives a shit about your internal clock there—everyone lives by the clock on the wall."

My jaw drops down. "How did you hide it from me so well?"

"Because when I'm with you, I can sleep. Like, *really* sleep." He's watching me intensely.

"Wow." I slowly look him up and down. "I'm sorry. You look like shit, by the way."

"Thanks, baby." He chuckles. "I haven't slept in months. Well, I've crashed, but it's not the same thing." My heart skips a beat at his 'baby,' and I try to squash it.

"Doesn't really explain anything."

"Right." He scratches his chin, which looks to have a

three-day beard, and it looks awfully sexy on him. "I crashed that night, and that woman you saw—she was in town, and we used to hook up years ago."

"Jake says it was at the same time we were together," I whisper.

"Right. Fuckin' Jake." He closes his eyes, takes a deep breath, and opens them. "He knows where the spare key is, and he let her in, hoping I'd fuck her when I woke up." I wince at his bluntness, but he continues. "You need to hear this. I haven't been with anyone for a very long time, Kay. A very long time. Long before we had something, I couldn't even look at anyone else. And after..." He shakes his head. "And do you really think that after I had you, I'd be able to look at someone else? Did I really give you that impression?"

"You did," I answer honestly, my voice small. This story is too surreal to be true. And at the same time, it's too surreal to be made up.

"I'm sorry, Kay. I'm really sorry." He makes a move to come to me but stops himself mid-step. "I hope one day you will be able to forgive me for all the shit I've done. All of it. And I'm ready to prove to you every single day that I'm an idiot. Every single day for the rest of my life." His eyes are full of pain and remorse, his Adam's apple bobbing in harsh swallows.

"What are you saying, Justin?" My voice is barely above a whisper.

"I'm saying that I love you. I think I've loved you for a very long time." He inches closer to me, but not close enough, giving me the power to decide our distance.

"Months?" My heart starts singing before he even replies.

"Years."

"Oh." My eyes widen—how is that possible? "You sure?" Such a stupid question.

"I'm very sure." He chuckles. "You're my home."

I feel a hot tear escape my eye and run down my cheek. "Why are you crying, Kay? What happened?" He finally steps closer and gently wipes the tear away with one knuckle. It's the first physical contact I've experienced with him in forever, and my body's weeping for more. A stopper's been pulled, opening a waterfall in my eyes, and I can't control myself anymore.

Justin grabs my hand and pulls me into him, enveloping me in his powerful embrace. I wrap my arms around his torso and feel how much weight he's really lost. I need to feed him. Pronto.

"Do you really love me?" I mumble into his chest.

"I do." The confidence in his tone ignites a fire in my belly.

"You have no idea how long I've been waiting for you to say that." I let out an embarrassing giggle, but I sober up quickly, remembering what he mentioned earlier. "Wait, you said you've been to Boston recently?"

"Yeah, I was at fuckface's house and then at the parlor." He tells me as he makes small circles on my back with his hand.

I lift my face up, looking into his eyes. "Why didn't you say anything to me then?"

"I dunno." He shrugs. "You looked so happy, so content. You were doing something you've been dreaming about for so long. I didn't want to take it from you."

"Oh, Justin," I sniffle. "You dumbass. I could have done both." I wipe my nose with the back of my hand.

"What?" He rears back. "What do you mean?"

"I could go to school and be with you at the same time.

People date and stay in school, you know." I poke his right pectoral.

"What—" He cuts himself off, looking up at the sky. "That fuckface!"

"What?"

"Never mind."

"What do you mea—"

He cuts me off with a hot kiss of his warm lips on mine, his delicious tongue enveloping my own. His hands pulling me into him. His scent assaulting my nose. His chest under my hands. His whole being surrounding me in a bubble of happiness and serenity that I was missing. That feeling of perfect belonging with the person who feels like home —*your* home. Justin was right—we're home.

"I've missed you," he says into my mouth.

"Me too," I reply, pulling him back hungrily.

"You're moving in with me."

"No, I'm not. You're a slob."

"I'll change," he answers between nibbles on my neck.

"No, you won't," I affirm with a smile of acceptance.

"No one is perfect," he hums into my skin.

I giggle. "Yeah, I come with an entourage."

"Let me guess: Marina?" He pulls on my braid, causing my head to fall backward.

"And Frank."

"And Frank." He laughs. "Frank is practically family at this point."

"Couldn't agree more," I confirm with a smile.

JUSTIN

. . .

When I saw that piece of shit hitting her, I nearly died. There are very few times in my life I've been so scared, and that was just about to top the list. If Donna hadn't told me she saw Kayla's Jeep driving through Maine street, I'd never have known she was home and wouldn't have gotten here in time. I don't know what would have happened, but it would have been yet another woman in my life I was too late to save. I owe Donna a big one.

Kayla walks to the door of her trailer, unlocking it, and I trot behind her like a loyal dog. Because that's what I choose to be: a loyal and, well, she likes doggy style, so...

I glance behind me. All those months, I've been jealous over a moose. Go figure. And she calls him *Frank*.

Opening the door, Kayla moves to head inside when her ass is right in front of me. Her very plump and juicy ass squeezed in those tight pants: my dick stirs. Of course, it does. He missed her; we missed her. He hasn't seen any action besides my hand, and that can only get him so far. So when he saw the object of his desire, he woke up with a vengeance. And even though my body demands to throw her over my shoulder and have my way with her, my poor broken heart is just happy to see her. Any woman can give me an orgasm, but no one can give me that beautiful peace that Kayla brings me. No one.

I follow her inside and close the door. Even though the place is super clean, it seems abandoned without her. There is no Kayla spirit around. But I'm sure it will only take her a few minutes to get it back to its original glory. She bends over to do something under the sink, and my dick goes hard again. Fucking tight jeans. Should have bought a bigger size.

She washes her hands and turns to me.

"Thank you for helping me out there." She waves her hand toward the front of the trailer.

"No problem. Looked like you and Frank had everything under control."

Her lips twitch. "We did."

"So, when are you moving in?"

Her face contorts, confused. "Where?"

"To my place, of course." *Duh.*

She rears back. "I'm not moving into your place."

"Why not?" Now I'm the one confused.

She looks at me like I'm a lunatic. "Because I just came back, and we were apart for so long."

"Exactly." I spread my arms. "Why waste more time?" In my opinion, my words are very reasonable.

"We need to get to know each other again!" She throws her hands out in front of her.

"What's the best way to know each other than to live together?" I feel my face stretch into a huge smile—*what does she have to say to that, huh?*

She places her hands on her hips, and I notice a new tattoo on her right thumb. It's a black arrow piercing a crimson, bleeding heart. It's so delicate and so small, yet so meaningful and bright, just like my Kayla.

"You're a slob, and your place is a dumpster!" She reprimands me, but I can't help but smile. I can't take my eyes off that tattoo. It represents her so well. And the bleeding heart over there? Well, that's me. She pierced right through me, and if she pulls the arrow out, I'll bleed to death.

"I'll clean it." I bite my lip. Her cheeks are adorably pink, and I fuckin' love that.

"You slept with half the town on that mattress." The light in her eyes dims a little. I can't change my past, but I can shape the future.

"I'll buy a new one. And a new bedframe. And a couch.

We can gut the whole place if you want to." I take a step toward her.

"And new sheets?" She looks at me from under her lashes.

"Especially them." I nod a few times like a dummy toy.

"And a new dresser?"

"Yes. Two dressers." Another tiny step.

"Why two dressers?" A line forms between her eyebrows.

"Because one will be filled with all the sexy lingerie I've bought for you." I wink at her.

"Oh." Her mouth opens a little, and I can see the tip of her pink tongue. "You bought me underwear?"

"Yes, I did. I ruined some, remember?" I've bought her half the damn stores in Maine. I'll buy her more if she wants me to. I'll get her the fuckin' moon if it makes her happy.

"Yeah, I do." She nods a few times, not comprehending what's happening. I understand: I had months to get myself ready for the big move, live with the idea, and wait for her to come home so my dream could come true, and for her, it's been ten minutes.

All right, I decide to give her five more minutes before I throw her over my shoulder and carry her sexy ass to her new home. "But what about my trailer? I'm not leaving it here." She looks around apologetically, as if the trailer can hear her.

"Pff." I roll my eyes. "I'd never leave the place I popped my woman's cherry here in the wild. It's *our* place. I don't want anyone to ruin it."

"You're so crude." Her cheeks pinken even more, but she glances toward where we had sex for the first time, and she bites her lower lip. Oh, she remembers, all right, and she loves me being dirty, I know.

"That's right, I am." Another step places me right in front of her. "I've missed you, Kayla." I push a strand of her hair behind her ear. Today, she's got dark blue streaks. I think it means she's sad. "I've missed you so much."

"I've missed you too." She puts her hands on my chest and lifts her face to mine, whispering, "And I've missed your inches." Her eyes sparkle with mischief.

A familiar, sharp jealousy pinches my chest. "How many other inches have you had in Boston?" I ask. It was the question that had been bothering me. I'm scared to hear the answer, but I still need to know. I just have to. I'm a masochist like that.

"Wouldn't you like to know?" Her eyes narrow, and a small smirk dances on her lips.

"Kayla," I growl as I wrap an arm behind her lower back and pull her to me. Her body becomes flush with mine, and I instantly sing a victory song. She *fits*.

"We-e-e-ell," she singsongs and taps her finger on her chin. "Let me think." I'm getting myself ready for a horror story. My body goes rigid, and she laughs. "Relax, Jus, you're so wound up."

"Kayla." My voice drops lower, and she laughs.

"No one, Justin. And even though I don't owe you an explanation, there was no one since you."

I let out a breath I didn't know I was holding and move my hand lower to cover her pussy. "This all is mine. From now on, I don't want to have to ask that question ever again. You are mine. Do you understand?" Even though my words sound confident, I'm anything but. I know Kayla, and I know she's been on her own for a long time. She isn't used to answering to anyone, but I can't do half-measures with her. I want her fully and utterly *mine*.

I see a storm brewing behind her narrowed eyes; she

opens her delicious mouth to rip me a new one, but she surprises me. Of course, she does. "If I'm yours, you are mine. You got it?"

A warm sensation blooms in my chest, and I nod. "Got it, ma'am."

Her mouth thins as she continues. "I'm not joking."

"Neither am I." I feel my face stretch in a wide smile. She doesn't know about the ring I got for her the day I left Boston. It has a giant ruby in it, matching the stripes in her hair when she's in her feistiest mood, my favorite one. I got it because I knew if it wouldn't be her, it wouldn't be anyone else. I'd die a bachelor with blisters. I don't understand why Alex is waiting for so long to propose to Freya—everyone knows they're perfect for each other. When you know she's the one, you know. I know, and I'm confident in my decision, but I won't ask just yet. I'll give her time to adjust to me always being around. I've never known myself to be such a possessive fucker, but I've never wanted anyone like I want her.

"You can move your hand now." She lifts her eyebrows.

"Alright." I bite my lip and move my hand up her body to the zipper on her pants and unbutton it. Her eyes go round.

"What are you doing?"

"What do you think I am doing?" I counter while I pull on the fly of her pants.

"Trying to get me naked?" A mischievous light in her eyes is enough of a green light for me.

"Your assumption would be correct." When her fly is open, I move my hand inside them, moving lower until I'm in her panties and find her wet. Not wet, no, completely *soaked*. "You are a dirty girl, Kayla Attleborough," I say as I dip my finger inside her.

Her breath catches but not from the reason I think. "What?" She freezes.

And I freeze. *Fuck. Shit.* Did I just call her Kayla Attleborough? So much for fucking keeping it locked down for now.

"What did you say, Justin?" Her eyes are enormous, her hands frozen on my shoulders.

"I mean—" Heat warms my cheeks. "I mean, I meant—" I clear my throat. "Fuck it. Will you marry me?" I blurt and stop breathing. I don't know what she'll answer; I honestly don't. Kayla's mind is a mystery to me. If she says 'no,' I'll spend the rest of my life convincing her to change her mind.

"What—" She blinks a few times. "Are you high?"

"On testosterone? Most likely." I cackle. "A man can go only so long without sex, and I haven't had any since you."

"Since me?" Her mouth is a cute *o*.

"Yeah," I nod. "It's been you for a long time, and I want it to be only you. Will you marry me to keep me out of my misery?" I sound more confident now. I know what I want, and I go after it.

Her lips stretch in that beautiful smile I've missed so much. "I think I can do that. Just so I can keep you out of your misery, you know."

"I don't give a shit why." I bring my hands under her ass, lifting her up and placing her on the counter where I fucked up so much the first time. "As long as it's a 'yes,' I'll take it."

She's feverishly licking her lips, her pupils are dilated, and I can tell she wants—*needs*—what I need right now, so I get rid of her pants, pulling them off of her. Unzipping my pants, I place myself between her legs. "Baby, I wish I could play with you for hours, but I don't think I can right now. I need you so fucking bad."

"I don't need foreplay now. Just all your inches.

C'mere." She grabs the undone belt of my pants and pulls me to her. Her quick hands dive inside my jeans and pull my dick out, hard as steel. It nearly weeps at the contact. Scratch that; it weeps. The precum wets the tip of it, and she spreads it around the extra sensitive head. It nearly makes me come, and I pull away.

"Kay, baby, not now, or it's about to be done before it even starts," I beg hoarsely.

She giggles as she opens her legs wider, grabs my dick again, and leads me toward her soaked center. My cock twitches, my balls tighten before it even touches her, and I understand it's time to take it in my hands, or it will be over. Quite literally.

I grab the base of my cock with one hand and make little circles on her clit with another. Kayla's breathing quickens, and she closes her eyes. I align myself with her pussy and push in. Now, since my hand is free, I grab her ass and pull her toward me. The moment I'm fully sheathed inside her, I let out a loud moan. *Fu-u-uck.* That's what home feels like.

I begin moving my hips in slow, shallow thrusts, trying to prolong the pleasure, but Kayla grabs my ass with her hands, digging her fingers into my flesh, and orders in a low voice that comes out only when she is on the verge of losing it.

"Justin, damn it, fuck me like you mean it."

That's all I needed to hear.

I speed up the tempo, thrusting deeper. My hands roam her back, my lips on her neck, sucking on her tasty, slightly salty skin. I know it will leave bruises, but I want them to be there. I want everyone to see who she belongs to.

"Justin." Her pleading voice reaches my nearly gone mind.

"Yes, baby, what do you want?"

"I want your hand on my neck," she whispers through my thrusts. Way more confident than she did the first time she asked for that.

"Happy to oblige." I was hoping it wasn't a fluke before, and she really likes it. I'm a lucky motherfucker.

I wrap my hand around the base of her throat, slightly pressing on the windpipe. The moment I do that, she bursts in flames. Her tight pussy squeezes my cock, and I come inside her like a fucking fountain.

My orgasm is never-ending as I keep thrusting in, and she cries out again, digging her hands into my ass cheeks.

We are a sweaty, happy mess as we hold on to each other. I'm never letting this woman go.

Later that day, with the help of a few orgasms, I manage to convince Kayla to move her trailer to my backyard as soon as possible, refusing to wait any longer. ASAP meaning like tonight. I'd never tell her, but if she refused, I'd be camping here for a long time until she caved. After the situation with Caroline and her buddies, I'll never feel comfortable with Kayla staying even one night in such a secluded location alone. She agreed to move her trailer tomorrow but agreed to move in *tonight*. I'm a happy man.

She can use my cards and fix up the place any way she wants; she can buy all the mismatched dishware and furniture in the world and make our home her cozy little haven. She can do anything she wants, as long as I get to keep her.

She's asleep in bed with my ring on her finger when I hear banging on the back door. Who the fuck is here so late?

I walk to the door with the confidence that I'm about to beat someone's ass when I see Frank beating his hoof on the wood. I carefully open it and step outside. I still can't erase from my mind how I almost pissed my pants when the moose came and nudged Kayla's shoulder. I was ready to take him on when he was just flirting with my woman.

"Sup, Frank?" He beats a hoof on the ground and lets out a loud exhale. "Alright, boy. I got it; you want to warn me about your friend, right?" He beats his hoof again but doesn't repeat any aggravated noises. "Alright, let's make one thing clear: she is mine." I watch him, and I swear he just rolled his eyes. "Yes, she's mine, and I'll take care of her, but I thank you for the save today. I owe you." Another hoofbeat. "Alright, all the bushes around are yours." He beats again. "Fine!" I throw my hands up in defeat. "You can visit anytime." He lets out a long exhale from his nose that I can somehow read as satisfaction and nods his head. His big eyes are trained on me, then squinted—I swear the fuckin' moose squints his eyes at me—before he turns around and leaves.

I watch him disappear into the night. Did I just have a standoff with a moose? I think I did. Well, he is Frank, so I'll deal with it.

I take a deep breath and return home to the woman in my bed who represents everything I thought I'd never have, and yet here I am, blessed with her presence in my life that I nearly fucked over. Never again. She is mine, and I'm a possessive motherfucker, as it turns out.

I jog upstairs and slide back into bed, where Kayla murmurs something unintelligible as she snuggles into my side. I hug her, pulling her warm body closer, and sniff her hair. Strawberry is my favorite fruit.

I'm asleep five minutes later.

Epilogue

A *lmost a year later*

JUSTIN

Today is a Star Wars–themed night at Dancing Pony, and I'm extremely nervous because it's the first time Alicia's coming out with us. Coming out to mingle with people, that is—not just with us, period.

A small hand lands on my knee, stopping it from jerking.

"Relax, Jus. She'll be fine." Kayla's voice always soothes me. Unless we're in the bedroom, of course—there, she turns into a little minx. She figured out how much I love dirty talking and uses it on me as her choice weapon of total destruction. You won't find me complaining, though. "She's doing better, and she brought up going all on her own. No one is forcing her. She's doing better, I promise."

"I trust you, baby. I'm just worried." I take her hand in mine and bring it to my lips for a kiss.

"I know you do. And that's one of the reasons I love you," she coos.

I quickly glance at her before returning my attention back to the road. "What are the others?"

"Hmm. Let me think." She taps her finger on her chin. "Your nine inches? I love all of them."

I let out a loud laugh. "Anything else?" I'm totally fishing here.

"Hmm... nope." She chuckles.

"Alright. Let's see if you change your mind later once I start withholding my inches until you find other reasons—since you're only using me for sex," I pretend to complain, suppressing my grin.

"I so am," she confirms with a devious smirk as she places her hand over my crotch.

I laugh again and smack her hand away—said inches roaring to life, just like every time Kayla's around, and the timing couldn't be more awkward.

"We're almost there. I'm not planning to walk around with a woody. That designer lady might notice." I pout, making Kayla laugh before her face turns serious.

"Oh, hell no. She'd better keep her hands off." Kayla's lips turn into a genuine pout, and it's adorable. She still has my ring on her finger, but the little minx refuses to set a date. I keep quiet because I want her to finish school and all the classes she signed up for, but after that, if she still refuses, we're eloping to Vegas.

We're at the Dancing Pony, and the street in front of it is fully packed with vehicles of all sorts. We park, and I get our bag from the back seat containing our costumes. I've never gone to a costume party here before—I guess I was *'too cool'* for that—but the preparations of the outfits turned out to be a lot of fun. A couple of years ago, Alex fucked up and had to dress as a hobbit just to go with Freya, so if he could do that, it might not be that bad.

As for me, all my fun started when Kayla was trying on different outfits, and some of them were really slutty. It was the best day of my life. She ended up dressing as Rey in this tight gray costume, showcasing her gorgeous body and the tattoos that the real Rey lacked. While I was busy ogling her dancing around the room in her tight pants, she coaxed me into playing Kylo Ren, telling me that I'm missing only the helmet because his snobbish attitude is my default setting.

The inn is full of people. I've heard that Emma throws... all sorts of parties, but I have never been to any of the *special ones*. Even with my reputation—scratch that, my *old* reputation—of a sex addict (which is absolutely far from the truth), I shudder at the thought. I don't want to end up in the same space as Paul swinging his dick around like a sword, since I've heard he and Marina attend those parties together.

I shudder again and secure the plastic sword on my hip. The real sword, not the other kind. *Ugh*.

"Here they are!" Freya singsongs from her chair when she sees us. She's dressed like that little green dude with cute ears, while Alex wears a black helmet and a black batman-like outfit. I only know it's him because his frame is unmistakable. I have no idea who their characters are, even though Freya looks like an overgrown Yoda.

"Who?" Alex asks, turning around too fast. His shoulders are far too broad for such a narrow space, though, and he knocks a lamp from the accent wall down with his elbow. It falls on the floor and shatters into pieces.

Everyone around groans. Everyone.

"Another victim of the serial killer," Freya says as she stands from the chair and wraps a hand around Alex's arm, cooing sweetly to him, "It's okay, Boo Bear. You'll be fine." She pats his belly where the material of his costume has stretched so much it's nearly bursting, and Kayla lets out a giggle.

"Boo Bear?" she repeats.

Freya shrugs with a smile. "Seems fitting."

"It sure does." Donna winks at her, appearing out of thin air. "Look at you two," she gushes, turning to Kayla and me. "dressing to match. Cutie pies!" She pats my cheek, and I'm about to throw up. *Cutie pies?*

Kayla winks back. "We're trying." I feel betrayed.

"Well, good for you. Happy you two finally got together; you made me a lot of money! That pool was intense!" She laughs as she waves, leaving us with our mouths hanging open.

"There was a pool about us? Besides my mom's bet?" I ask no one in particular.

"There was," answers Alicia, appearing next to us. She's dressed in the iconic white Princess Leia costume. I haven't seen my sister in anything but sweatpants for a long time; this ridiculous outfit is the best thing she could possibly have picked today. My heart swells in my chest, and I swallow a huge lump in my throat. "I feel left out for not participating. Should have thrown my money in too." She smiles, and there's a little sliver of the smile she had *before*.

"Figures. Small towns and bored folks." Kayla rolls her eyes, and I give her a kiss on her cheek.

"That, and you were both kind of funny with all your

mutual growling and chemistry. Oof." She dramatically fans herself with her hand. "I gotta write a book about you."

"Stop right there," I groan. "That's just gross."

She only laughs, then turns to address Freya. "I wanted to ask you something about the center. Can we have a quick chat later?"

Freya throws me a curious look and answers, "Sure! Anytime." Then she picks up two glasses from the table filled with something that looks like mimosas and passes them to Kayla and Alicia.

"Cool," Alicia answers with a genuine smile. She looks relaxed, not cornered like she usually does with a lot of people besides her family in the room. "By the way, Mrs. Jenkins moved in with her daughter, and I rented out her place," Alicia announces proudly just as Kayla takes a sip of her drink—she spits it out once Alicia's words register. Her eyes bulge as she tries to cough the remaining liquid out. She looks at Alicia with shocked eyes and swallows nervously.

What is happening? What did I miss?

Acknowledgments

No one likes reading acknowledgments but people like giving them. I, personally, love that because I get to express all the gratitude I feel. So please, be patient.

This time around, I want to thank all the people who helped me spread the word about the Little Hope series. Without you, all this would be impossible. Bookstagrammers, BookTokers, readers, reviewers. Thank you!

The following names have the same importance, but I can't put them all together because it doesn't work like that, duh, so one is going to follow another, but again, it absolutely DOES NOT mean that one is less important than the other.

To Sarah, my PA, of course. I don't know what I'd do without you. Like honestly. Who will cheer me up when I'm feeling down and share my happiness when I'm feeling high like you do? No one. Who can find *anything anywhere* like you do? No one.

To Hailey. You know your scene (you are very welcome and thank you, ha-ha) and one particular character is on you too. You'll know him when you'll meet him. He's my favorite so far. I think you'll love him too. Muse, I applaud you.

To Steph, the Deputy Mayor of Little Hope, my regular supplier of inspiration and pretty packages (*You got it, right?* Wink wink).

To Jennifer the Spreader of the Word. Thank you for

letting people know about Little Hope. Really MVP on the field.

To my ARC team. Thank you for reading my books and helping them to get *out there.*

To my street team (names are taken in order from the sign-up list), people (most of them) who stayed with me from the very beginning: Darlene (also known as my first ever IG friend, a fellow writer, and a fellow MA citizen), Clea (also known as a Facebook group moderator), Molly, Jennifer (also known as the Spreader of the Word, *that* Jennifer), Sarah, one more Sarah (yup, they signed up one after another, I think it was destiny), Heather, Leah, Batwoman, Rose, Hailey (also known as a Muse), Traci (also known as one of the Fae Guardians), Cheryl (also known as a super influential person), Samantha, Crystal (a fellow MA citizen and one of the first ever ARC readers), Andrea (also known as the first person who bought the discreet cover in Canada and who holds a special place in my heart because I just LOVE that cover), Christina (also known as Sovaria who has endless book recommendations), Anshul (who's known to be the sweetest person), Steph (also known as *that* deputy mayor), Jenn, one more Samantha, Zakerah, Preet (who is also known to be the person to excite me to write), Cassie (also known to give the best advice ever), one more Sarah (who is also known as a newest addition so let's welcome her). Thank you all!

To everyone who supports my crazy idea to become a writer.

And the most important one: the reader. Whoever reads this book is THE reader I dedicate my endless hours of work to. A reader who picked up this book among millions of amazing stories out there. That's why I decided to write: If my stories help you to get out of the problems in your head or forget the shitty moments you might have had even for a few minutes, that's why I write. Because that's why I read.

THANK YOU!

∼ With a lot of love (like *THAT* much love),
  Ariana

Also by Ariana Cane

The World of the Fallen Gates series

Dystopian, paranormal, urban fantasy romance series

Tale of the Deceived, Book 1 of the duet

Story of the Forsaken , Book 2 of the duet

-vampires, werewolves, faes

-true enemies to lovers

-the life after the World has ended

-super slow-burn

-one bed

-true series

-scorching tension

-tons of secrets

Little Hope Series

Small town, slow burn, contemporary romance stand-alones.

Haunted Hearts, Little Hope Series, Book 1

Alex and Freya,

-one bed

-grumpy-sunshine

-strangers to enemies to lovers

-an ex-navy veteran with PTSD

-woman on the run

- *woodchopping*
- *cabin in the woods*
- *damaged MMC*
- *all the bears of Maine*

Guilty Minds, Little Hope Series, Book 2

Justin and Kayla

- *true bully romance*
- *groveling*
- *tattoo artist-waitress/mechanic*
- -miscommunication for a good reason
- -wildlife of Maine

Broken Souls, Little Hope Series, Book 3

Mark and Alicia

- *fireman and author*
- *strangers to neighbors to lovers*
- *hurt/comfort*
- *trauma recovery*
- *man's best friend*
- *protective MMC*

Fragile Lives, Little Hope Series, Book 4

Archie and Leila

- *enemies to lovers*
- *one bed*
- *cabin in the woods*
- *age-gap*
- *brother's best friend*

-the most beloved character
-wildlife of Maine
-trauma recovery/PTSD (MMC)
-lots of tattoos and piercings (MMC)

Book 5, Kenneth's story, is coming soon...

They say the truth will set you free. But what about the ugly truth? The one that reveals pretty as damaging and ugly as redeeming?

Printed in Great Britain
by Amazon